MELLYBEAR

AND THE
WICKED WIZARD

WITHDRAWN

MIKE WHITE

RAZORBILL

RAZORBILL
An imprint of Penguin Random House LLC, New York

First published in the United States of America by Razorbill,
an imprint of Penguin Random House LLC, 2021

Visit us online at penguinrandomhouse.com.

Library of Congress Cataloging-in-Publication Data

Names: White, Mike (Children's author), author, illustrator.
Title: Mellybean and the wicked wizard / Mike White.
Description: New York : Razorbill, 2021. | Series: Mellybean; book 2 | Audience: Ages 8–12. |
Summary: Mellybean and the cats help their friends in a fantastical world from a wizard trying to steal the magic of all the other mythical creatures in order to become the greatest wizard ever.
Identifiers: LCCN 2020049220 | ISBN 9780593202814 (hardcover) | ISBN 9780593202838 (trade paperback) | ISBN 9780593202821 (ebook) | ISBN 9780593205754 (ebook) | ISBN 9780593205761 (ebook)
Subjects: LCSH: Graphic novels. | CYAC: Graphic novels. | Magic—Fiction. | Wizards—Fiction. | Dogs—Fiction. | Cats—Fiction. | Adventure and adventurers—Fiction.
Classification: LCC PZ7.7.W5415 Mg 2021 | DDC 741.5/973—dc23
LC record available at https://lccn.loc.gov/2020049220

Manufactured in China.

1 3 5 7 9 10 8 6 4 2

Design by Mike White.
Colors by Valery Kutz.
Text set in Evil Genius.

Dedicated to all my friends, past, present, and future.

With special thanks to Ali and Murti of Streamlabs (whose dog-friendly office enabled us to adopt Melly).

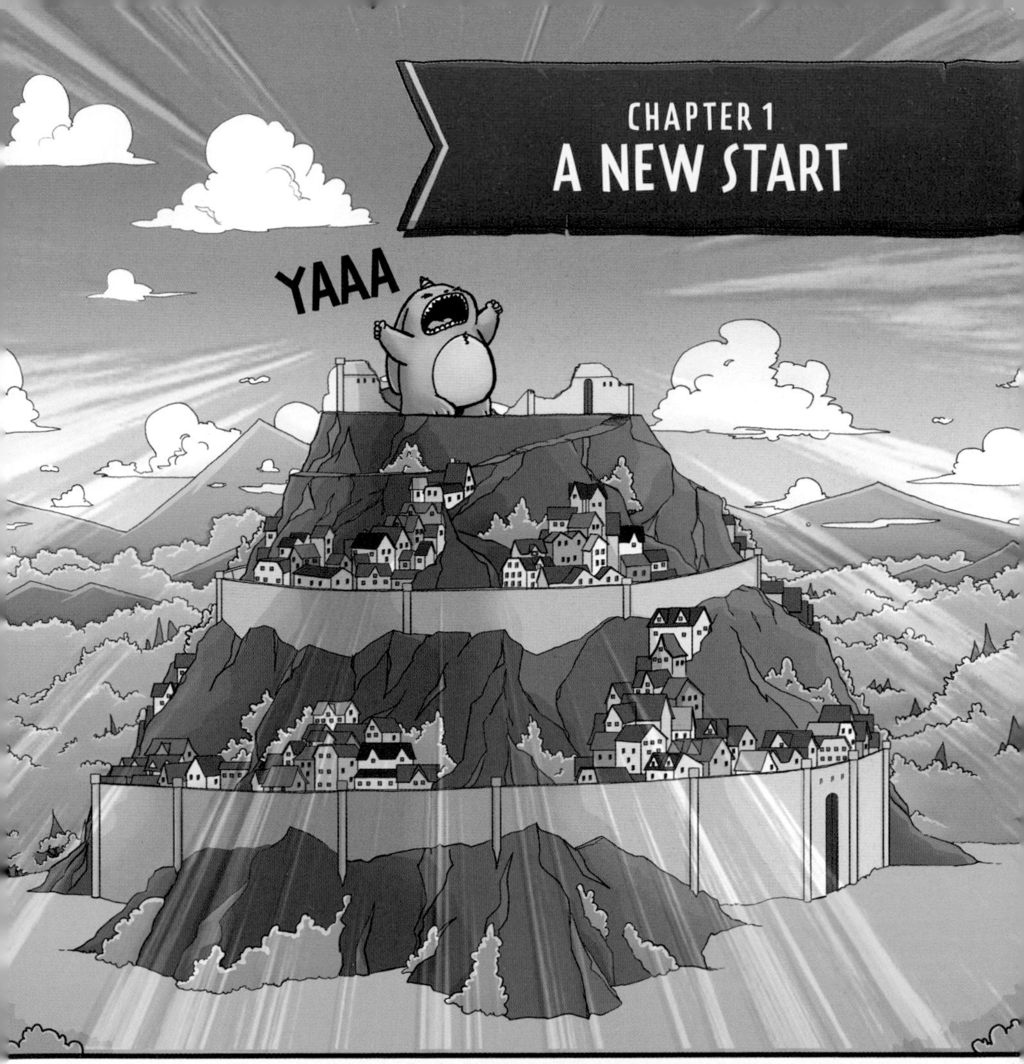
CHAPTER 1
A NEW START
YAAA

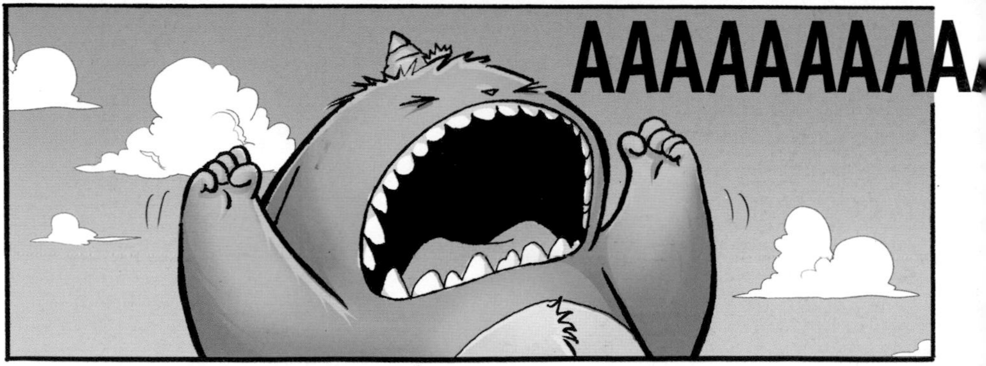
AAAAAAAAA

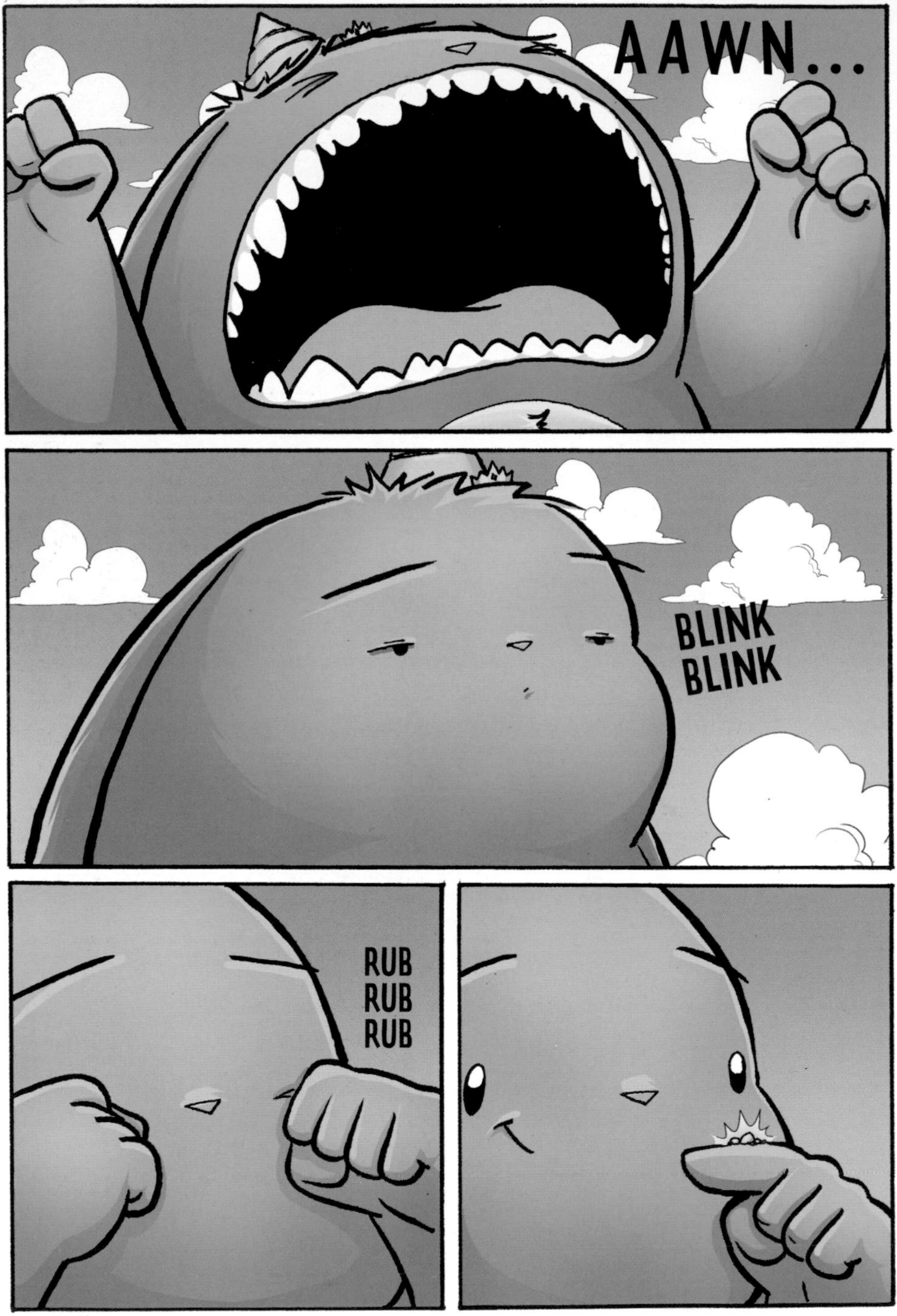
AAWN...
BLINK
BLINK
RUB
RUB
RUB

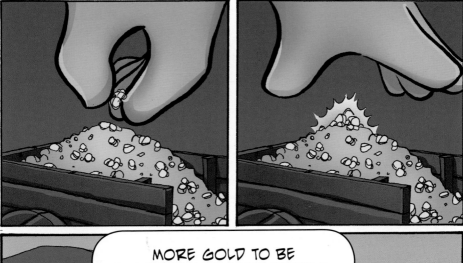

MORE GOLD TO BE SHARED AMONG THE PEOPLE.

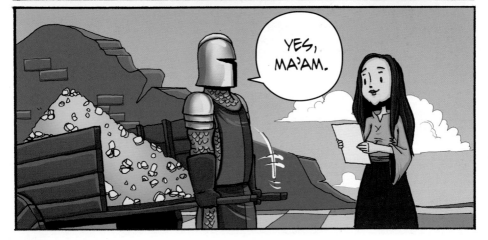

YES, MA'AM.

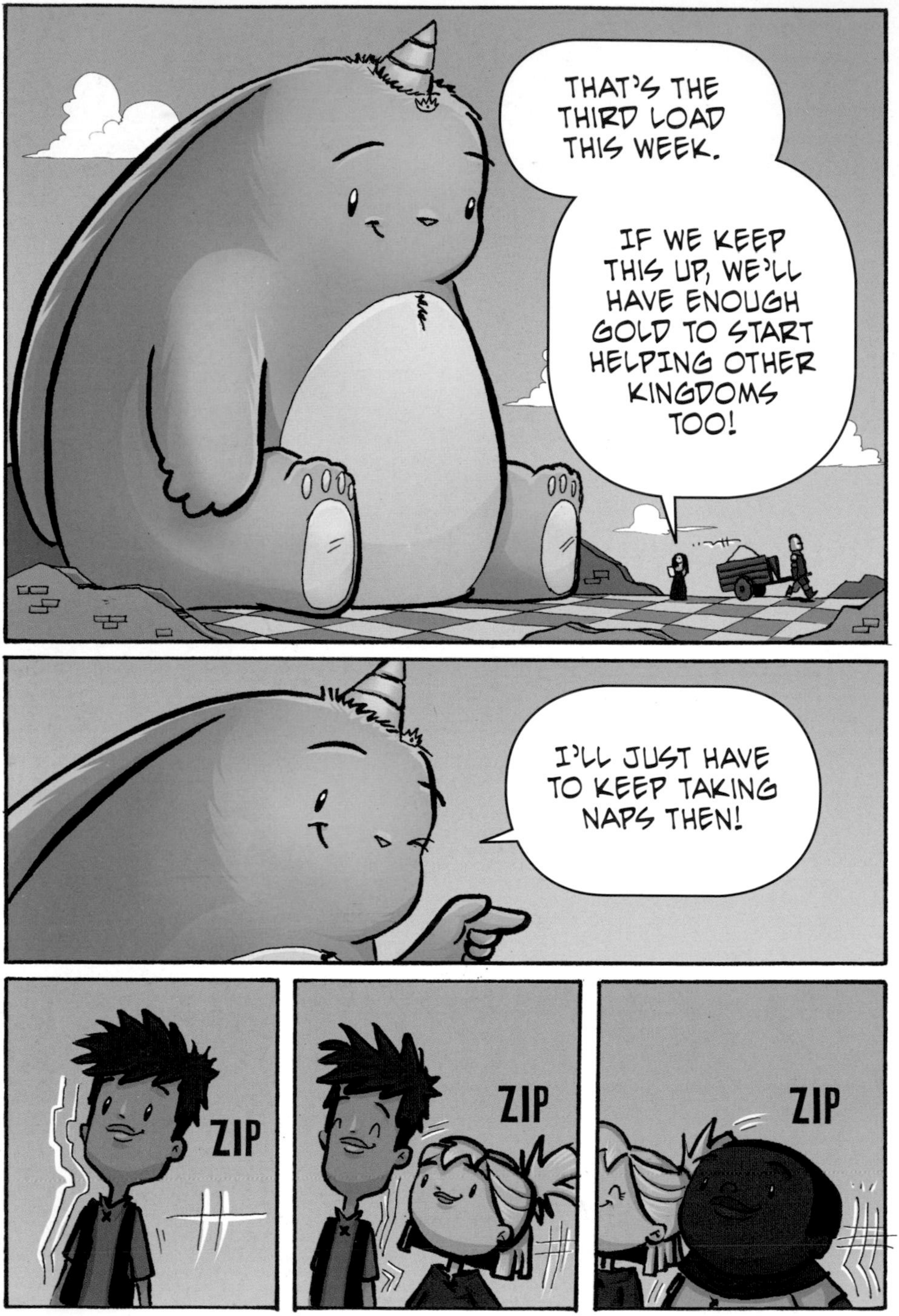
THAT'S THE THIRD LOAD THIS WEEK.
IF WE KEEP THIS UP, WE'LL HAVE ENOUGH GOLD TO START HELPING OTHER KINGDOMS TOO!
I'LL JUST HAVE TO KEEP TAKING NAPS THEN!
ZIP
ZIP
ZIP

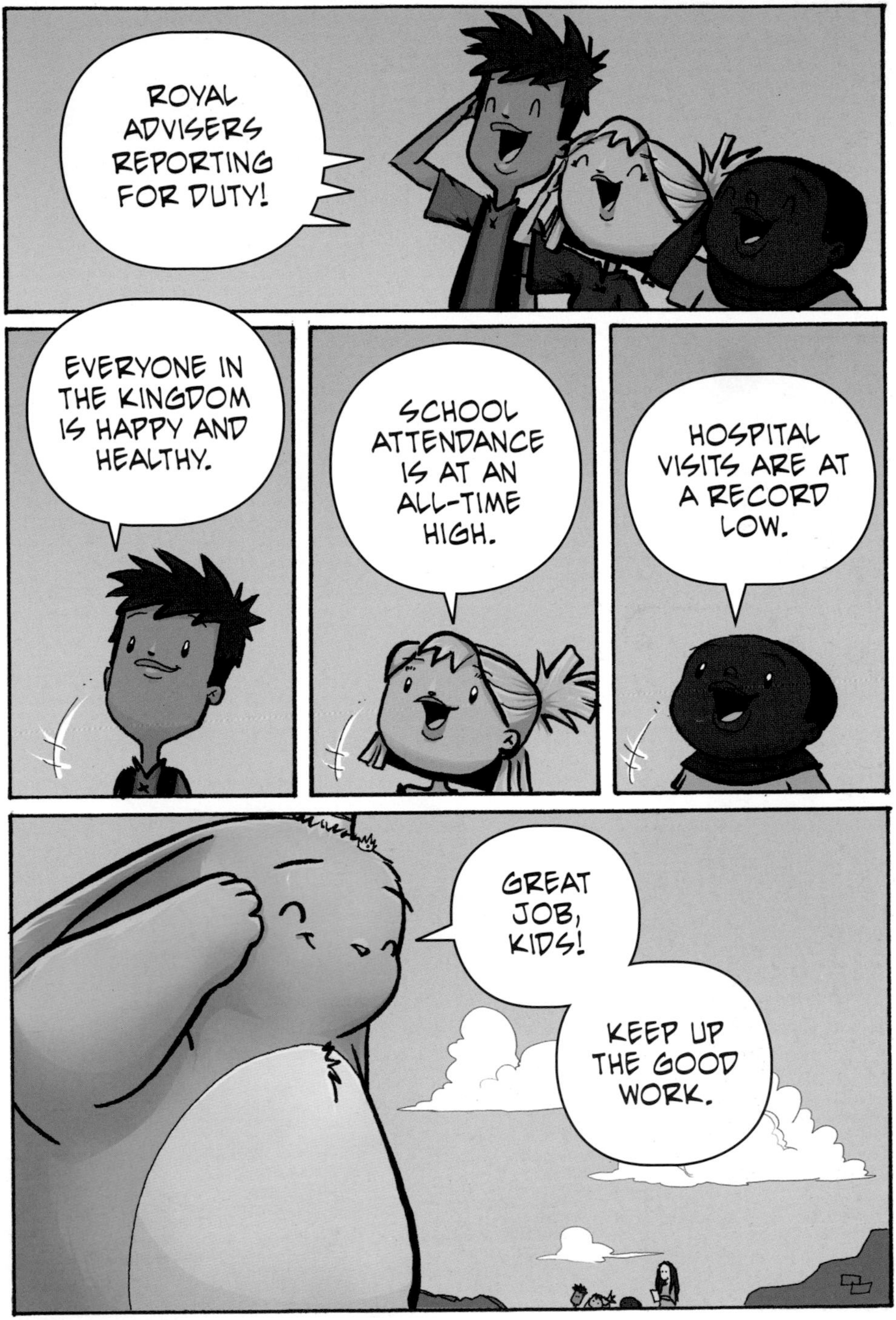
ROYAL ADVISERS REPORTING FOR DUTY!
EVERYONE IN THE KINGDOM IS HAPPY AND HEALTHY.
SCHOOL ATTENDANCE IS AT AN ALL-TIME HIGH.
HOSPITAL VISITS ARE AT A RECORD LOW.
GREAT JOB, KIDS!
KEEP UP THE GOOD WORK.

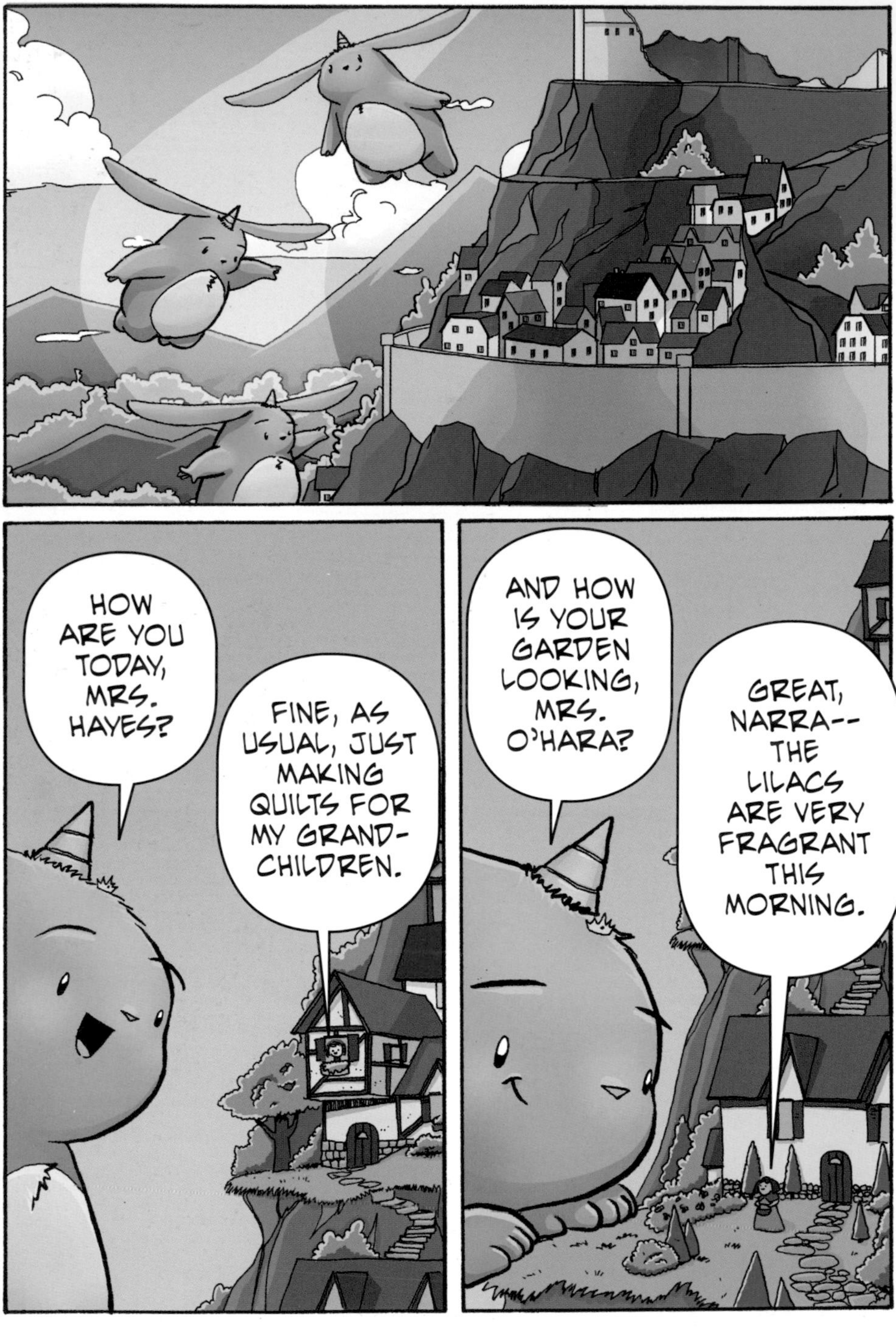
HOW ARE YOU TODAY, MRS. HAYES?
FINE, AS USUAL, JUST MAKING QUILTS FOR MY GRAND-CHILDREN.
AND HOW IS YOUR GARDEN LOOKING, MRS. O'HARA?
GREAT, NARRA-- THE LILACS ARE VERY FRAGRANT THIS MORNING.

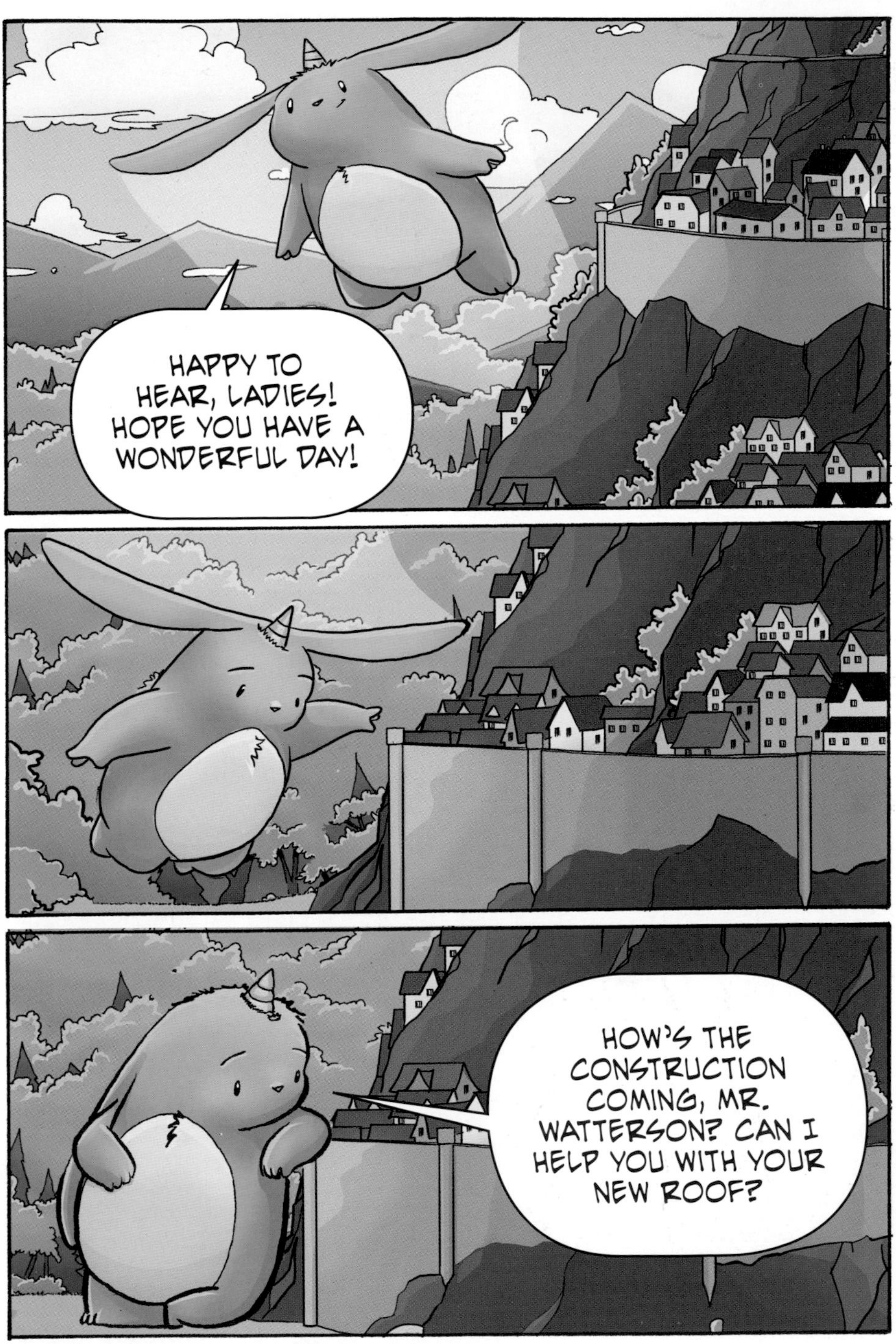
HAPPY TO HEAR, LADIES! HOPE YOU HAVE A WONDERFUL DAY!
HOW'S THE CONSTRUCTION COMING, MR. WATTERSON? CAN I HELP YOU WITH YOUR NEW ROOF?

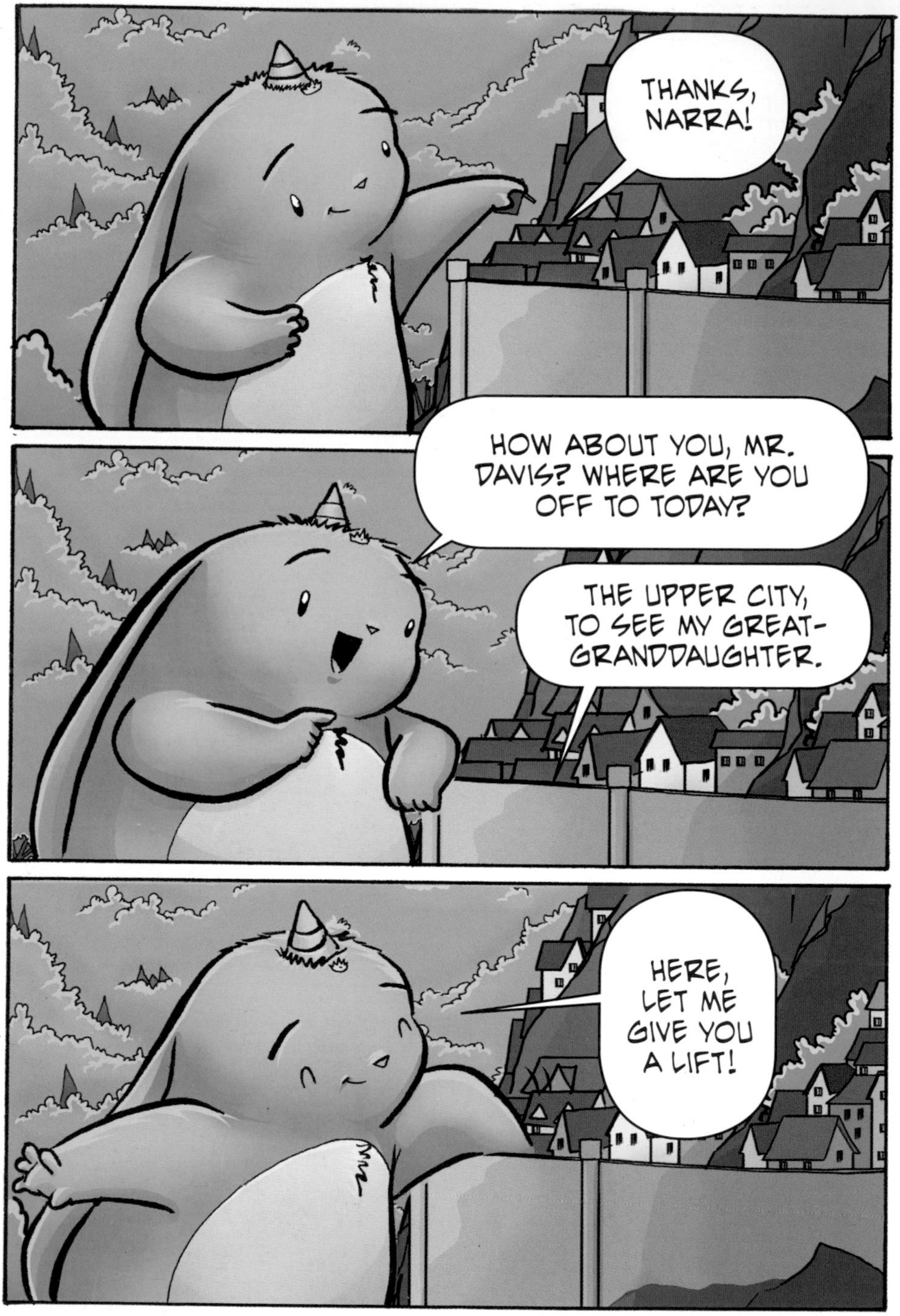
THANKS, NARRA!
HOW ABOUT YOU, MR. DAVIS? WHERE ARE YOU OFF TO TODAY?
THE UPPER CITY, TO SEE MY GREAT-GRANDDAUGHTER.
HERE, LET ME GIVE YOU A LIFT!

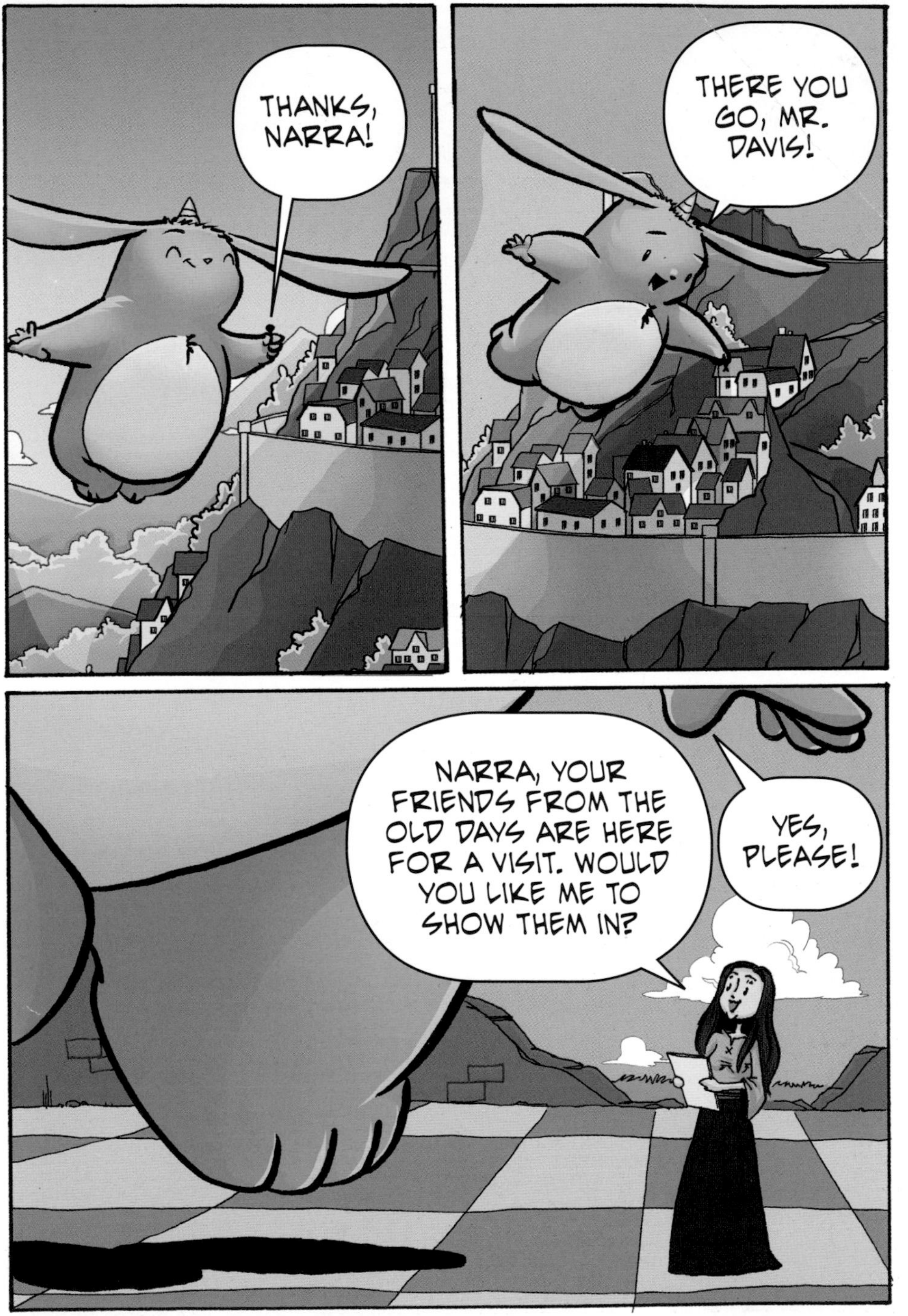
THANKS, NARRA!
THERE YOU GO, MR. DAVIS!
NARRA, YOUR FRIENDS FROM THE OLD DAYS ARE HERE FOR A VISIT. WOULD YOU LIKE ME TO SHOW THEM IN?
YES, PLEASE!

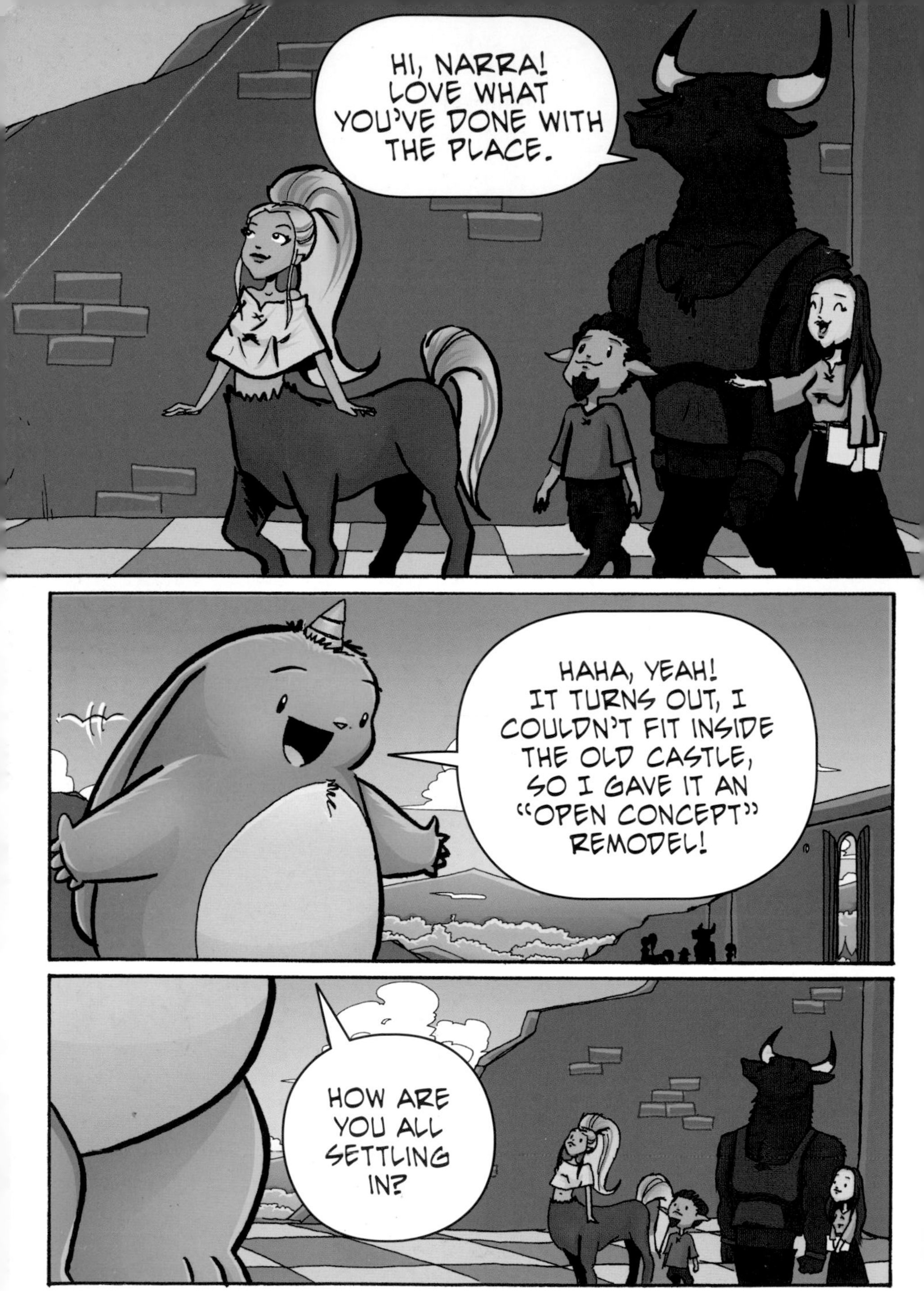
HI, NARRA! LOVE WHAT YOU'VE DONE WITH THE PLACE.
HAHA, YEAH! IT TURNS OUT, I COULDN'T FIT INSIDE THE OLD CASTLE, SO I GAVE IT AN "OPEN CONCEPT" REMODEL!
HOW ARE YOU ALL SETTLING IN?

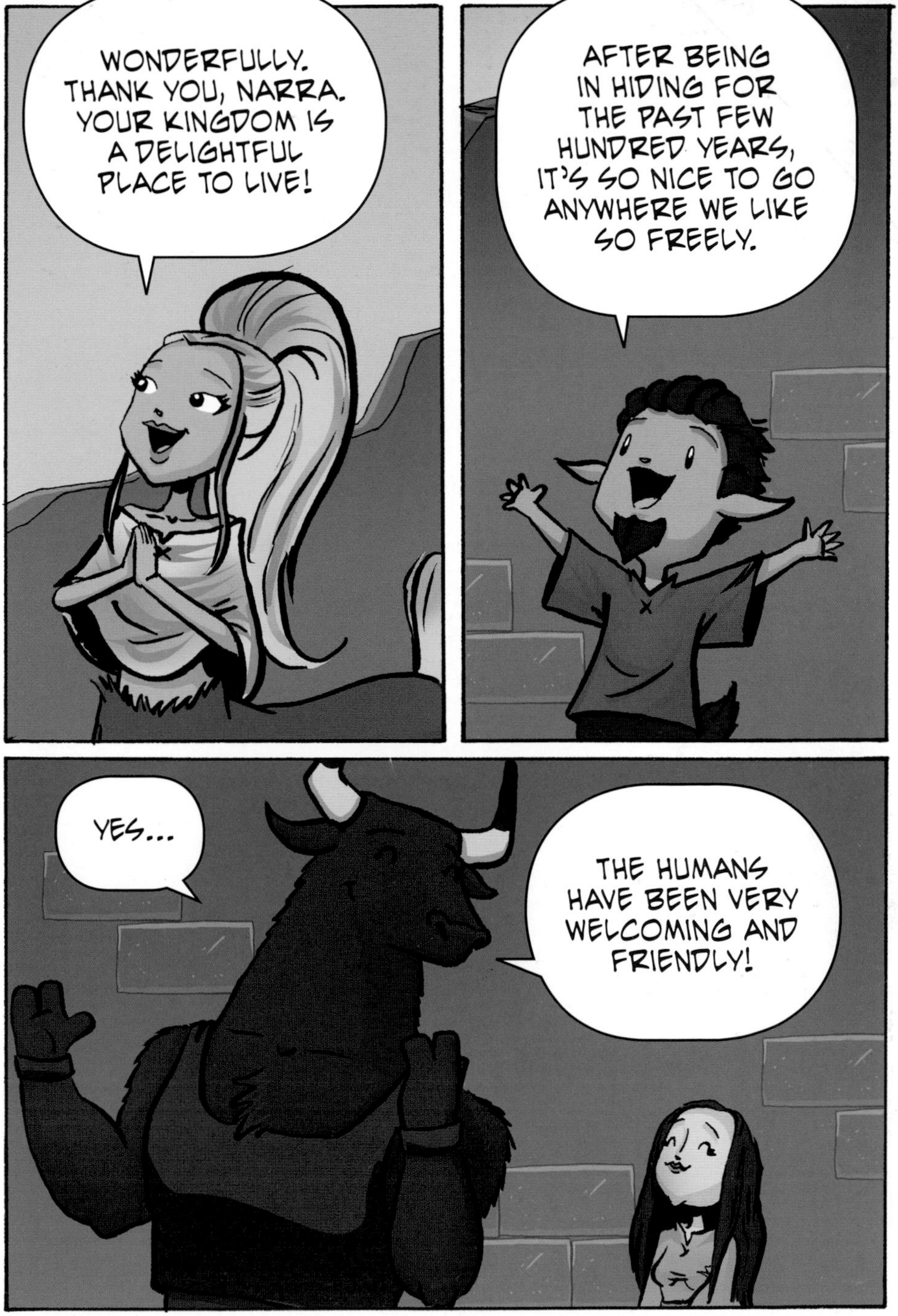
WONDERFULLY. THANK YOU, NARRA. YOUR KINGDOM IS A DELIGHTFUL PLACE TO LIVE!
AFTER BEING IN HIDING FOR THE PAST FEW HUNDRED YEARS, IT'S SO NICE TO GO ANYWHERE WE LIKE SO FREELY.
YES...
THE HUMANS HAVE BEEN VERY WELCOMING AND FRIENDLY!

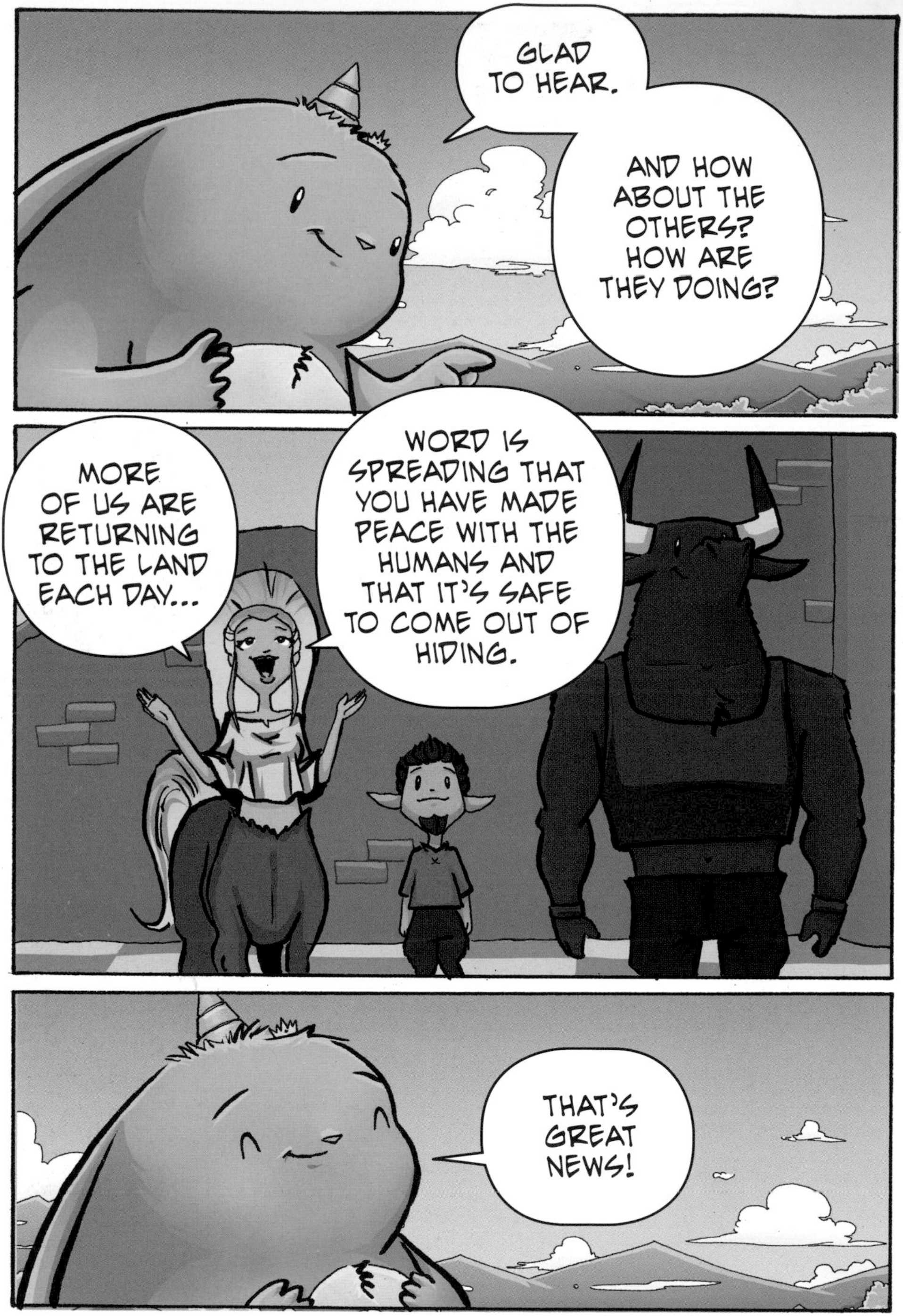
GLAD TO HEAR.
AND HOW ABOUT THE OTHERS? HOW ARE THEY DOING?
MORE OF US ARE RETURNING TO THE LAND EACH DAY...
WORD IS SPREADING THAT YOU HAVE MADE PEACE WITH THE HUMANS AND THAT IT'S SAFE TO COME OUT OF HIDING.
THAT'S GREAT NEWS!

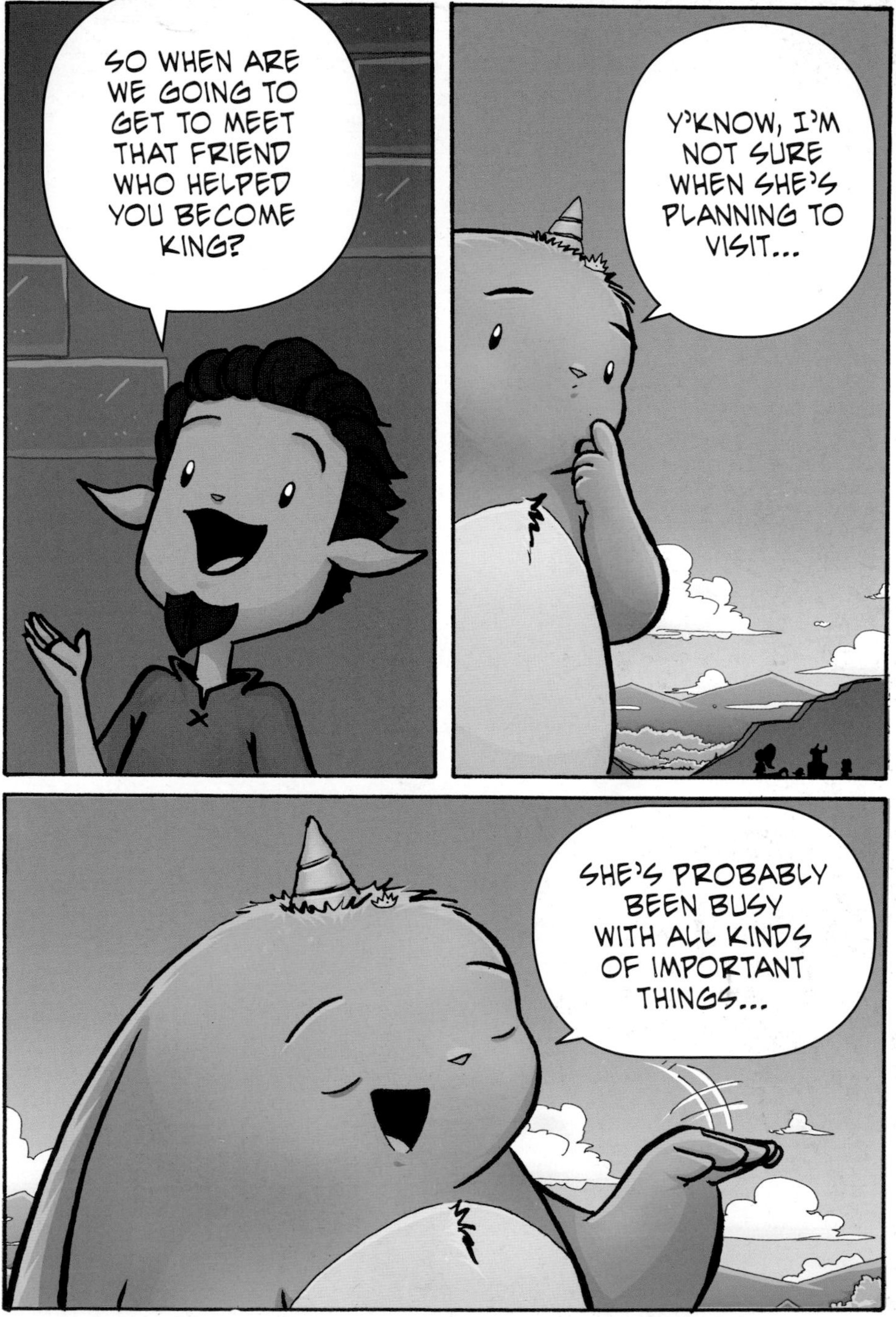
SO WHEN ARE WE GOING TO GET TO MEET THAT FRIEND WHO HELPED YOU BECOME KING?
Y'KNOW, I'M NOT SURE WHEN SHE'S PLANNING TO VISIT...
SHE'S PROBABLY BEEN BUSY WITH ALL KINDS OF IMPORTANT THINGS...

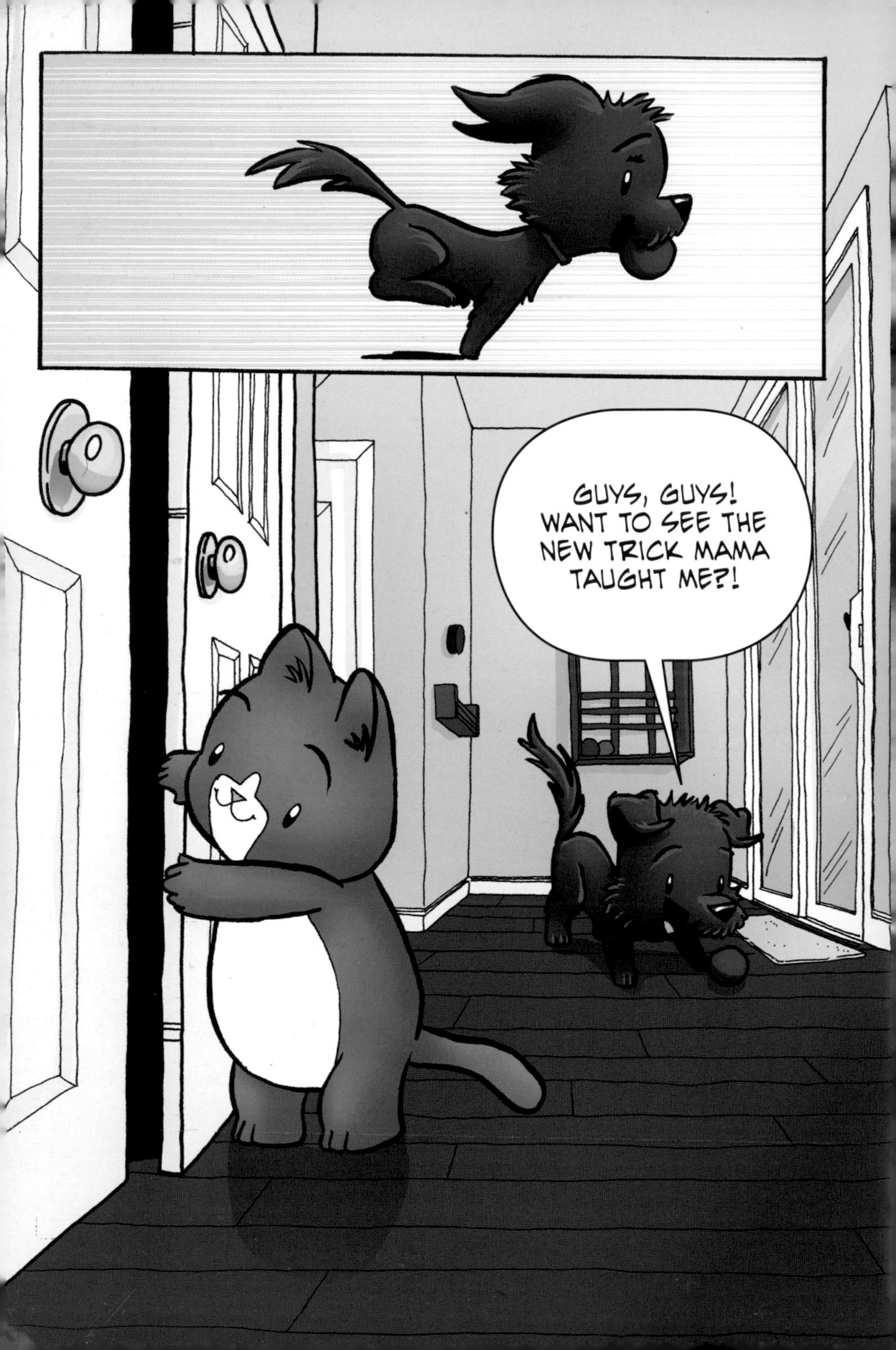
GUYS, GUYS! WANT TO SEE THE NEW TRICK MAMA TAUGHT ME?!

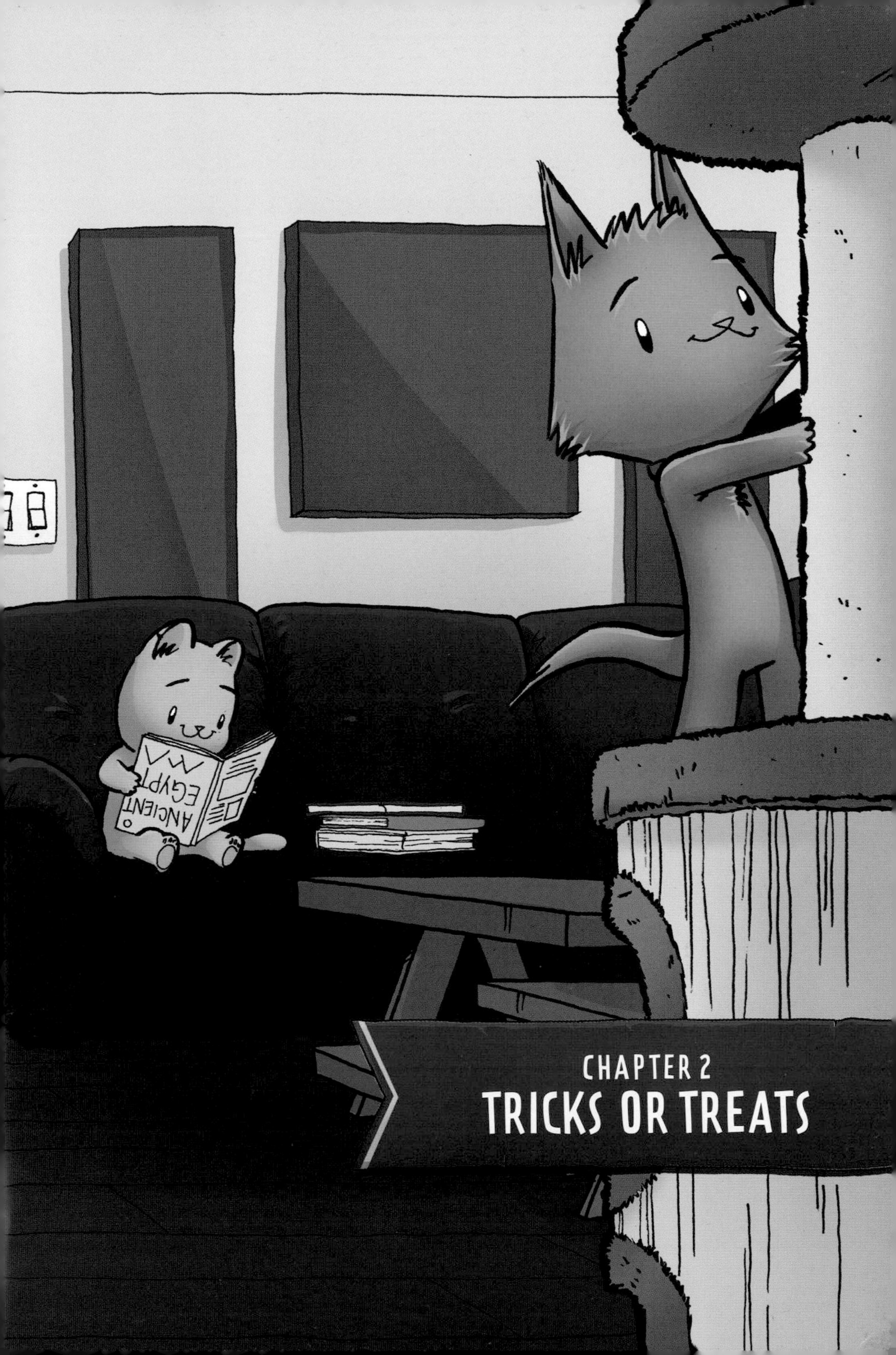
ANCIENT EGYPT

CHAPTER 2
TRICKS OR TREATS

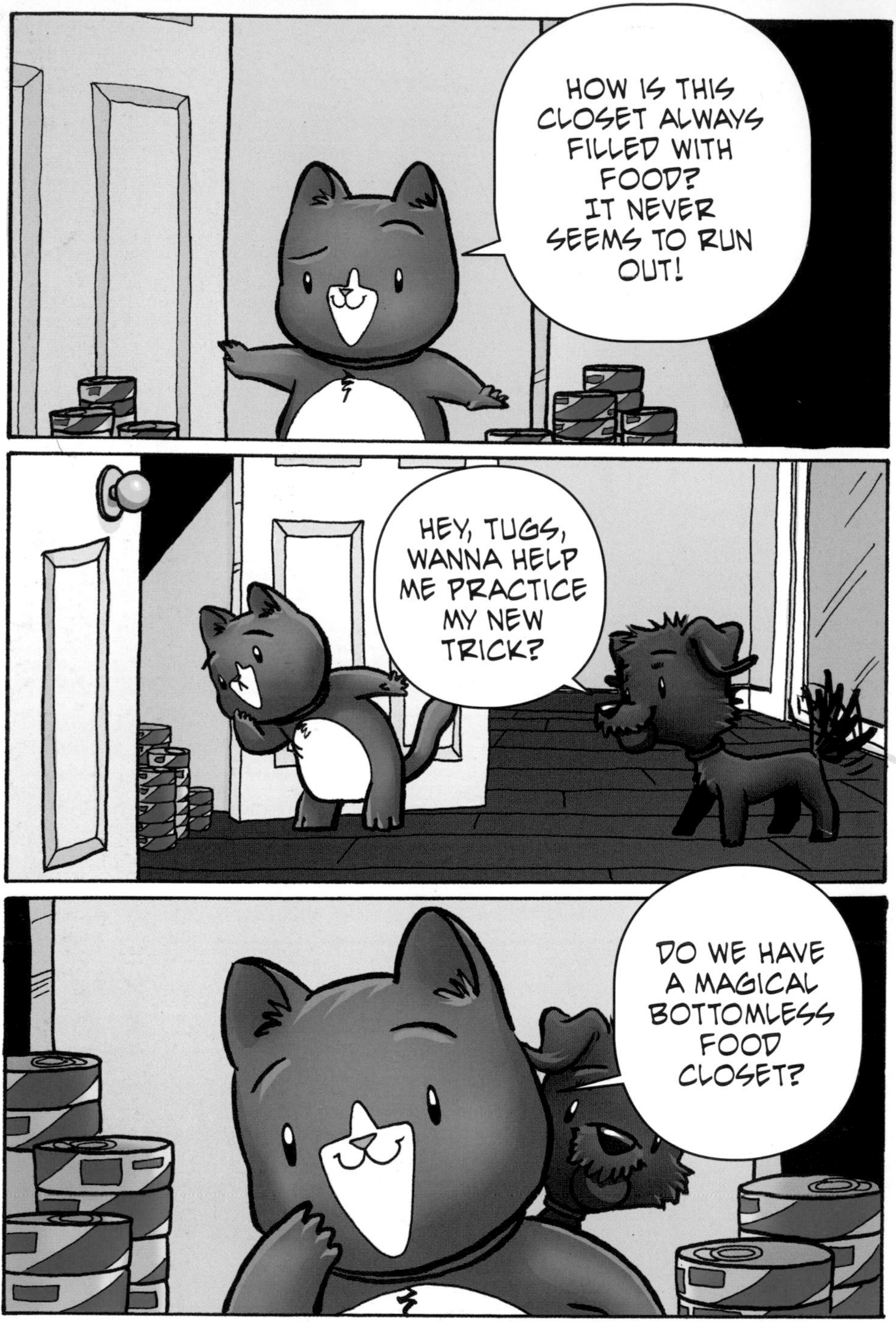
HOW IS THIS CLOSET ALWAYS FILLED WITH FOOD? IT NEVER SEEMS TO RUN OUT!
HEY, TUGS, WANNA HELP ME PRACTICE MY NEW TRICK?
DO WE HAVE A MAGICAL BOTTOMLESS FOOD CLOSET?

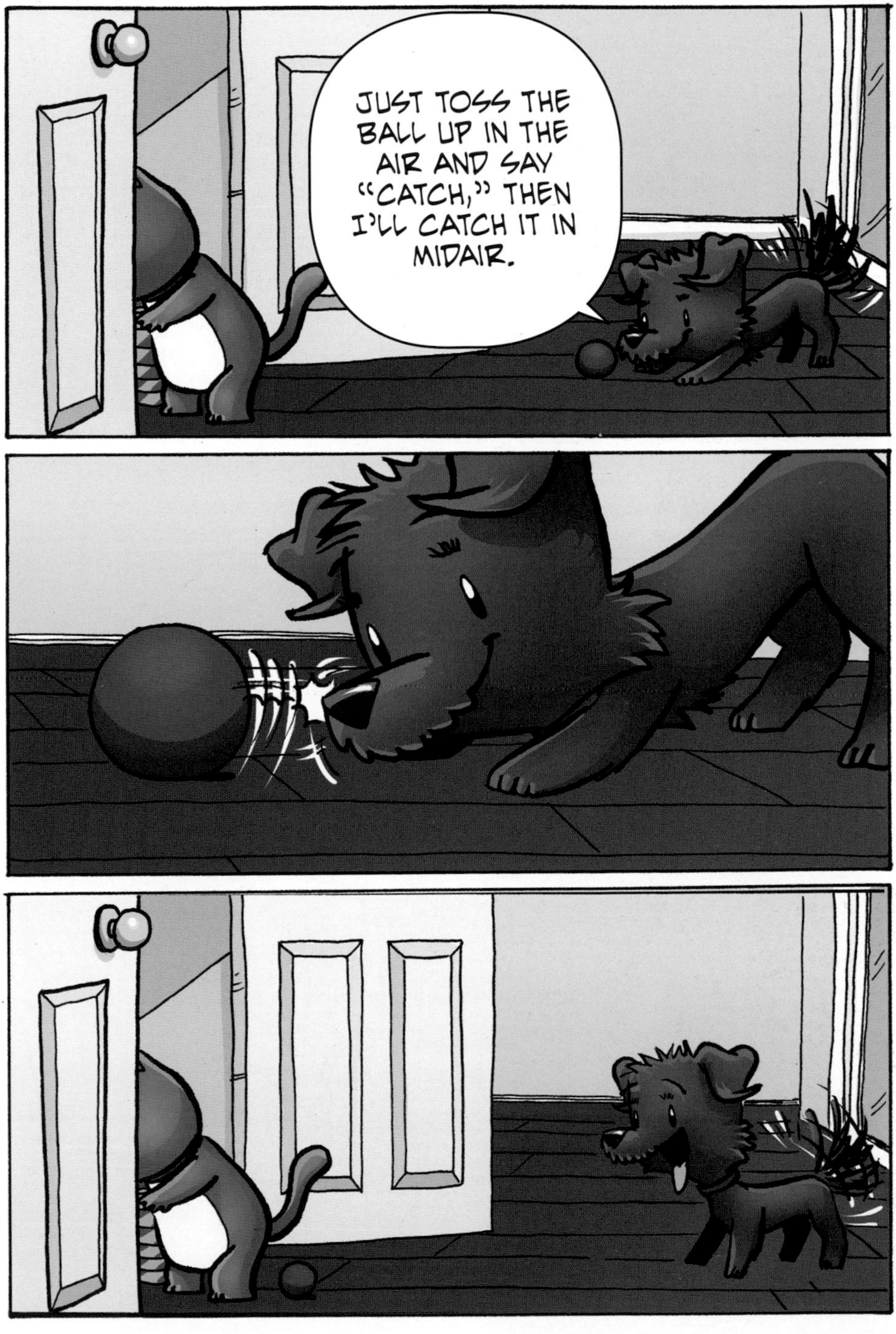

JUST TOSS THE BALL UP IN THE AIR AND SAY "CATCH," THEN I'LL CATCH IT IN MIDAIR.

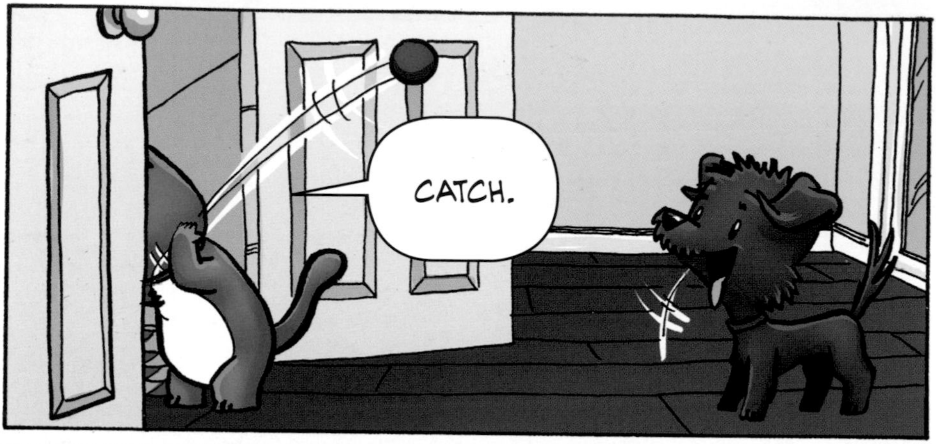
CATCH.

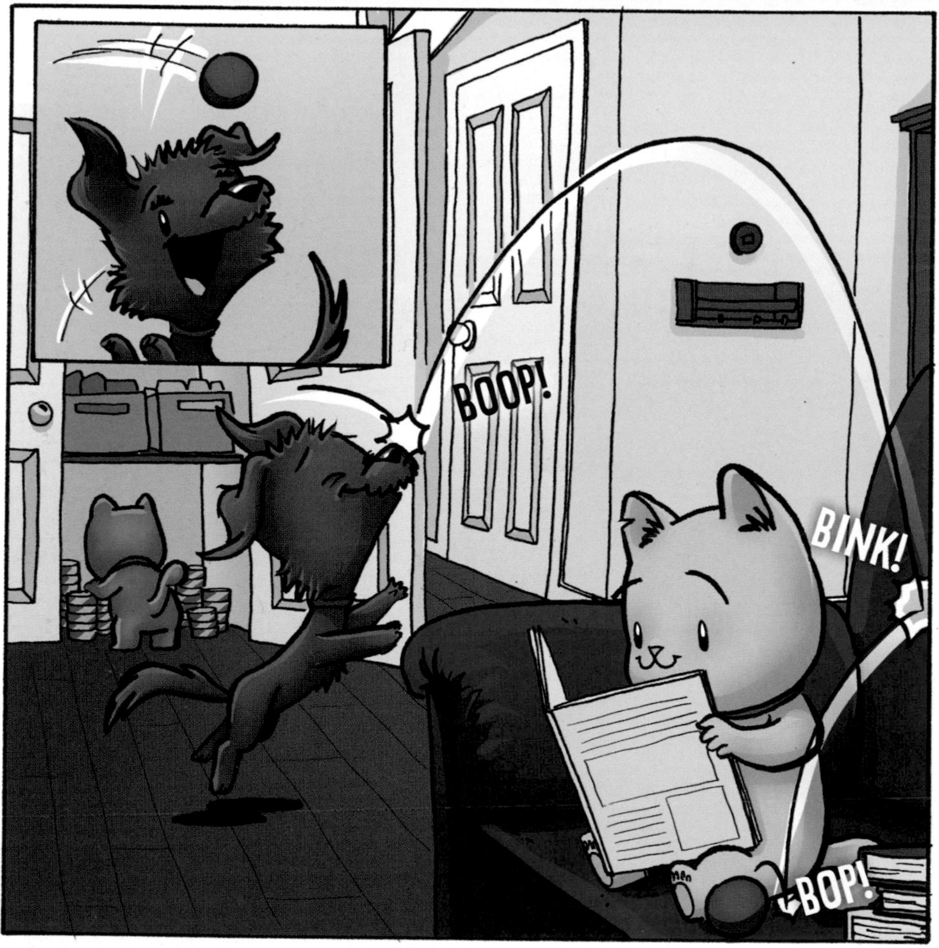
BOOP!
BINK!
BOP!

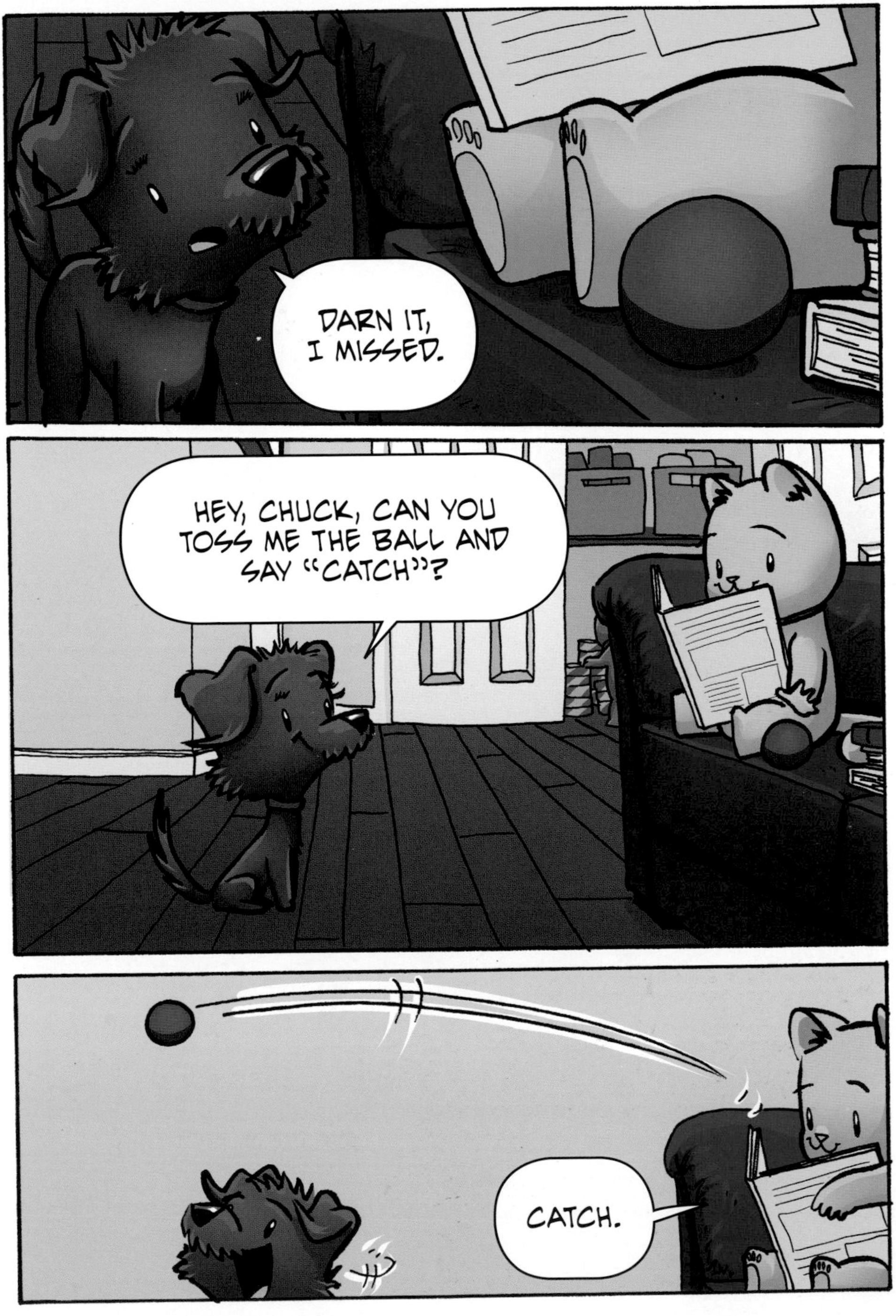
DARN IT, I MISSED.
HEY, CHUCK, CAN YOU TOSS ME THE BALL AND SAY "CATCH"?
CATCH.

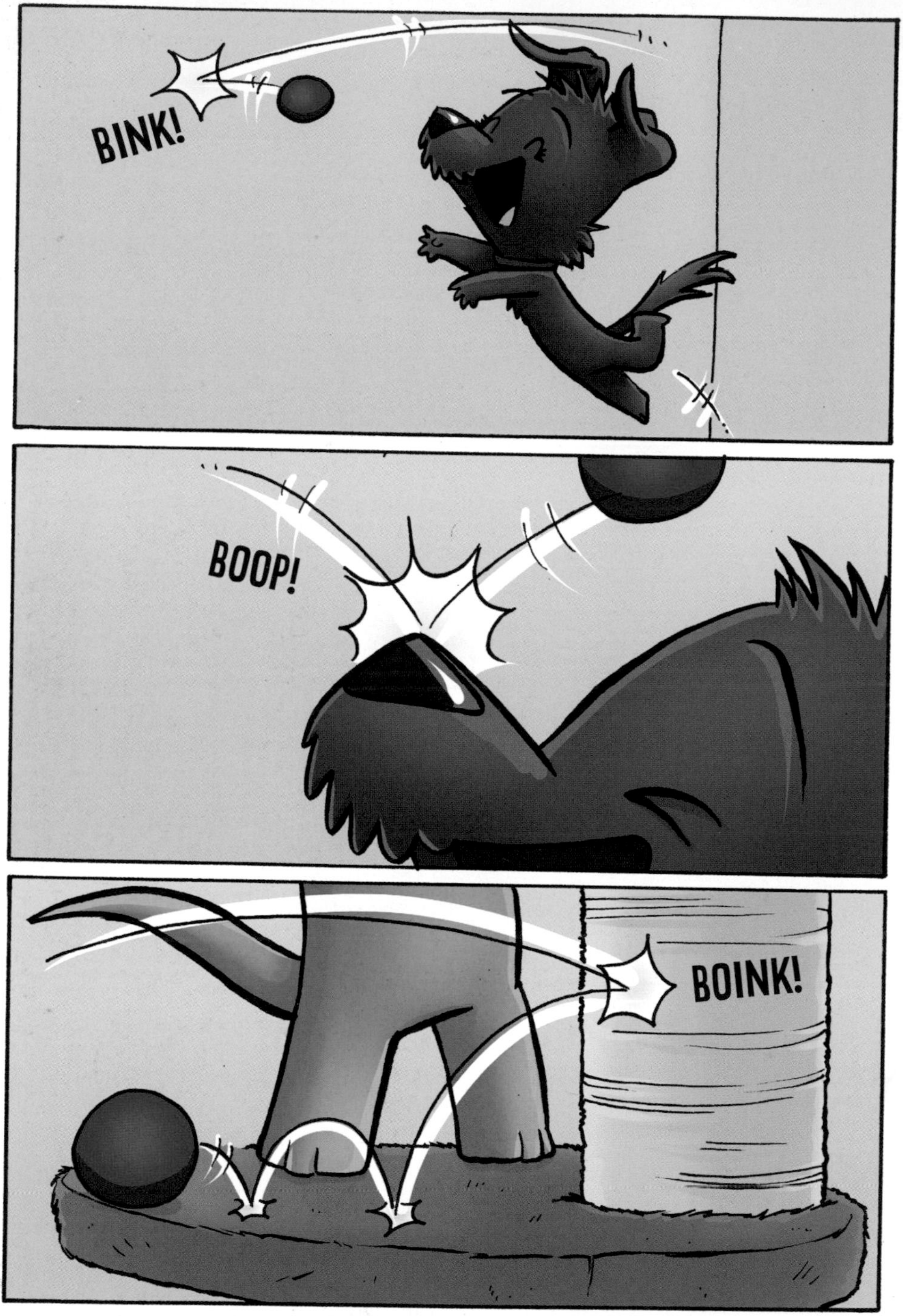
BINK!
BOOP!
BOINK!

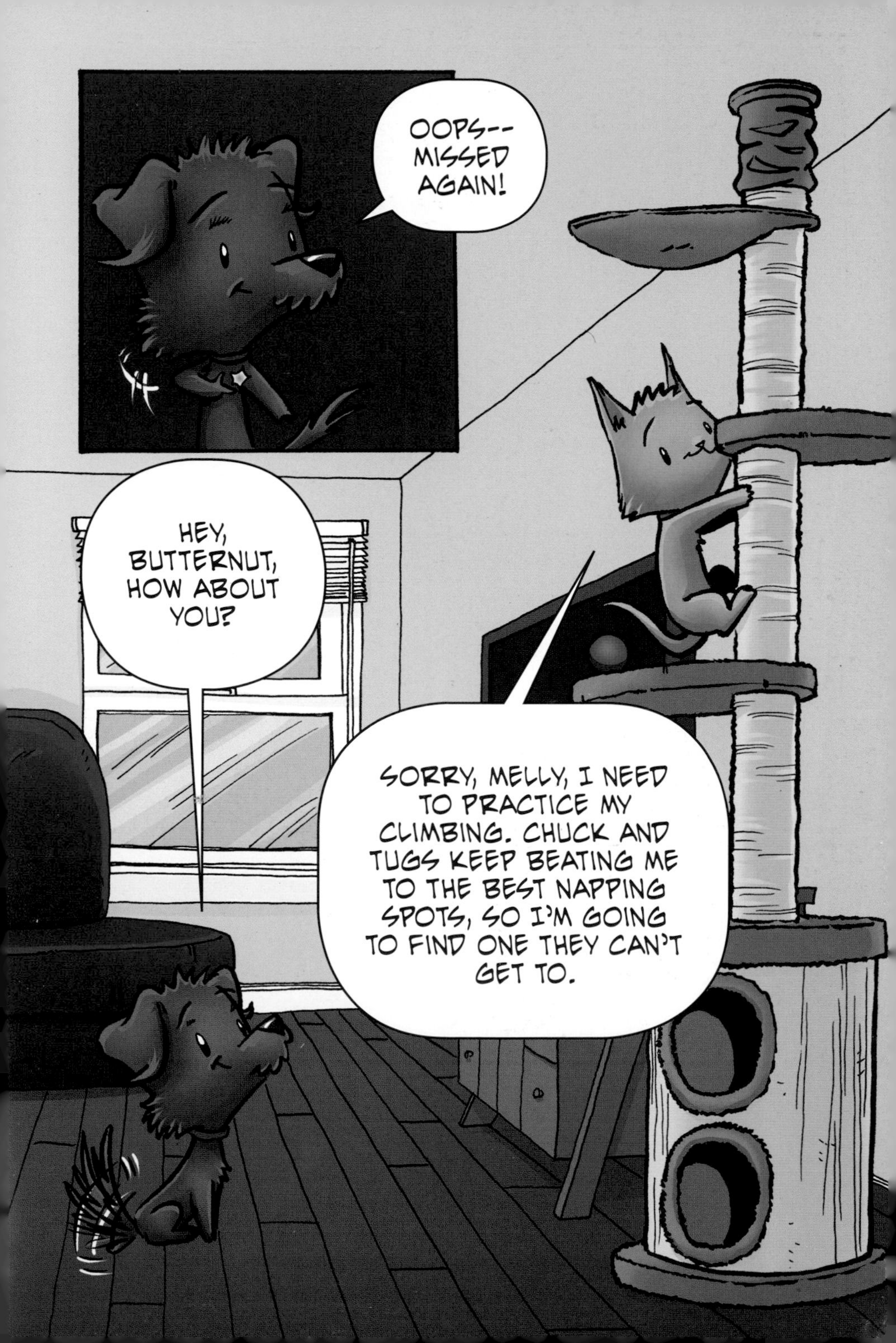
OOPS--
MISSED
AGAIN!
HEY, BUTTERNUT, HOW ABOUT YOU?
SORRY, MELLY, I NEED TO PRACTICE MY CLIMBING. CHUCK AND TUGS KEEP BEATING ME TO THE BEST NAPPING SPOTS, SO I'M GOING TO FIND ONE THEY CAN'T GET TO.

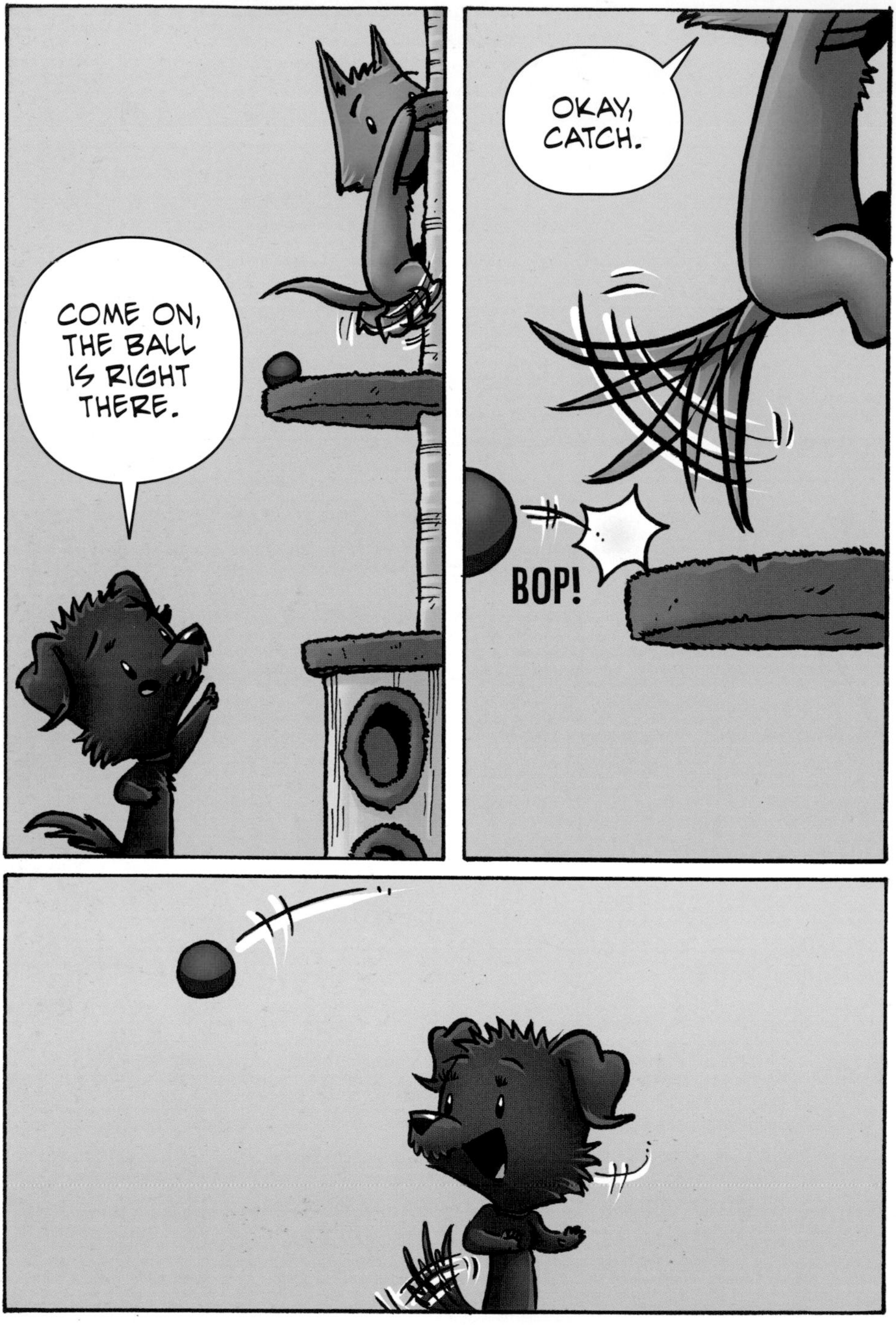
COME ON, THE BALL IS RIGHT THERE.
OKAY, CATCH.
BOP!

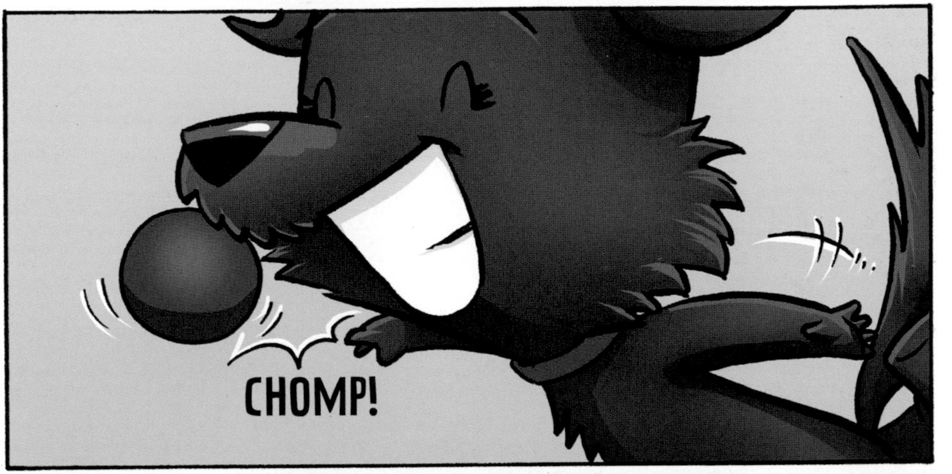
CHOMP!

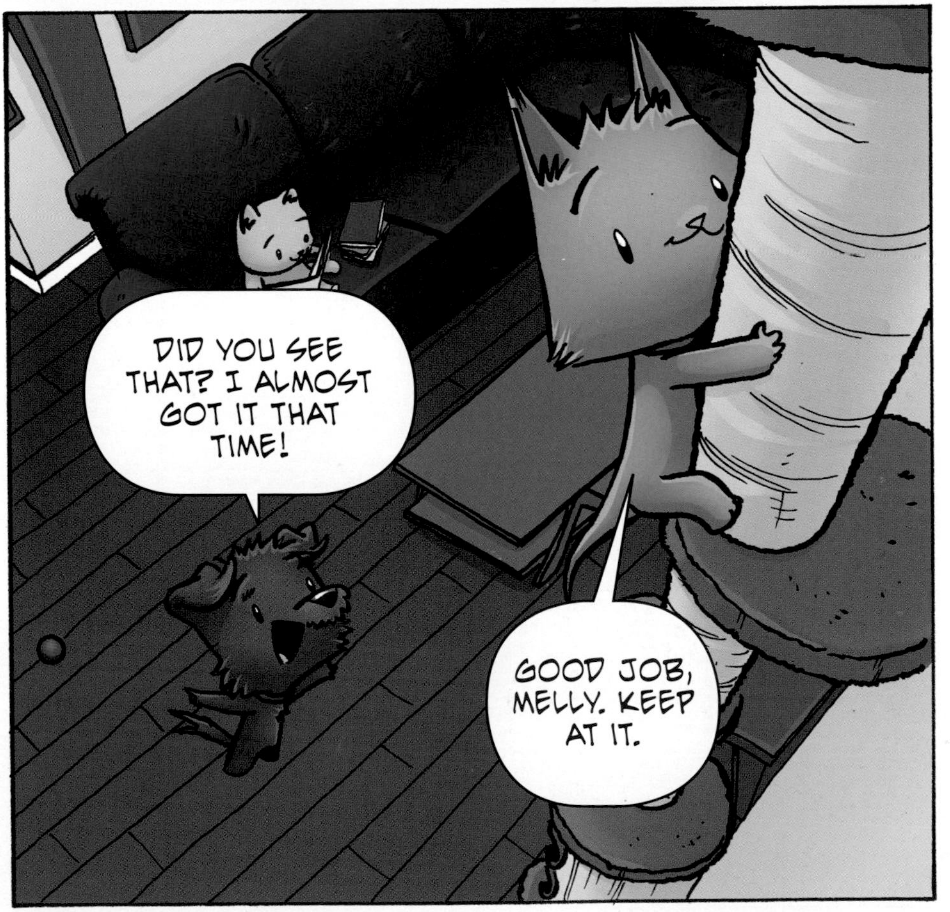
DID YOU SEE THAT? I ALMOST GOT IT THAT TIME!
GOOD JOB, MELLY. KEEP AT IT.

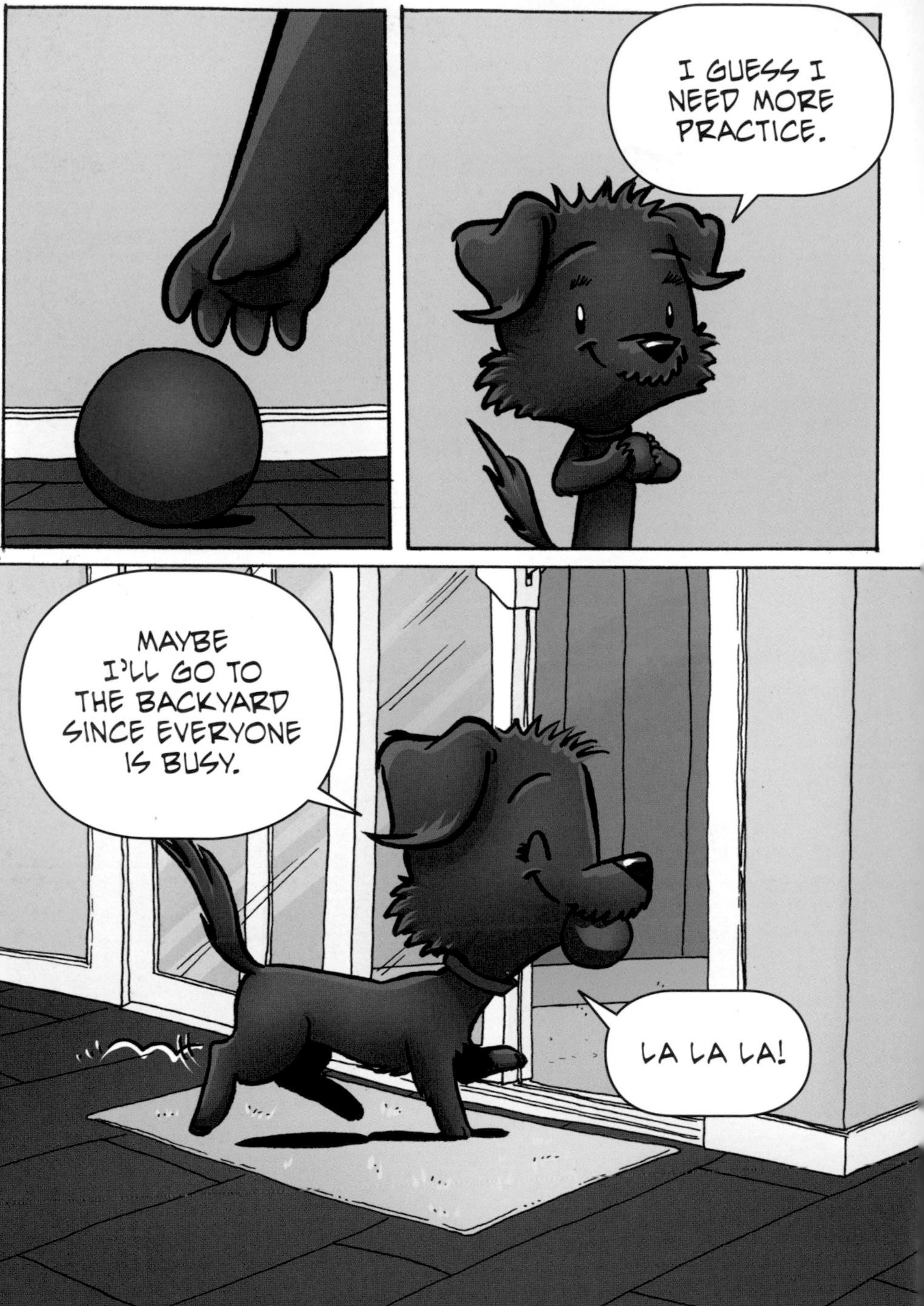
I GUESS I NEED MORE PRACTICE.
MAYBE I'LL GO TO THE BACKYARD SINCE EVERYONE IS BUSY.
LA LA LA!

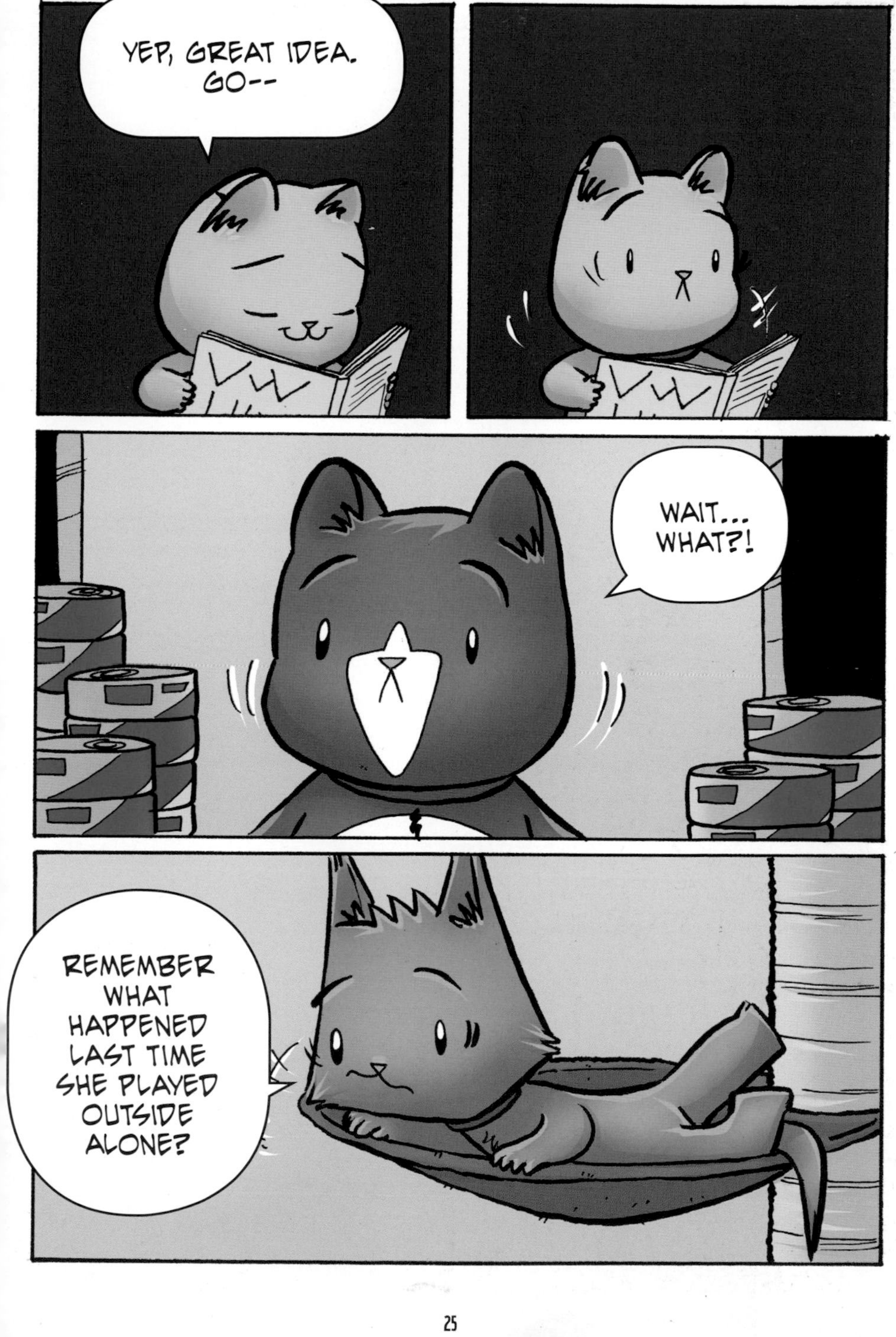
YEP, GREAT IDEA. GO--
WAIT... WHAT?!
REMEMBER WHAT HAPPENED LAST TIME SHE PLAYED OUTSIDE ALONE?

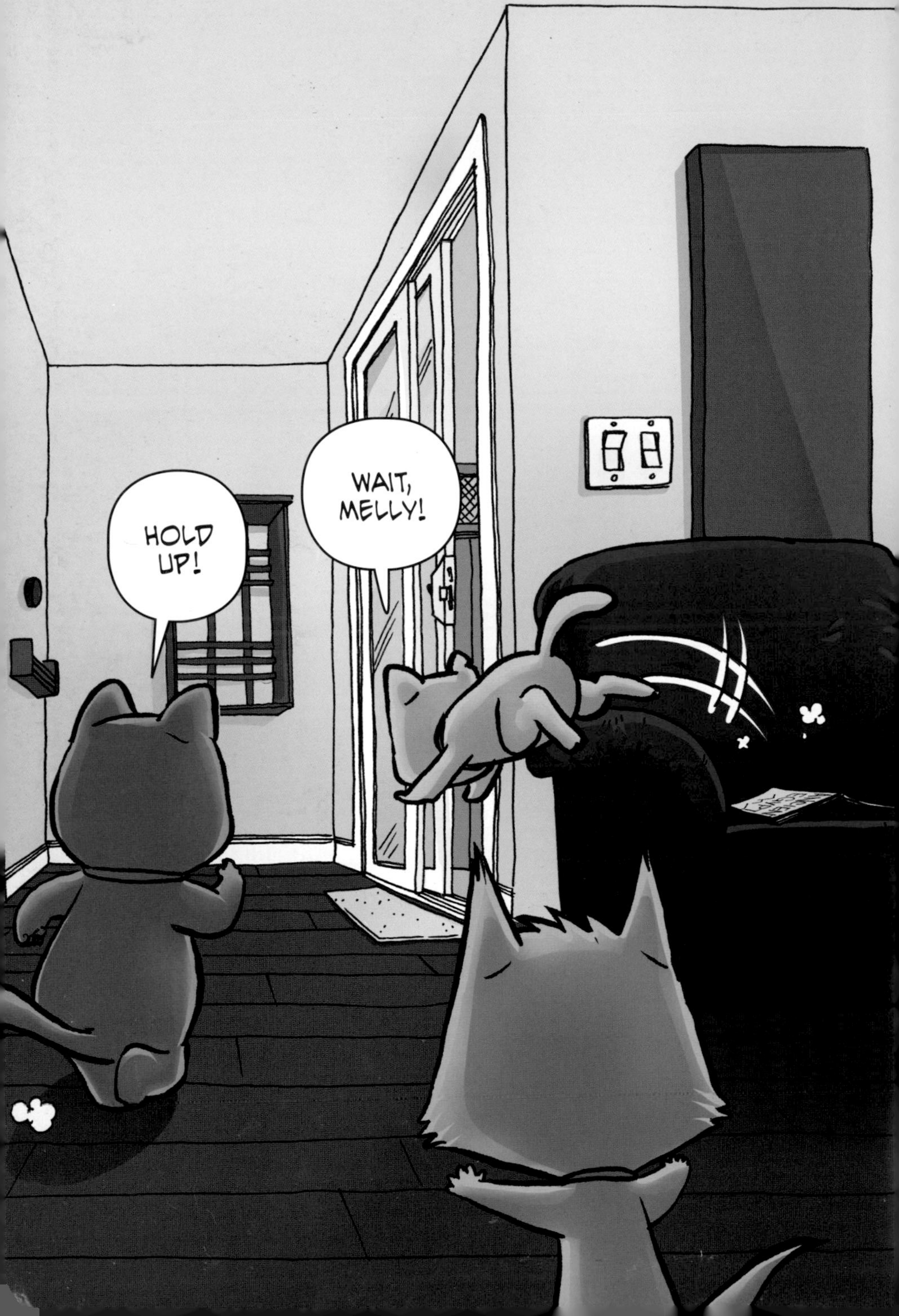
HOLD UP!
WAIT, MELLY!

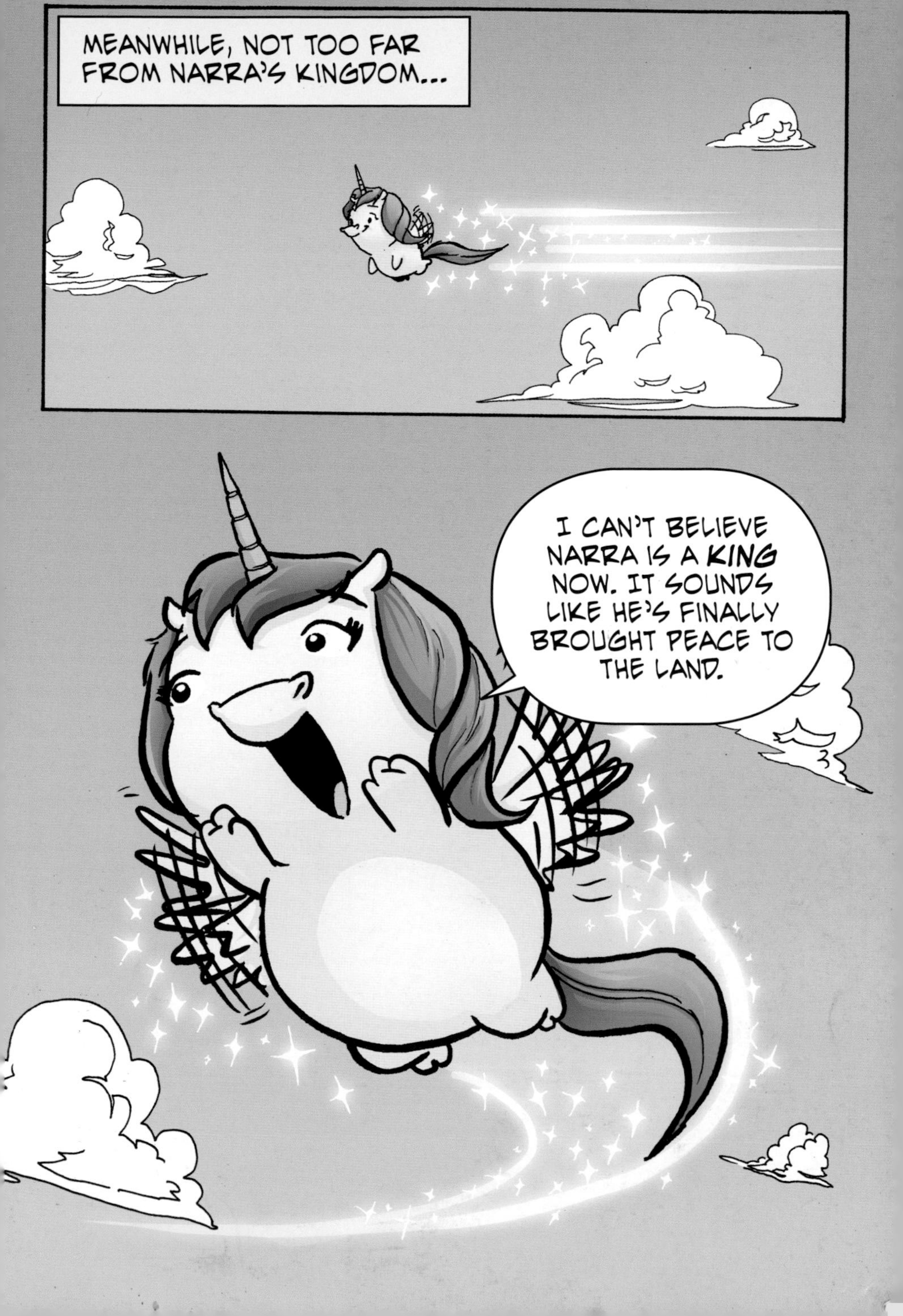
MEANWHILE, NOT TOO FAR FROM NARRA'S KINGDOM...
I CAN'T BELIEVE NARRA IS A **KING** NOW. IT SOUNDS LIKE HE'S FINALLY BROUGHT PEACE TO THE LAND.

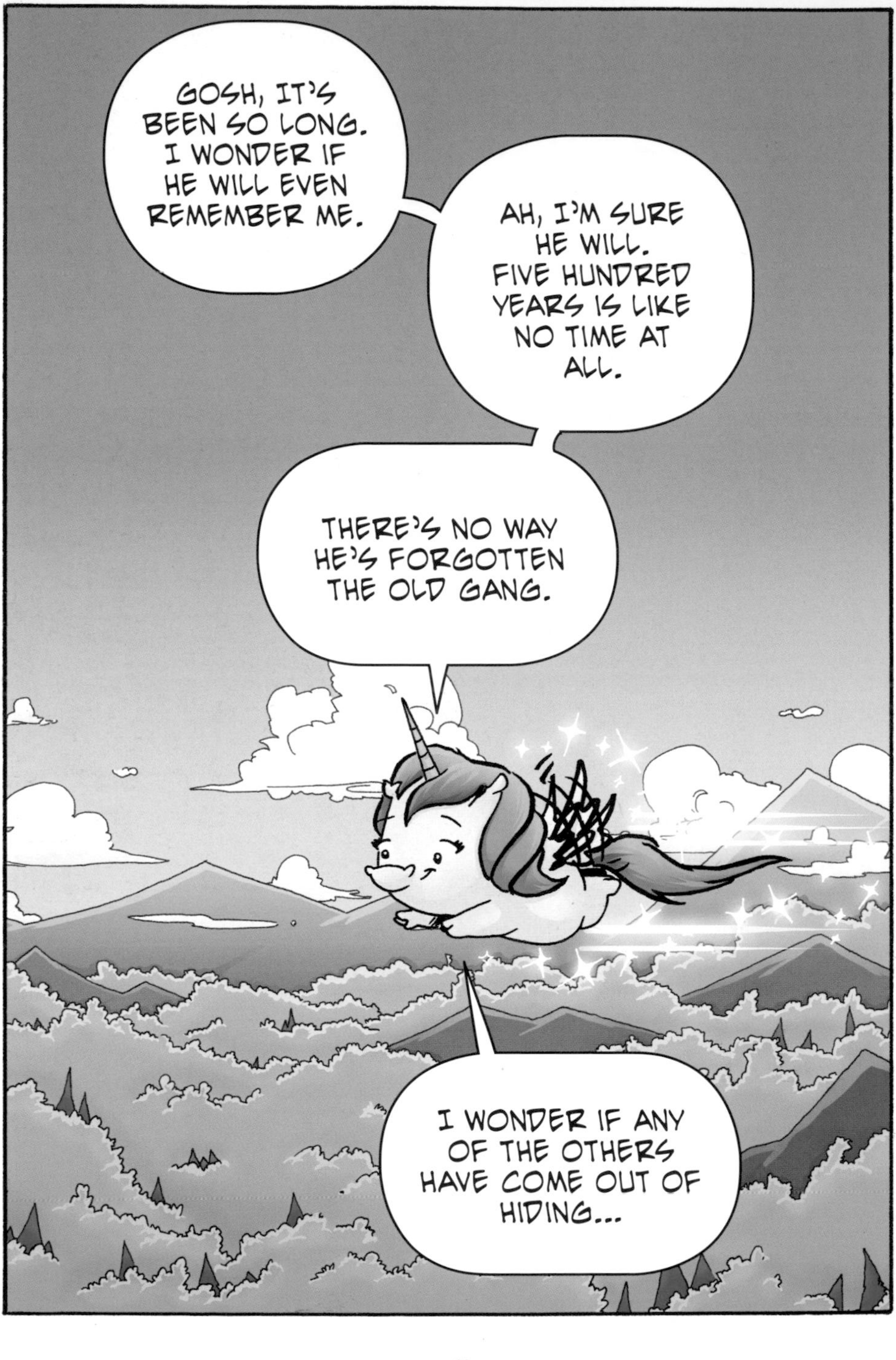
GOSH, IT'S BEEN SO LONG. I WONDER IF HE WILL EVEN REMEMBER ME.
AH, I'M SURE HE WILL. FIVE HUNDRED YEARS IS LIKE NO TIME AT ALL.
THERE'S NO WAY HE'S FORGOTTEN THE OLD GANG.
I WONDER IF ANY OF THE OTHERS HAVE COME OUT OF HIDING...

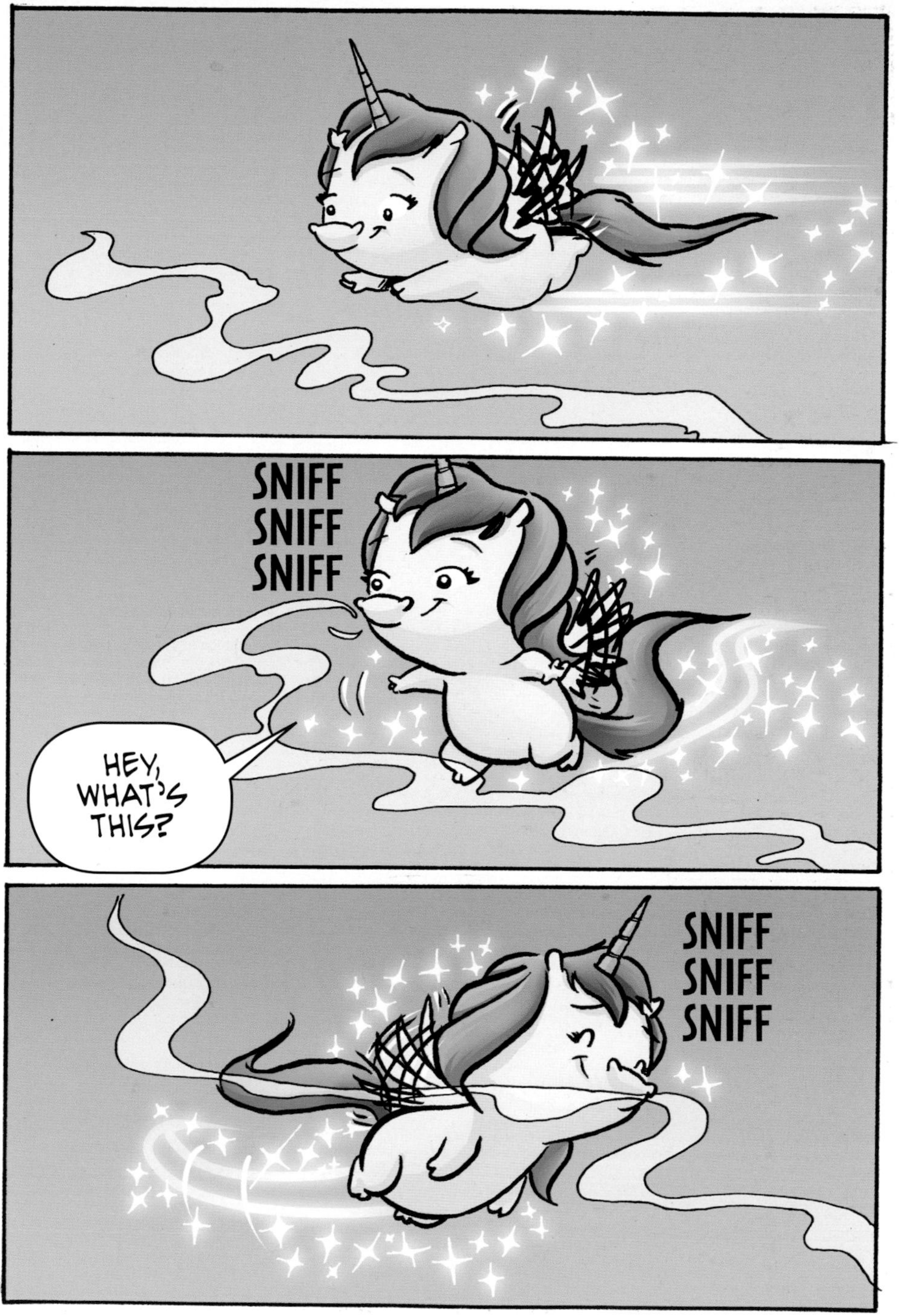
SNIFF
SNIFF
SNIFF
HEY, WHAT'S THIS?
SNIFF
SNIFF
SNIFF

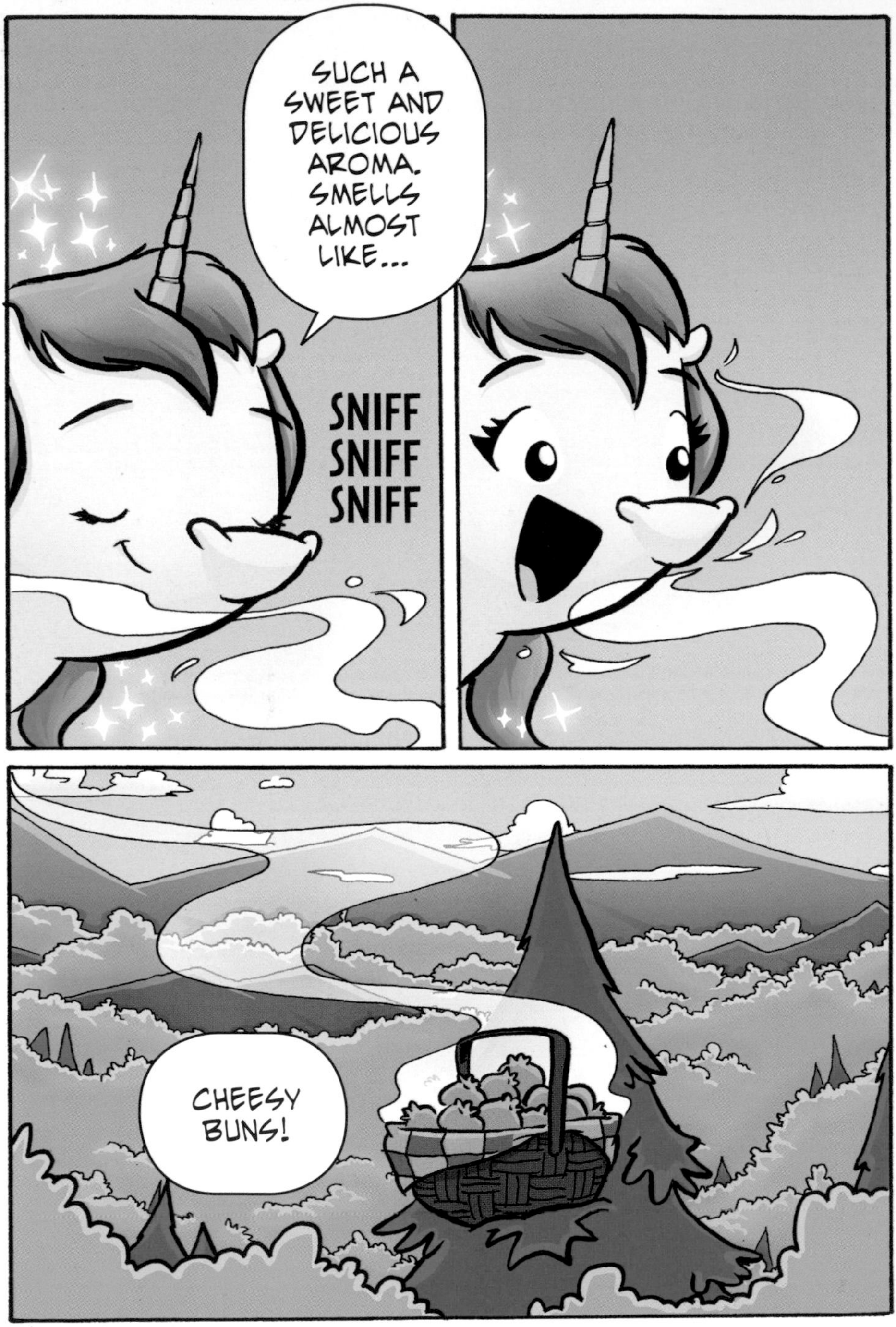
SUCH A SWEET AND DELICIOUS AROMA. SMELLS ALMOST LIKE...
SNIFF SNIFF SNIFF
CHEESY BUNS!

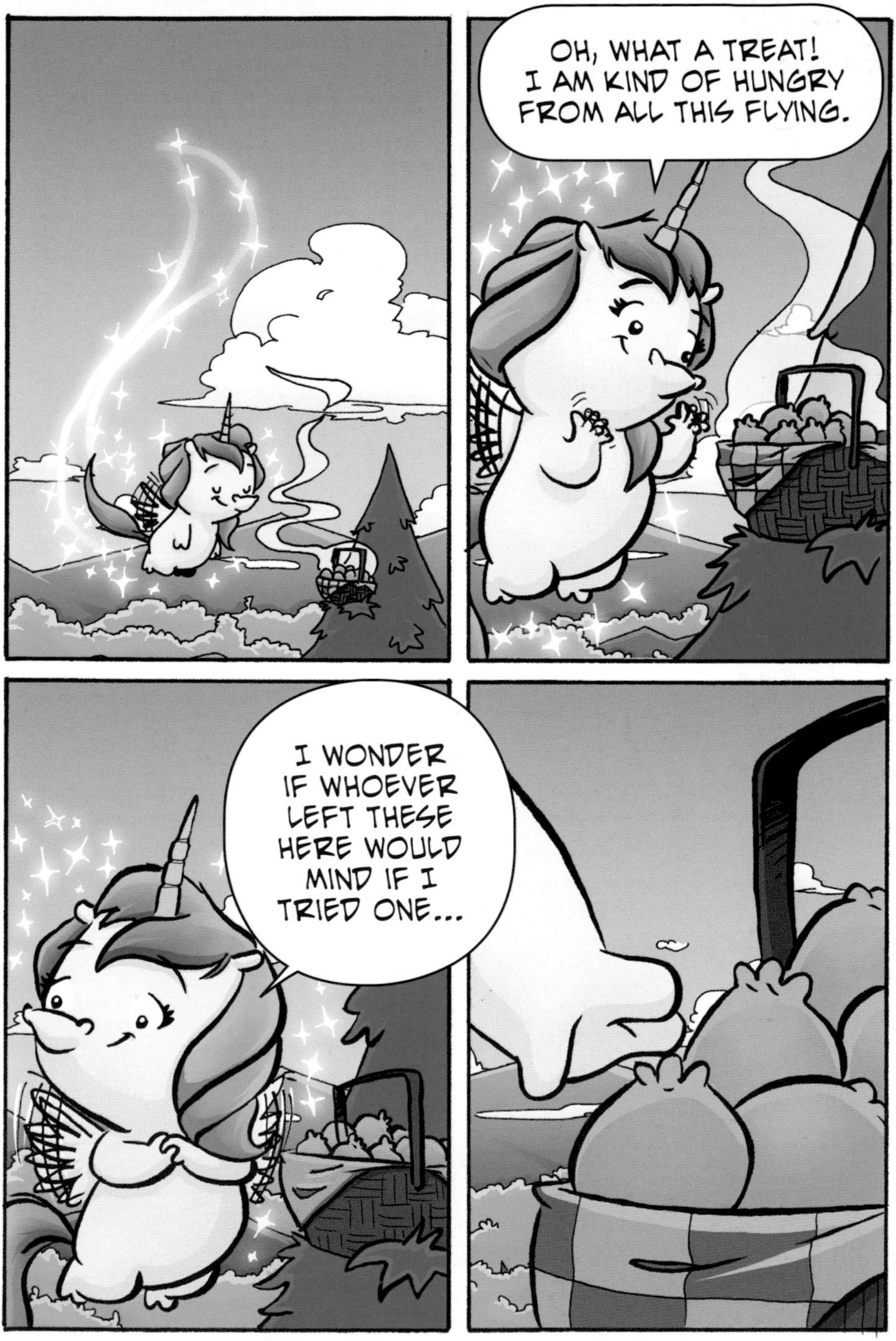
OH, WHAT A TREAT! I AM KIND OF HUNGRY FROM ALL THIS FLYING.
I WONDER IF WHOEVER LEFT THESE HERE WOULD MIND IF I TRIED ONE...

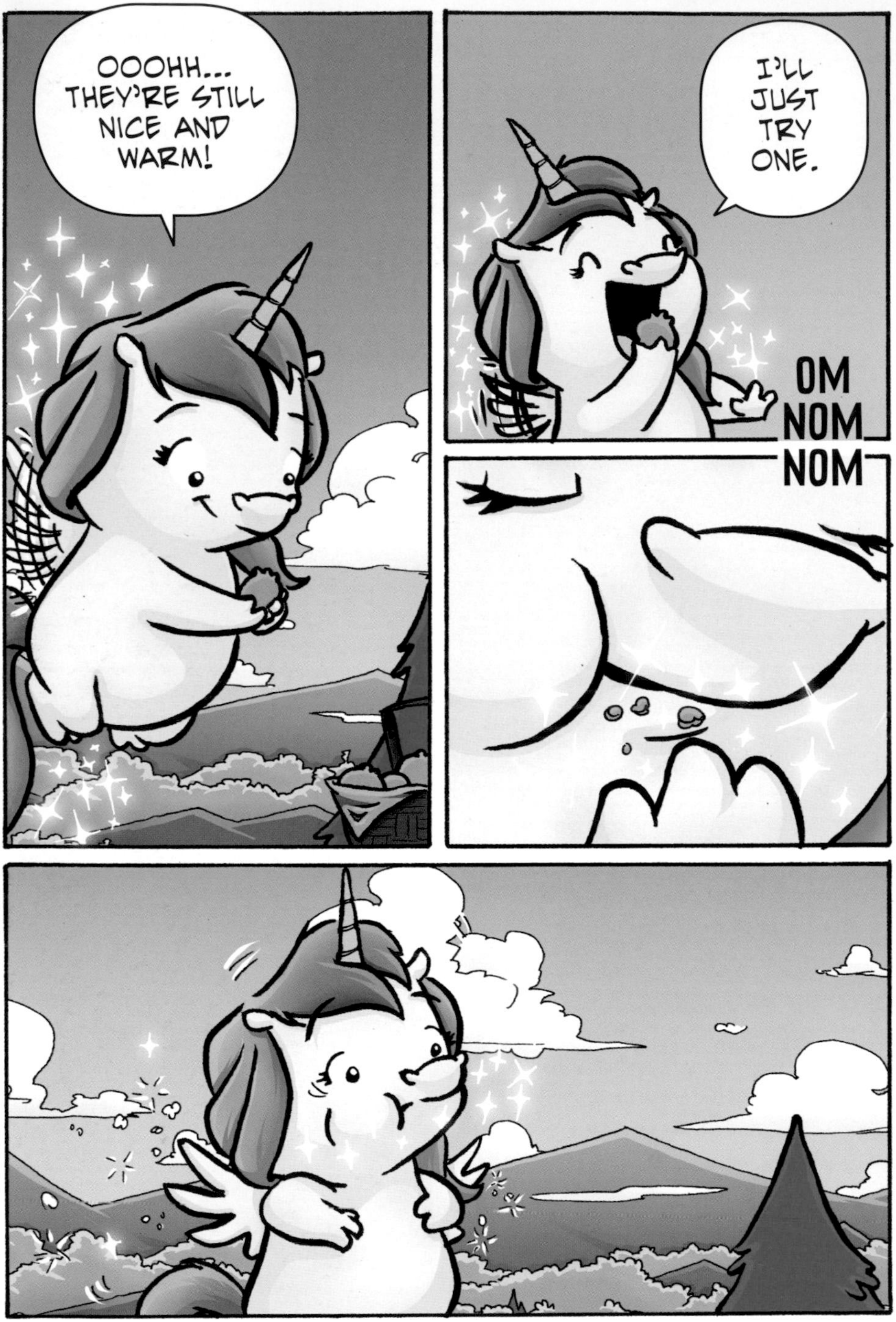
OOOHH... THEY'RE STILL NICE AND WARM!
I'LL JUST TRY ONE.
OM NOM NOM

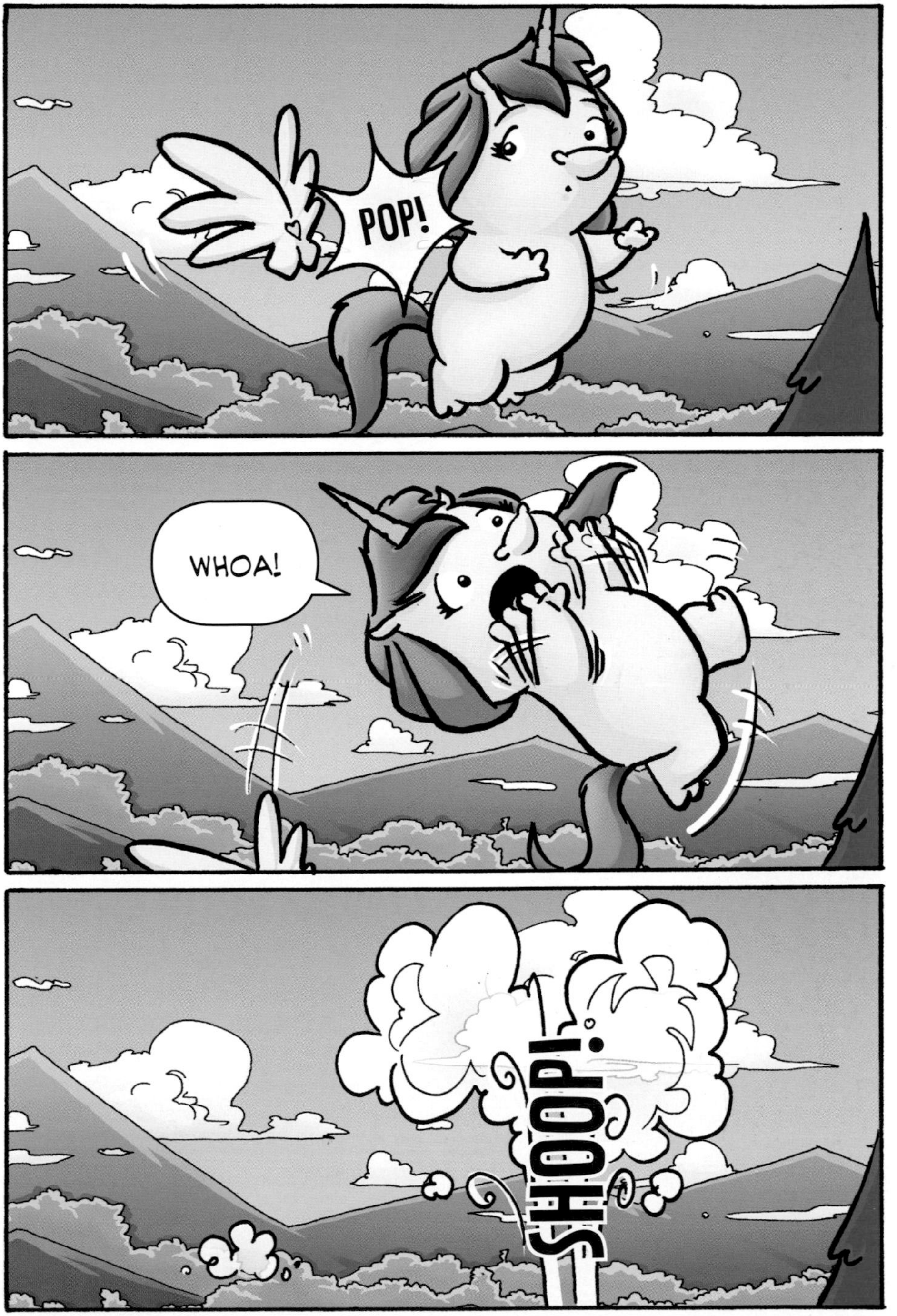
POP!
WHOA!
SHOOP!

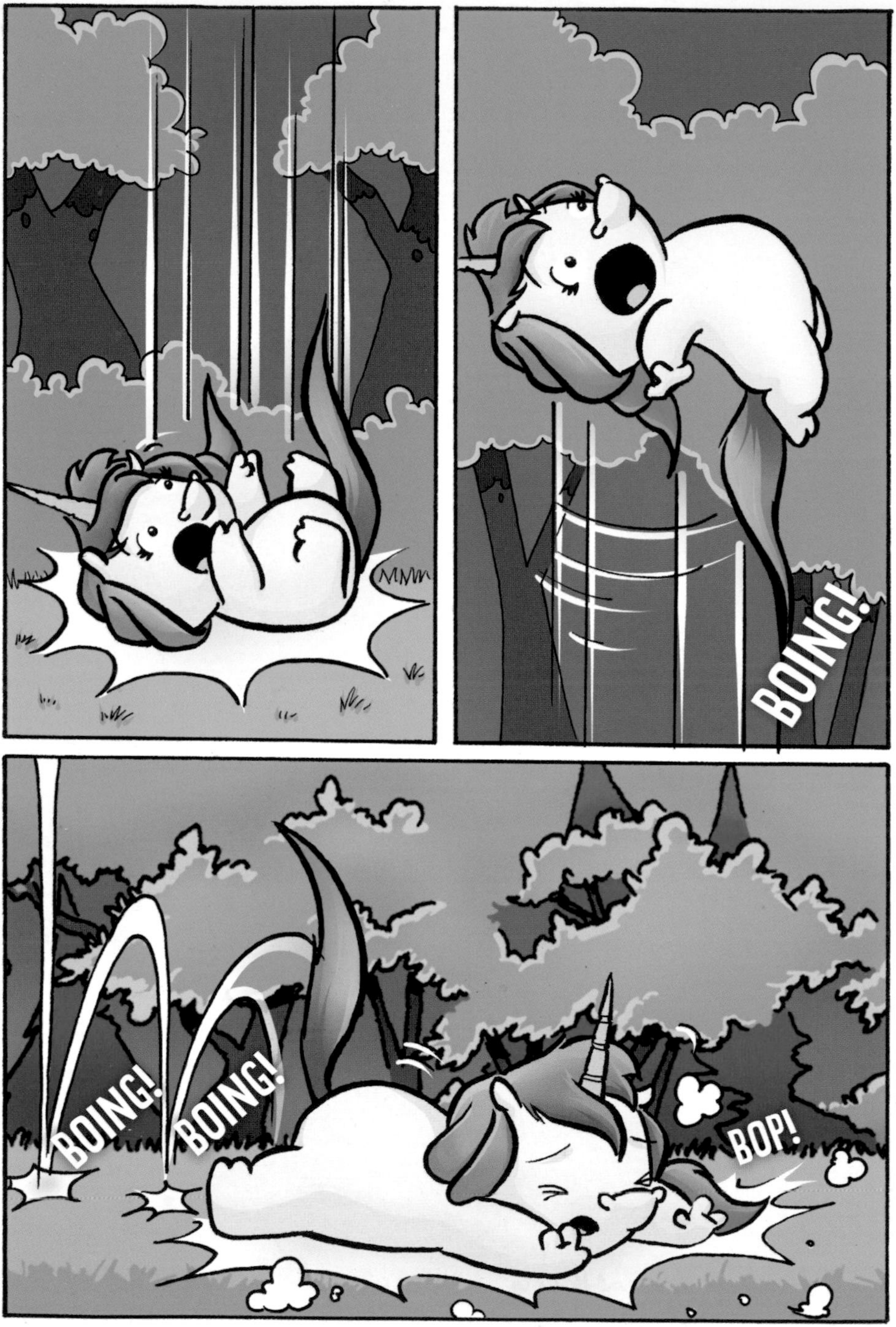
BOING!
BOING!
BOING!
BOP!

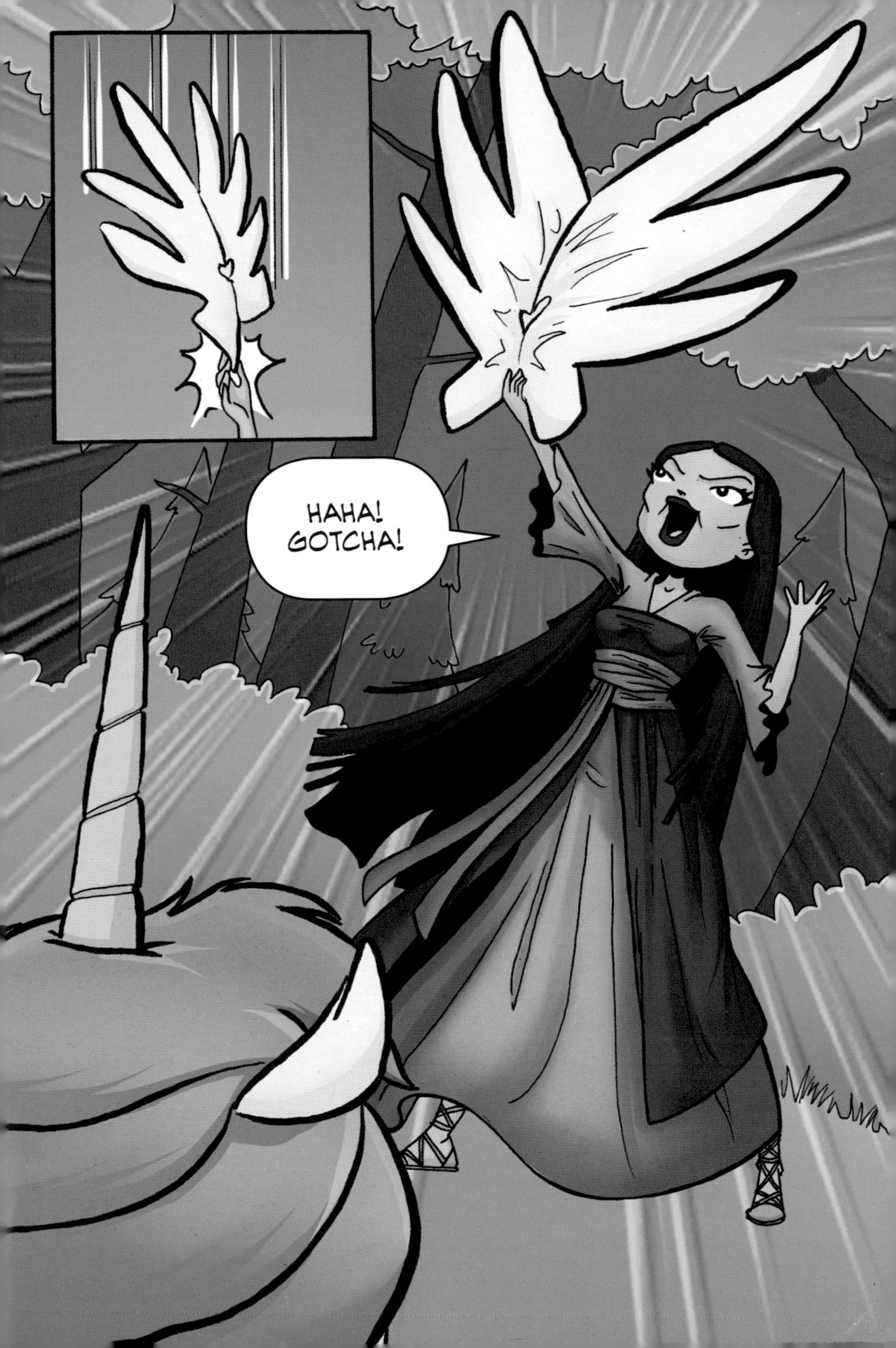
HAHA!
GOTCHA!

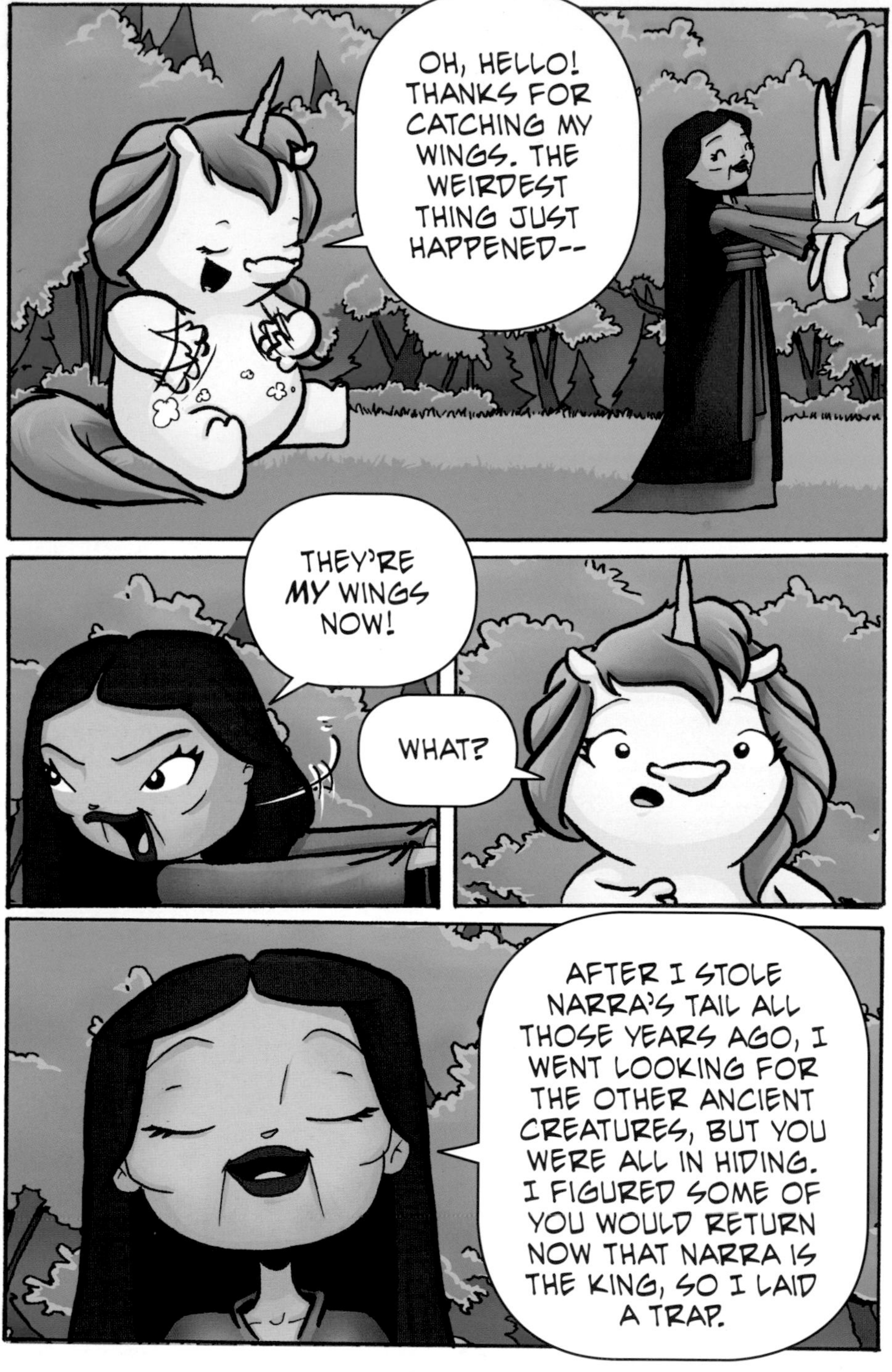
OH, HELLO! THANKS FOR CATCHING MY WINGS. THE WEIRDEST THING JUST HAPPENED--
THEY'RE MY WINGS NOW!
WHAT?
AFTER I STOLE NARRA'S TAIL ALL THOSE YEARS AGO, I WENT LOOKING FOR THE OTHER ANCIENT CREATURES, BUT YOU WERE ALL IN HIDING. I FIGURED SOME OF YOU WOULD RETURN NOW THAT NARRA IS THE KING, SO I LAID A TRAP.

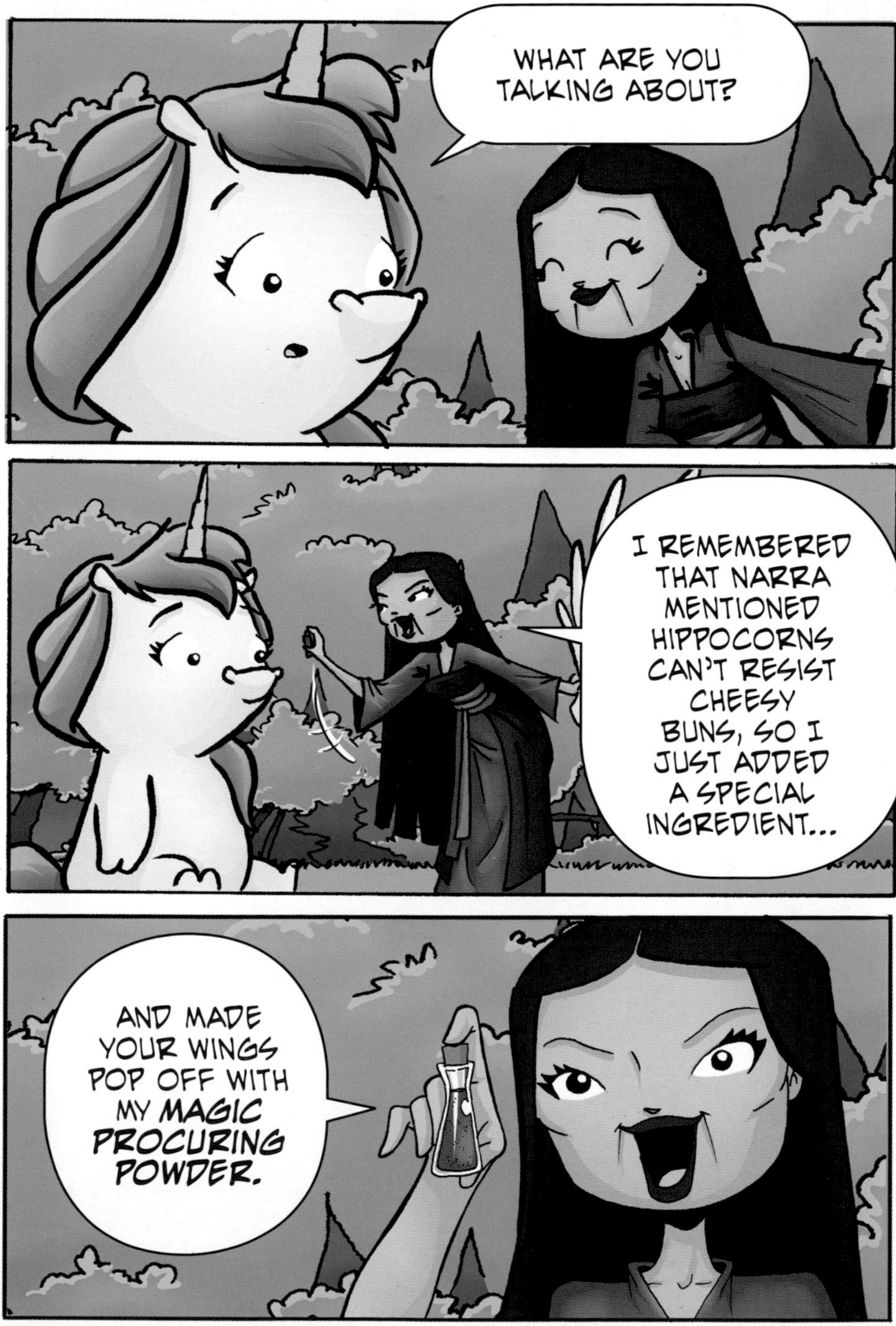
WHAT ARE YOU TALKING ABOUT?
I REMEMBERED THAT NARRA MENTIONED HIPPOCORNS CAN'T RESIST CHEESY BUNS, SO I JUST ADDED A SPECIAL INGREDIENT...
AND MADE YOUR WINGS POP OFF WITH MY **MAGIC PROCURING POWDER.**

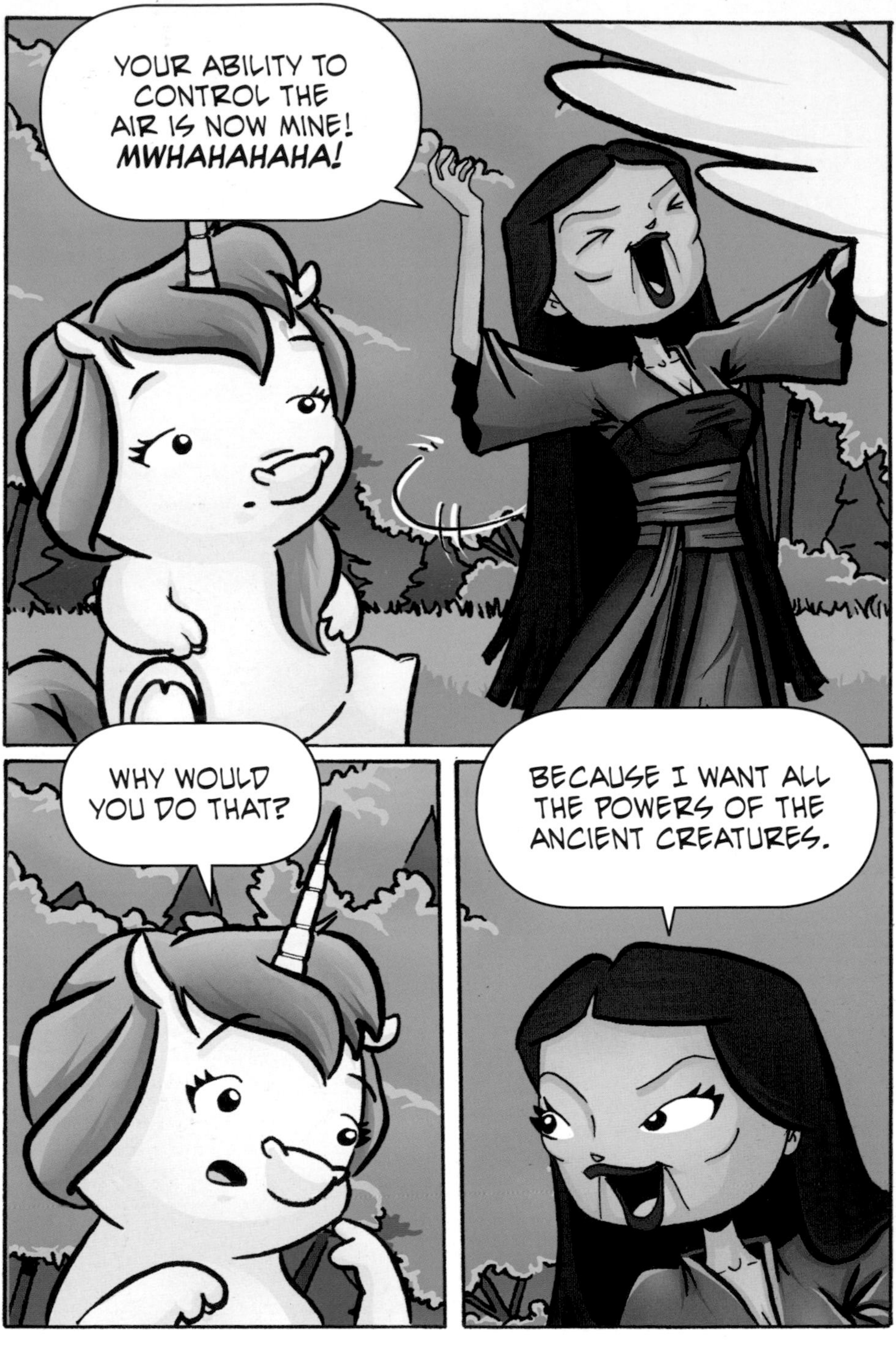
YOUR ABILITY TO CONTROL THE AIR IS NOW MINE! **MWHAHAHAHA!**
WHY WOULD YOU DO THAT?
BECAUSE I WANT ALL THE POWERS OF THE ANCIENT CREATURES.

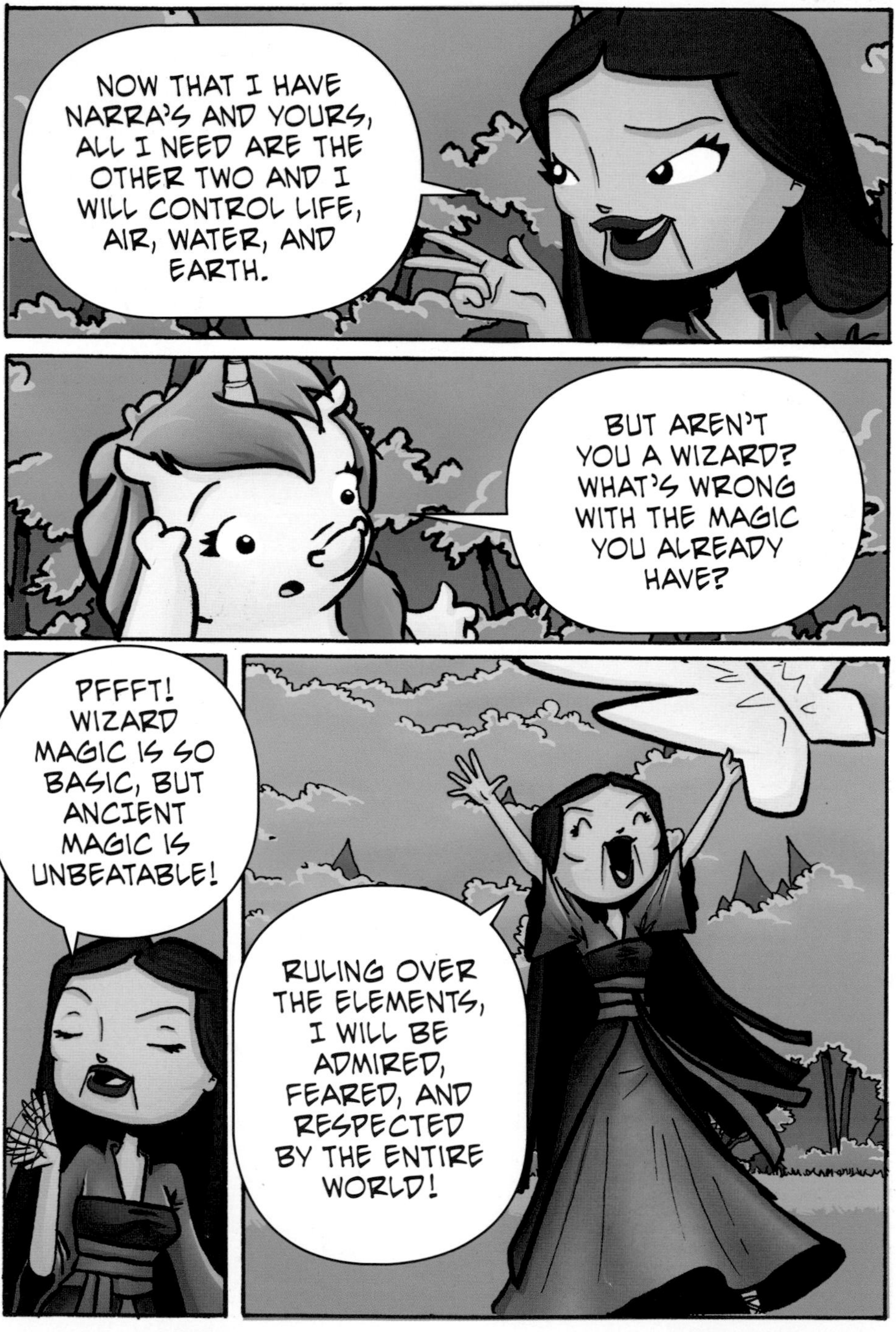
NOW THAT I HAVE NARRA'S AND YOURS, ALL I NEED ARE THE OTHER TWO AND I WILL CONTROL LIFE, AIR, WATER, AND EARTH.
BUT AREN'T YOU A WIZARD? WHAT'S WRONG WITH THE MAGIC YOU ALREADY HAVE?
PFFFT! WIZARD MAGIC IS SO BASIC, BUT ANCIENT MAGIC IS UNBEATABLE!
RULING OVER THE ELEMENTS, I WILL BE ADMIRED, FEARED, AND RESPECTED BY THE ENTIRE WORLD!

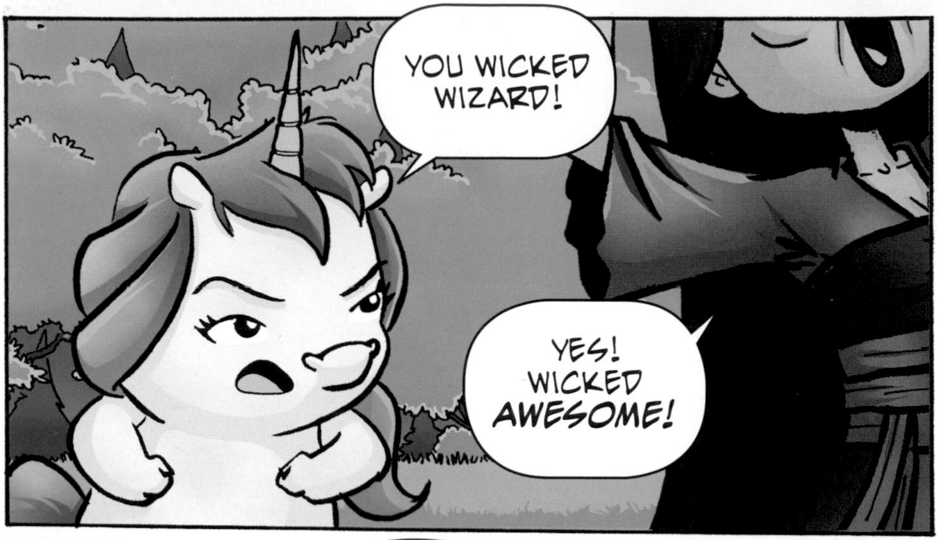
YOU WICKED WIZARD!
YES! WICKED AWESOME!

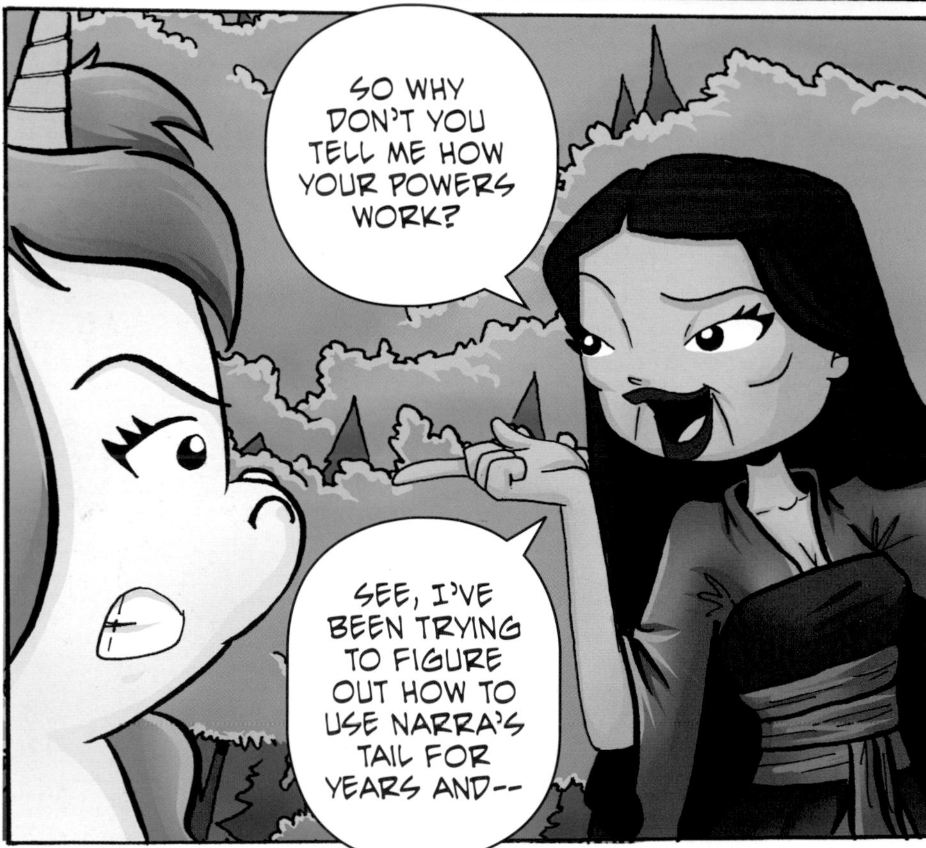
SO WHY DON'T YOU TELL ME HOW YOUR POWERS WORK?
SEE, I'VE BEEN TRYING TO FIGURE OUT HOW TO USE NARRA'S TAIL FOR YEARS AND--

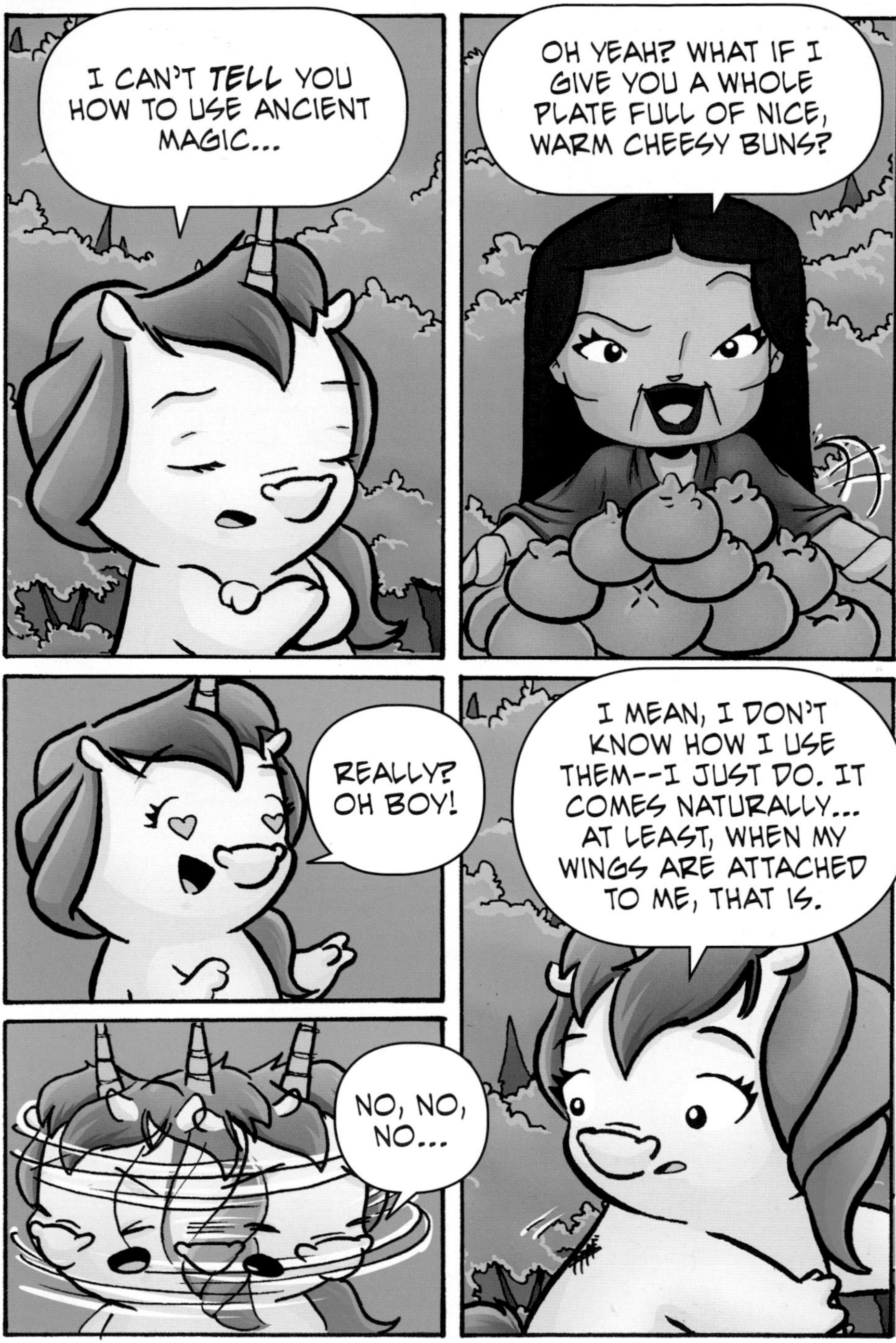
I CAN'T TELL YOU HOW TO USE ANCIENT MAGIC...
OH YEAH? WHAT IF I GIVE YOU A WHOLE PLATE FULL OF NICE, WARM CHEESY BUNS?
REALLY? OH BOY!
I MEAN, I DON'T KNOW HOW I USE THEM--I JUST DO. IT COMES NATURALLY... AT LEAST, WHEN MY WINGS ARE ATTACHED TO ME, THAT IS.
NO, NO, NO...

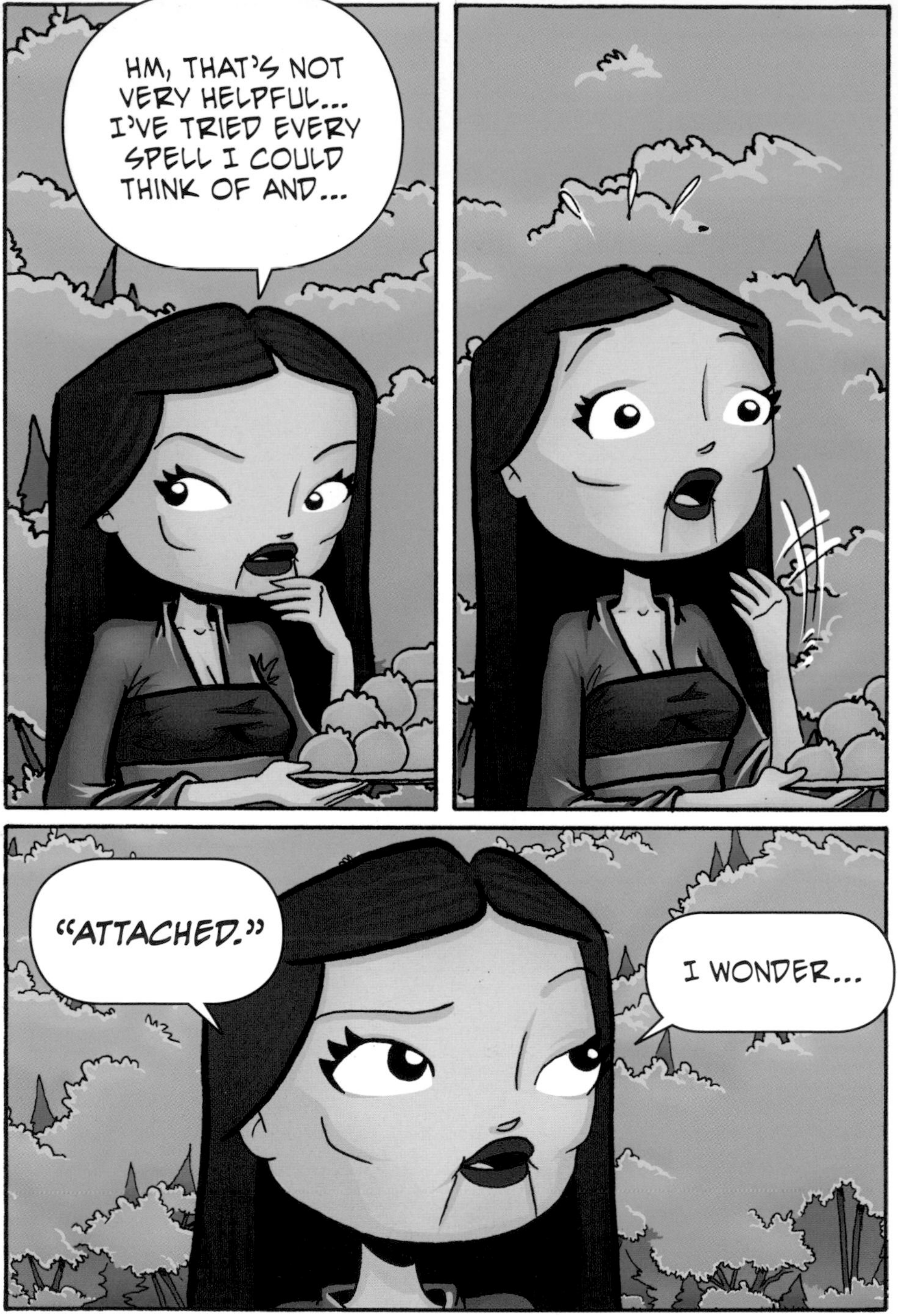
HM, THAT'S NOT VERY HELPFUL... I'VE TRIED EVERY SPELL I COULD THINK OF AND...
"ATTACHED."
I WONDER...

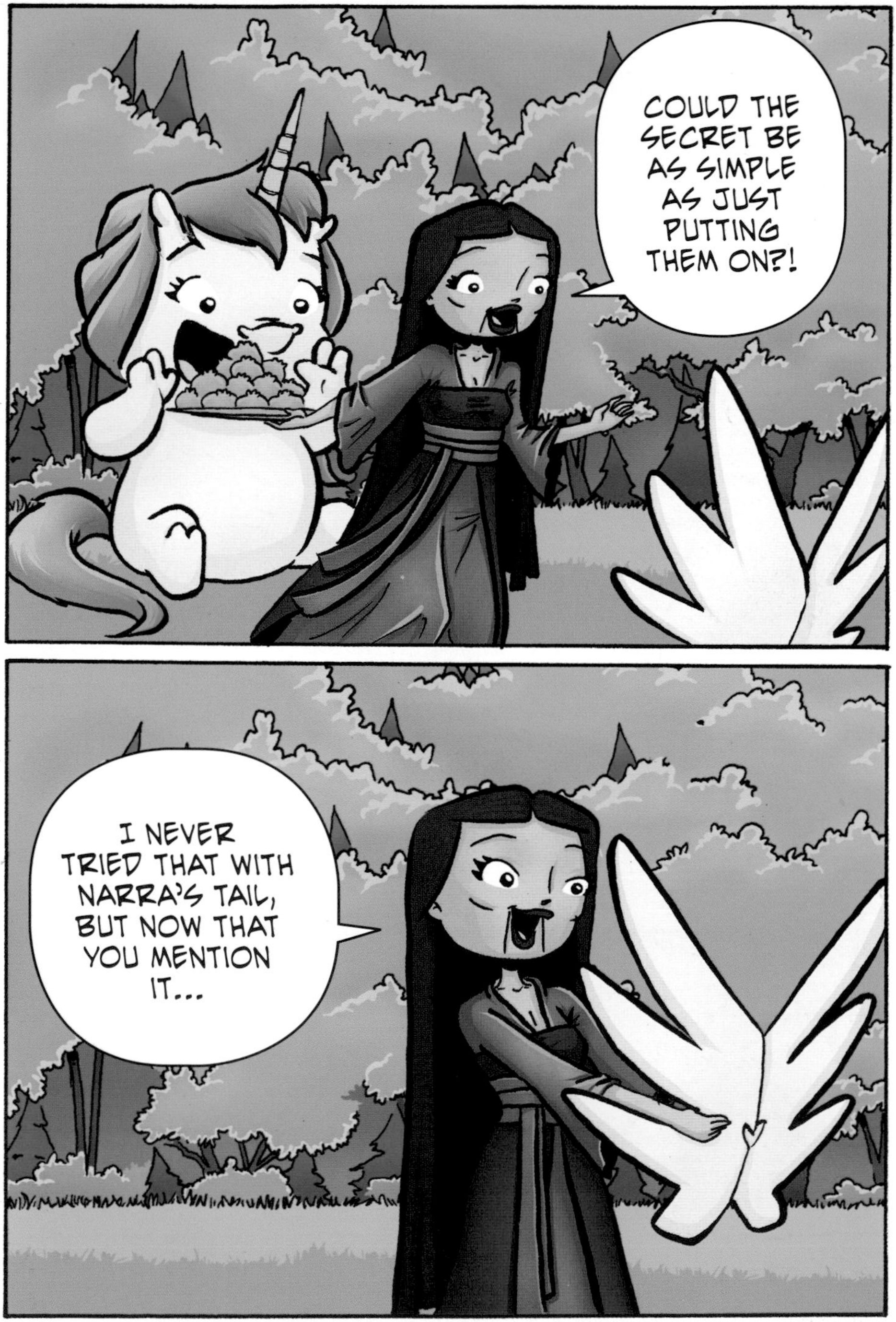
COULD THE SECRET BE AS SIMPLE AS JUST PUTTING THEM ON?!
I NEVER TRIED THAT WITH NARRA'S TAIL, BUT NOW THAT YOU MENTION IT...

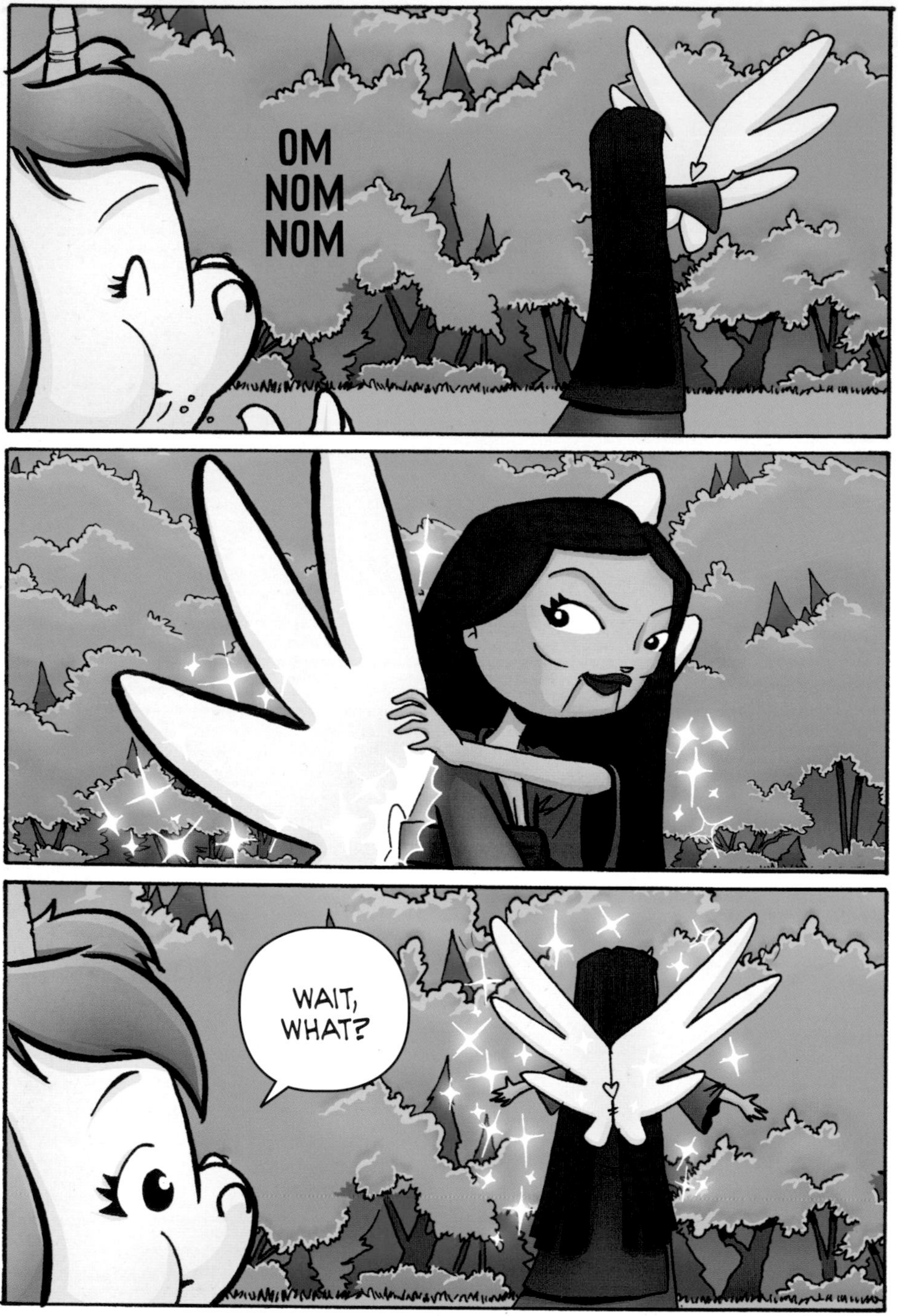
OM NOM NOM
WAIT, WHAT?

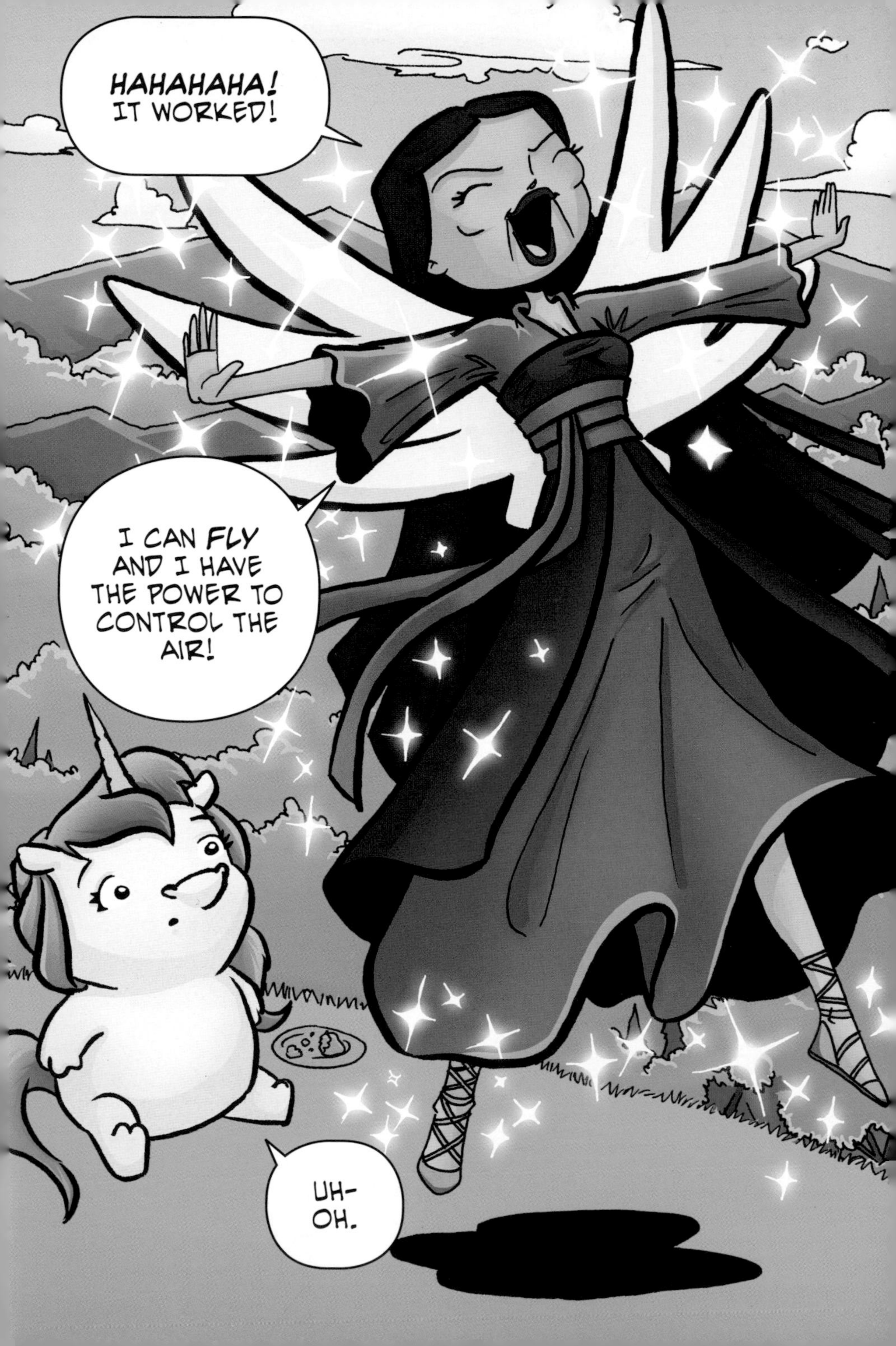
HAHAHAHA! IT WORKED!
I CAN FLY AND I HAVE THE POWER TO CONTROL THE AIR!
UH-OH.

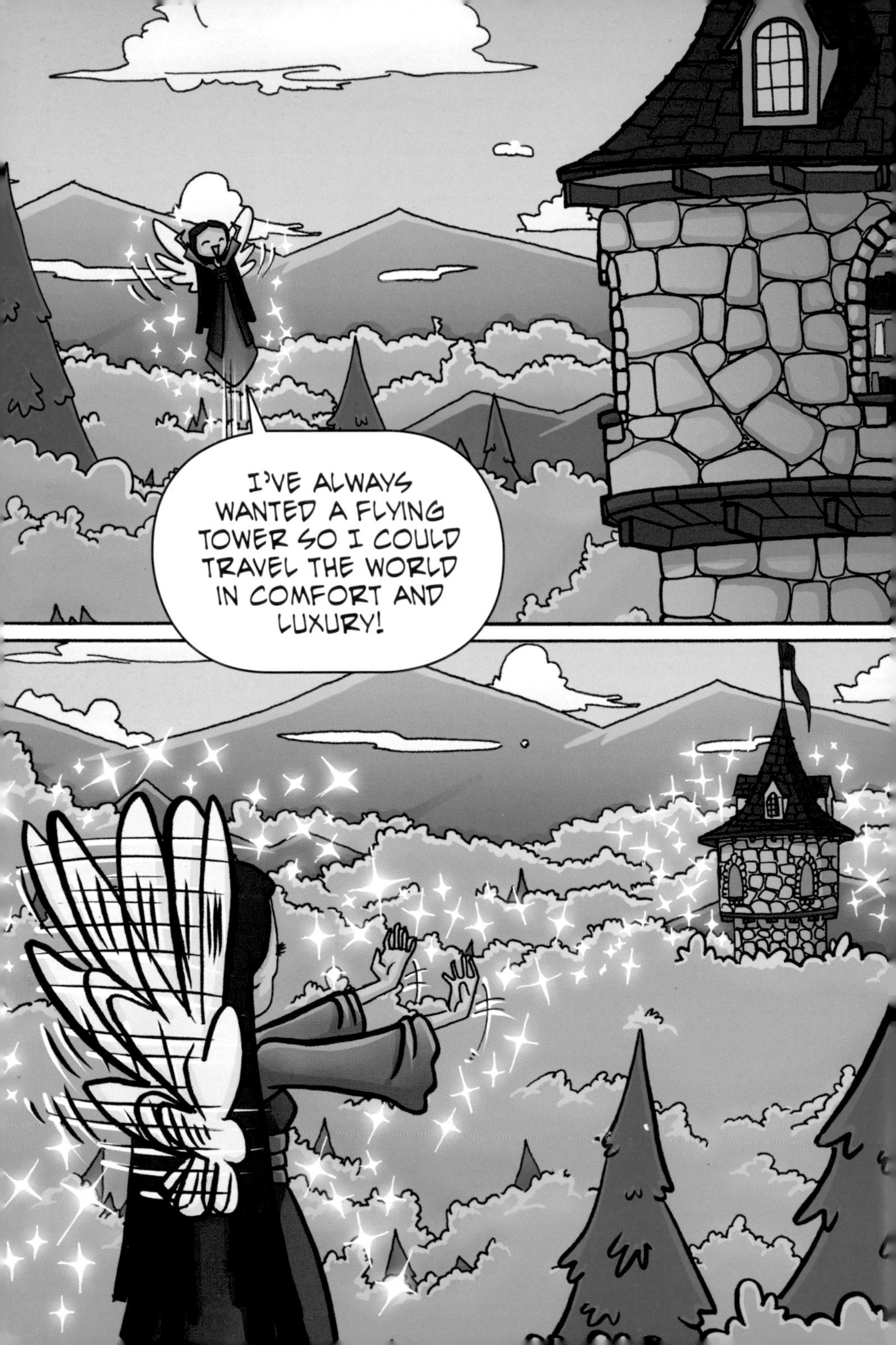
I'VE ALWAYS WANTED A FLYING TOWER SO I COULD TRAVEL THE WORLD IN COMFORT AND LUXURY!

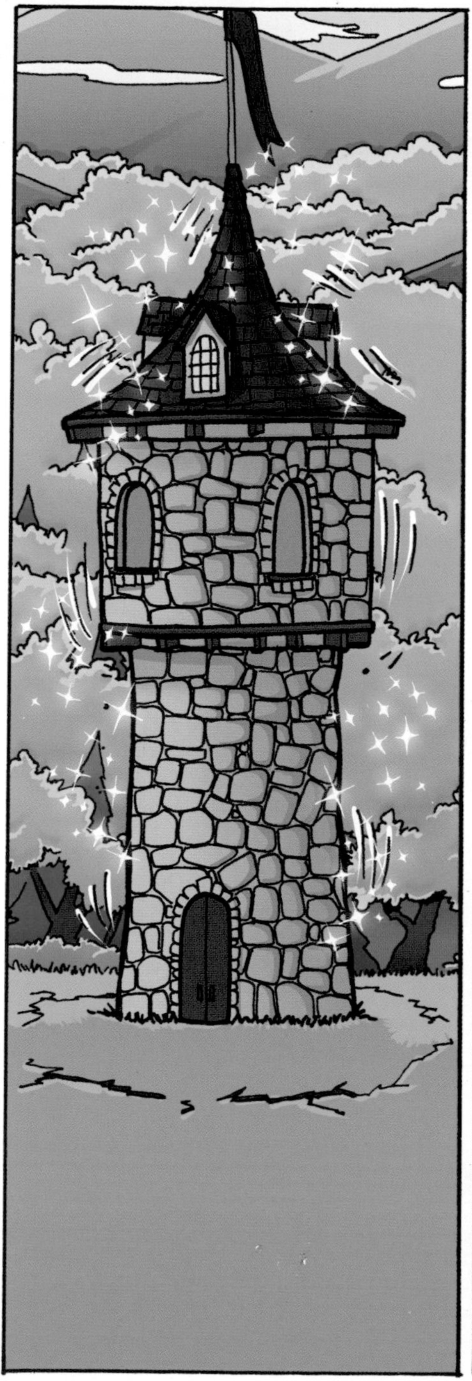
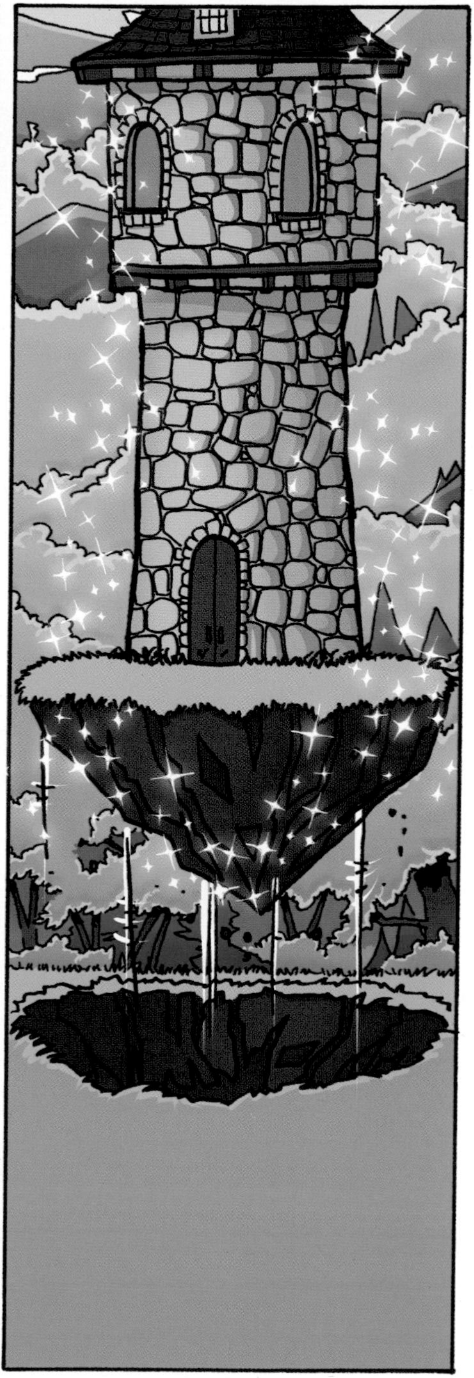

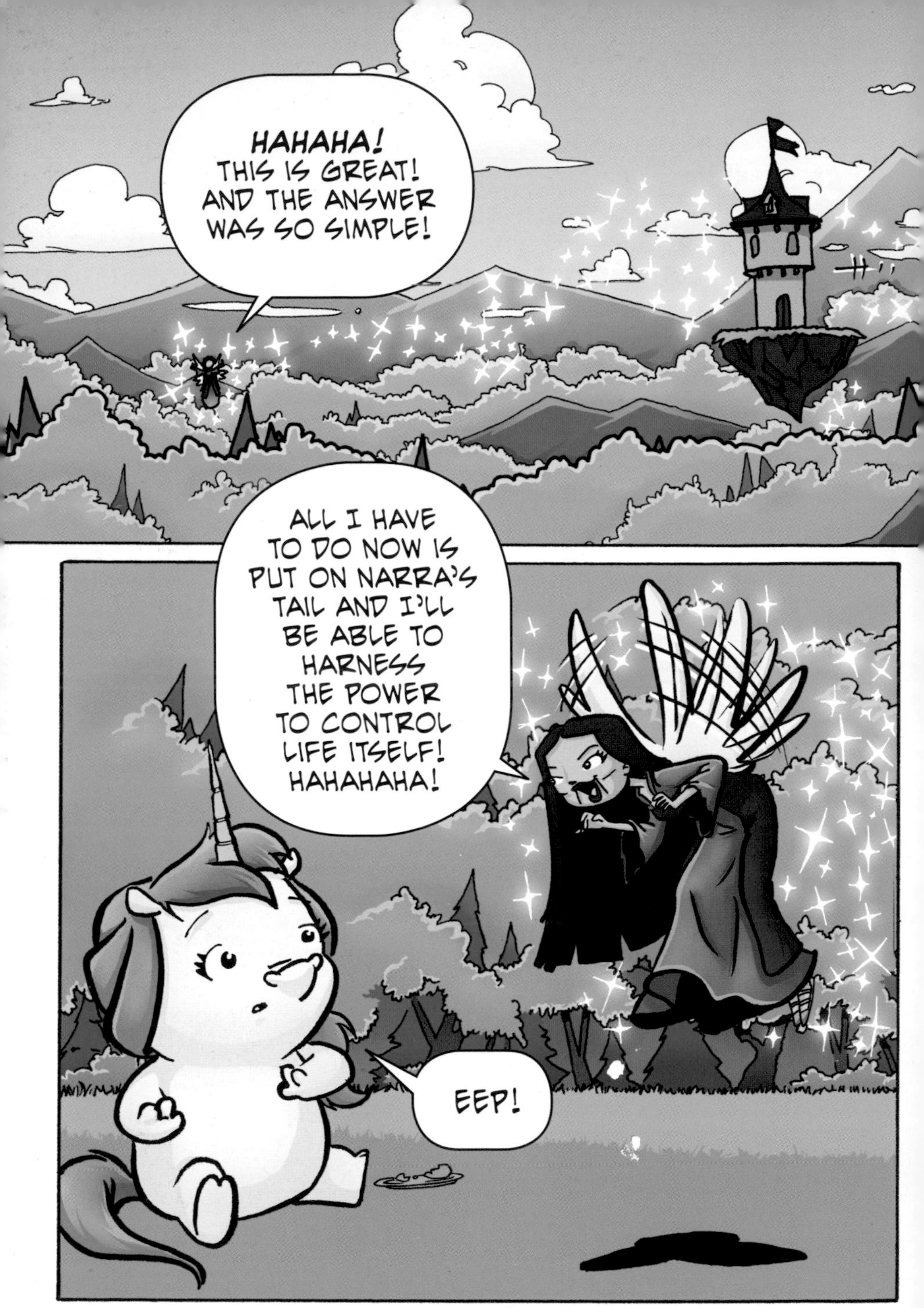
HAHAHA! THIS IS GREAT! AND THE ANSWER WAS SO SIMPLE!
ALL I HAVE TO DO NOW IS PUT ON NARRA'S TAIL AND I'LL BE ABLE TO HARNESS THE POWER TO CONTROL LIFE ITSELF! HAHAHAHA!
EEP!

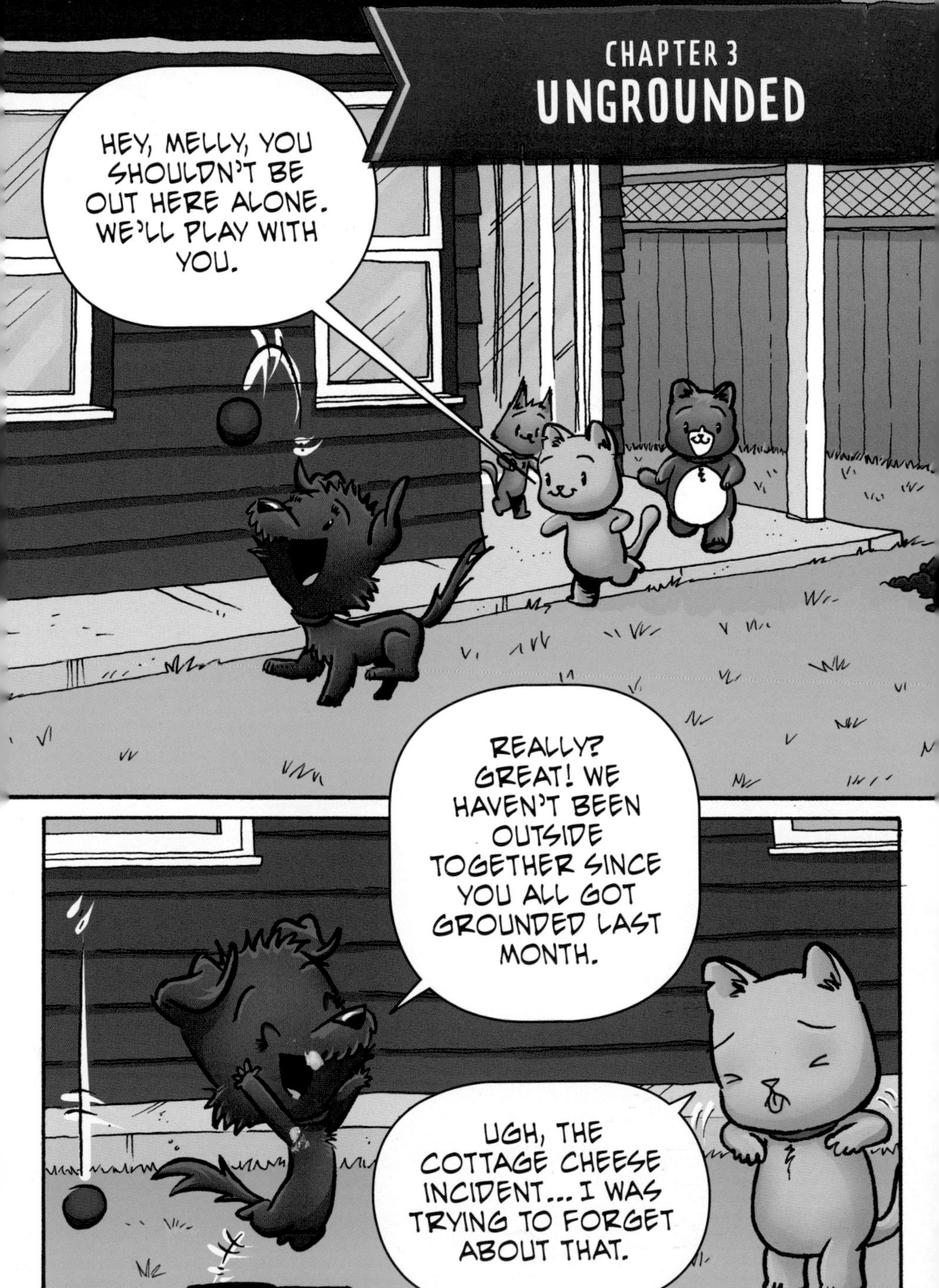
CHAPTER 3
UNGROUNDED
HEY, MELLY, YOU SHOULDN'T BE OUT HERE ALONE. WE'LL PLAY WITH YOU.
REALLY? GREAT! WE HAVEN'T BEEN OUTSIDE TOGETHER SINCE YOU ALL GOT GROUNDED LAST MONTH.
UGH, THE COTTAGE CHEESE INCIDENT... I WAS TRYING TO FORGET ABOUT THAT.

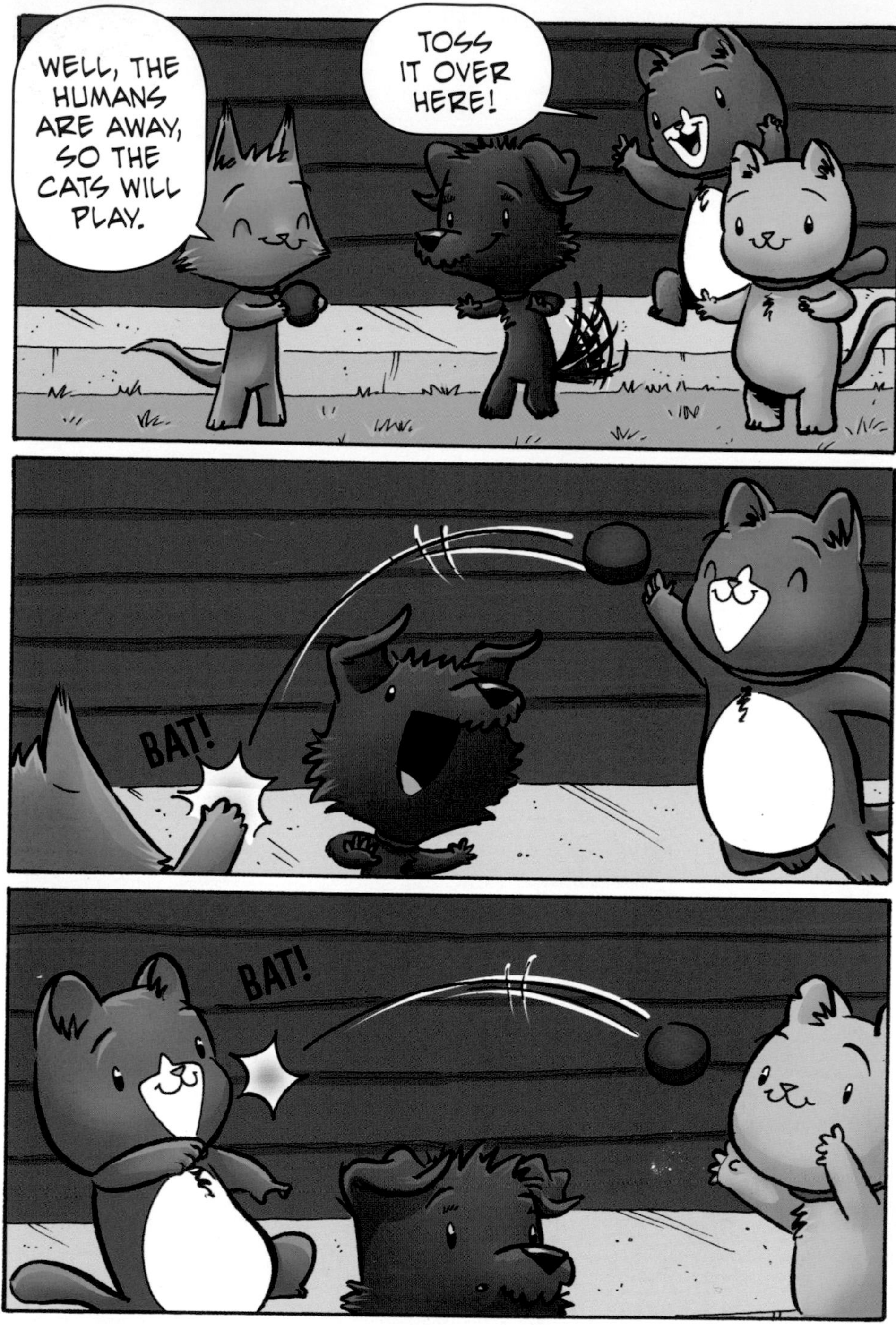
WELL, THE HUMANS ARE AWAY, SO THE CATS WILL PLAY.
TOSS IT OVER HERE!
BAT!
BAT!

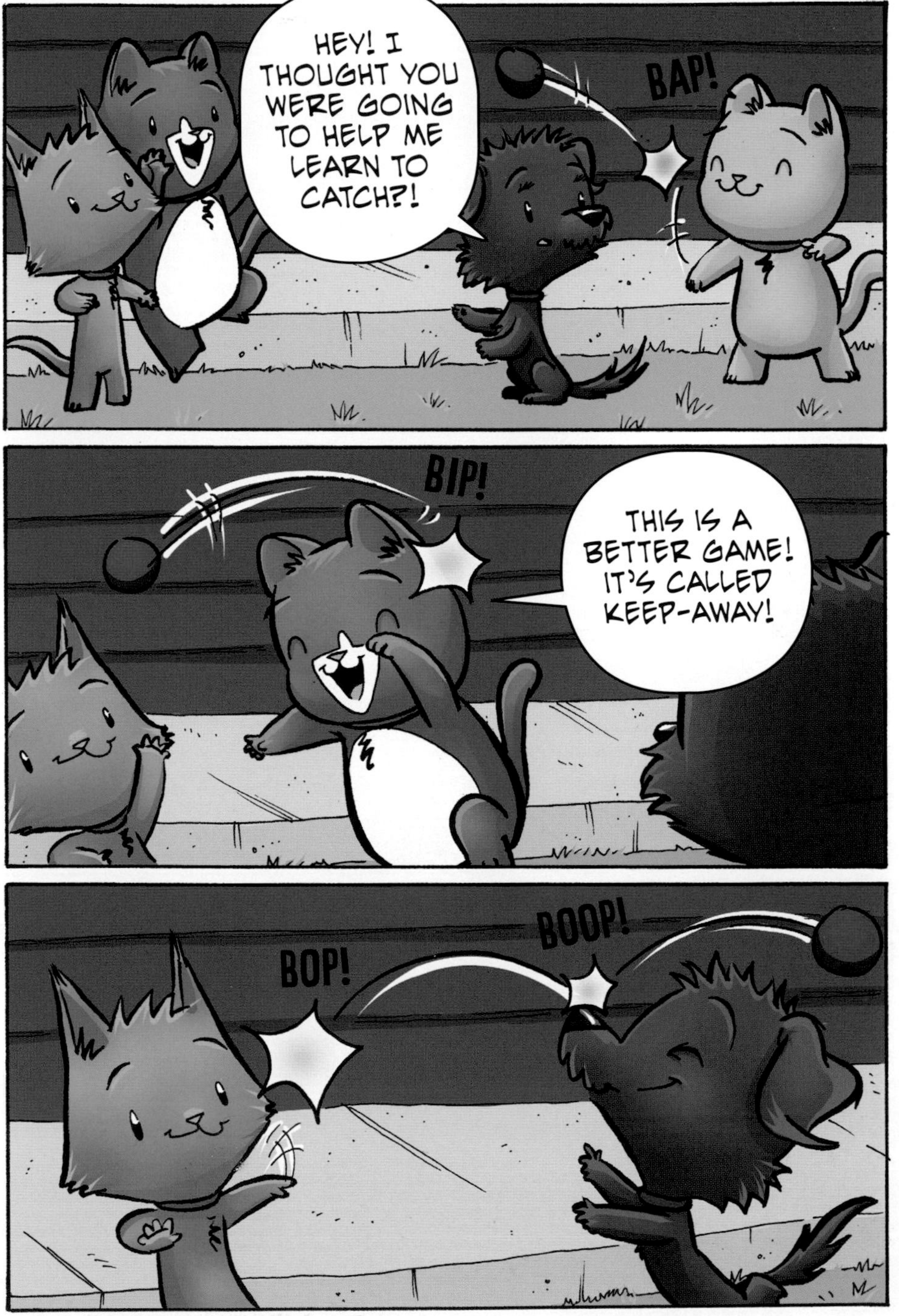
HEY! I THOUGHT YOU WERE GOING TO HELP ME LEARN TO CATCH?!
BAP!
BIP!
THIS IS A BETTER GAME! IT'S CALLED KEEP-AWAY!
BOP!
BOOP!

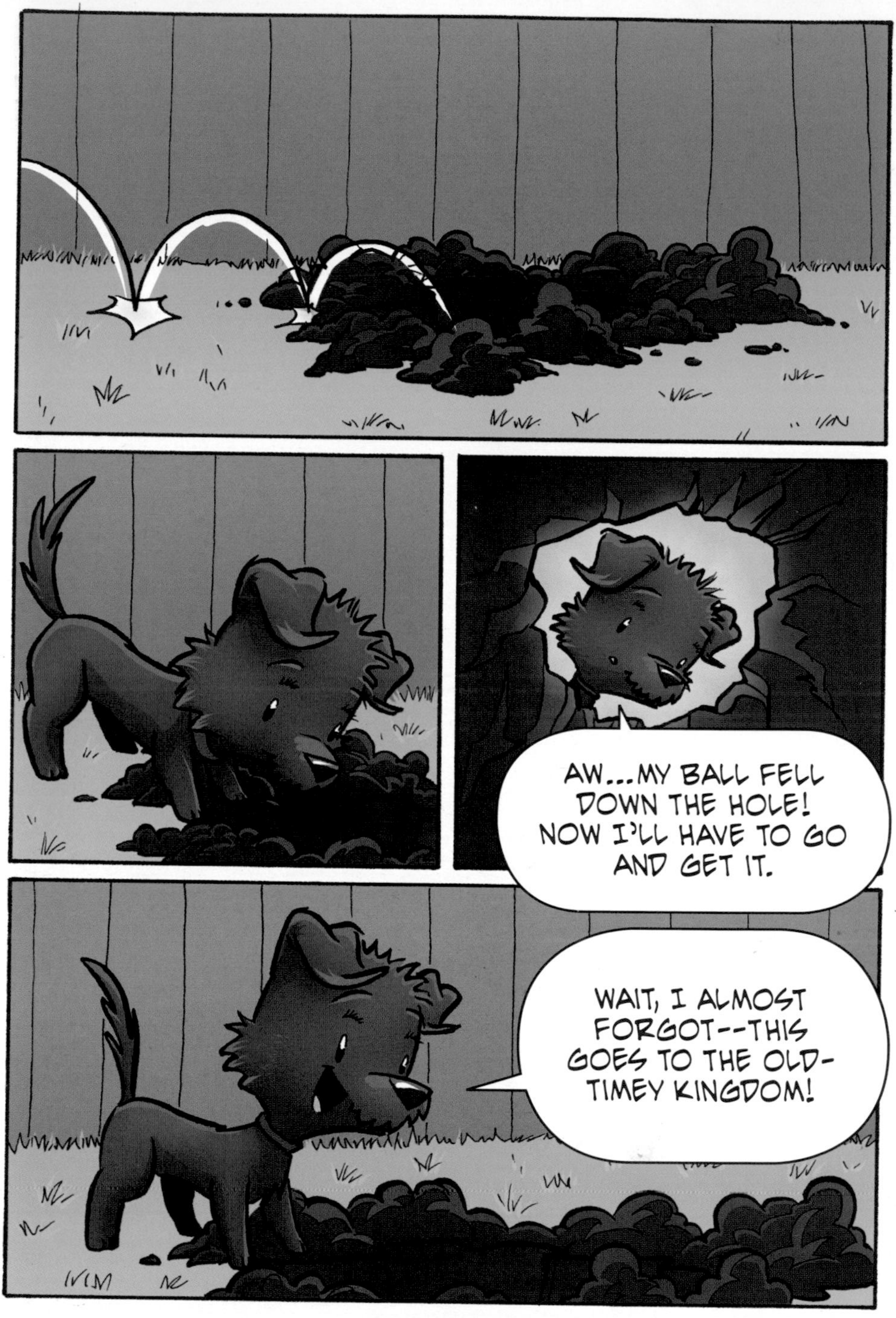
AW...MY BALL FELL DOWN THE HOLE! NOW I'LL HAVE TO GO AND GET IT.
WAIT, I ALMOST FORGOT--THIS GOES TO THE OLD-TIMEY KINGDOM!

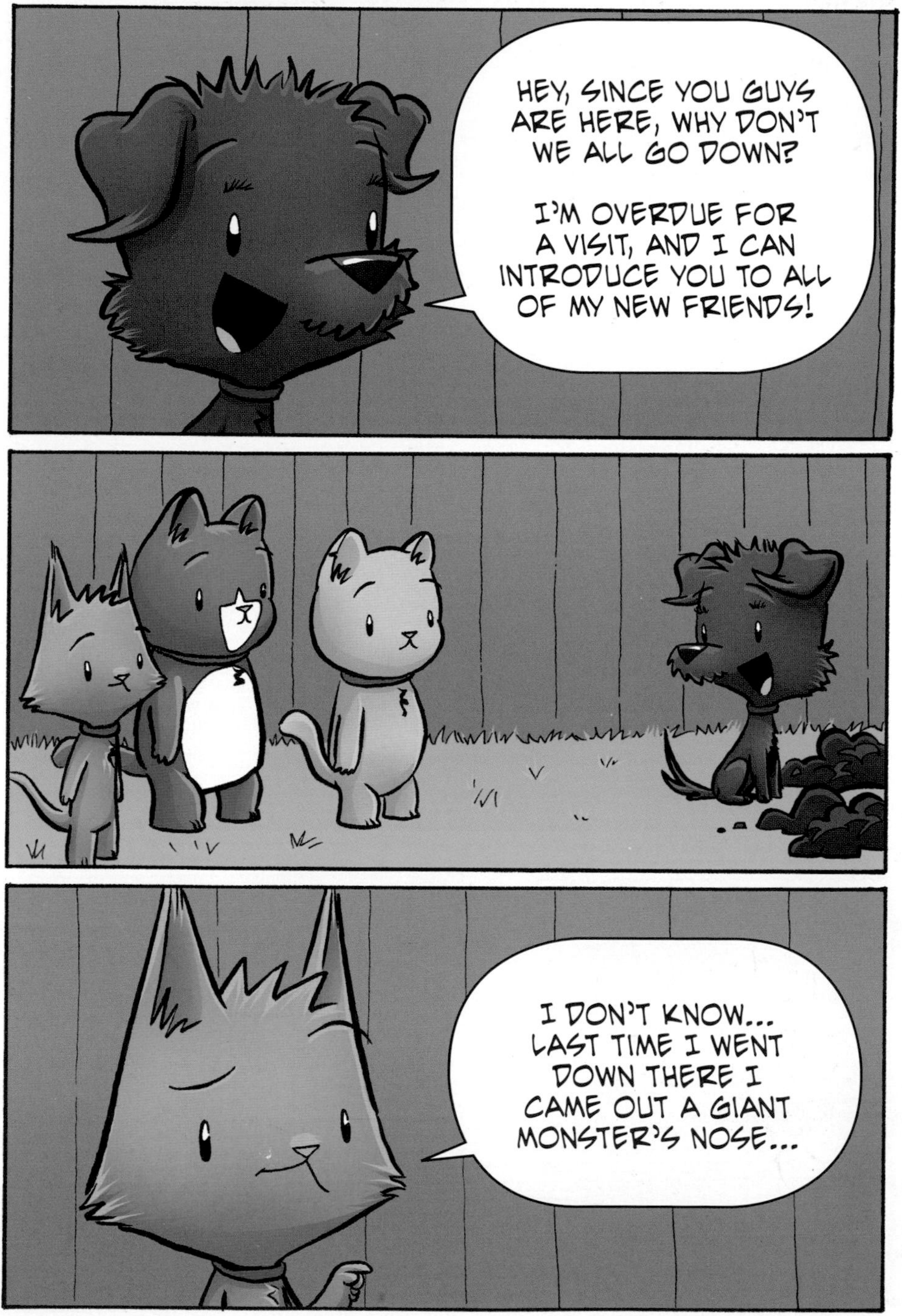
HEY, SINCE YOU GUYS ARE HERE, WHY DON'T WE ALL GO DOWN?
I'M OVERDUE FOR A VISIT, AND I CAN INTRODUCE YOU TO ALL OF MY NEW FRIENDS!
I DON'T KNOW... LAST TIME I WENT DOWN THERE I CAME OUT A GIANT MONSTER'S NOSE...

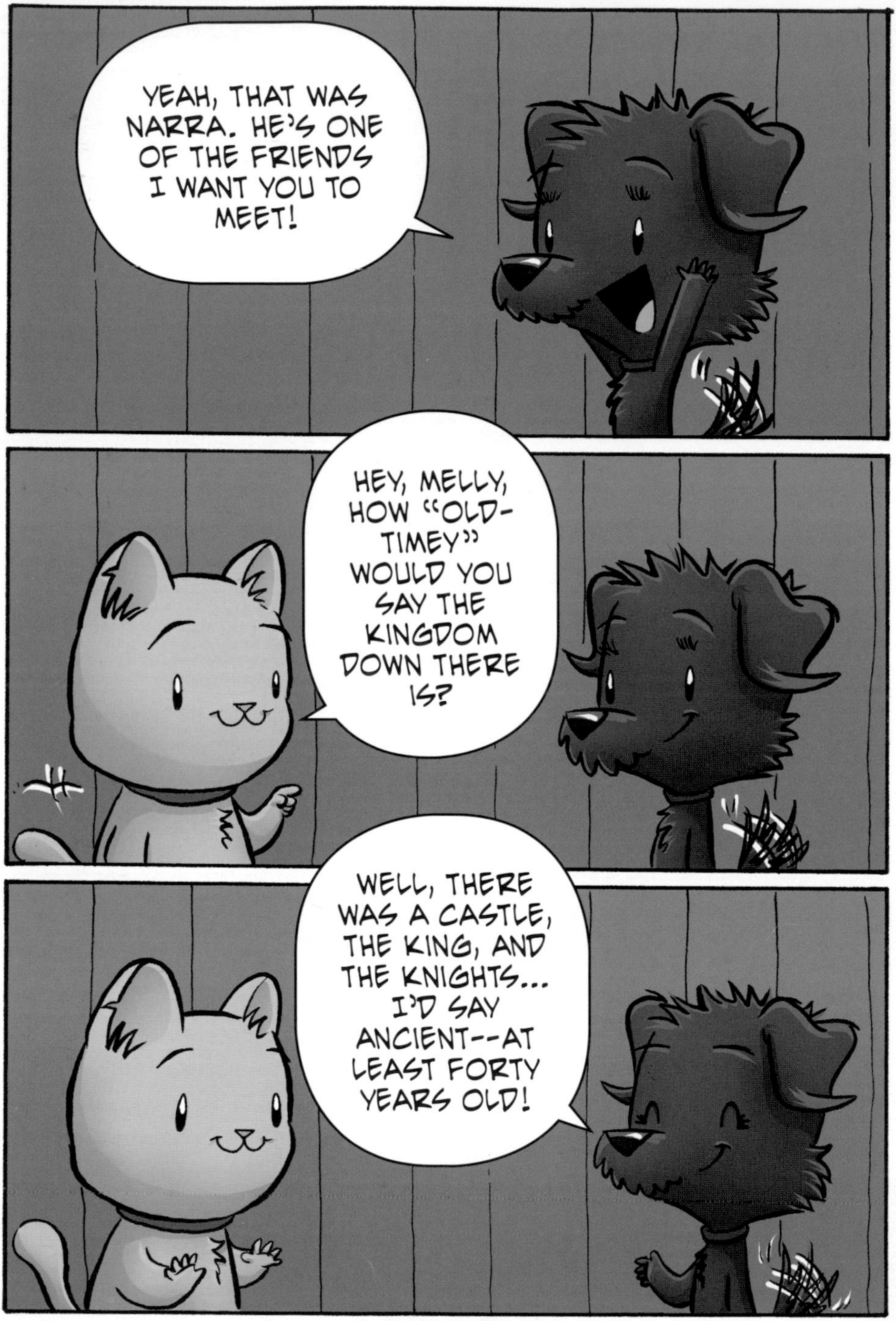
YEAH, THAT WAS NARRA. HE'S ONE OF THE FRIENDS I WANT YOU TO MEET!
HEY, MELLY, HOW "OLD-TIMEY" WOULD YOU SAY THE KINGDOM DOWN THERE IS?
WELL, THERE WAS A CASTLE, THE KING, AND THE KNIGHTS... I'D SAY ANCIENT--AT LEAST FORTY YEARS OLD!

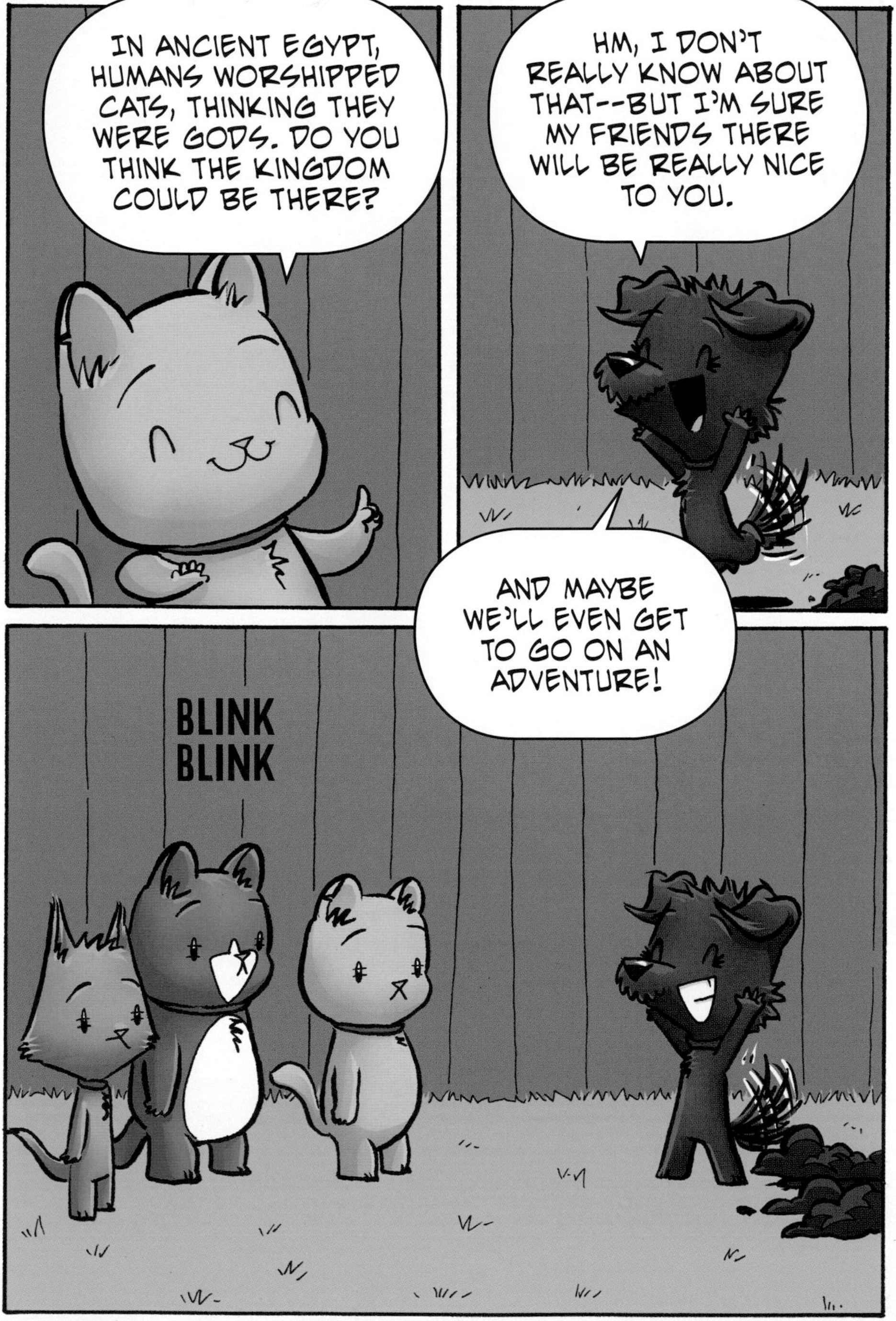
IN ANCIENT EGYPT, HUMANS WORSHIPPED CATS, THINKING THEY WERE GODS. DO YOU THINK THE KINGDOM COULD BE THERE?
HM, I DON'T REALLY KNOW ABOUT THAT--BUT I'M SURE MY FRIENDS THERE WILL BE REALLY NICE TO YOU.
AND MAYBE WE'LL EVEN GET TO GO ON AN ADVENTURE!
BLINK
BLINK

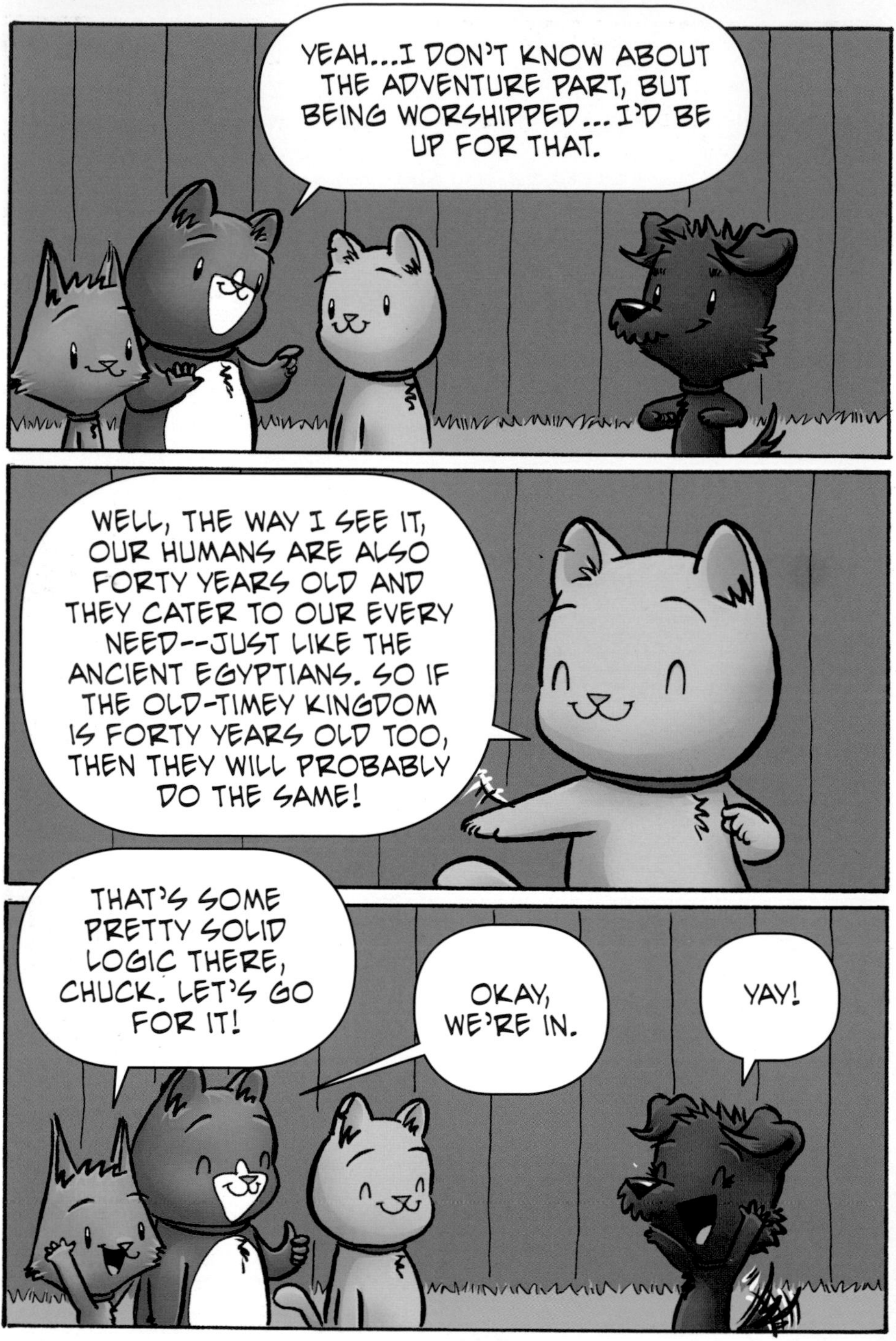
YEAH...I DON'T KNOW ABOUT THE ADVENTURE PART, BUT BEING WORSHIPPED... I'D BE UP FOR THAT.
WELL, THE WAY I SEE IT, OUR HUMANS ARE ALSO FORTY YEARS OLD AND THEY CATER TO OUR EVERY NEED--JUST LIKE THE ANCIENT EGYPTIANS. SO IF THE OLD-TIMEY KINGDOM IS FORTY YEARS OLD TOO, THEN THEY WILL PROBABLY DO THE SAME!
THAT'S SOME PRETTY SOLID LOGIC THERE, CHUCK. LET'S GO FOR IT!
OKAY, WE'RE IN.
YAY!

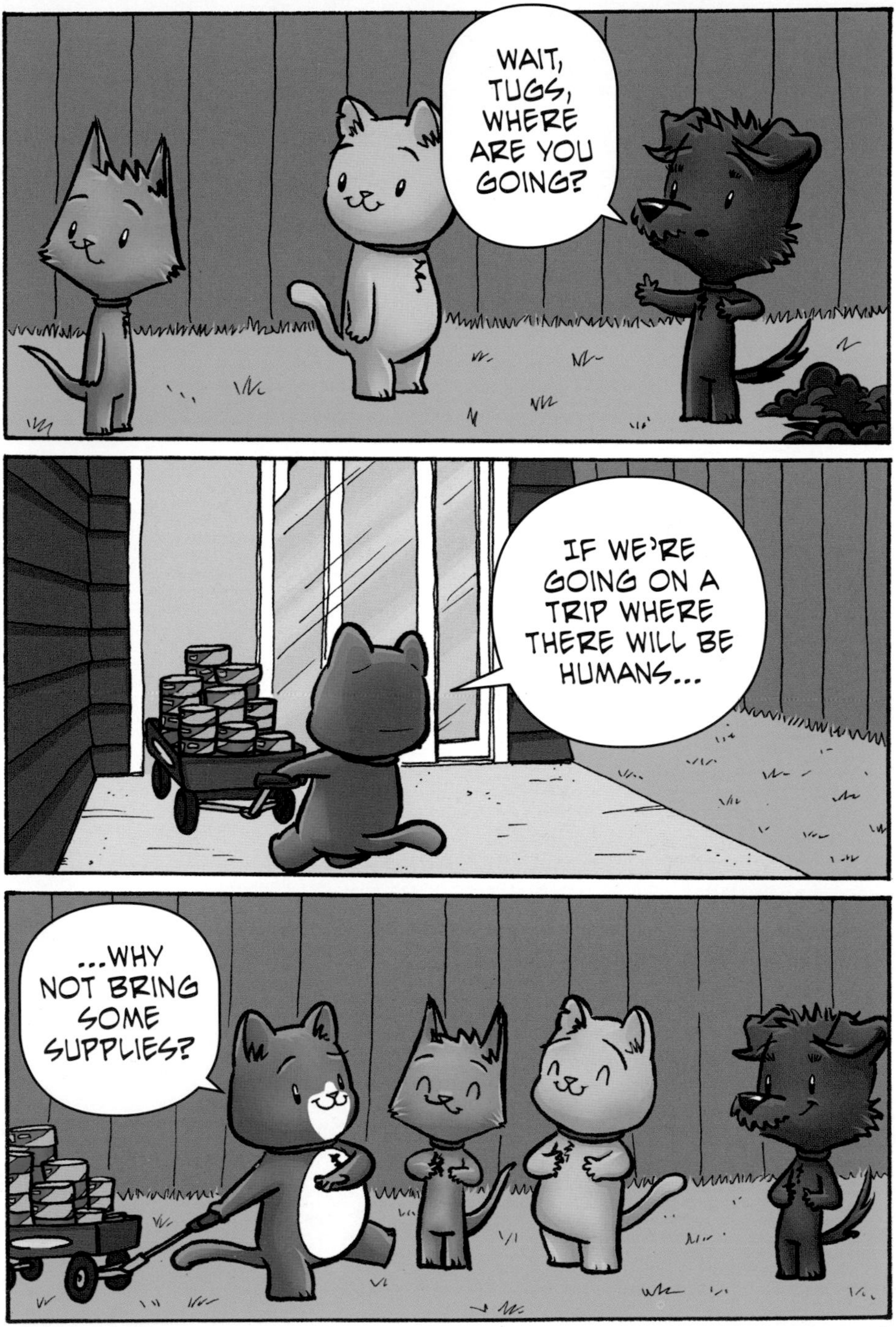
WAIT, TUGS, WHERE ARE YOU GOING?
IF WE'RE GOING ON A TRIP WHERE THERE WILL BE HUMANS...
...WHY NOT BRING SOME SUPPLIES?

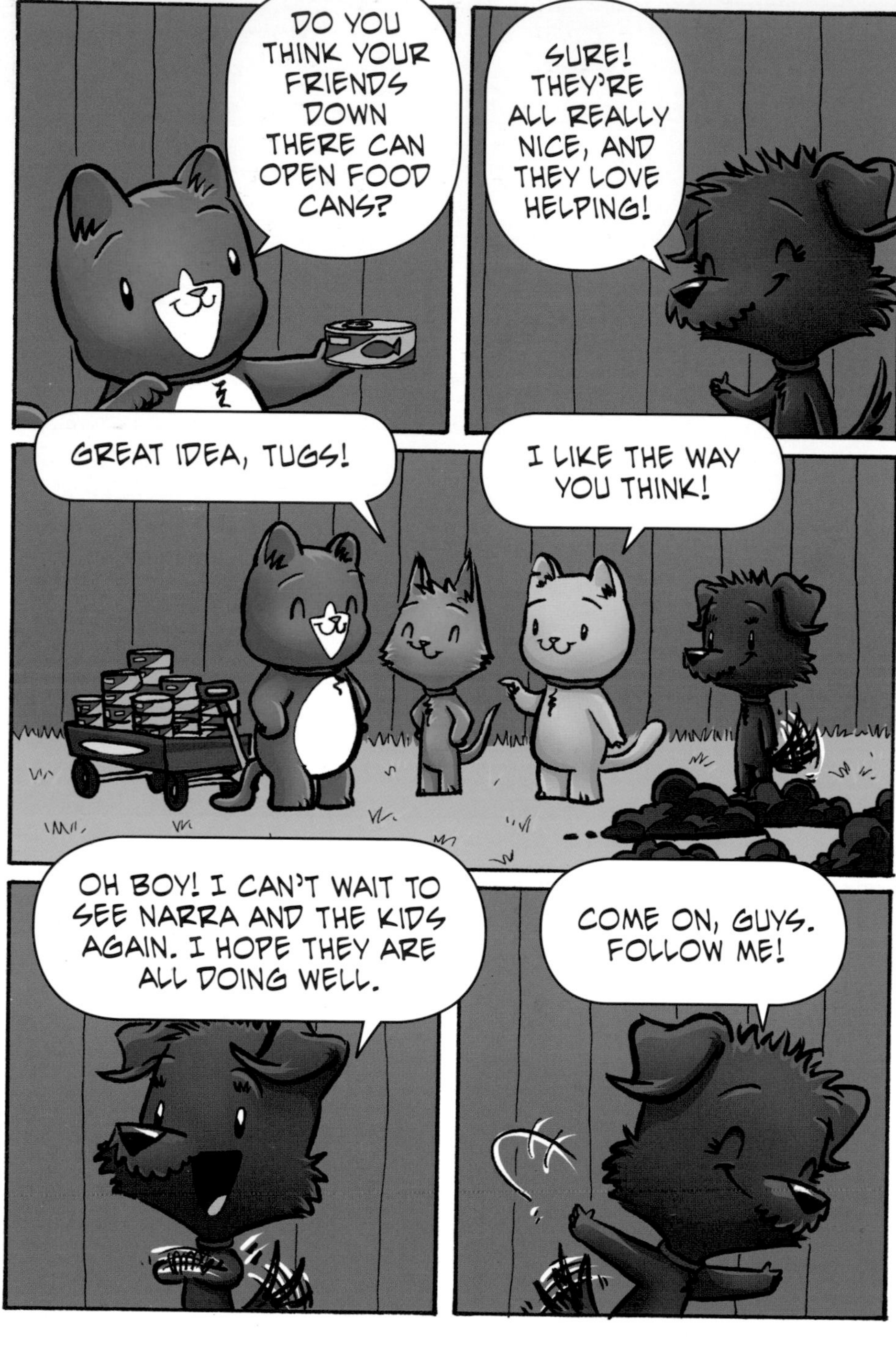
DO YOU THINK YOUR FRIENDS DOWN THERE CAN OPEN FOOD CANS?
SURE! THEY'RE ALL REALLY NICE, AND THEY LOVE HELPING!
GREAT IDEA, TUGS!
I LIKE THE WAY YOU THINK!
OH BOY! I CAN'T WAIT TO SEE NARRA AND THE KIDS AGAIN. I HOPE THEY ARE ALL DOING WELL.
COME ON, GUYS. FOLLOW ME!

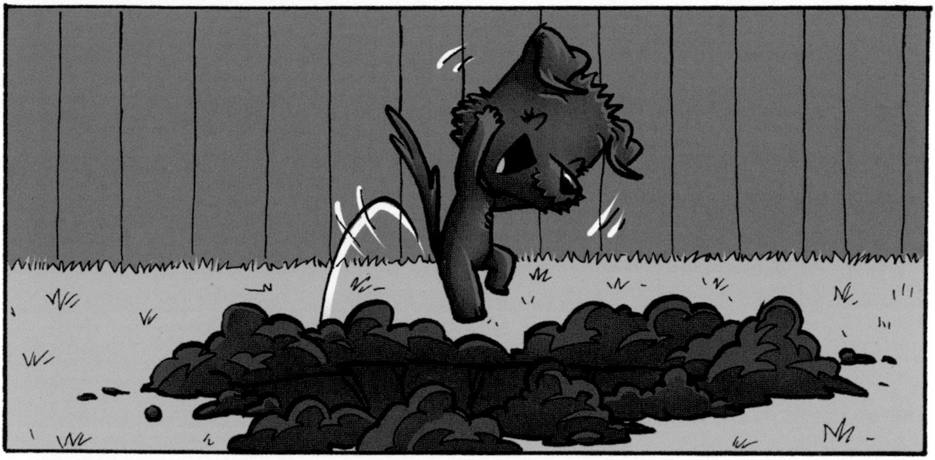
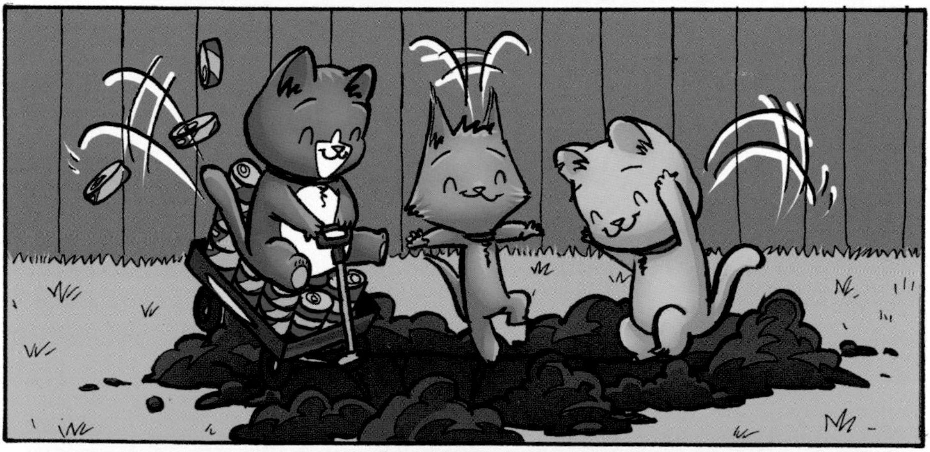
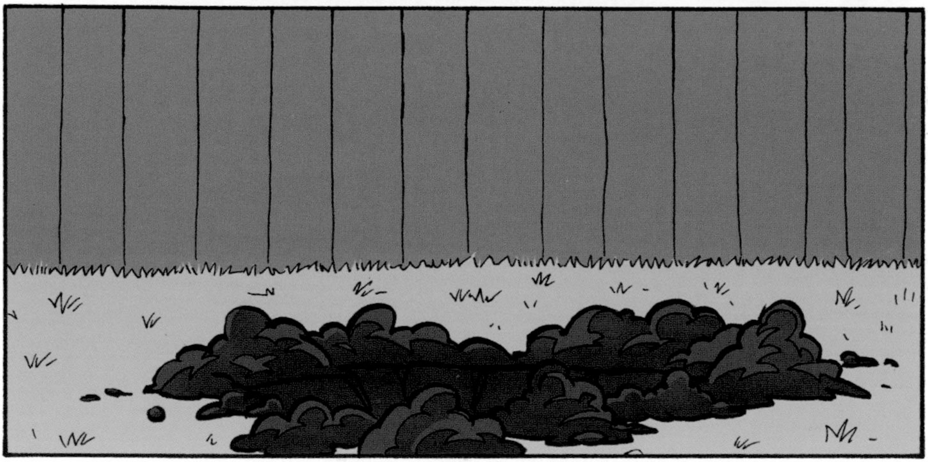

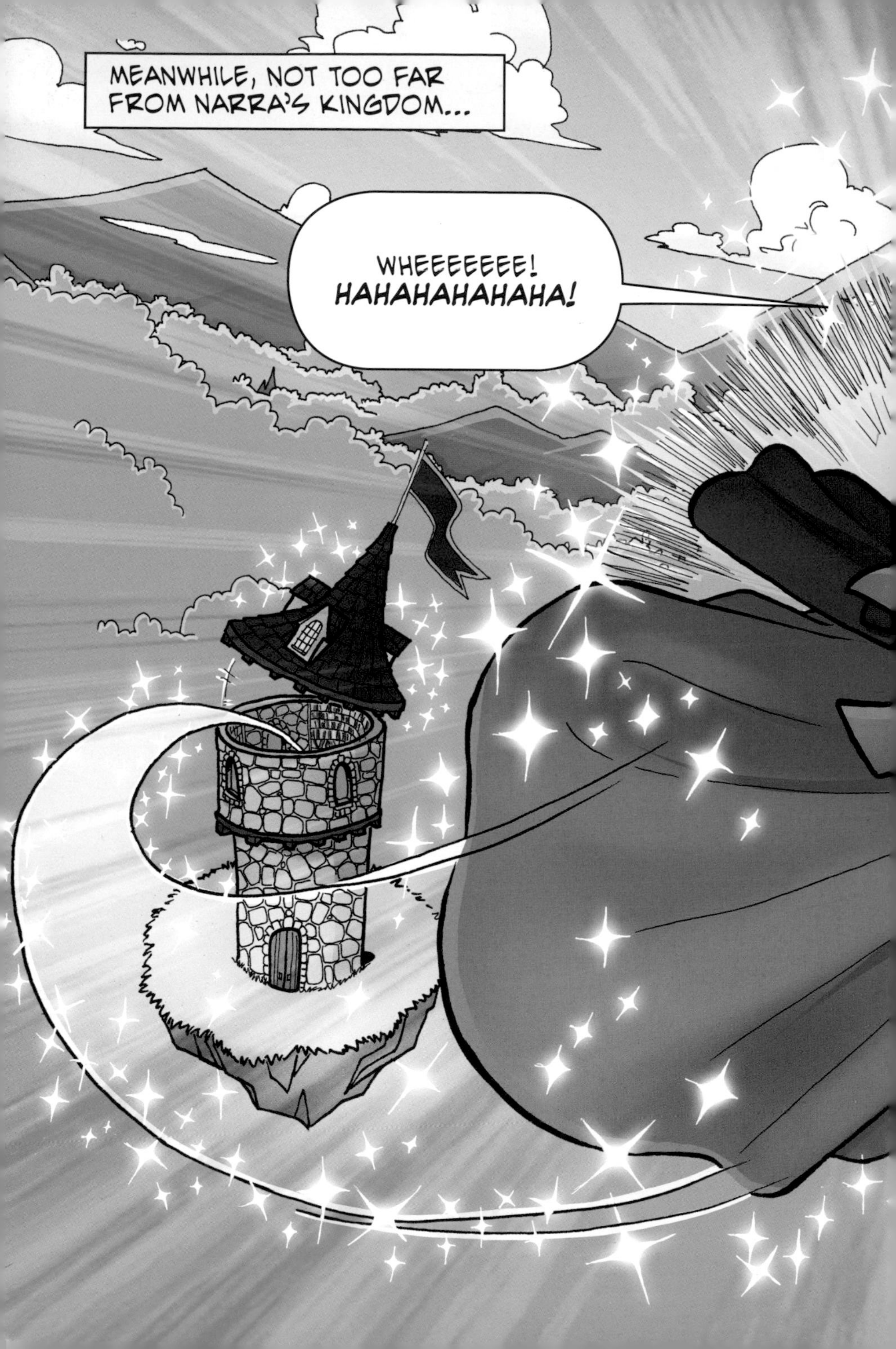
MEANWHILE, NOT TOO FAR FROM NARRA'S KINGDOM...
WHEEEEEEEE! HAHAHAHAHAHA!

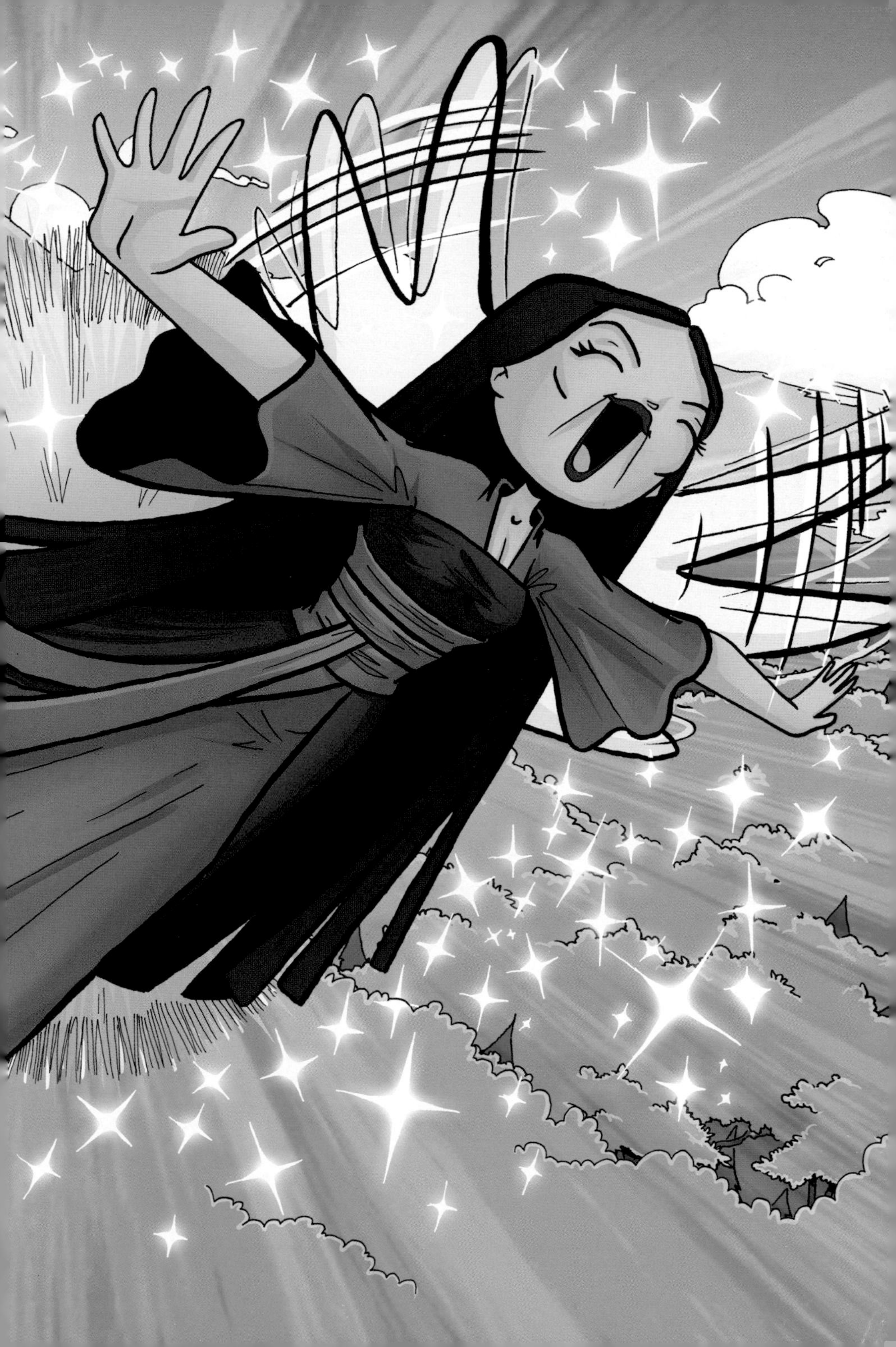

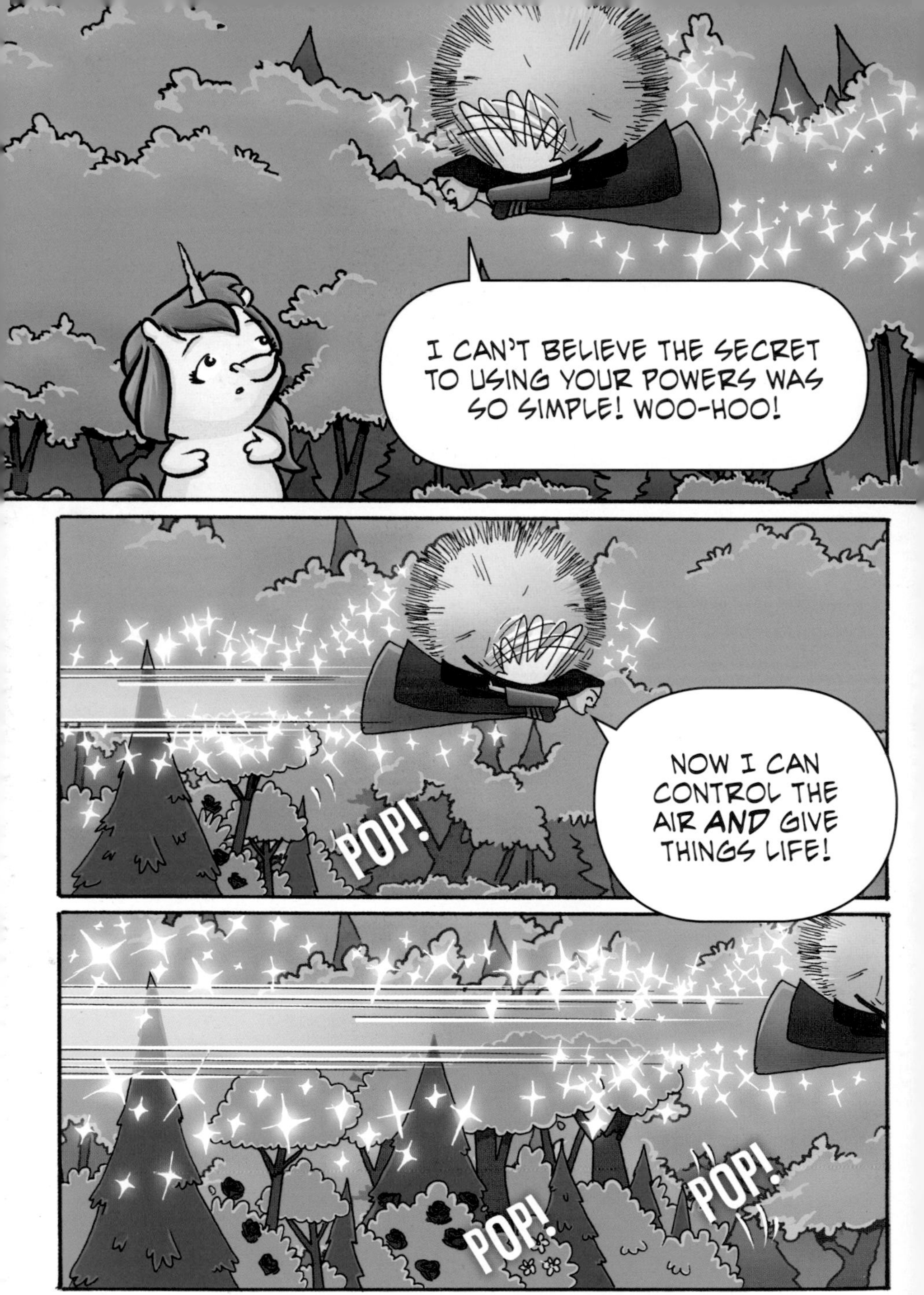
I CAN'T BELIEVE THE SECRET TO USING YOUR POWERS WAS SO SIMPLE! WOO-HOO!
NOW I CAN CONTROL THE AIR **AND** GIVE THINGS LIFE!
POP!
POP!
POP!

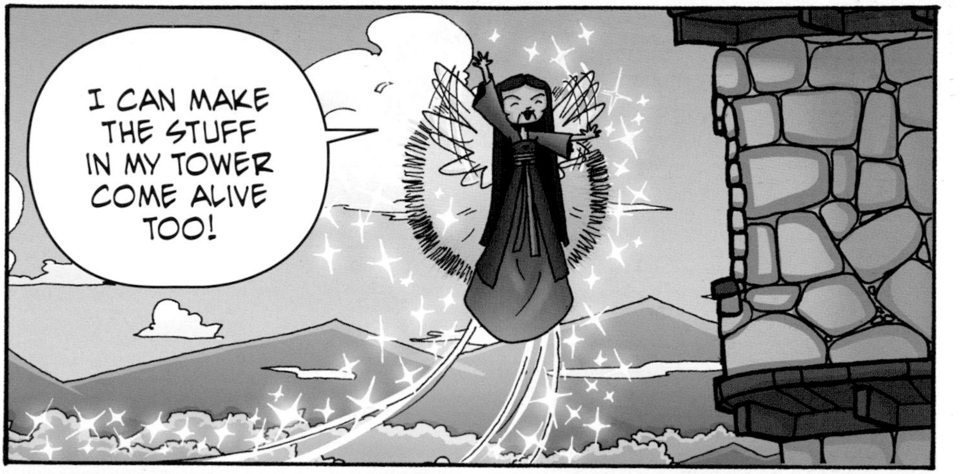
I CAN MAKE THE STUFF IN MY TOWER COME ALIVE TOO!

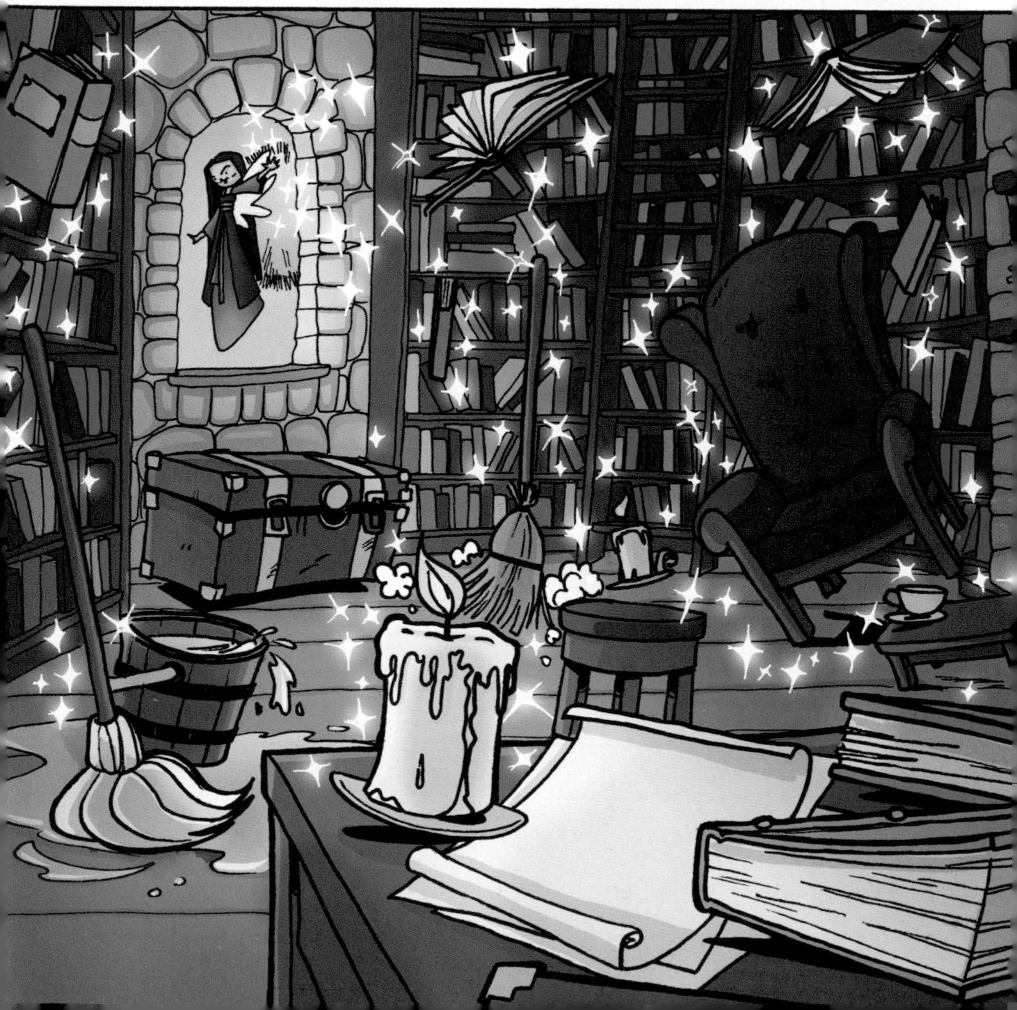

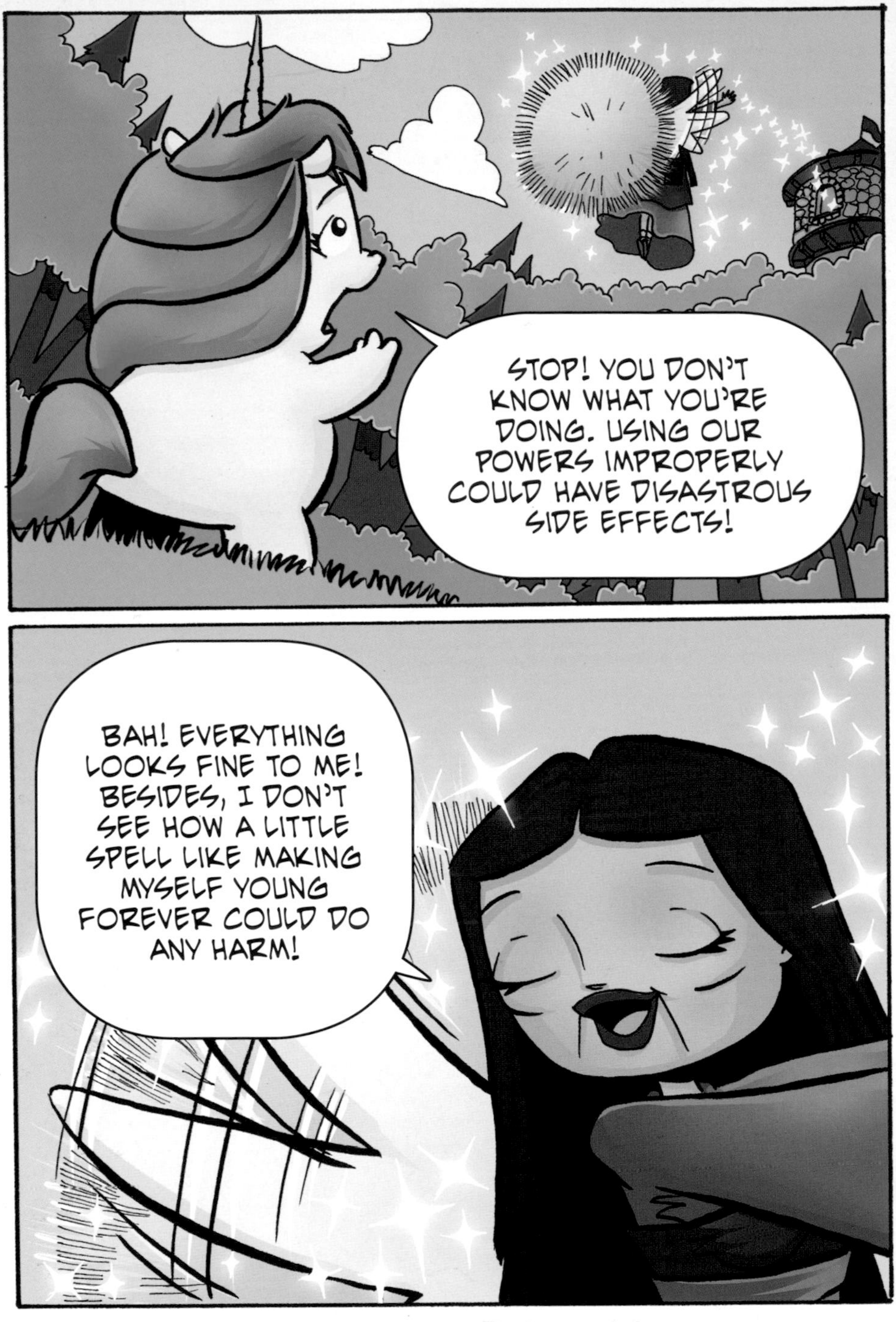
STOP! YOU DON'T KNOW WHAT YOU'RE DOING. USING OUR POWERS IMPROPERLY COULD HAVE DISASTROUS SIDE EFFECTS!
BAH! EVERYTHING LOOKS FINE TO ME! BESIDES, I DON'T SEE HOW A LITTLE SPELL LIKE MAKING MYSELF YOUNG FOREVER COULD DO ANY HARM!

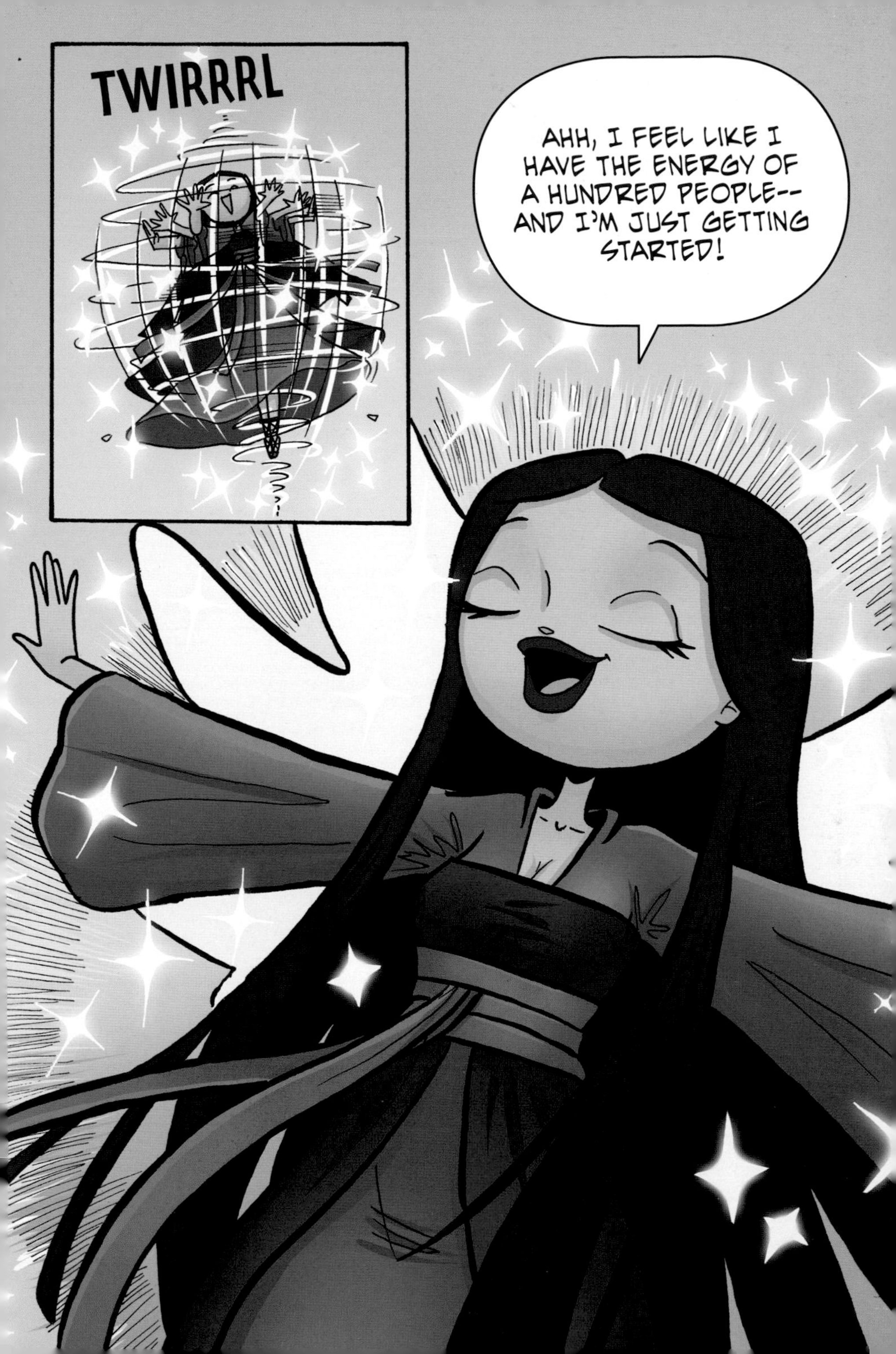
TWIRRRL
AHH, I FEEL LIKE I HAVE THE ENERGY OF A HUNDRED PEOPLE--AND I'M JUST GETTING STARTED!

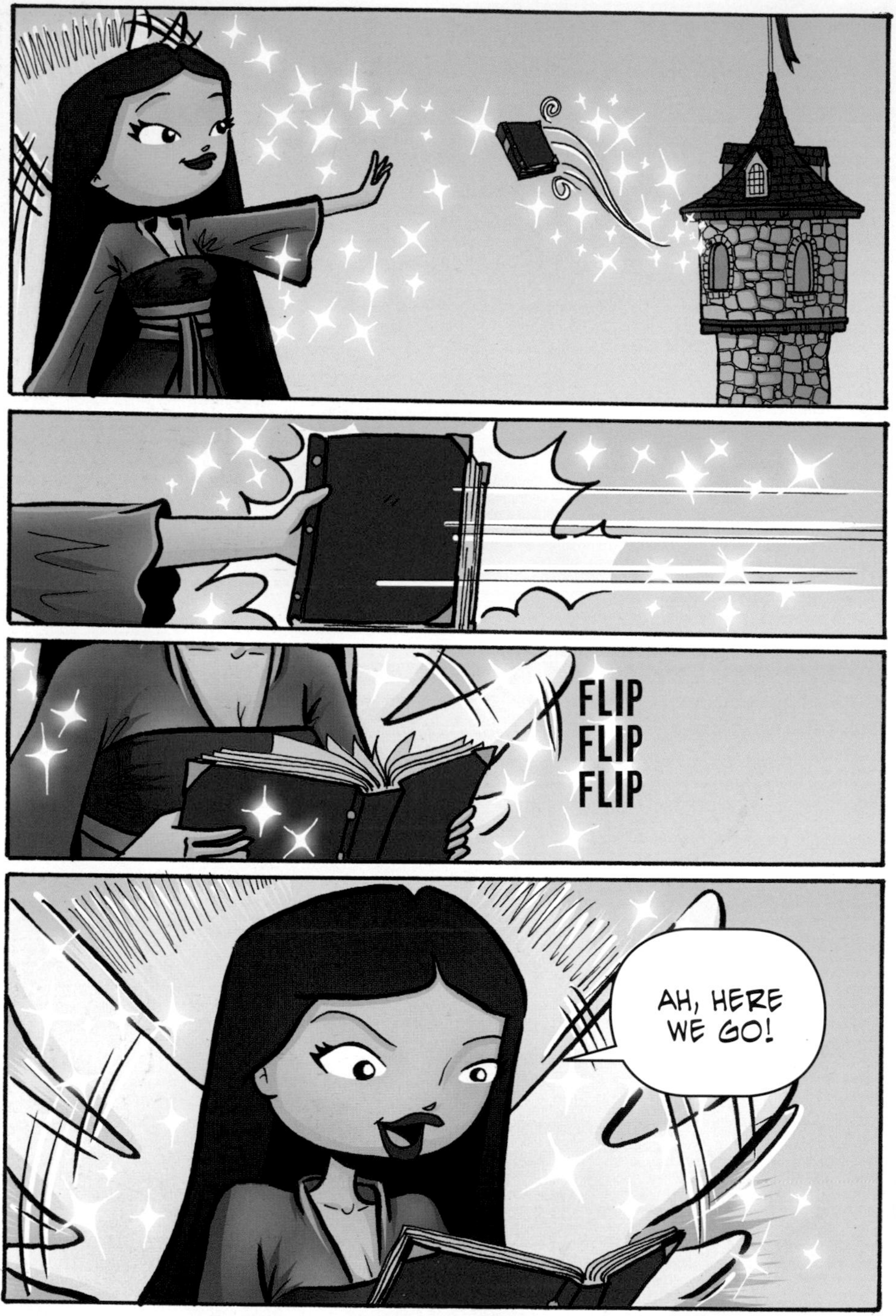
FLIP
FLIP
FLIP
AH, HERE WE GO!

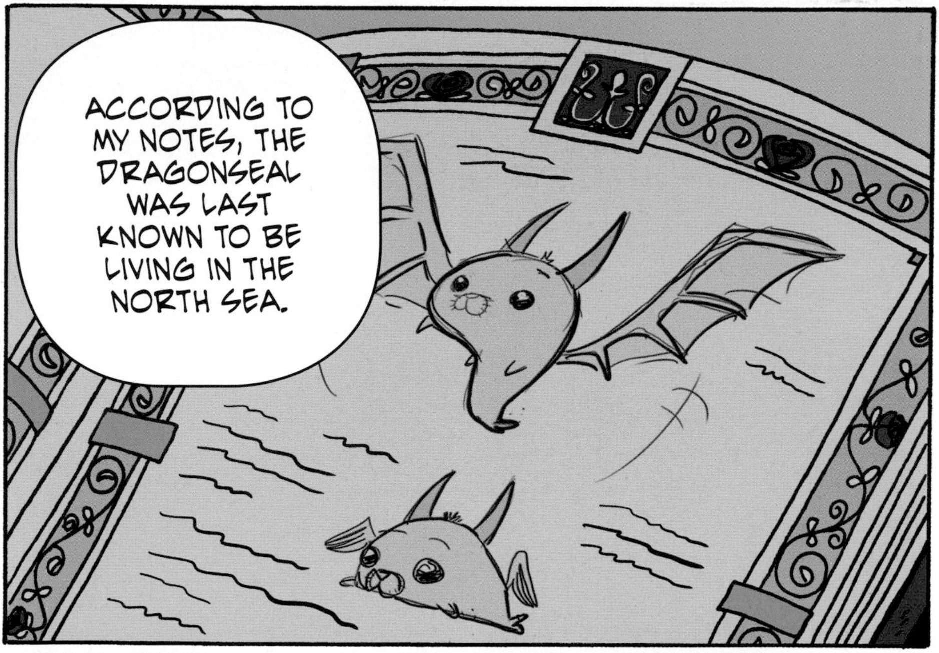
ACCORDING TO MY NOTES, THE DRAGONSEAL WAS LAST KNOWN TO BE LIVING IN THE NORTH SEA.

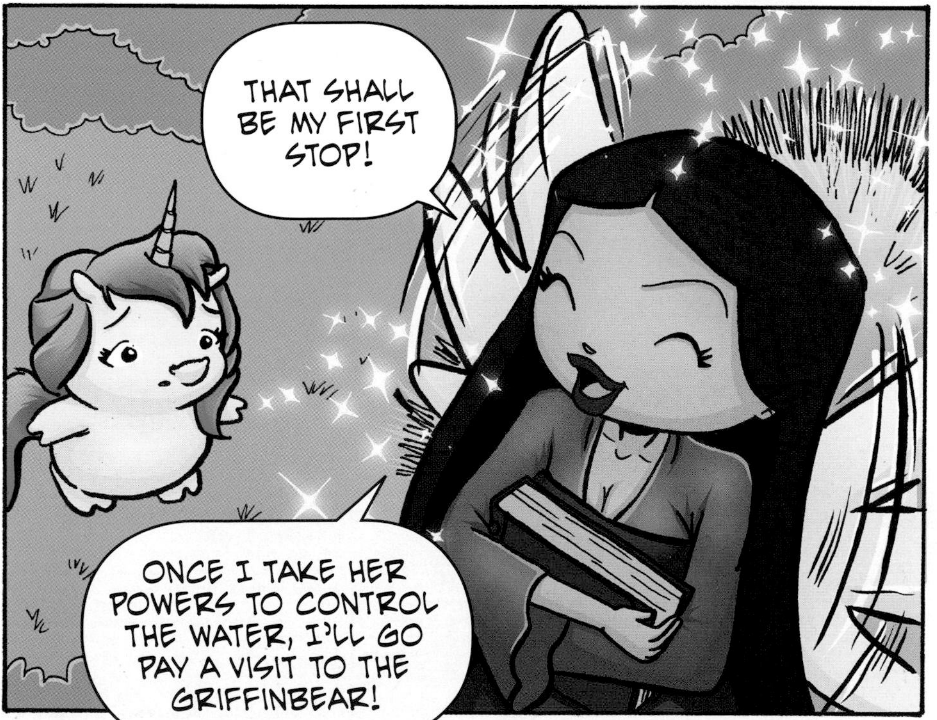
THAT SHALL BE MY FIRST STOP!
ONCE I TAKE HER POWERS TO CONTROL THE WATER, I'LL GO PAY A VISIT TO THE GRIFFINBEAR!

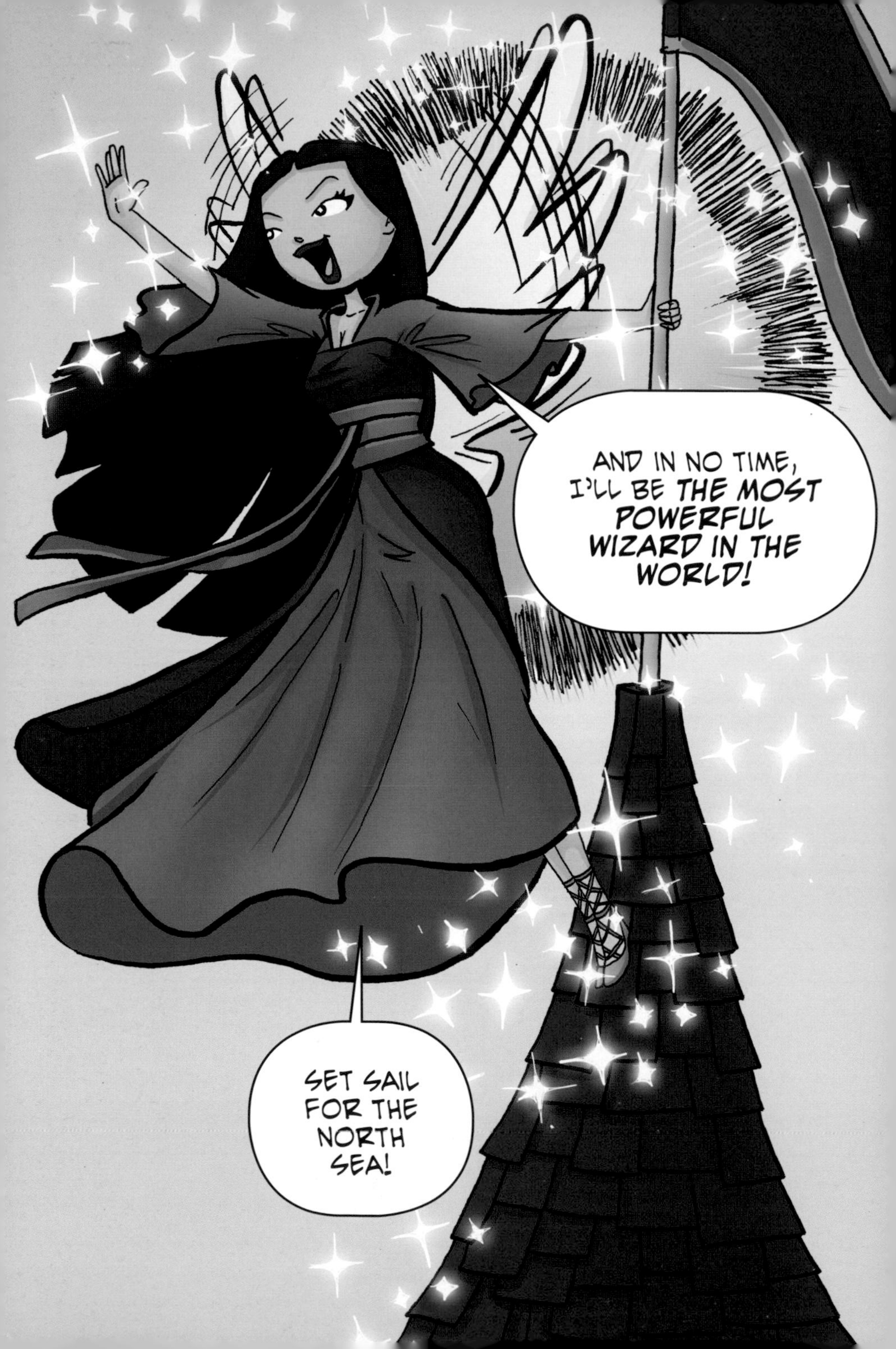
AND IN NO TIME, I'LL BE THE MOST POWERFUL WIZARD IN THE WORLD!
SET SAIL FOR THE NORTH SEA!

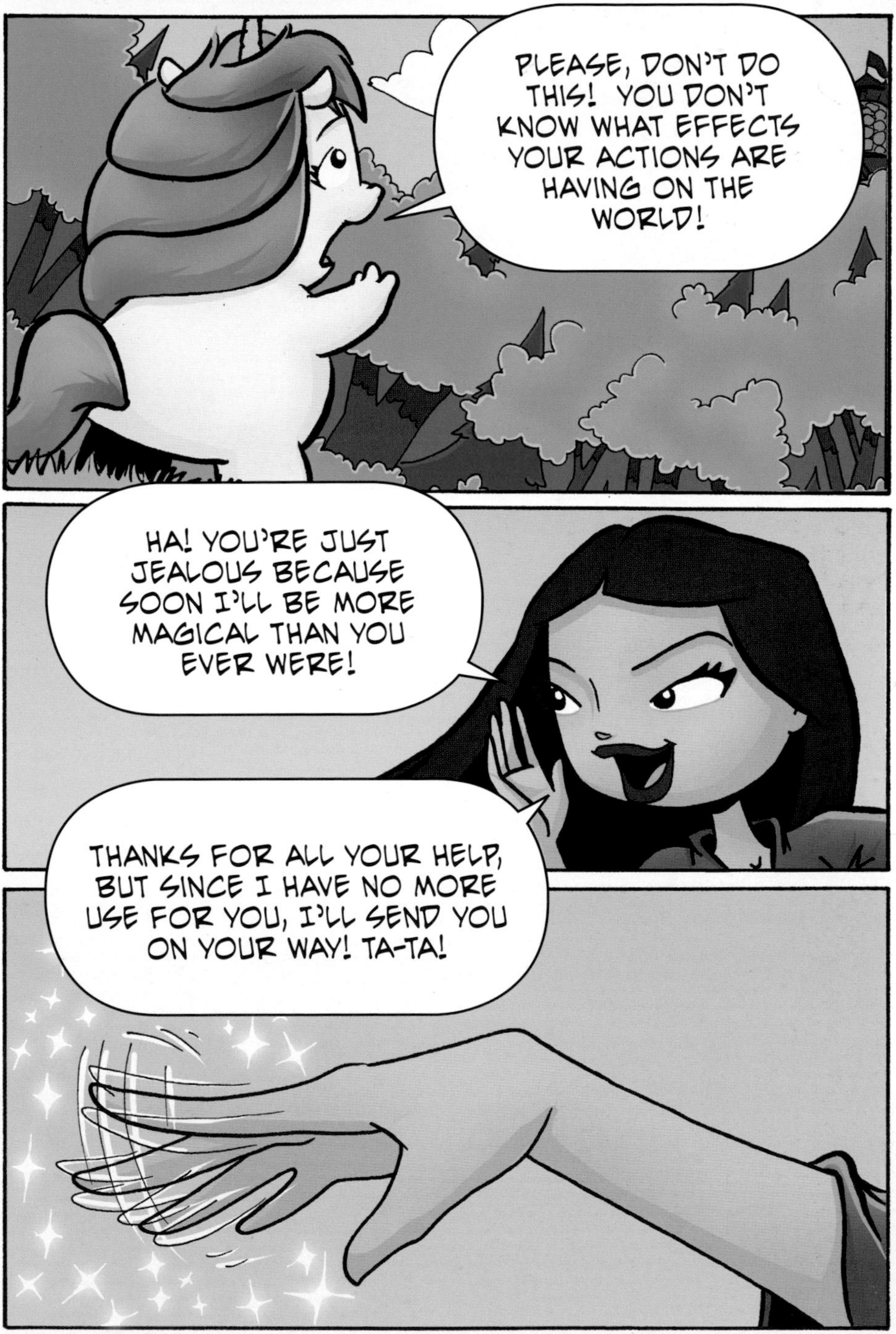
PLEASE, DON'T DO THIS! YOU DON'T KNOW WHAT EFFECTS YOUR ACTIONS ARE HAVING ON THE WORLD!
HA! YOU'RE JUST JEALOUS BECAUSE SOON I'LL BE MORE MAGICAL THAN YOU EVER WERE!
THANKS FOR ALL YOUR HELP, BUT SINCE I HAVE NO MORE USE FOR YOU, I'LL SEND YOU ON YOUR WAY! TA-TA!

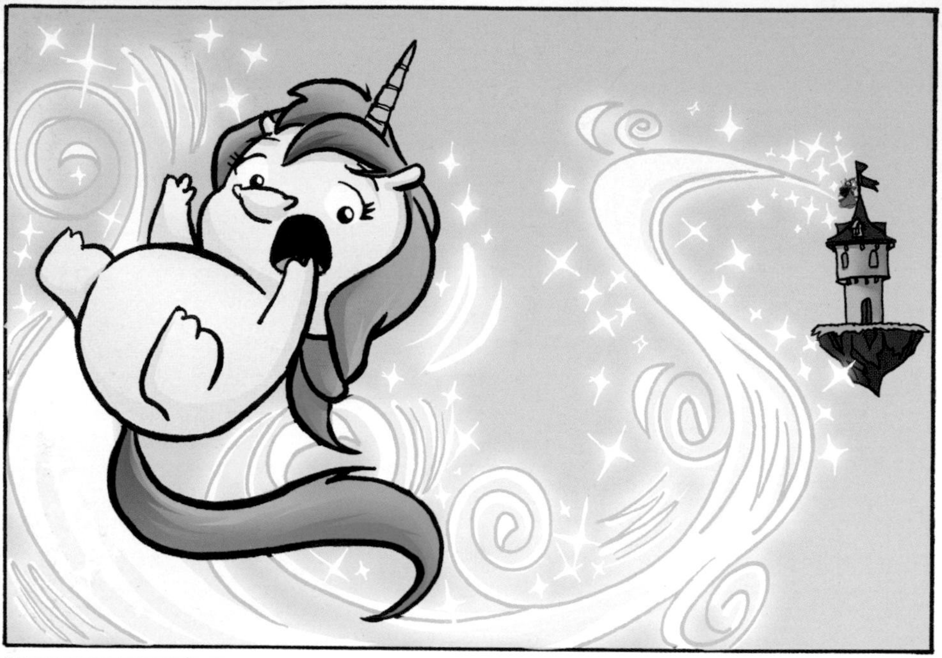

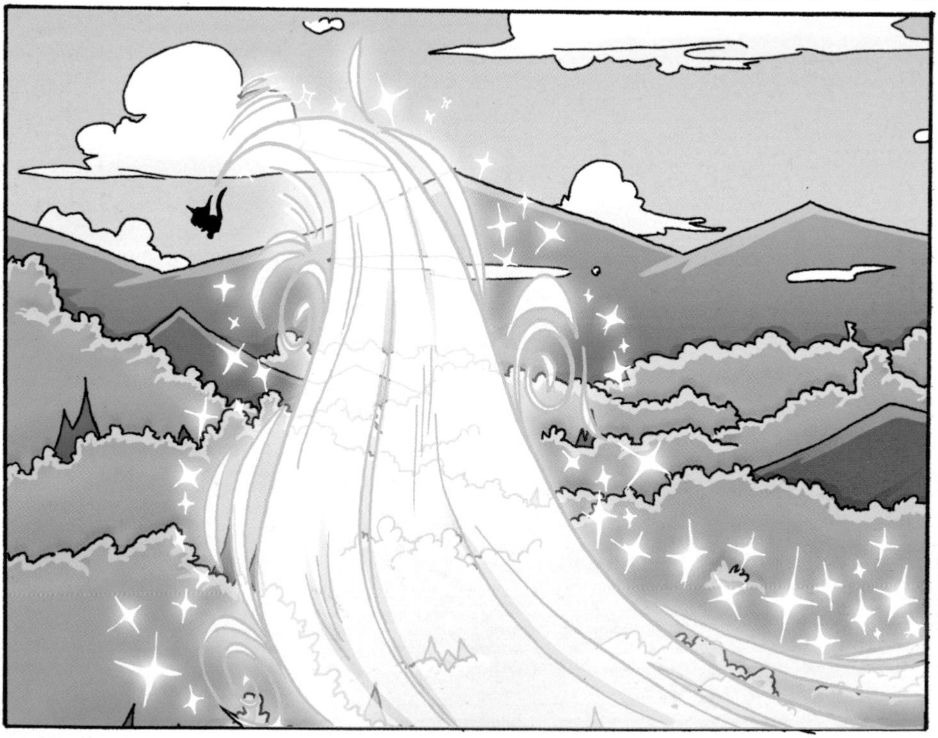

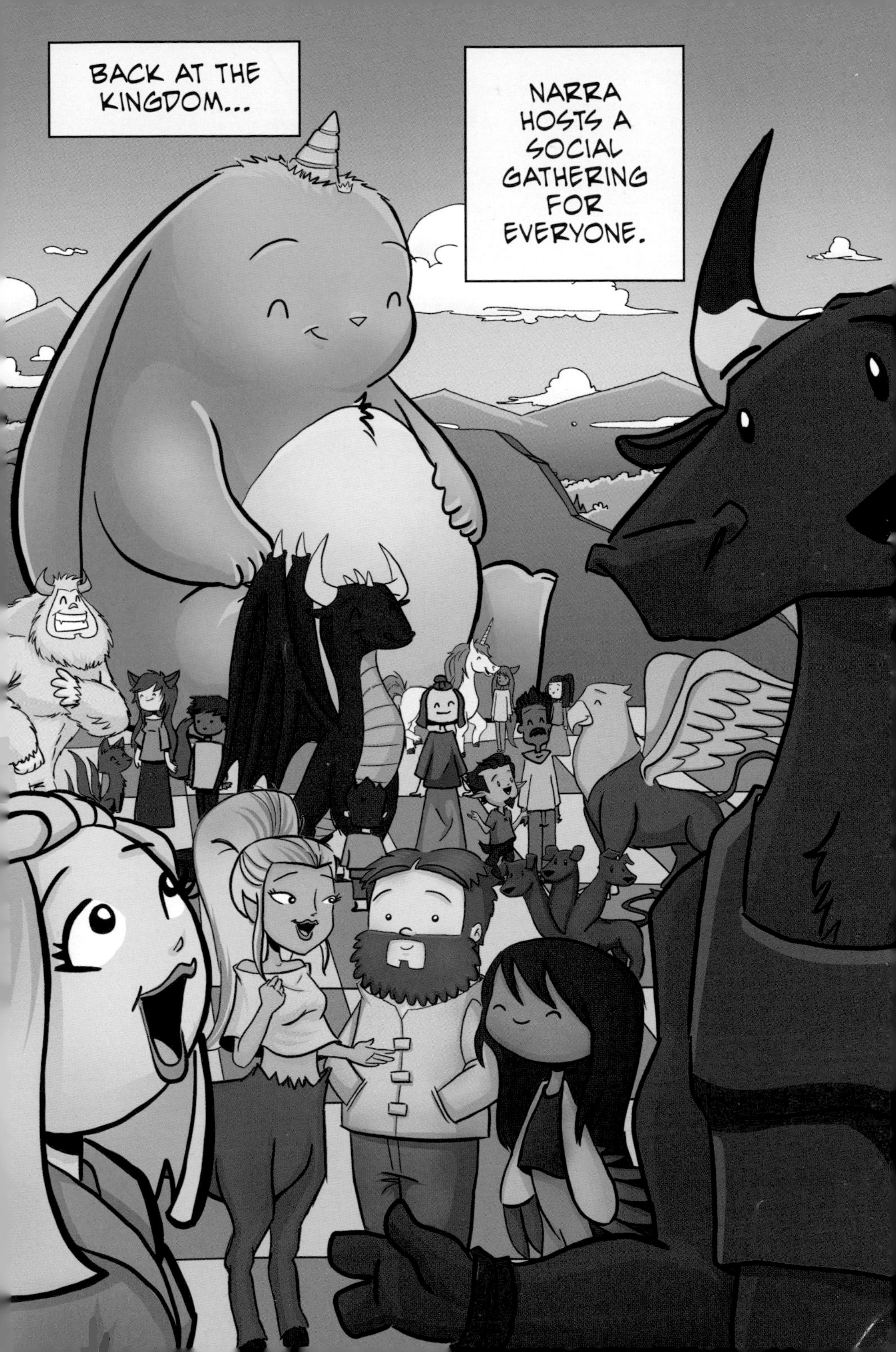
BACK AT THE KINGDOM...
NARRA HOSTS A SOCIAL GATHERING FOR EVERYONE.

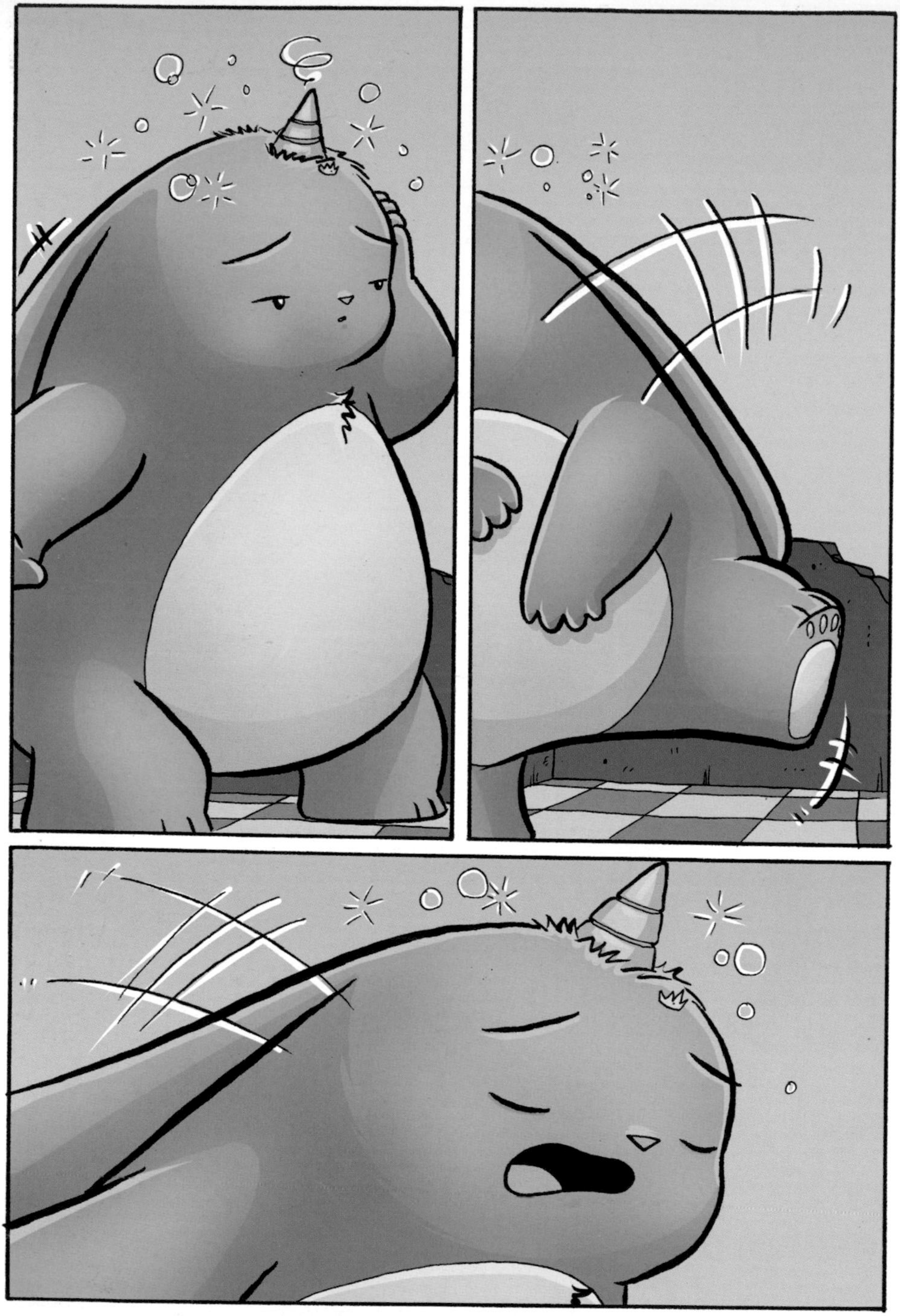

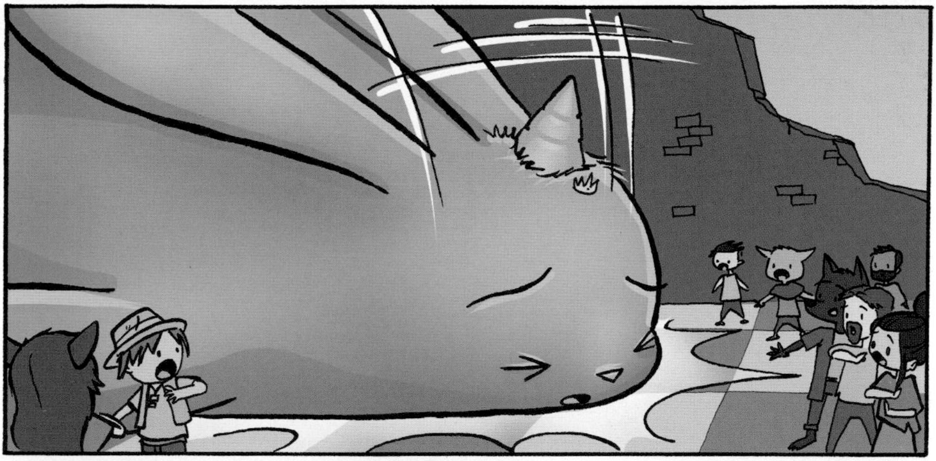

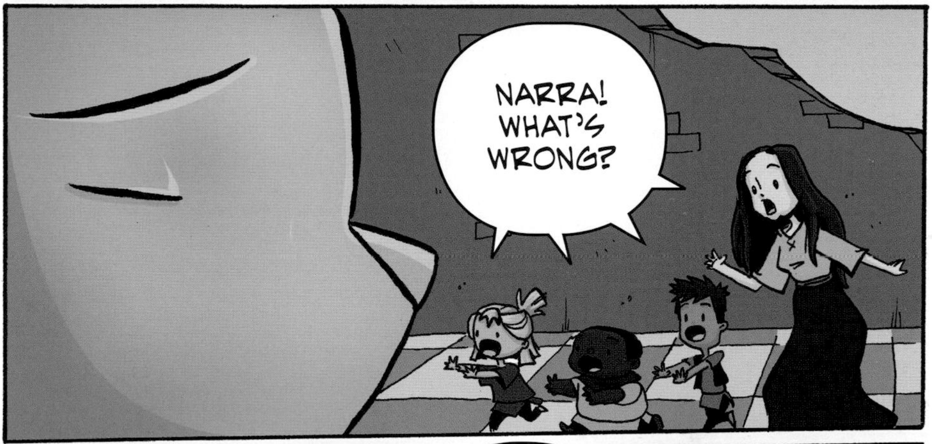
NARRA! WHAT'S WRONG?

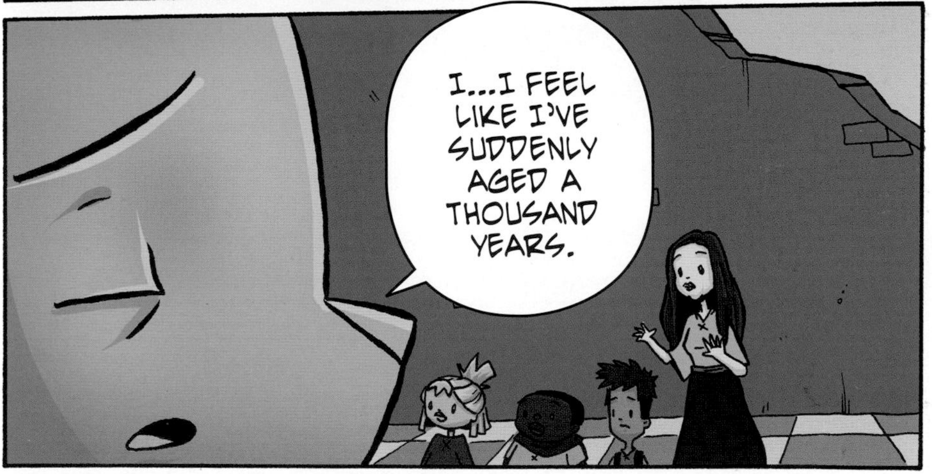
I...I FEEL LIKE I'VE SUDDENLY AGED A THOUSAND YEARS.

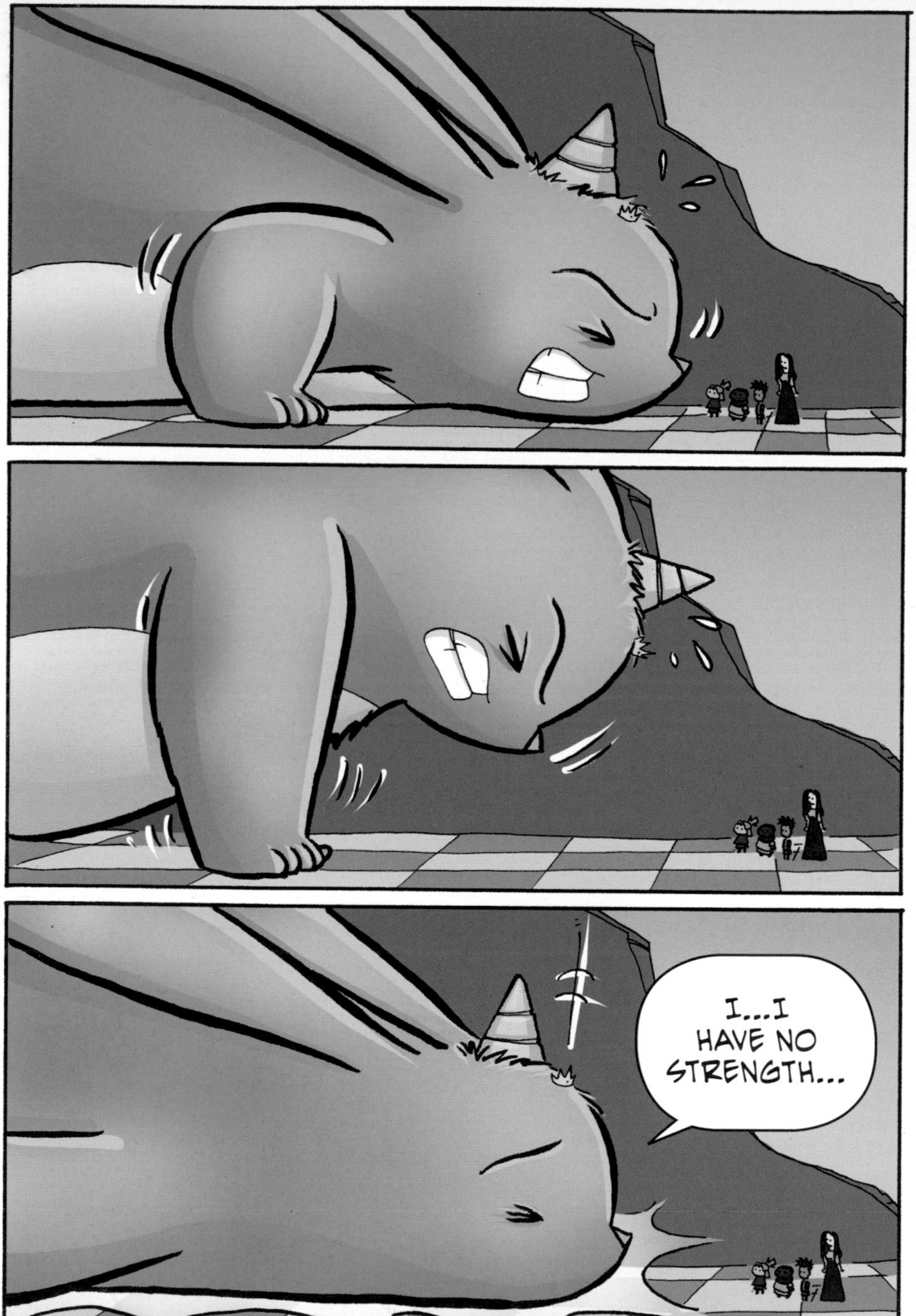
I...I
HAVE NO
STRENGTH...

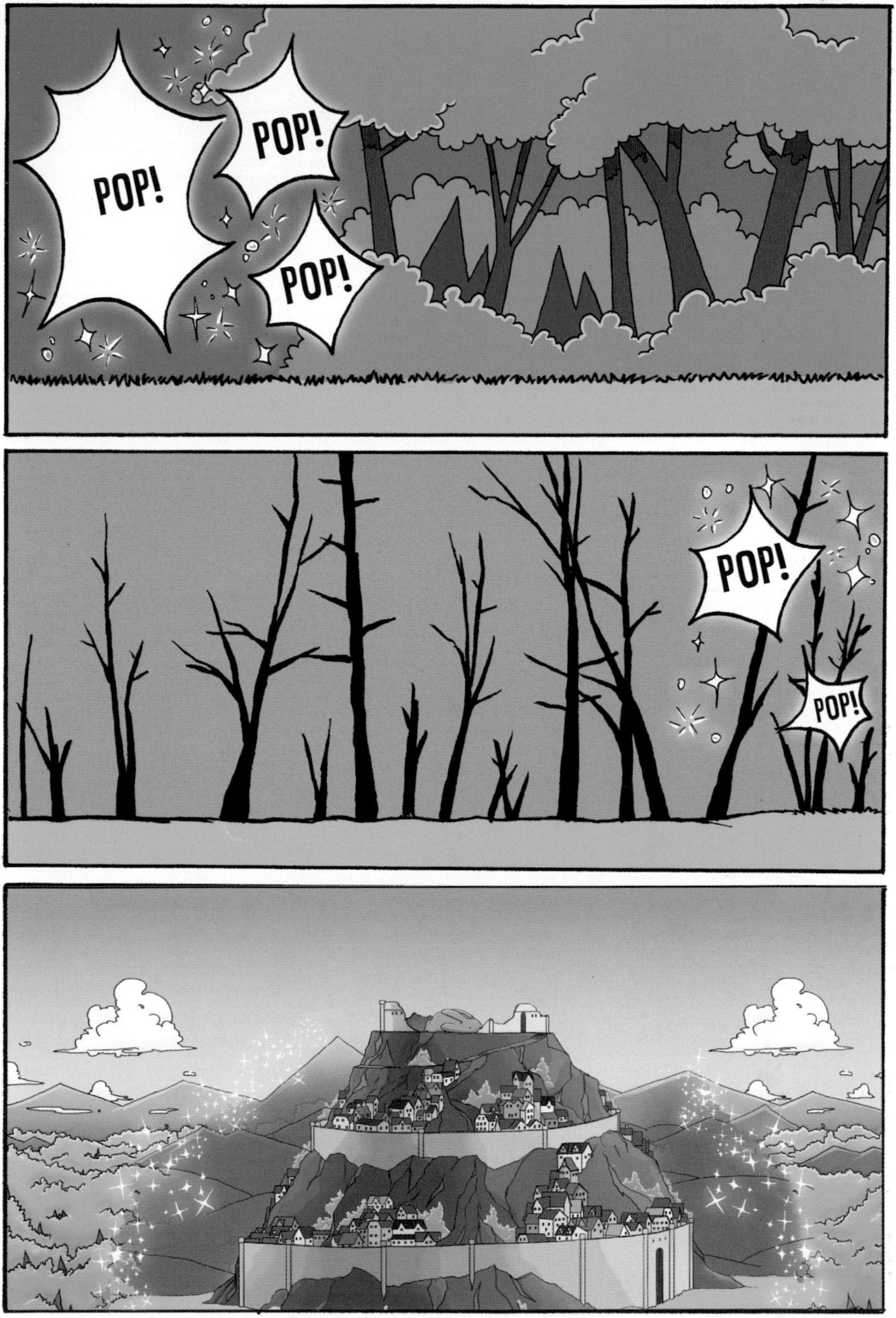
POP!
POP!
POP!
POP!
POP!

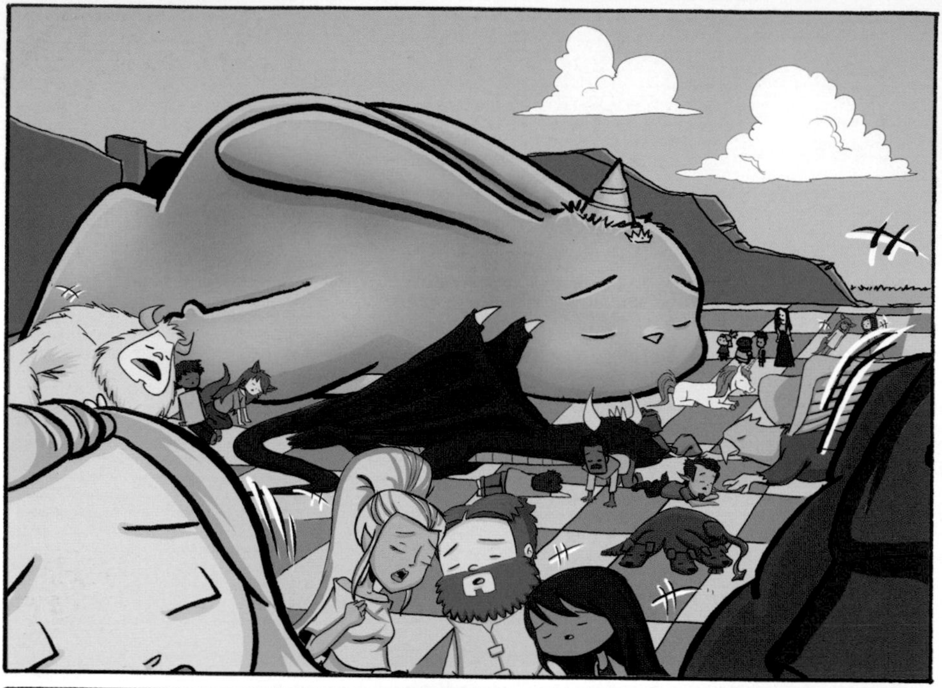

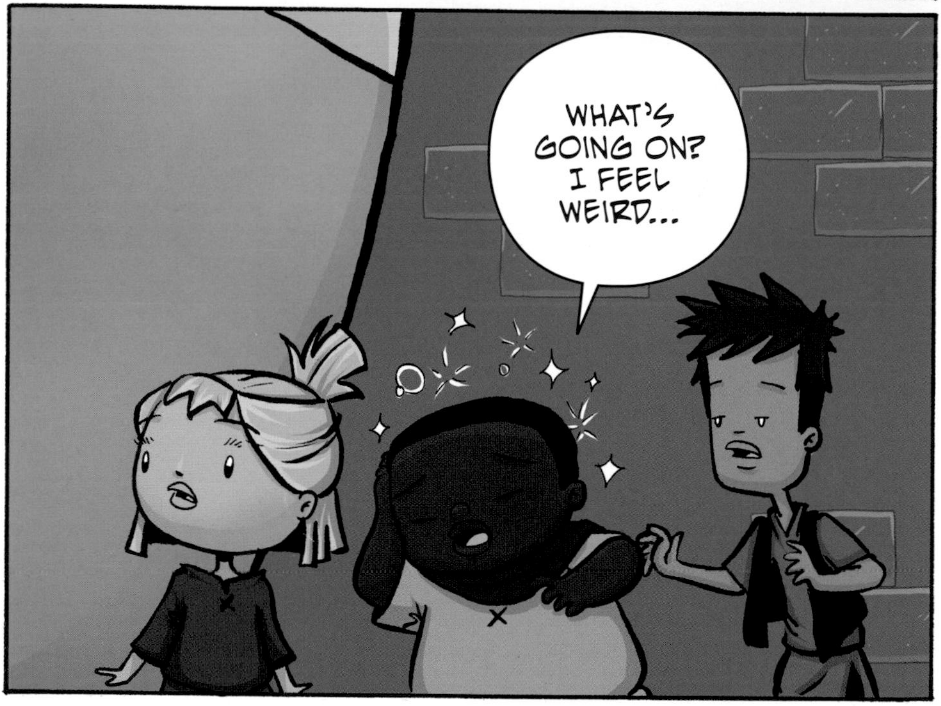
WHAT'S GOING ON? I FEEL WEIRD...

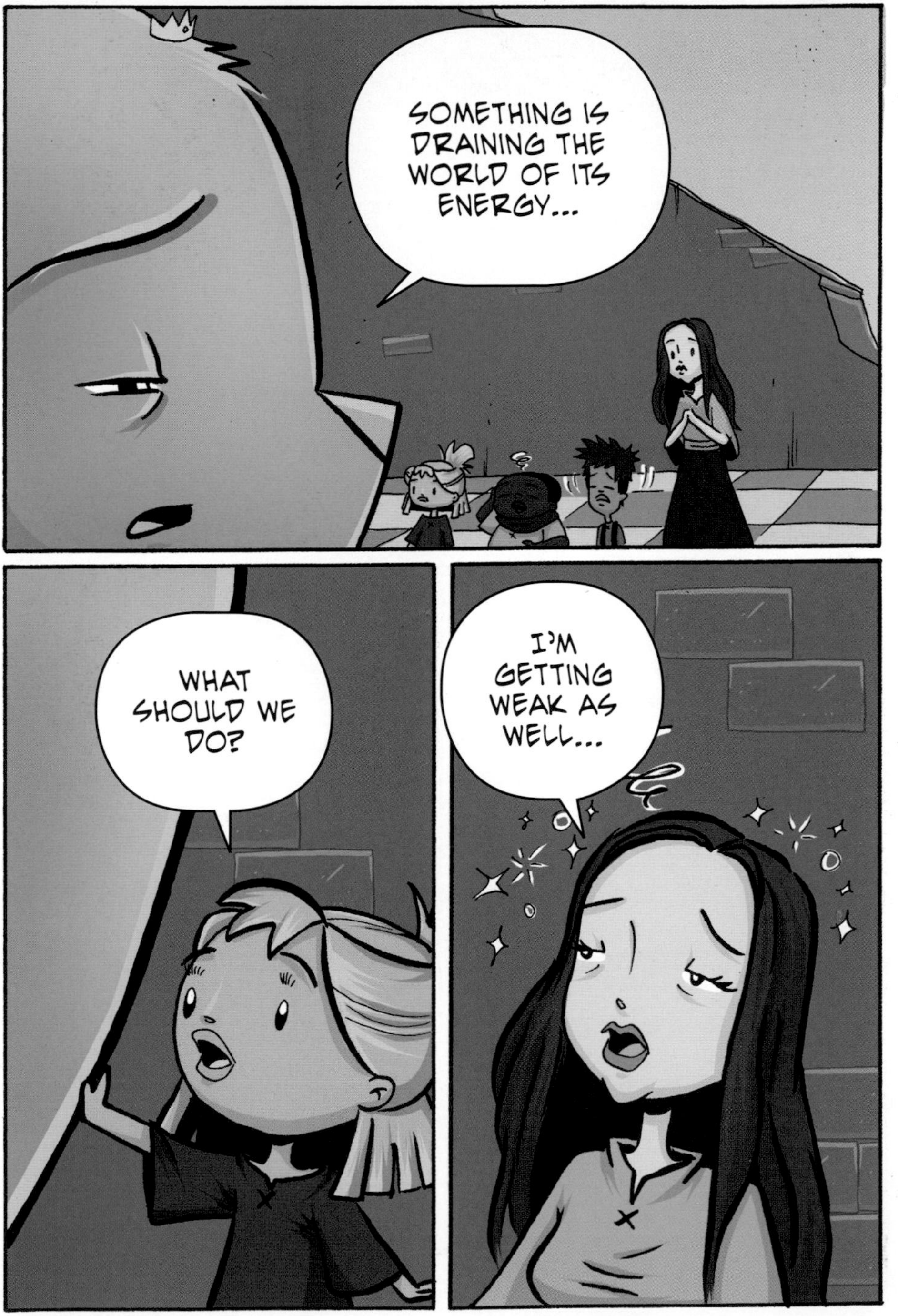
SOMETHING IS DRAINING THE WORLD OF ITS ENERGY...
WHAT SHOULD WE DO?
I'M GETTING WEAK AS WELL...

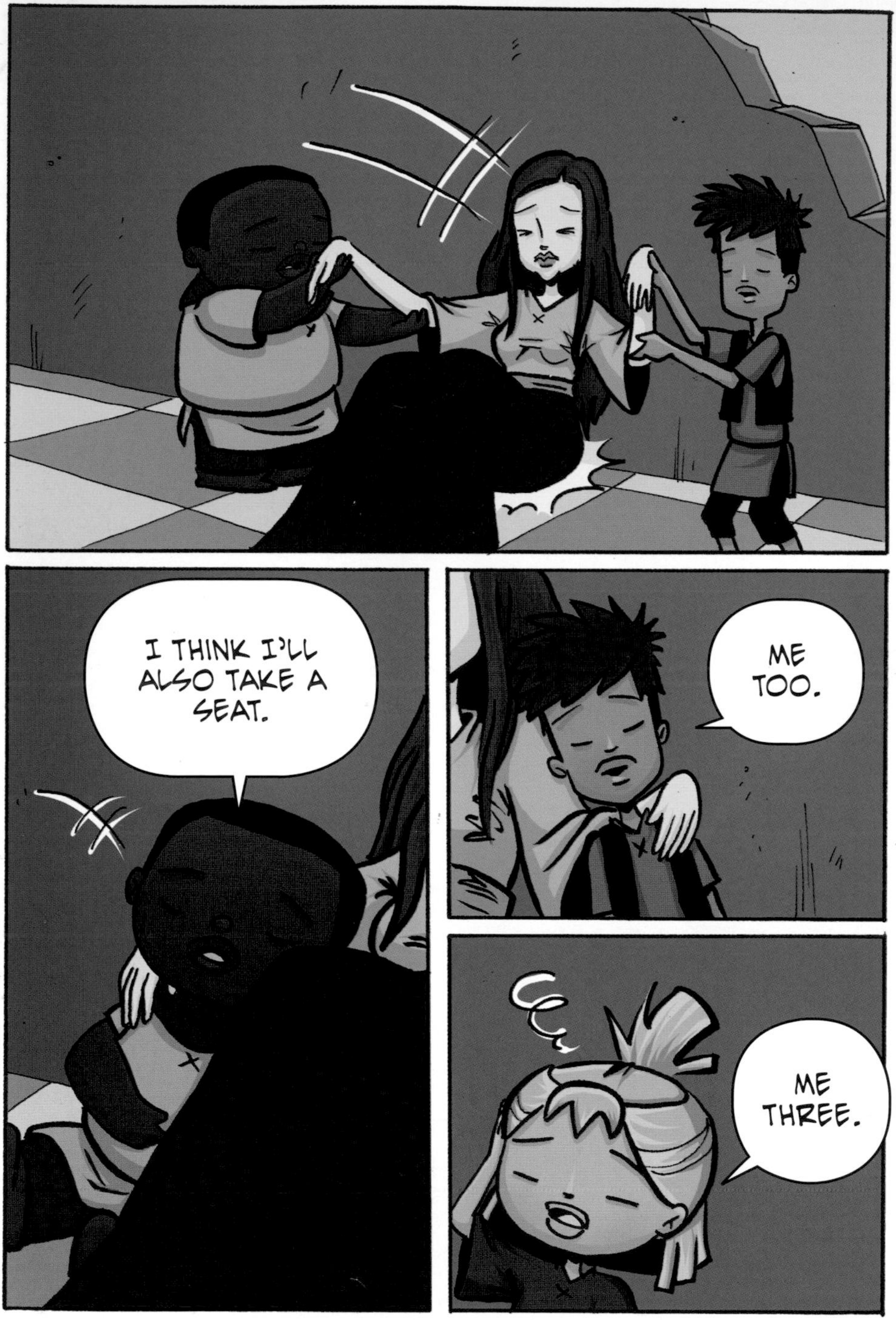
I THINK I'LL ALSO TAKE A SEAT.
ME TOO.
ME THREE.

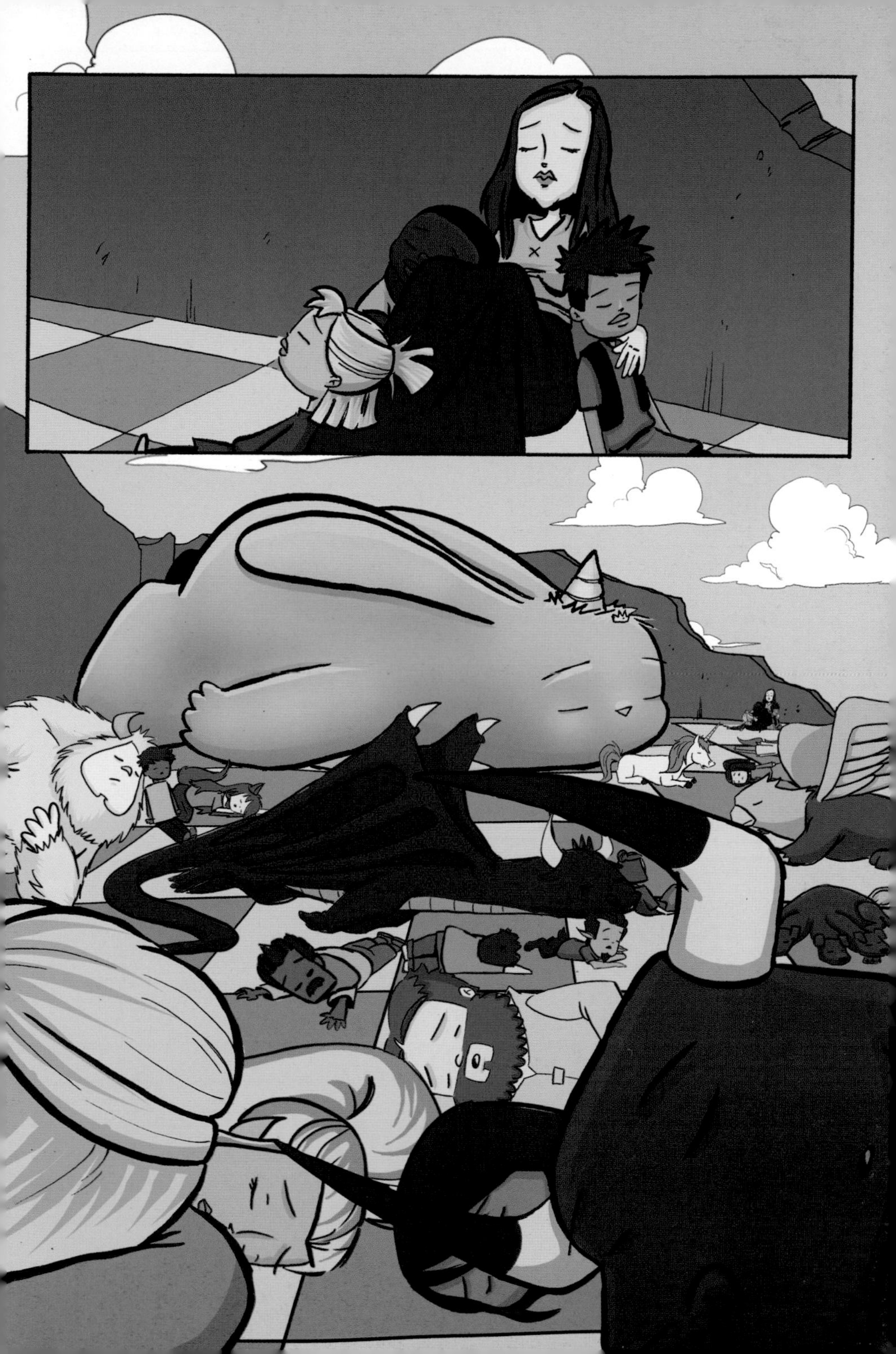

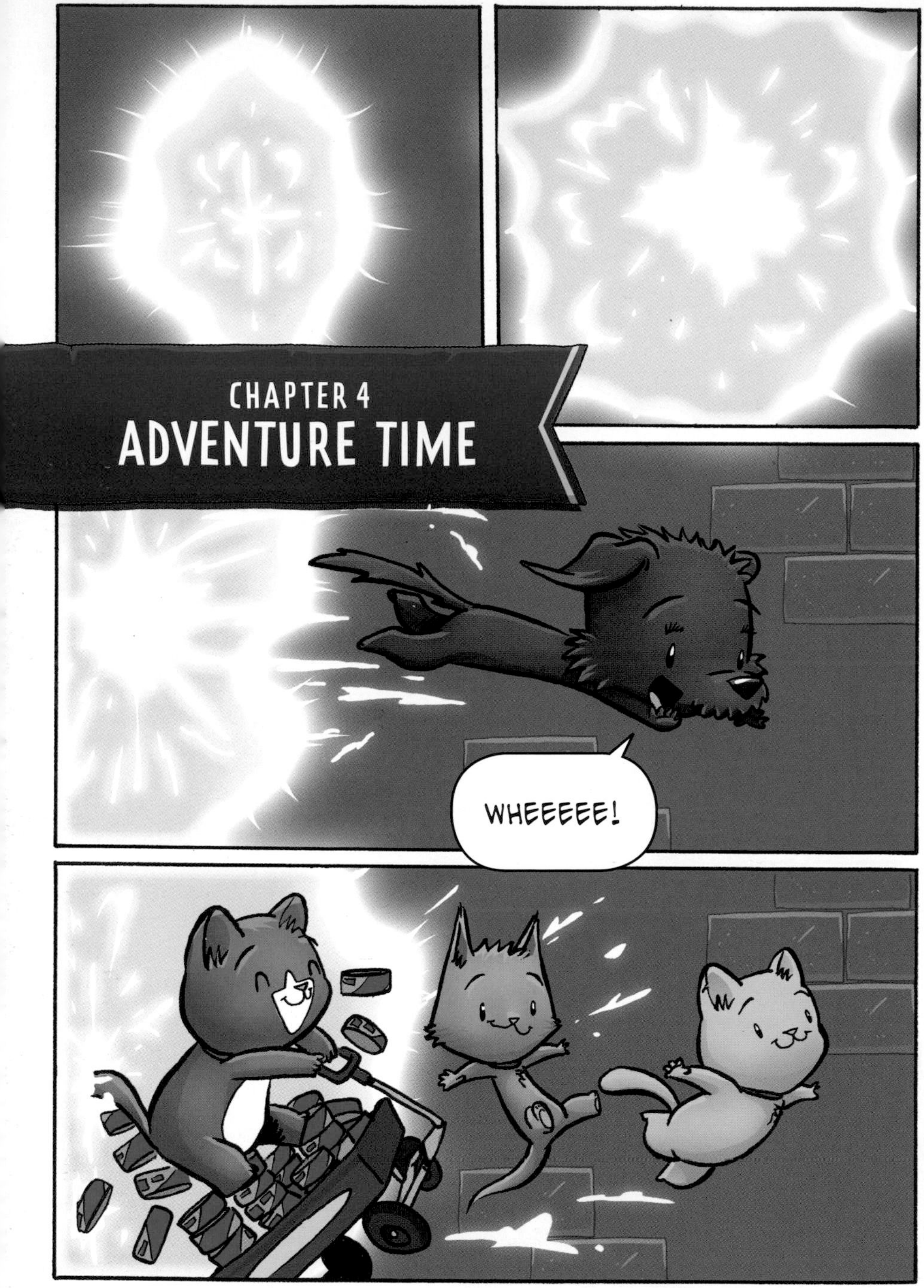
CHAPTER 4
ADVENTURE TIME
WHEEEEEE!

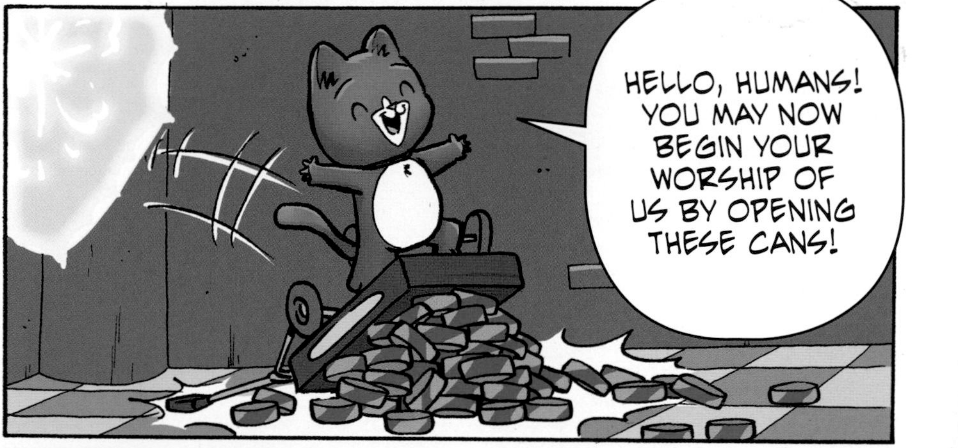
HELLO, HUMANS! YOU MAY NOW BEGIN YOUR WORSHIP OF US BY OPENING THESE CANS!

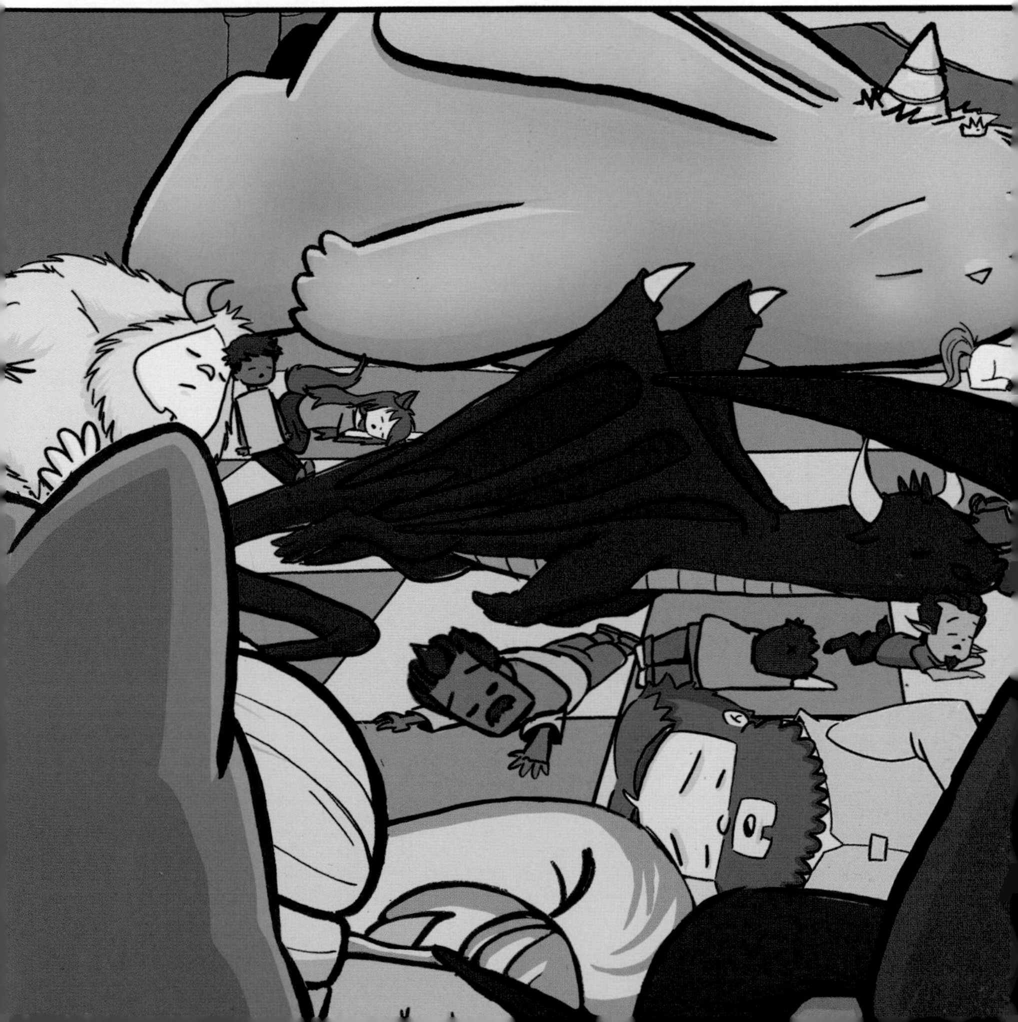

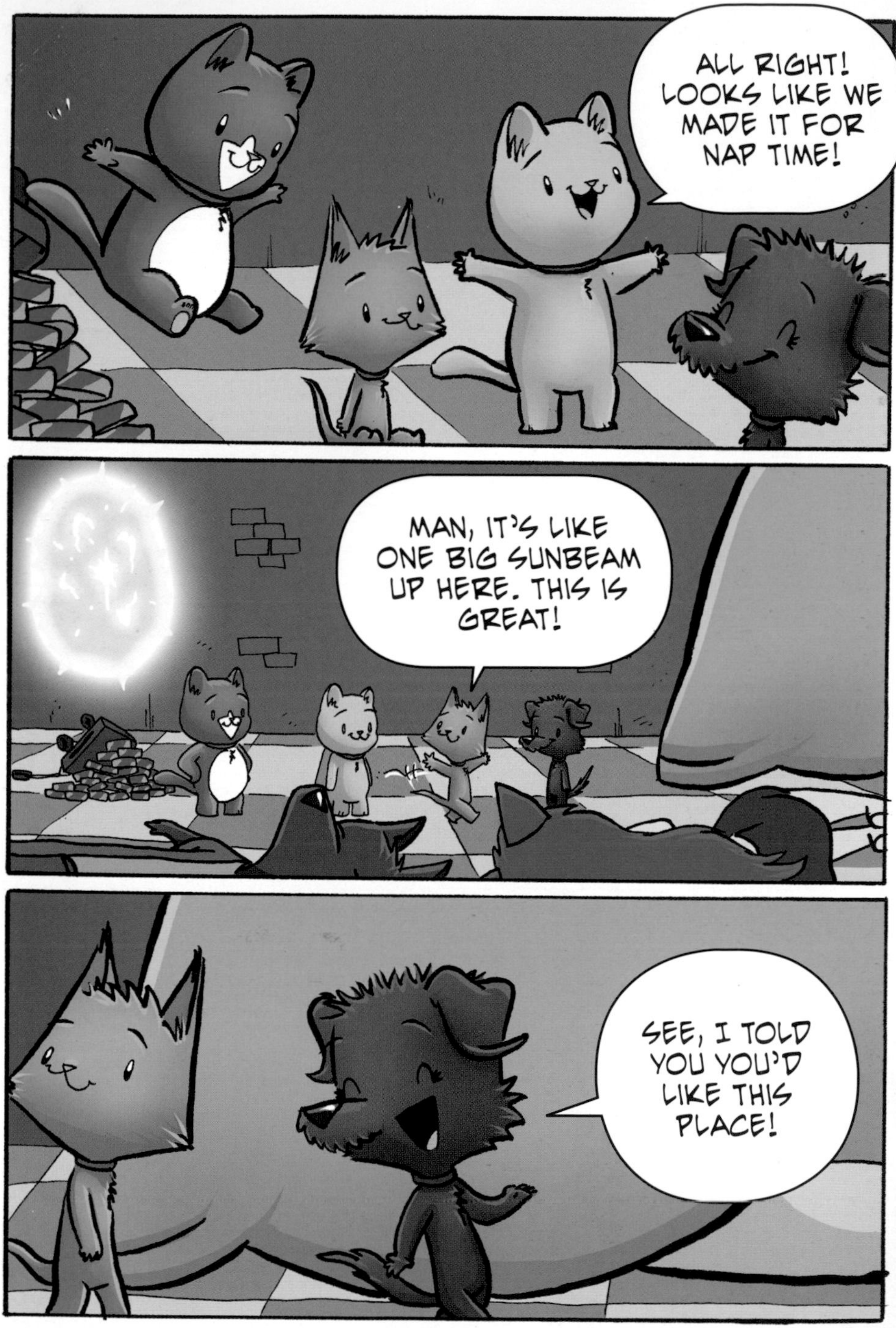
ALL RIGHT! LOOKS LIKE WE MADE IT FOR NAP TIME!
MAN, IT'S LIKE ONE BIG SUNBEAM UP HERE. THIS IS GREAT!
SEE, I TOLD YOU YOU'D LIKE THIS PLACE!

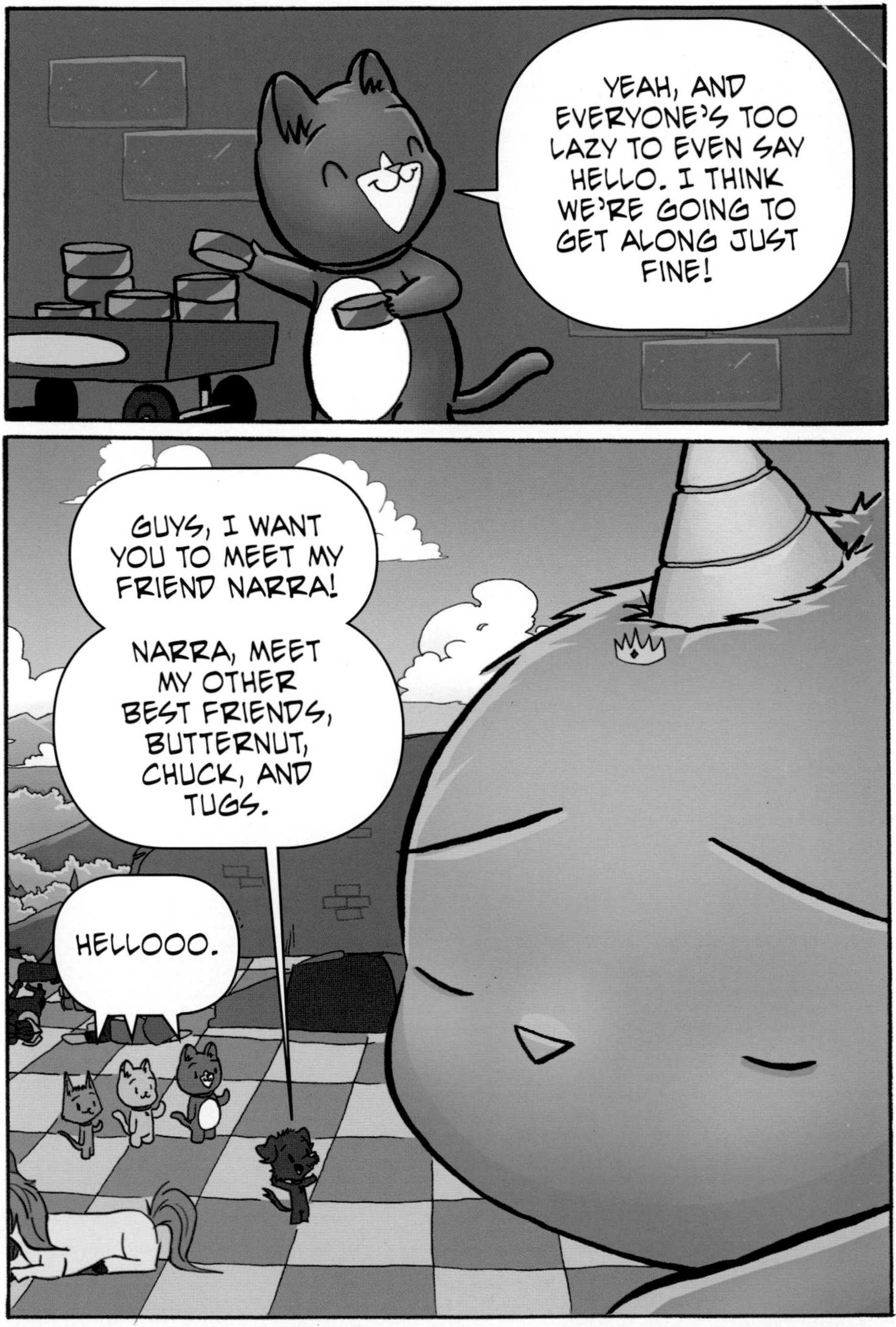
YEAH, AND EVERYONE'S TOO LAZY TO EVEN SAY HELLO. I THINK WE'RE GOING TO GET ALONG JUST FINE!
GUYS, I WANT YOU TO MEET MY FRIEND NARRA!
NARRA, MEET MY OTHER BEST FRIENDS, BUTTERNUT, CHUCK, AND TUGS.
HELLOOO.

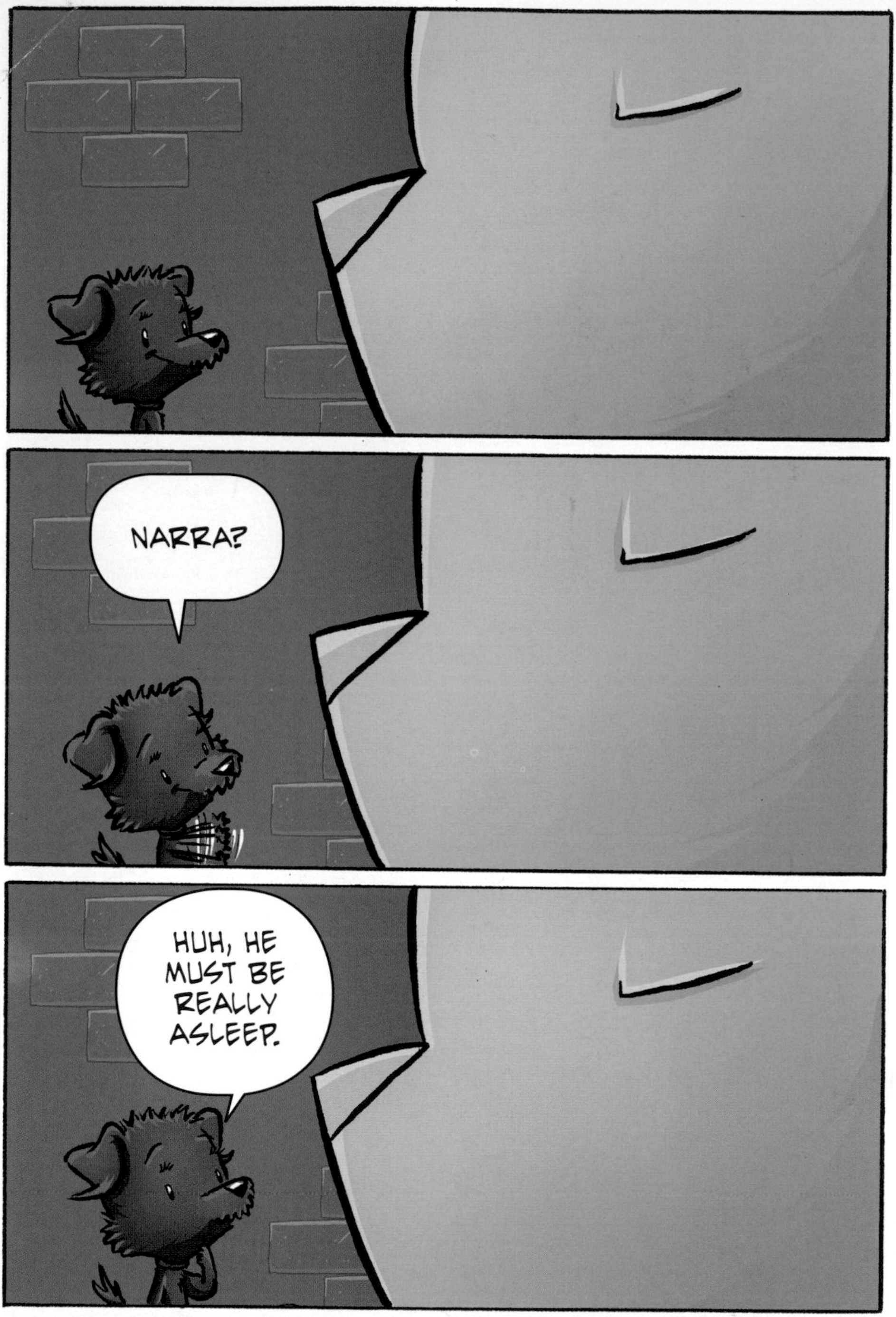
NARRA?
HUH, HE MUST BE REALLY ASLEEP.

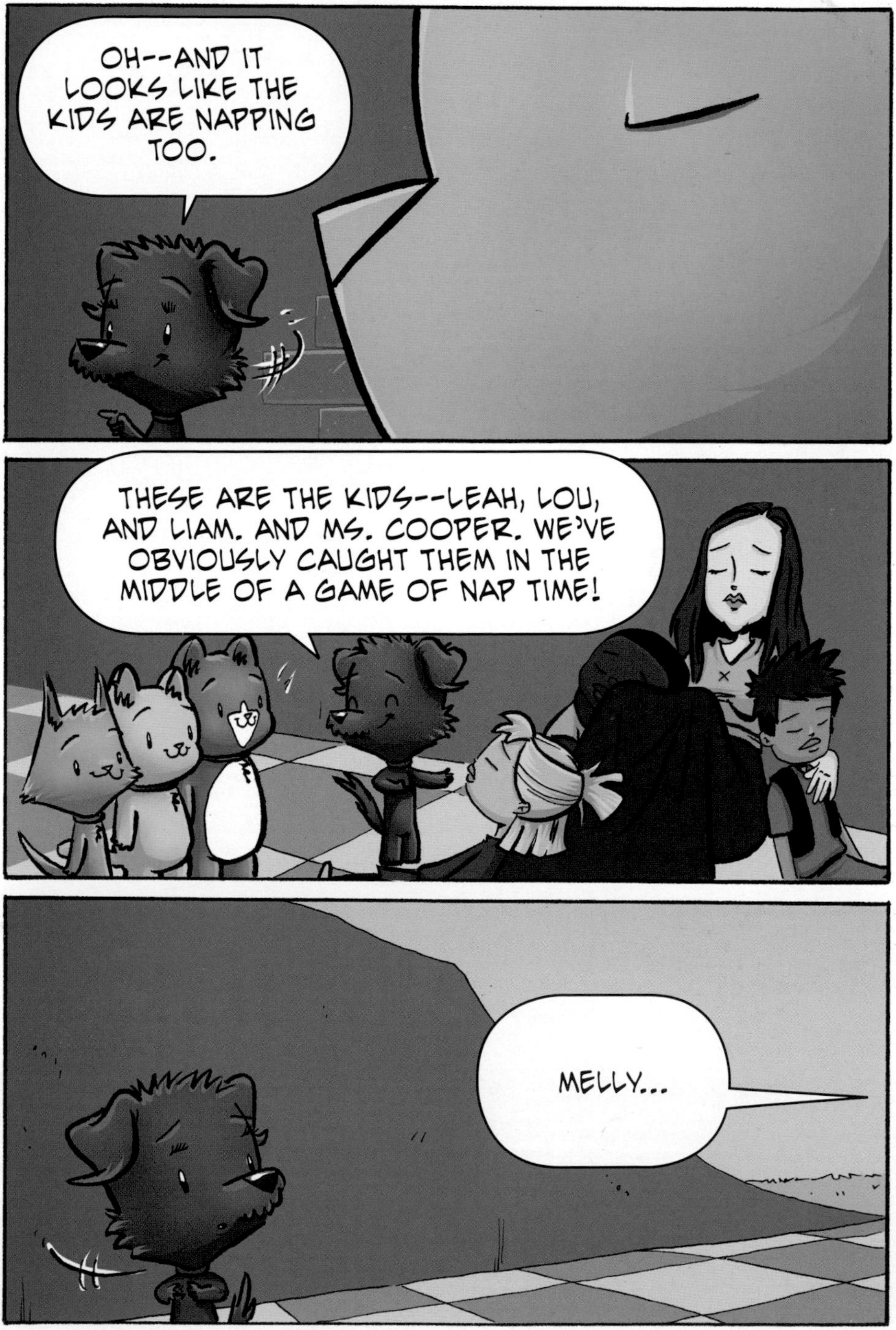
OH--AND IT LOOKS LIKE THE KIDS ARE NAPPING TOO.
THESE ARE THE KIDS--LEAH, LOU, AND LIAM. AND MS. COOPER. WE'VE OBVIOUSLY CAUGHT THEM IN THE MIDDLE OF A GAME OF NAP TIME!
MELLY...

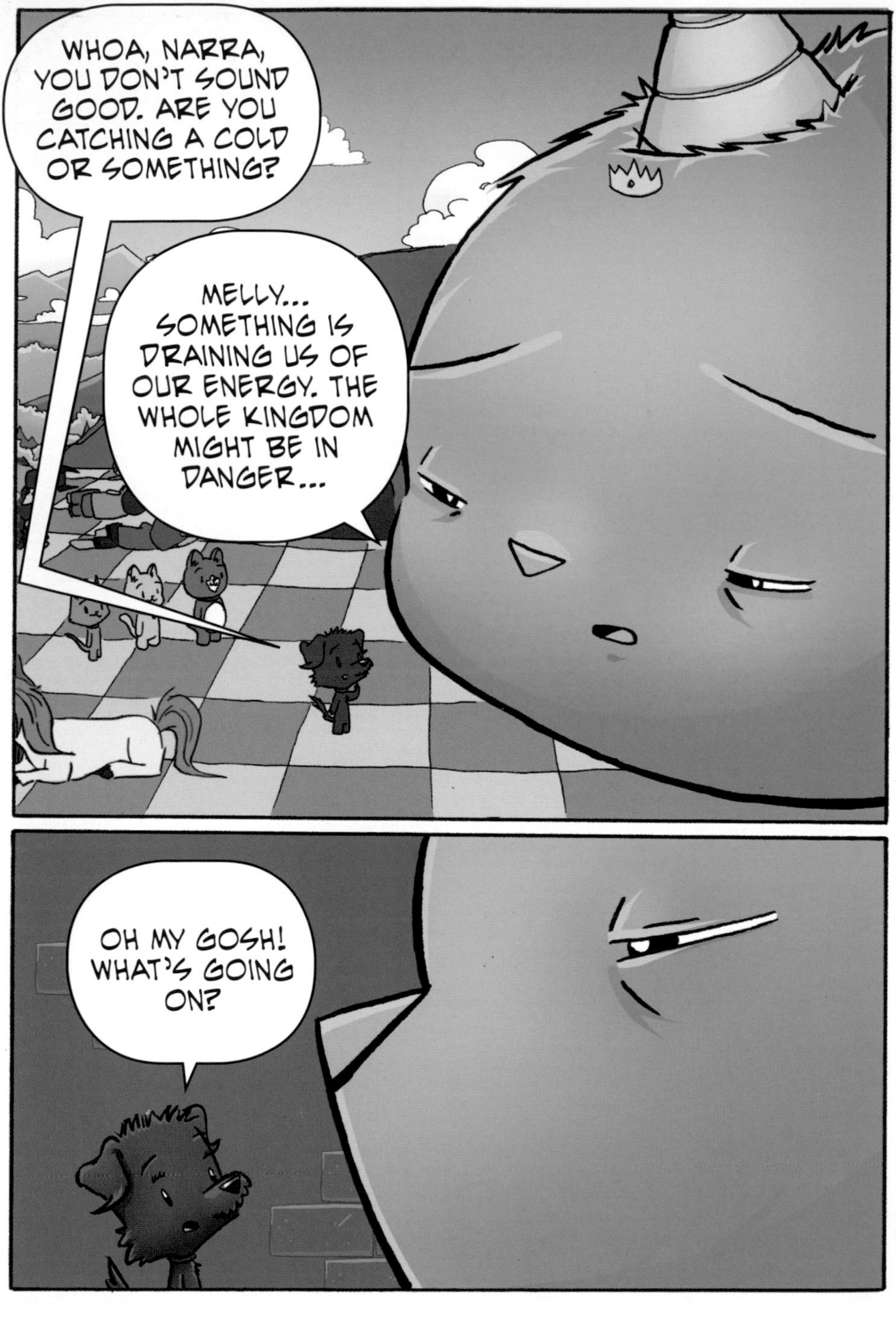
WHOA, NARRA, YOU DON'T SOUND GOOD. ARE YOU CATCHING A COLD OR SOMETHING?
MELLY... SOMETHING IS DRAINING US OF OUR ENERGY. THE WHOLE KINGDOM MIGHT BE IN DANGER...
OH MY GOSH! WHAT'S GOING ON?

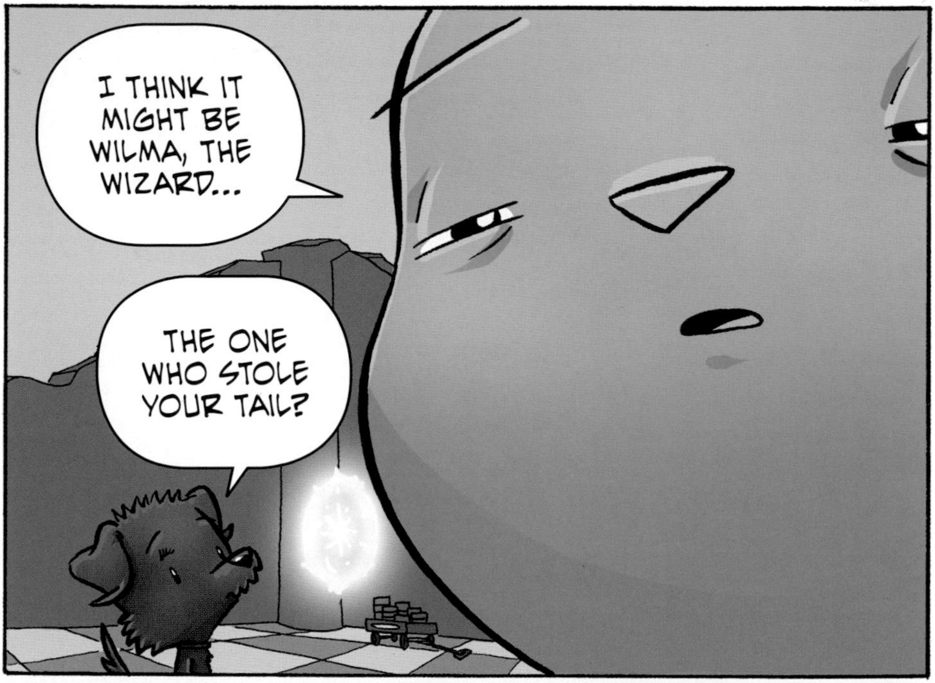
I THINK IT MIGHT BE WILMA, THE WIZARD...
THE ONE WHO STOLE YOUR TAIL?

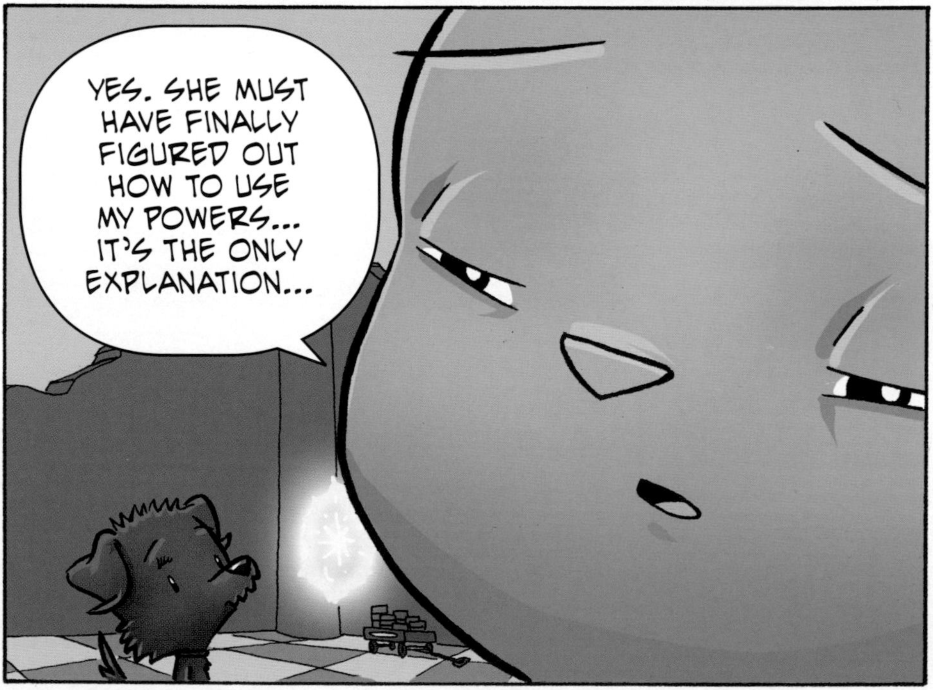
YES. SHE MUST HAVE FINALLY FIGURED OUT HOW TO USE MY POWERS... IT'S THE ONLY EXPLANATION...

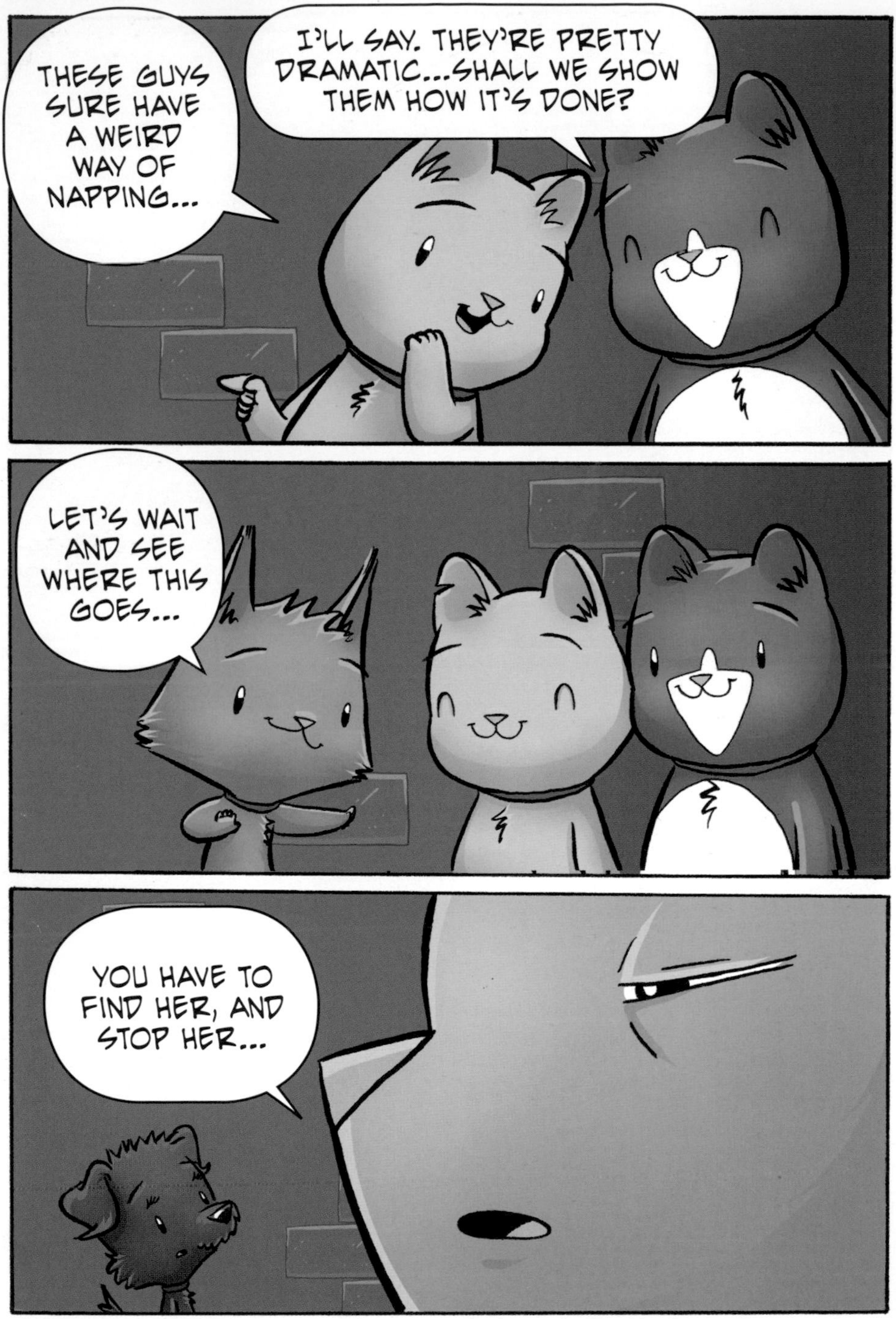
THESE GUYS SURE HAVE A WEIRD WAY OF NAPPING...
I'LL SAY. THEY'RE PRETTY DRAMATIC...SHALL WE SHOW THEM HOW IT'S DONE?
LET'S WAIT AND SEE WHERE THIS GOES...
YOU HAVE TO FIND HER, AND STOP HER...

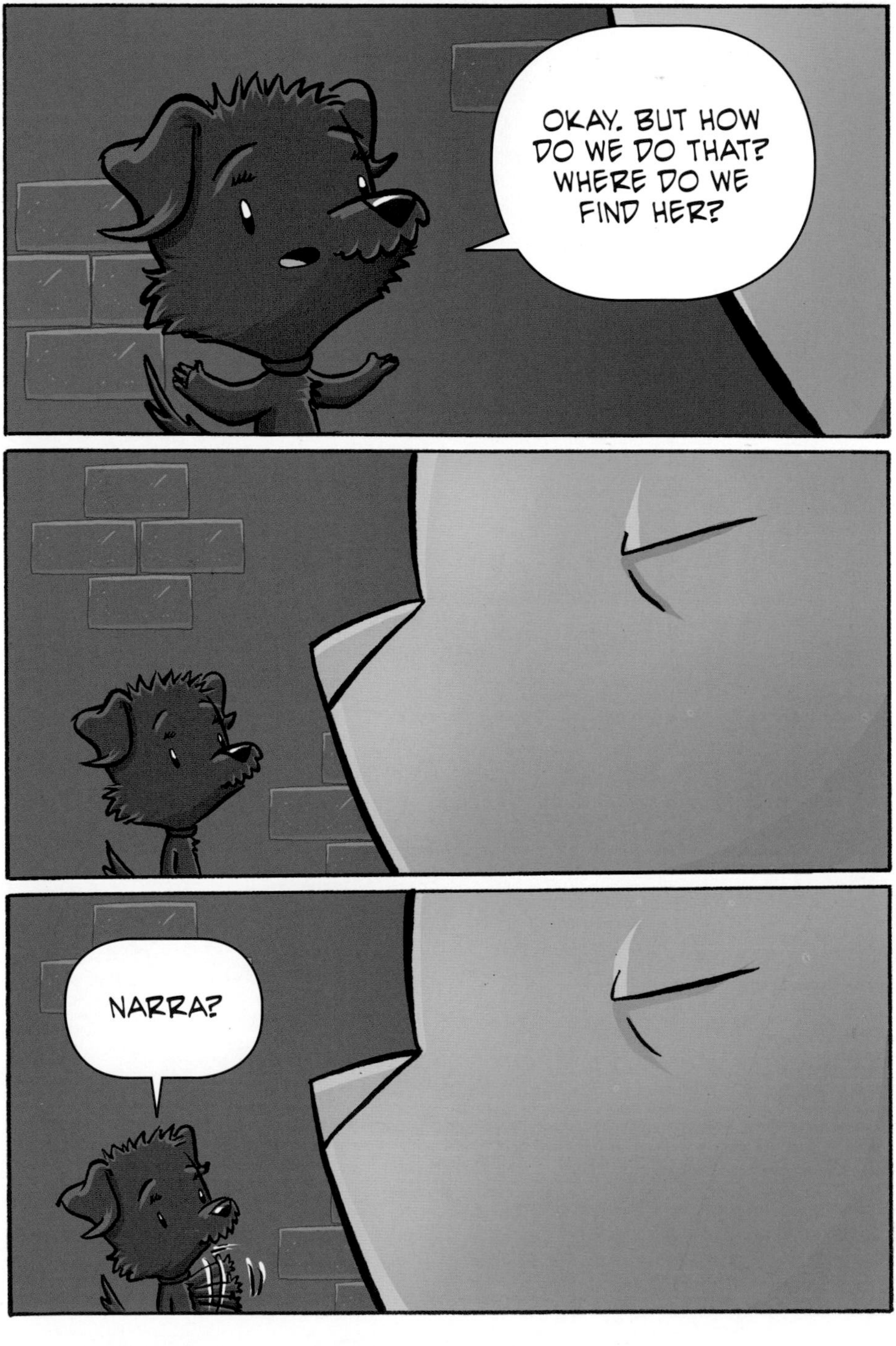
OKAY. BUT HOW DO WE DO THAT? WHERE DO WE FIND HER?
NARRA?

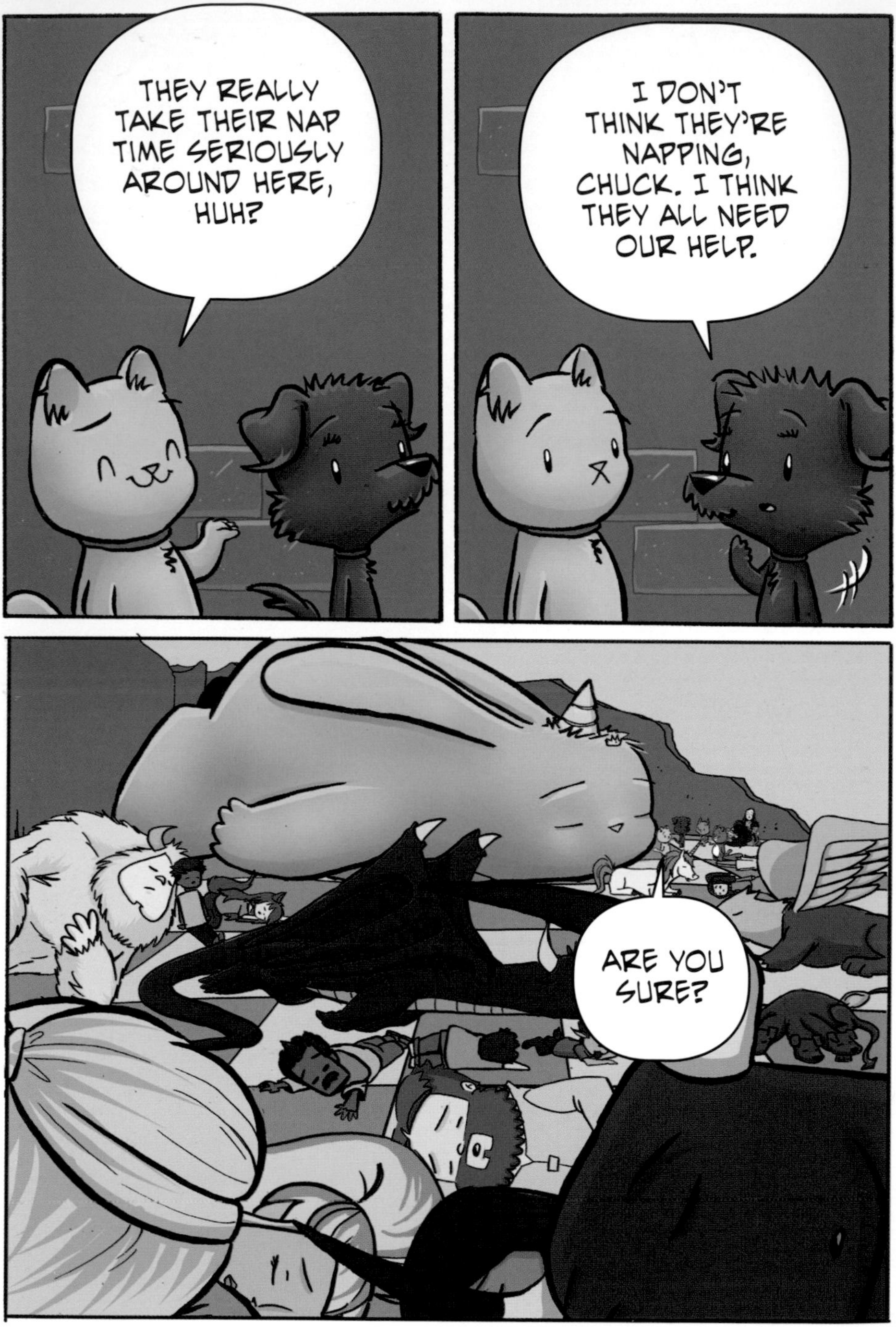
THEY REALLY TAKE THEIR NAP TIME SERIOUSLY AROUND HERE, HUH?
I DON'T THINK THEY'RE NAPPING, CHUCK. I THINK THEY ALL NEED OUR HELP.
ARE YOU SURE?

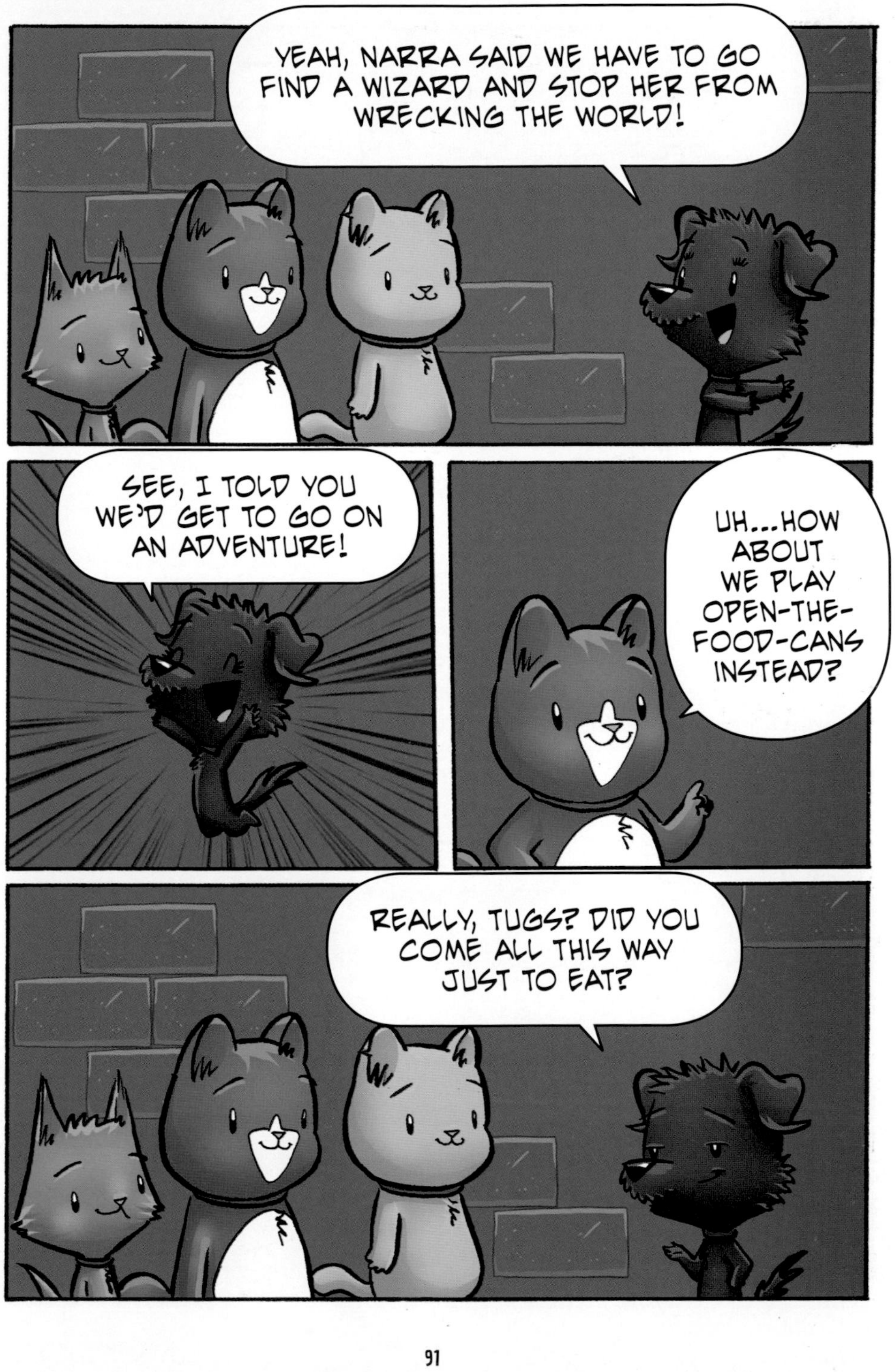
YEAH, NARRA SAID WE HAVE TO GO FIND A WIZARD AND STOP HER FROM WRECKING THE WORLD!
SEE, I TOLD YOU WE'D GET TO GO ON AN ADVENTURE!
UH...HOW ABOUT WE PLAY OPEN-THE-FOOD-CANS INSTEAD?
REALLY, TUGS? DID YOU COME ALL THIS WAY JUST TO EAT?

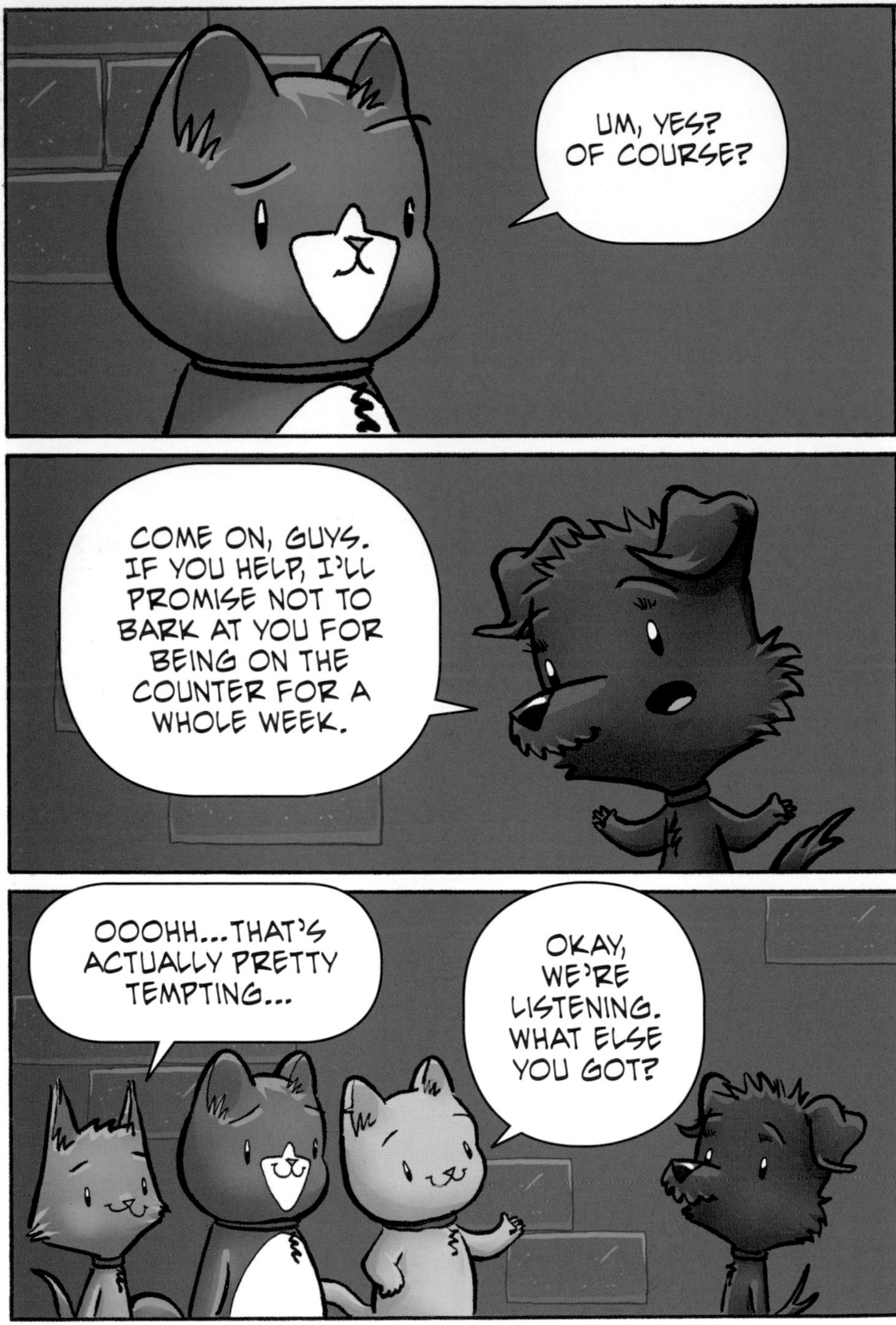
UM, YES? OF COURSE?
COME ON, GUYS. IF YOU HELP, I'LL PROMISE NOT TO BARK AT YOU FOR BEING ON THE COUNTER FOR A WHOLE WEEK.
OOOHH...THAT'S ACTUALLY PRETTY TEMPTING...
OKAY, WE'RE LISTENING. WHAT ELSE YOU GOT?

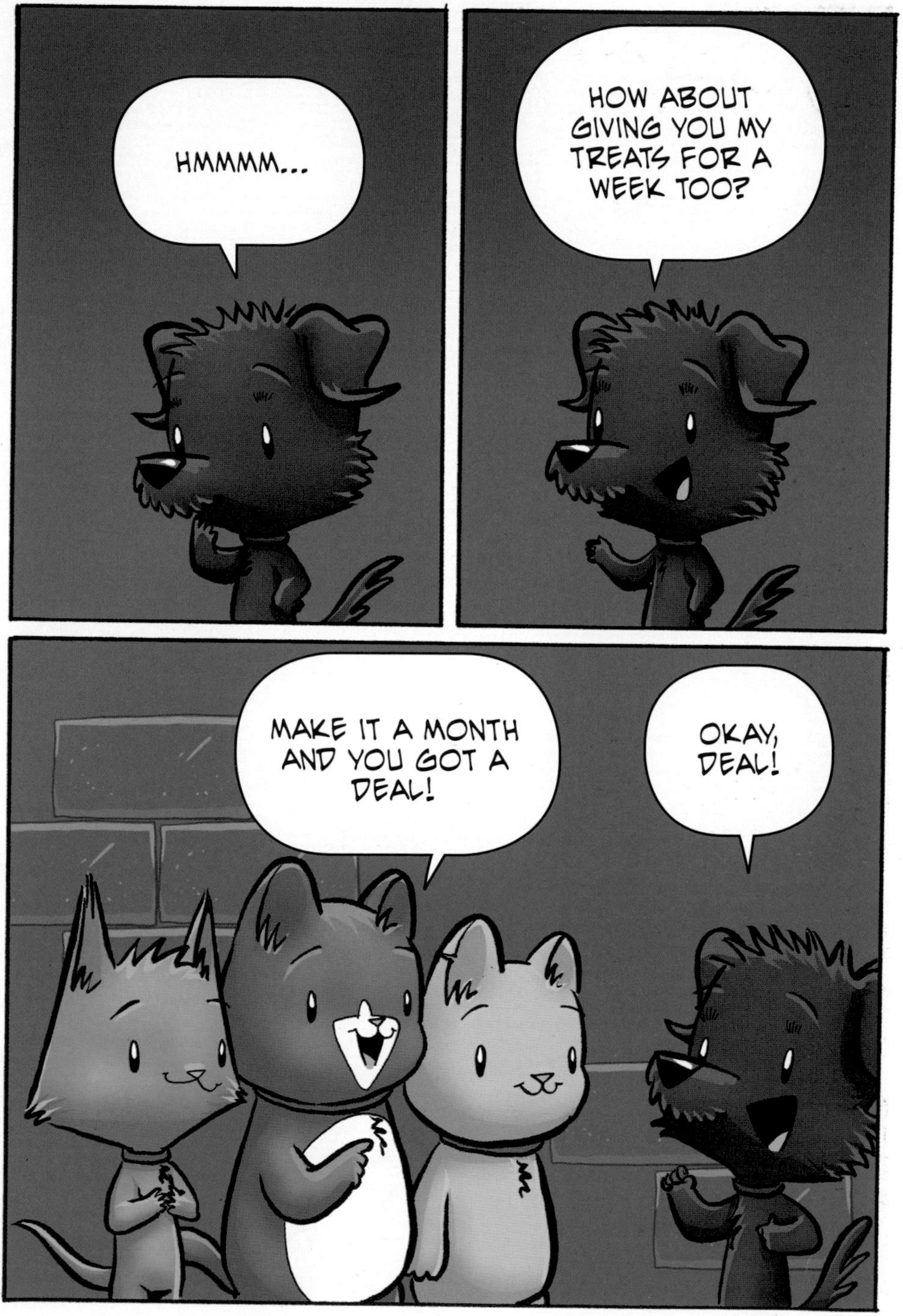
HMMMM...
HOW ABOUT GIVING YOU MY TREATS FOR A WEEK TOO?
MAKE IT A MONTH AND YOU GOT A DEAL!
OKAY, DEAL!

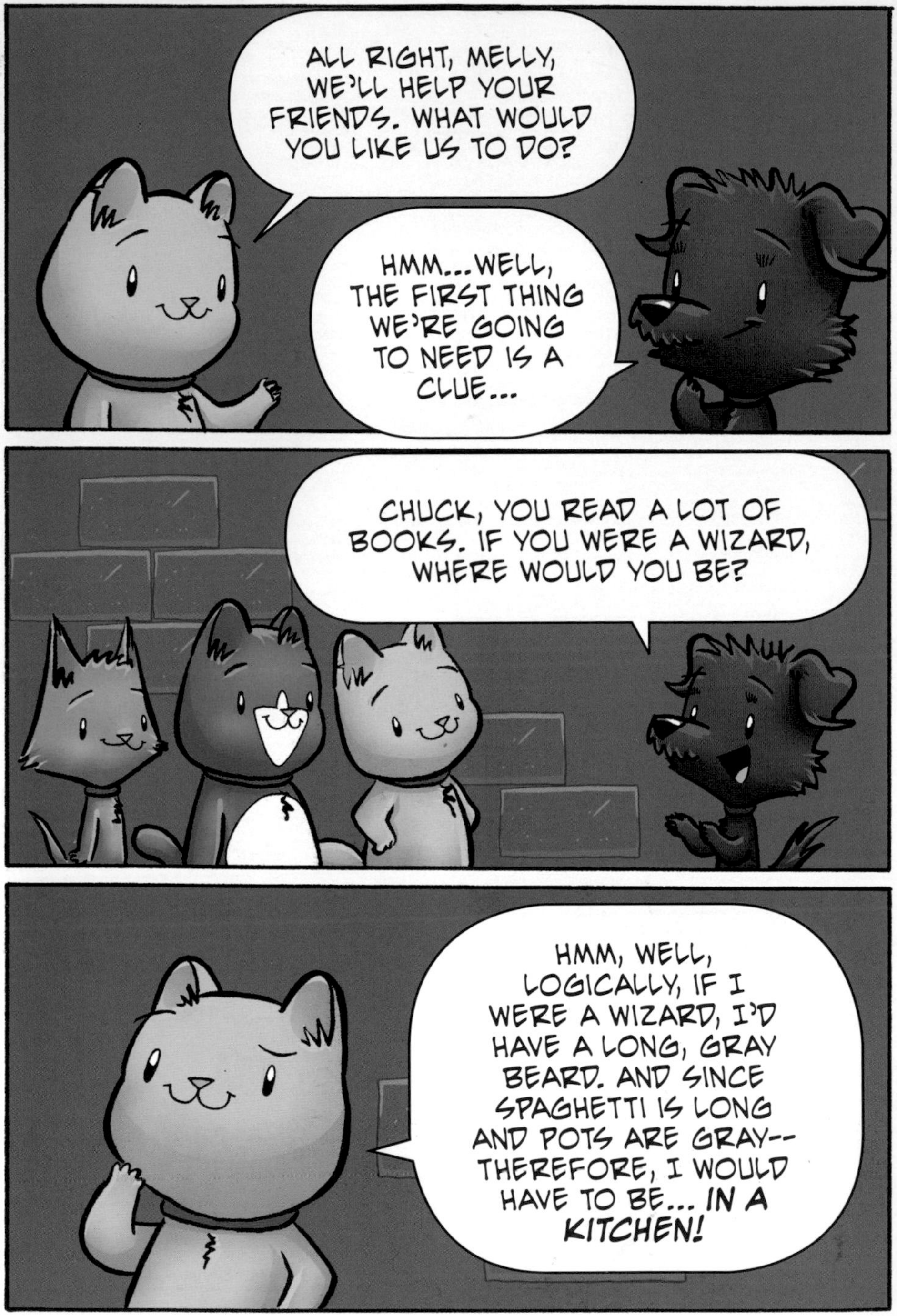
ALL RIGHT, MELLY, WE'LL HELP YOUR FRIENDS. WHAT WOULD YOU LIKE US TO DO?
HMM...WELL, THE FIRST THING WE'RE GOING TO NEED IS A CLUE...
CHUCK, YOU READ A LOT OF BOOKS. IF YOU WERE A WIZARD, WHERE WOULD YOU BE?
HMM, WELL, LOGICALLY, IF I WERE A WIZARD, I'D HAVE A LONG, GRAY BEARD. AND SINCE SPAGHETTI IS LONG AND POTS ARE GRAY--THEREFORE, I WOULD HAVE TO BE... *IN A KITCHEN!*

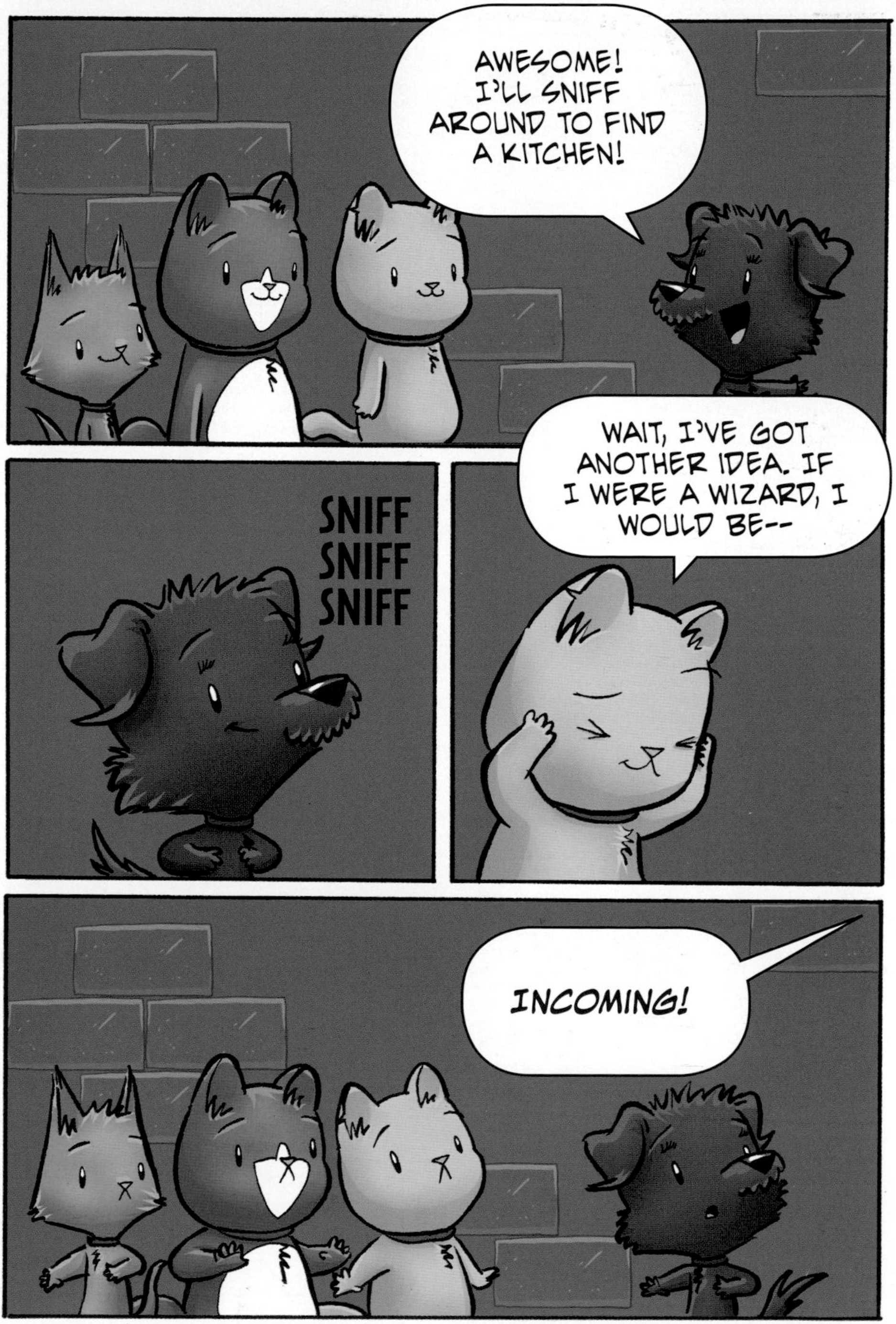
AWESOME! I'LL SNIFF AROUND TO FIND A KITCHEN!
SNIFF SNIFF SNIFF
WAIT, I'VE GOT ANOTHER IDEA. IF I WERE A WIZARD, I WOULD BE--
INCOMING!

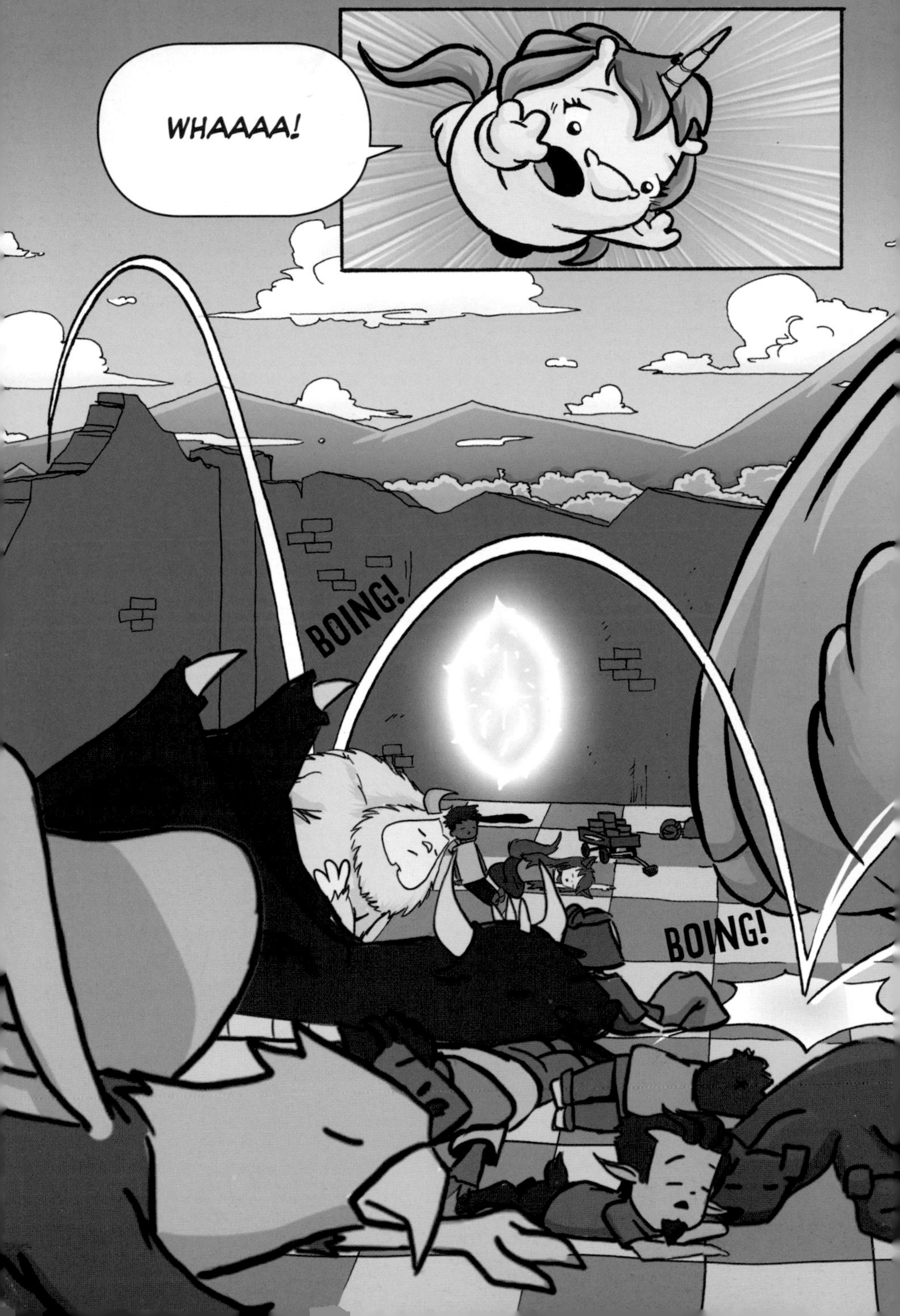
WHAAAA!
BOING!
BOING!

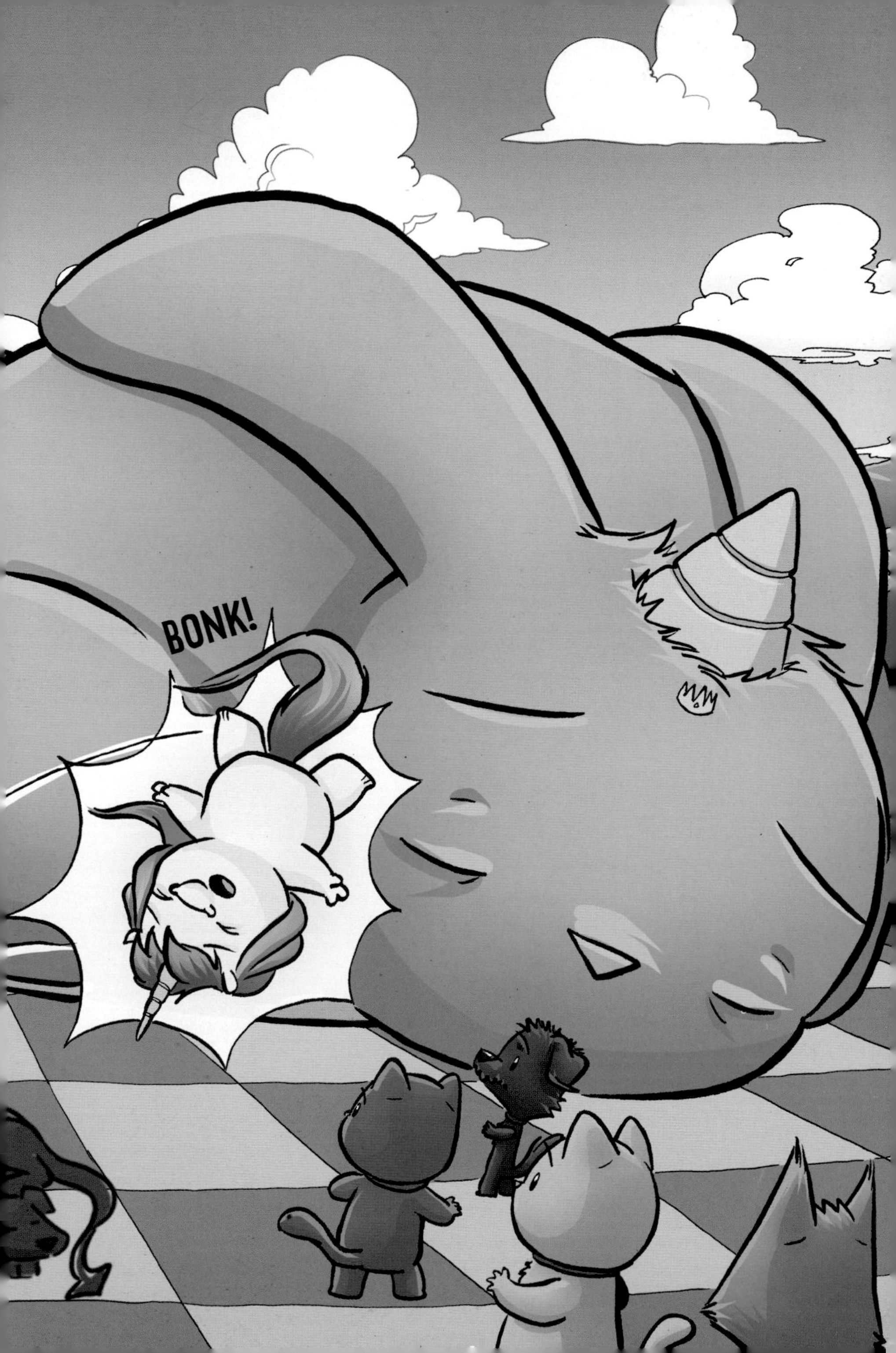
BONK!

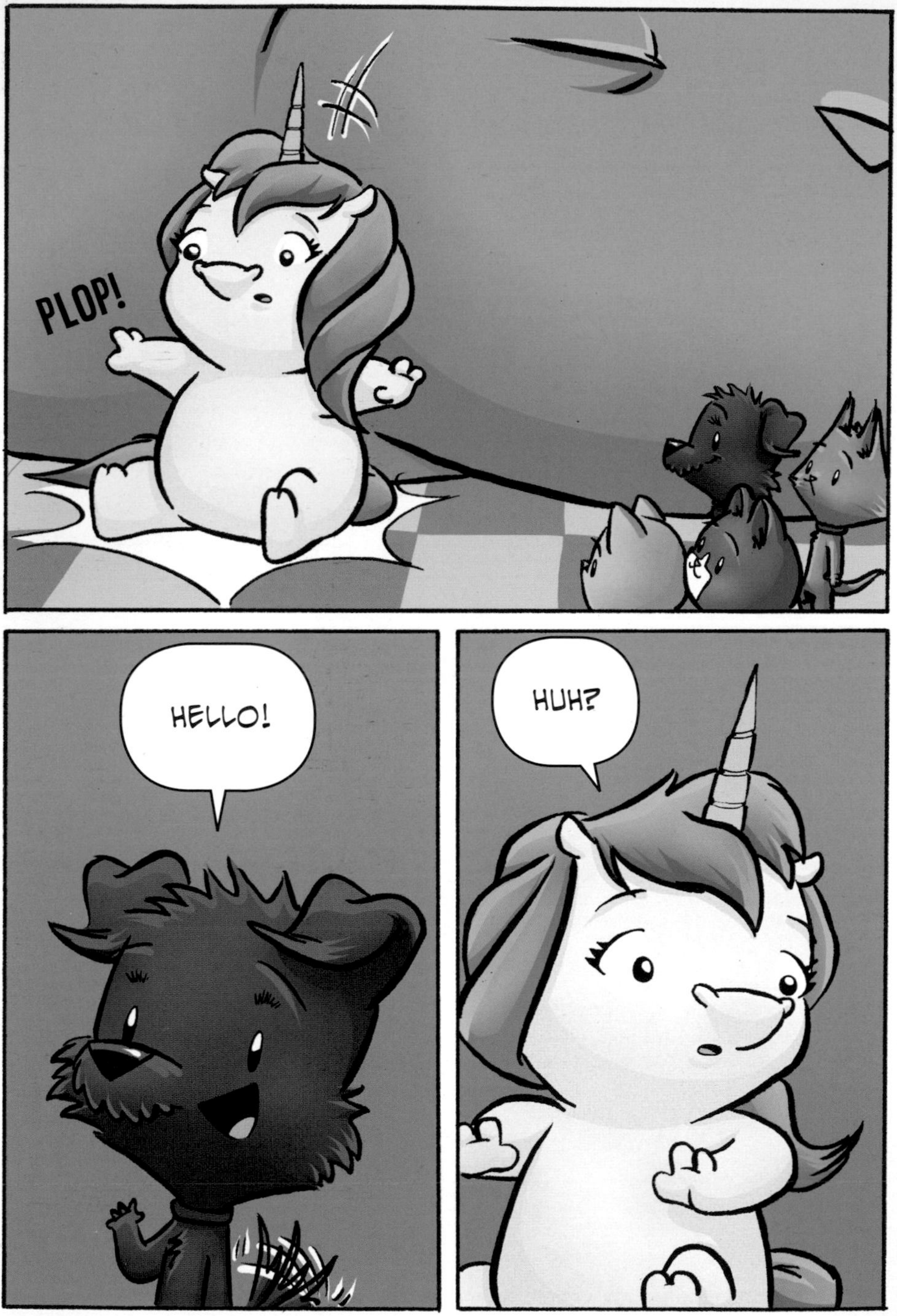
PLOP!
HELLO!
HUH?

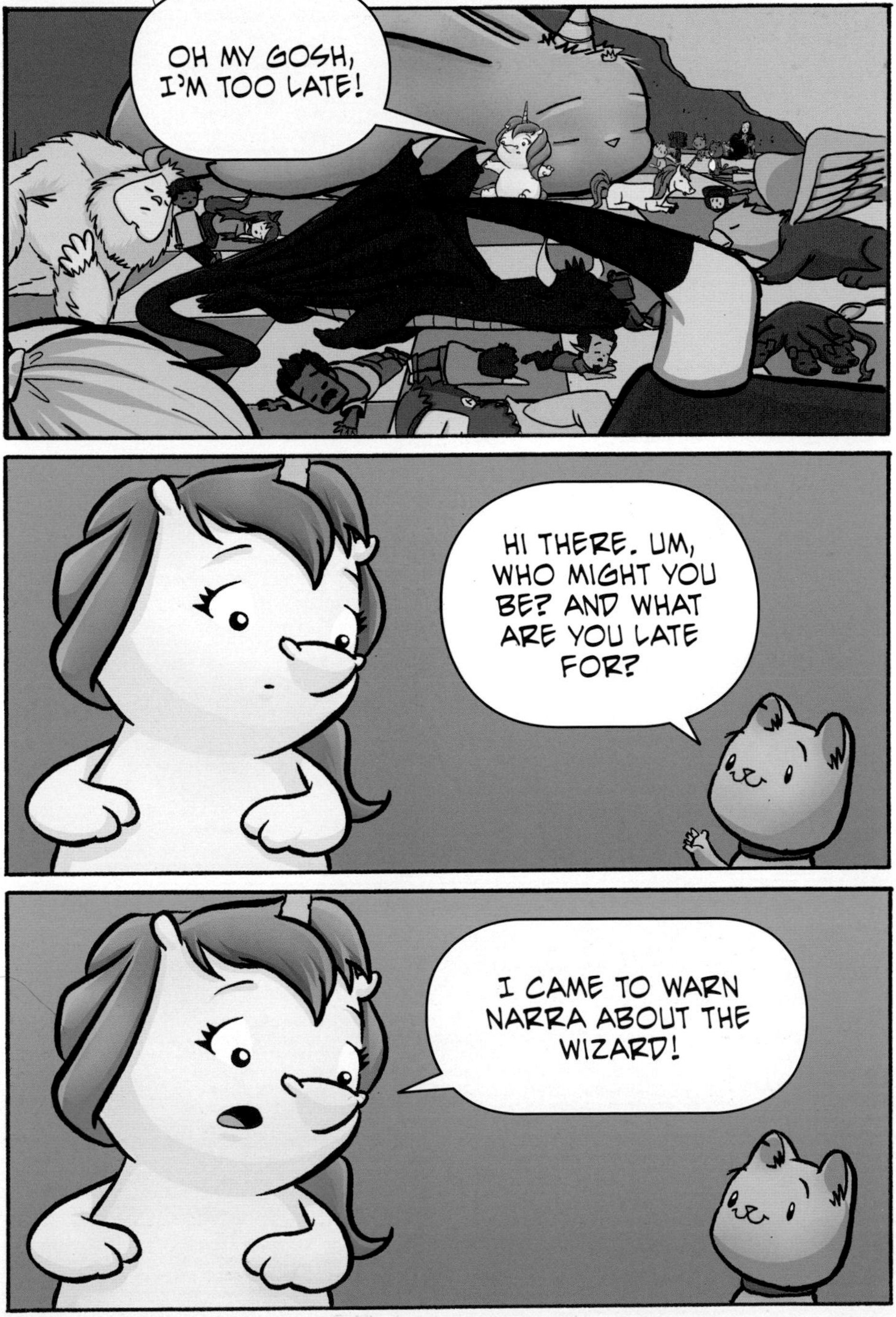
OH MY GOSH, I'M TOO LATE!
HI THERE. UM, WHO MIGHT YOU BE? AND WHAT ARE YOU LATE FOR?
I CAME TO WARN NARRA ABOUT THE WIZARD!

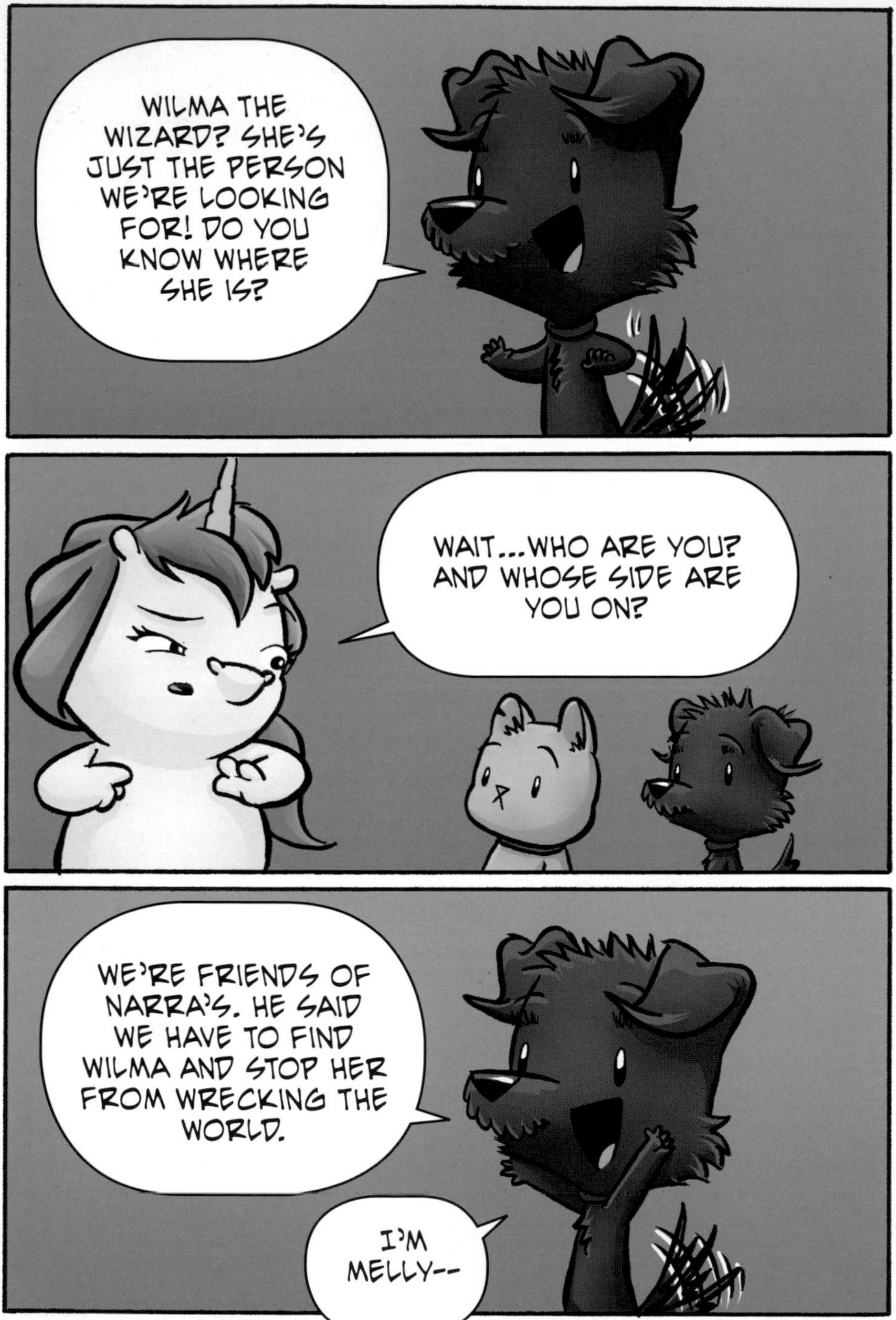
WILMA THE WIZARD? SHE'S JUST THE PERSON WE'RE LOOKING FOR! DO YOU KNOW WHERE SHE IS?
WAIT...WHO ARE YOU? AND WHOSE SIDE ARE YOU ON?
WE'RE FRIENDS OF NARRA'S. HE SAID WE HAVE TO FIND WILMA AND STOP HER FROM WRECKING THE WORLD.
I'M MELLY--

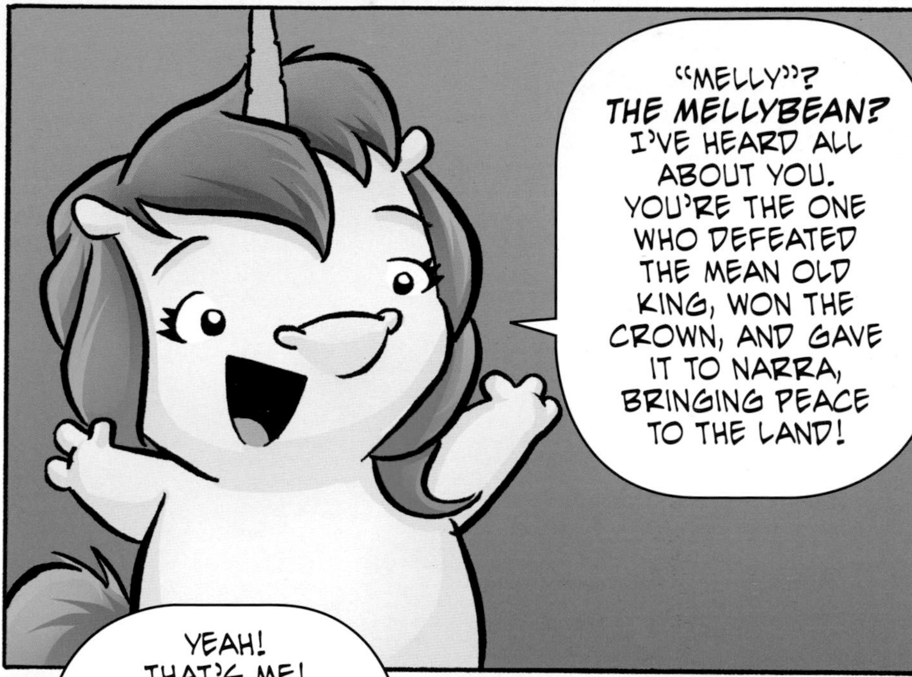
"MELLY"? **THE MELLYBEAN?** I'VE HEARD ALL ABOUT YOU. YOU'RE THE ONE WHO DEFEATED THE MEAN OLD KING, WON THE CROWN, AND GAVE IT TO NARRA, BRINGING PEACE TO THE LAND!

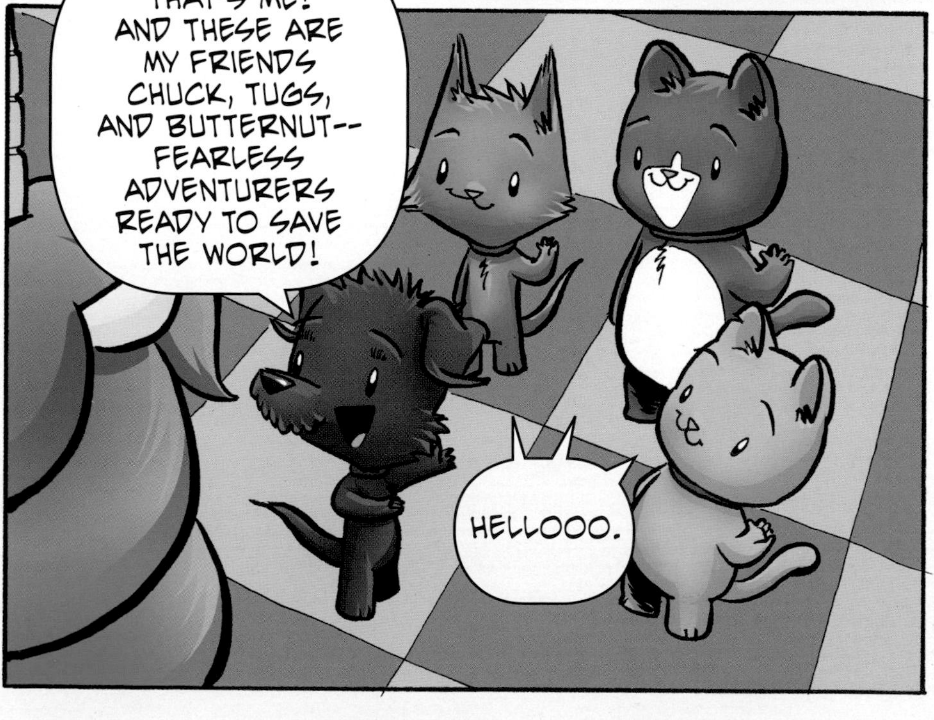
YEAH! THAT'S ME! AND THESE ARE MY FRIENDS CHUCK, TUGS, AND BUTTERNUT--FEARLESS ADVENTURERS READY TO SAVE THE WORLD!
HELLOOO.

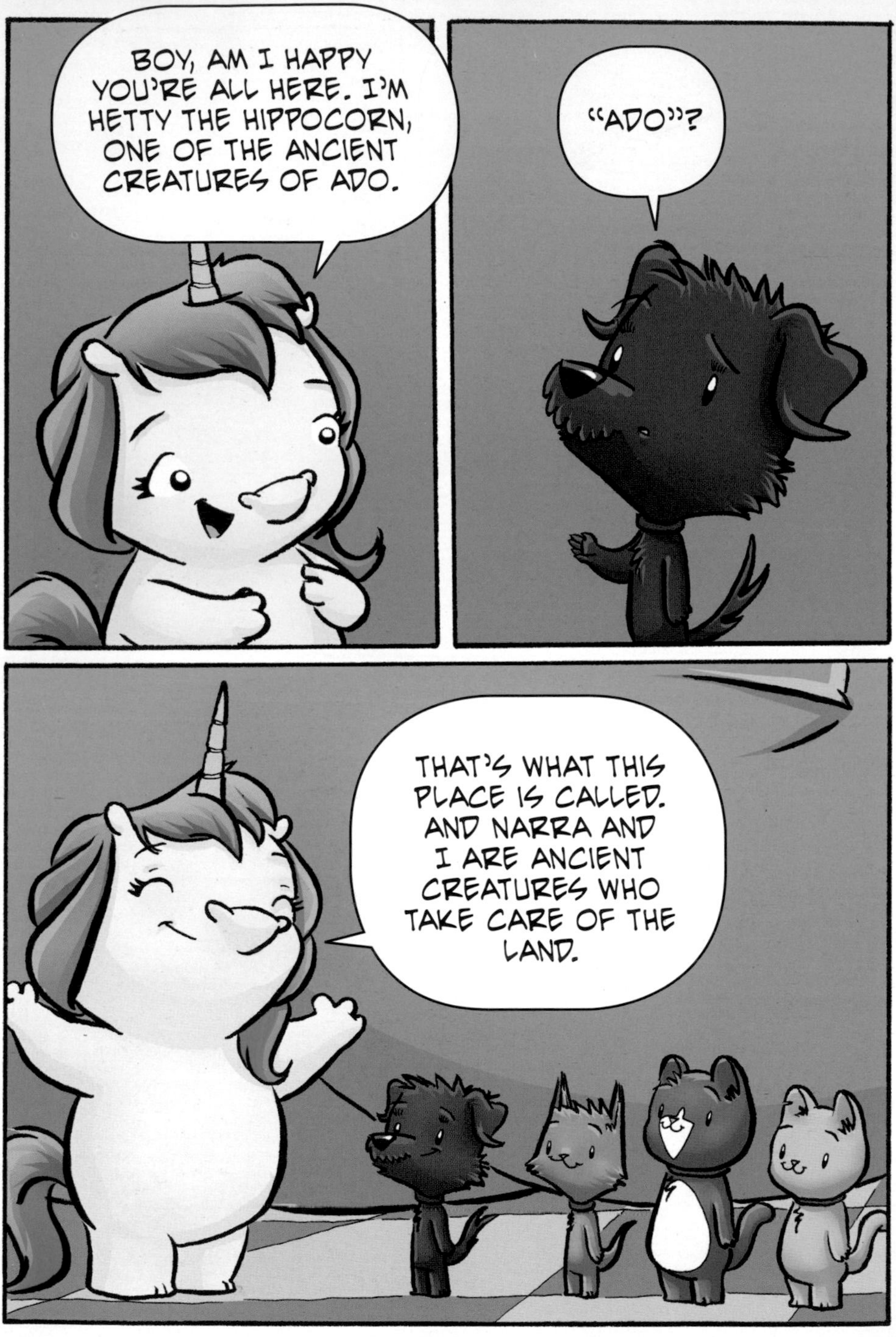
BOY, AM I HAPPY YOU'RE ALL HERE. I'M HETTY THE HIPPOCORN, ONE OF THE ANCIENT CREATURES OF ADO.
"ADO"?
THAT'S WHAT THIS PLACE IS CALLED. AND NARRA AND I ARE ANCIENT CREATURES WHO TAKE CARE OF THE LAND.

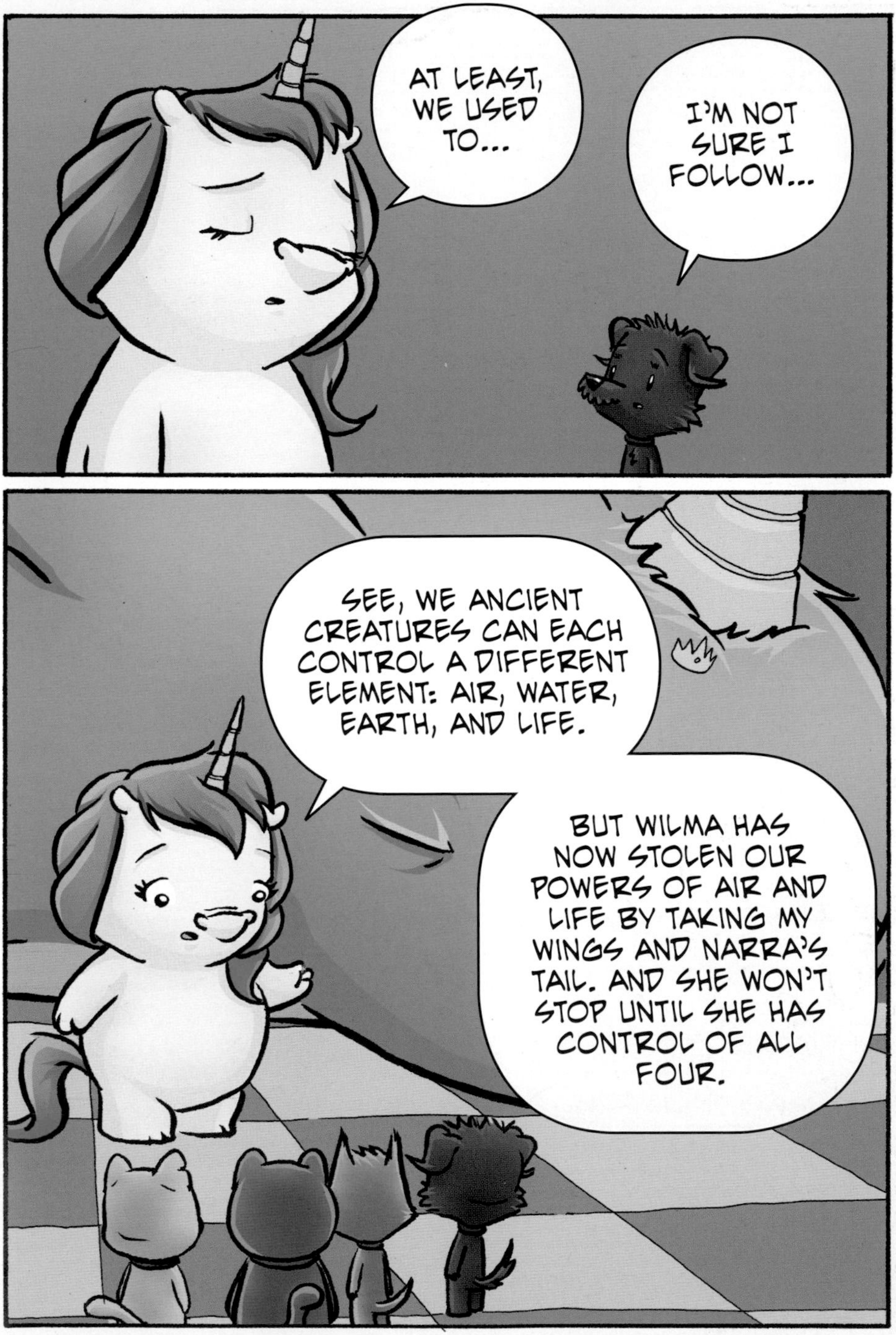
AT LEAST, WE USED TO...
I'M NOT SURE I FOLLOW...
SEE, WE ANCIENT CREATURES CAN EACH CONTROL A DIFFERENT ELEMENT: AIR, WATER, EARTH, AND LIFE.
BUT WILMA HAS NOW STOLEN OUR POWERS OF AIR AND LIFE BY TAKING MY WINGS AND NARRA'S TAIL. AND SHE WON'T STOP UNTIL SHE HAS CONTROL OF ALL FOUR.

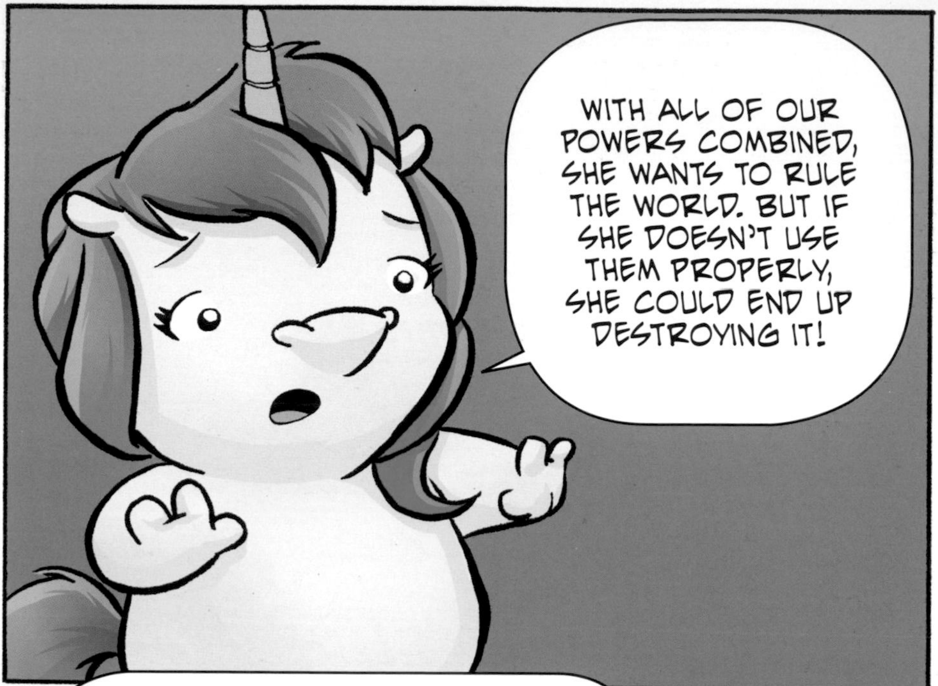
WITH ALL OF OUR POWERS COMBINED, SHE WANTS TO RULE THE WORLD. BUT IF SHE DOESN'T USE THEM PROPERLY, SHE COULD END UP DESTROYING IT!

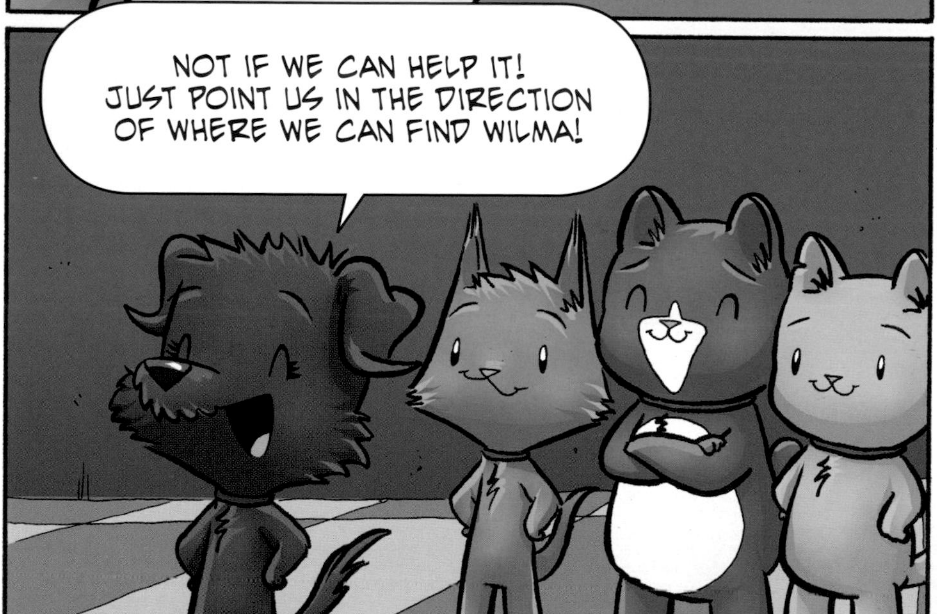
NOT IF WE CAN HELP IT! JUST POINT US IN THE DIRECTION OF WHERE WE CAN FIND WILMA!

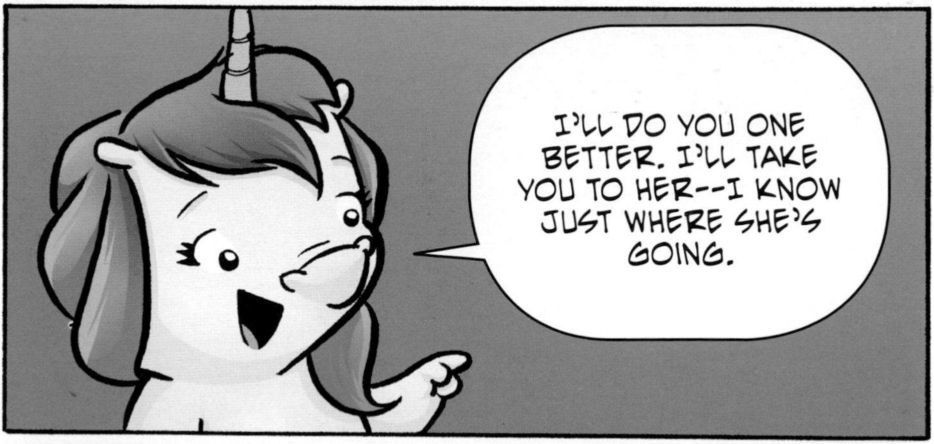
I'LL DO YOU ONE BETTER. I'LL TAKE YOU TO HER--I KNOW JUST WHERE SHE'S GOING.

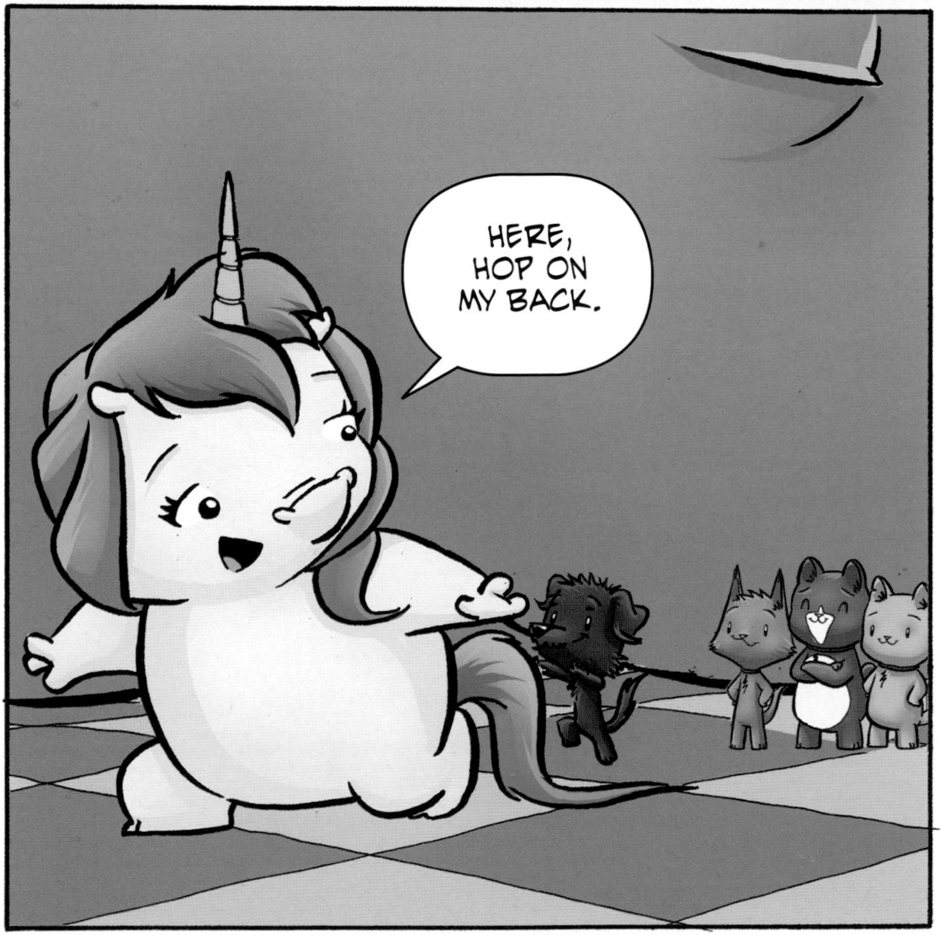
HERE, HOP ON MY BACK.

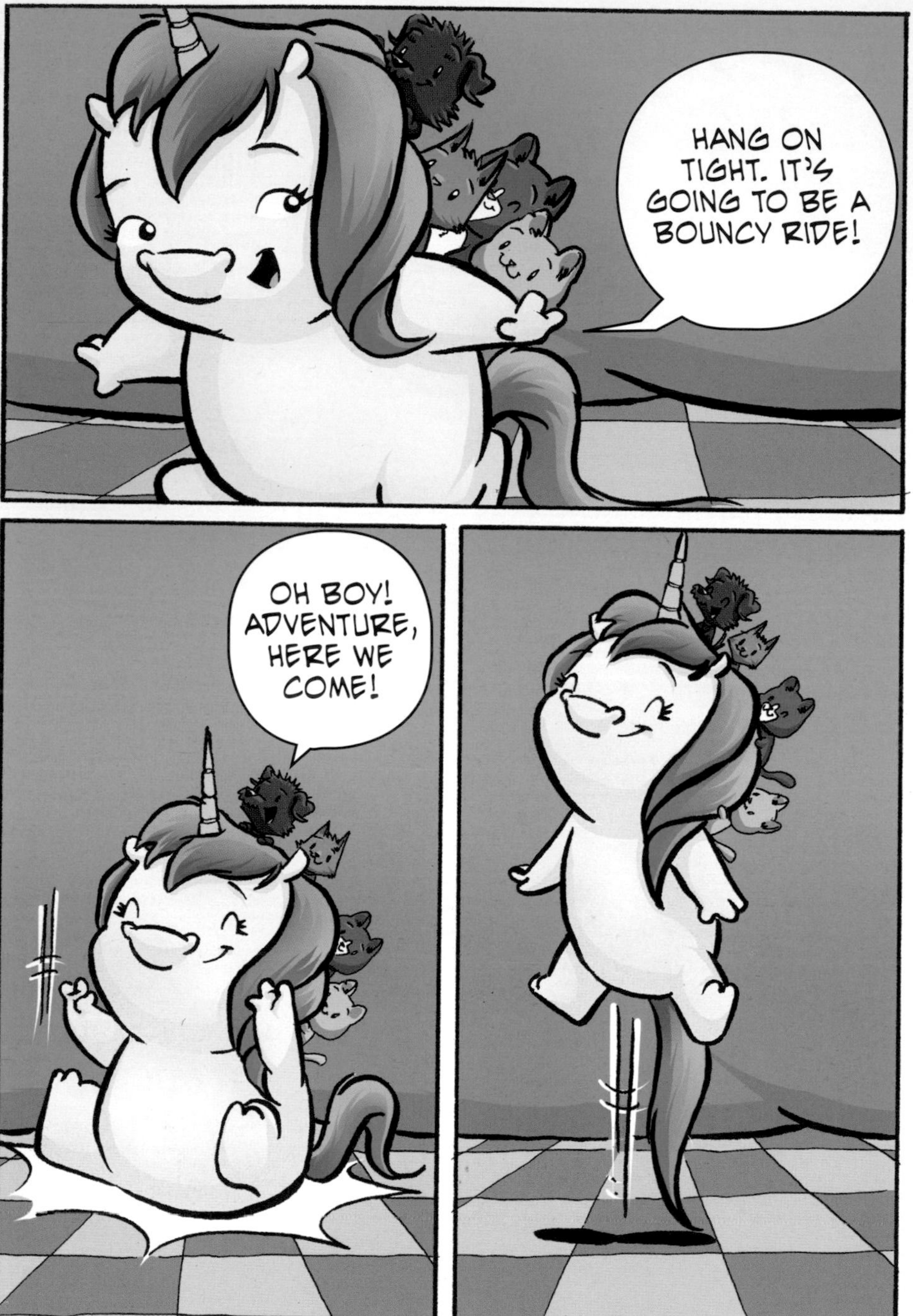
HANG ON TIGHT. IT'S GOING TO BE A BOUNCY RIDE!
OH BOY! ADVENTURE, HERE WE COME!

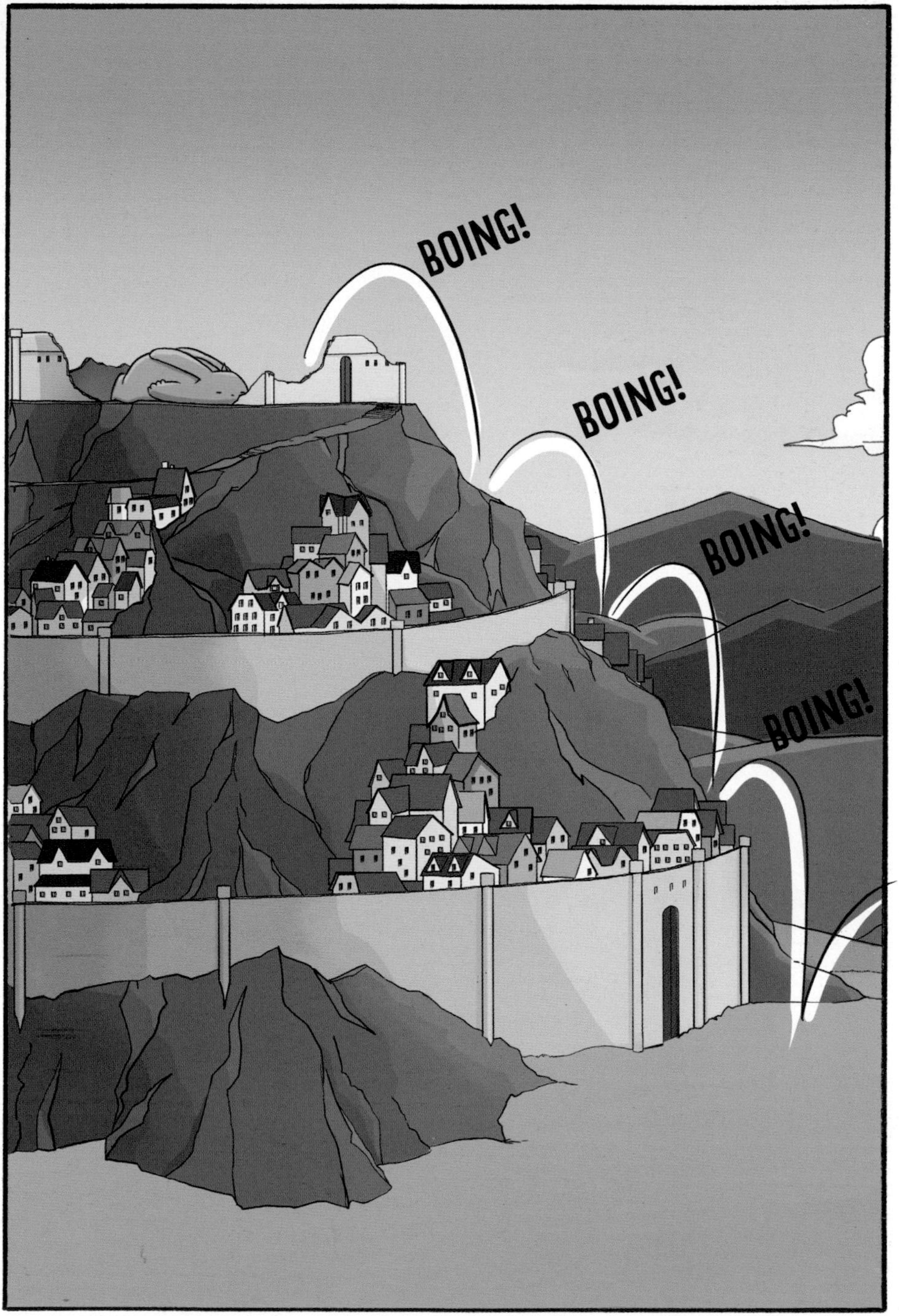
BOING!
BOING!
BOING!
BOING!

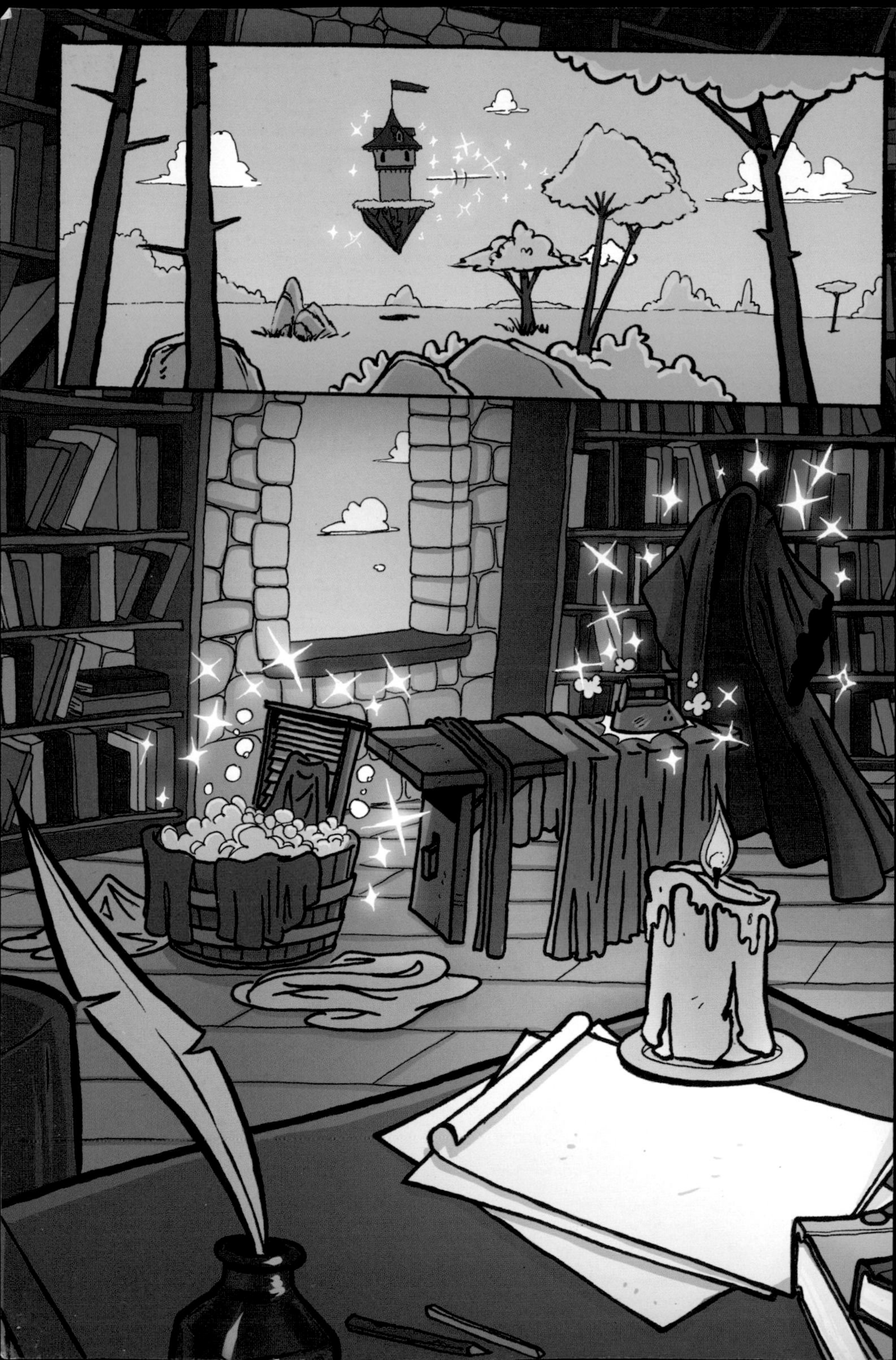

CHAPTER 5
GRAND PLANS

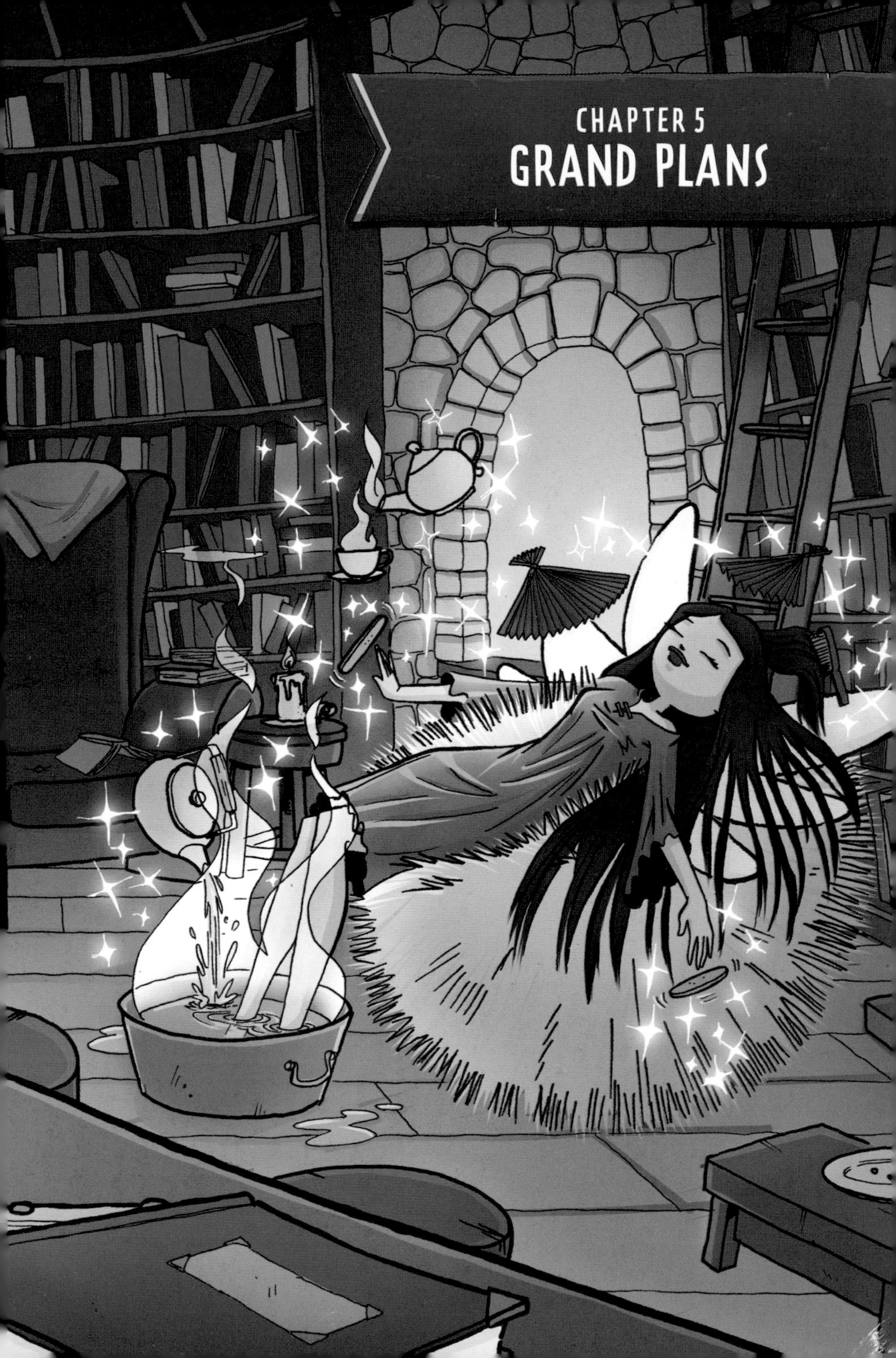

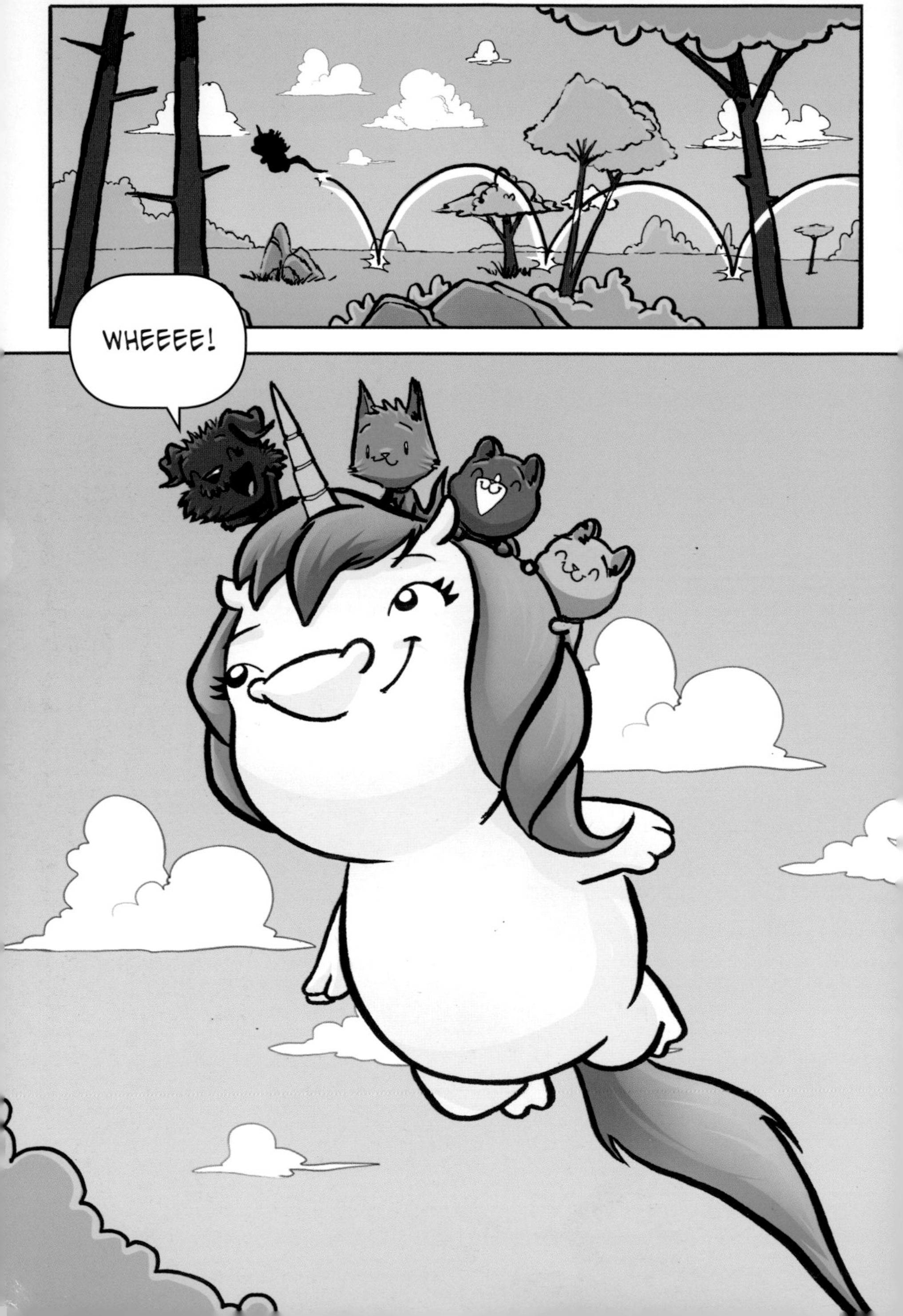
WHEEEEE!

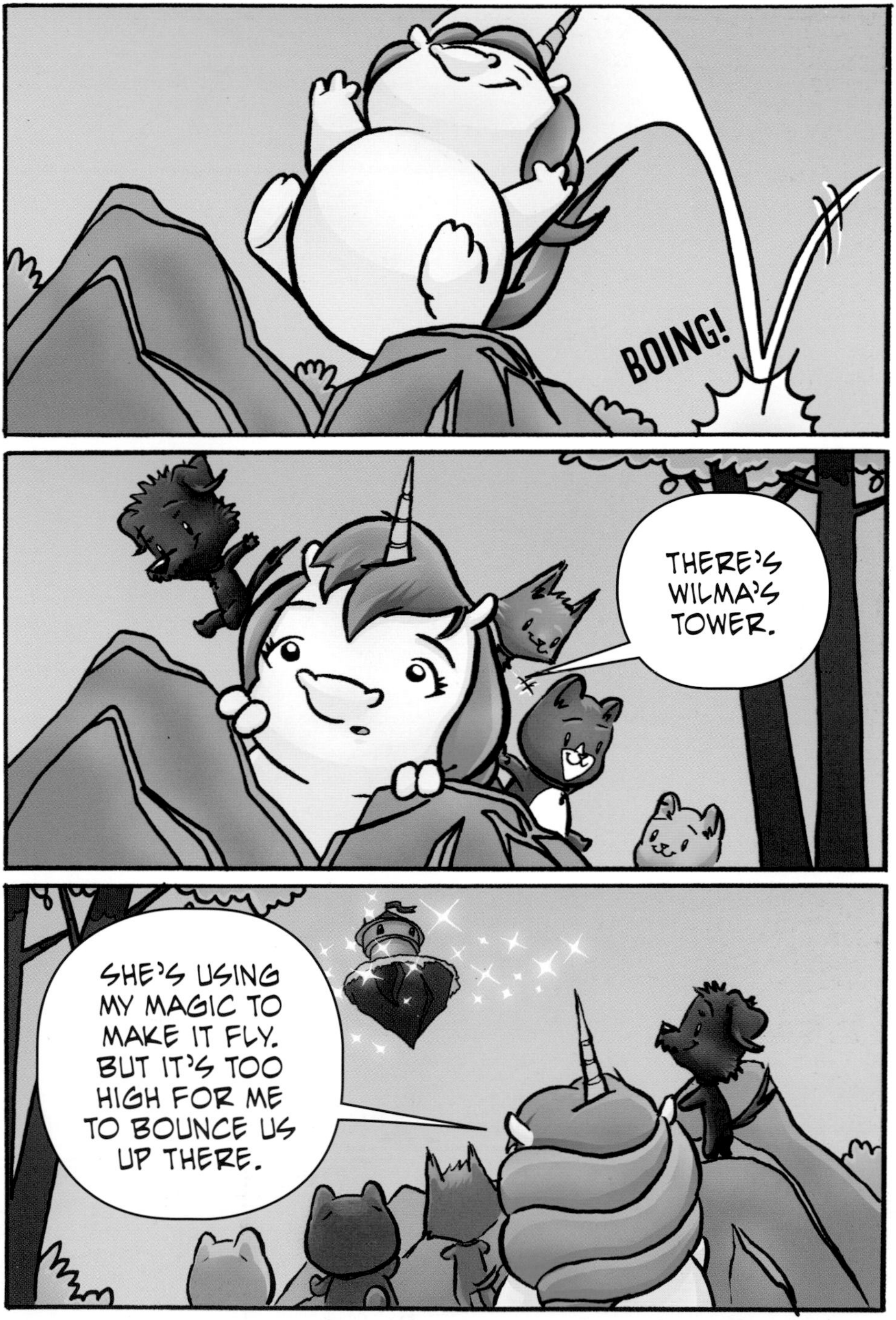
BOING!
THERE'S WILMA'S TOWER.
SHE'S USING MY MAGIC TO MAKE IT FLY. BUT IT'S TOO HIGH FOR ME TO BOUNCE US UP THERE.

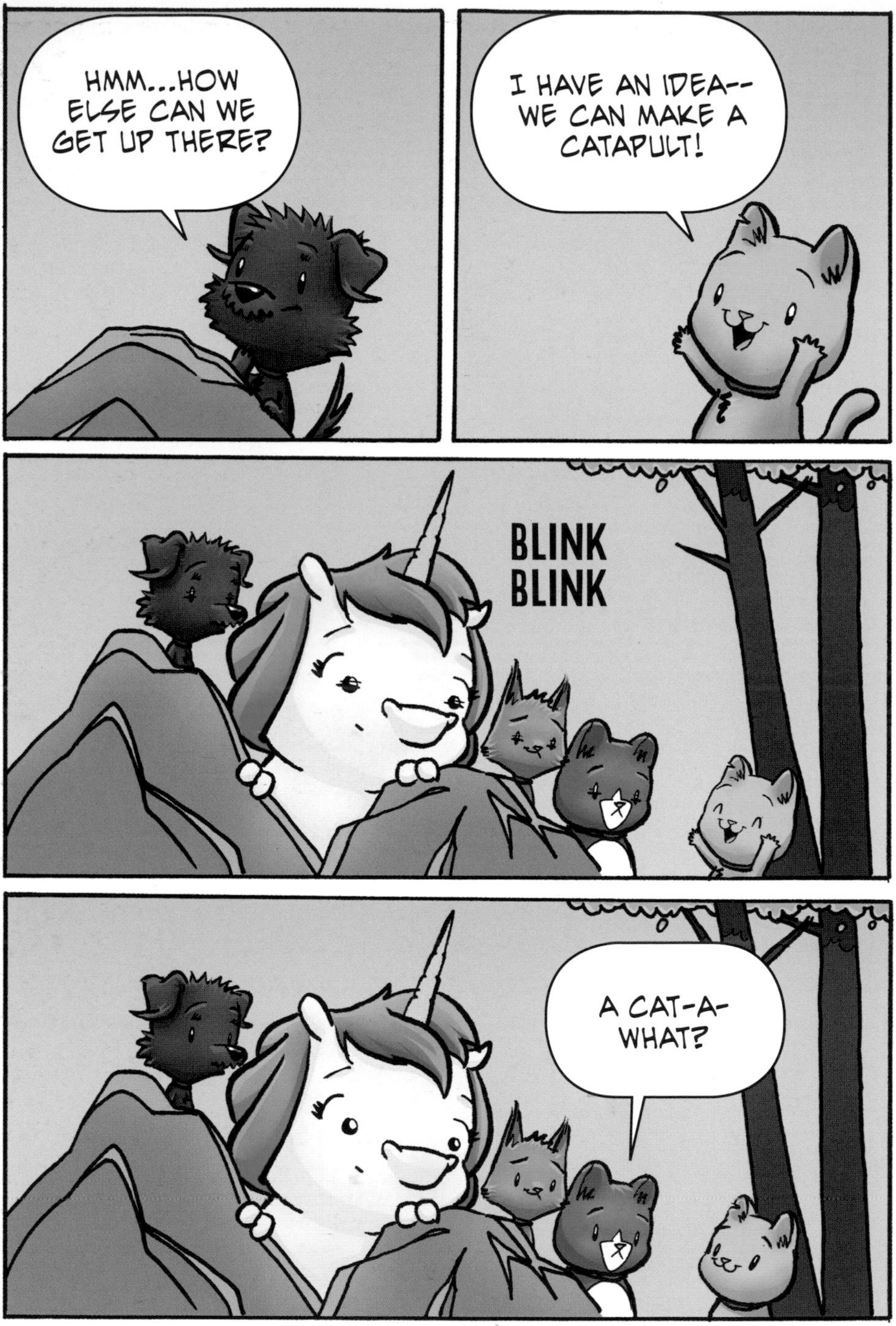
HMM...HOW ELSE CAN WE GET UP THERE?
I HAVE AN IDEA-- WE CAN MAKE A CATAPULT!
BLINK BLINK
A CAT-A-WHAT?

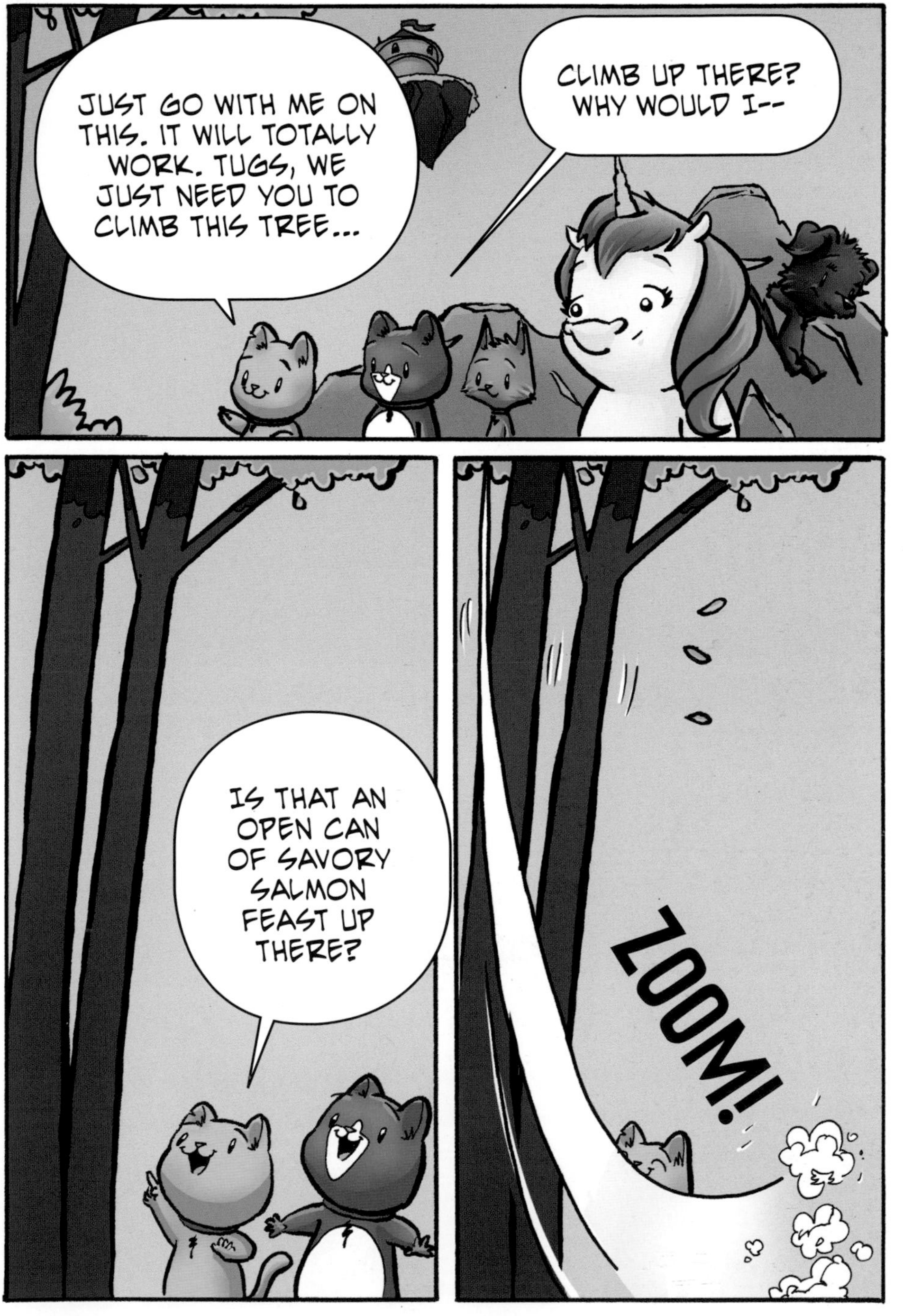
JUST GO WITH ME ON THIS. IT WILL TOTALLY WORK. TUGS, WE JUST NEED YOU TO CLIMB THIS TREE...
CLIMB UP THERE? WHY WOULD I--
IS THAT AN OPEN CAN OF SAVORY SALMON FEAST UP THERE?
ZOOM!

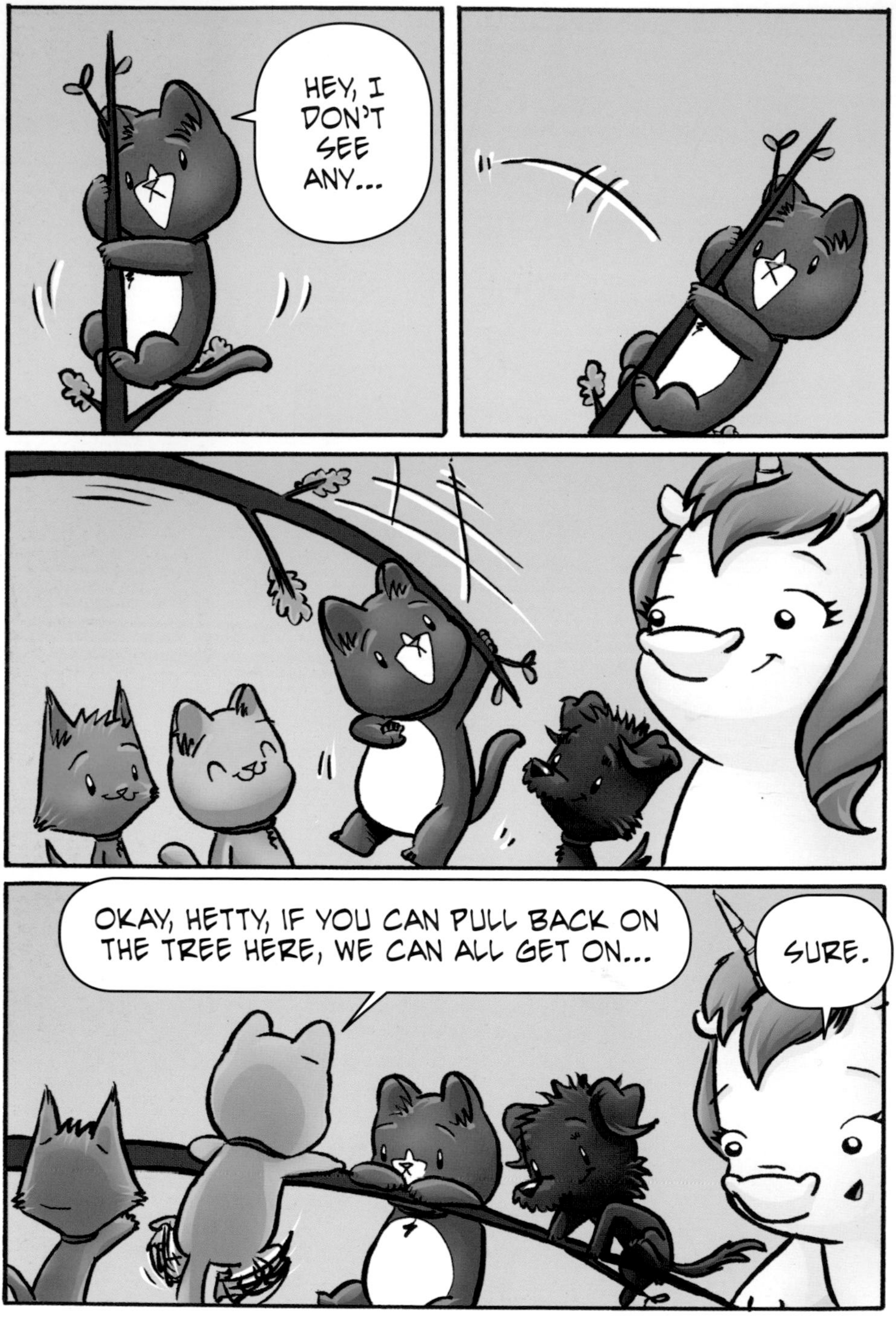
HEY, I DON'T SEE ANY...
OKAY, HETTY, IF YOU CAN PULL BACK ON THE TREE HERE, WE CAN ALL GET ON...
SURE.

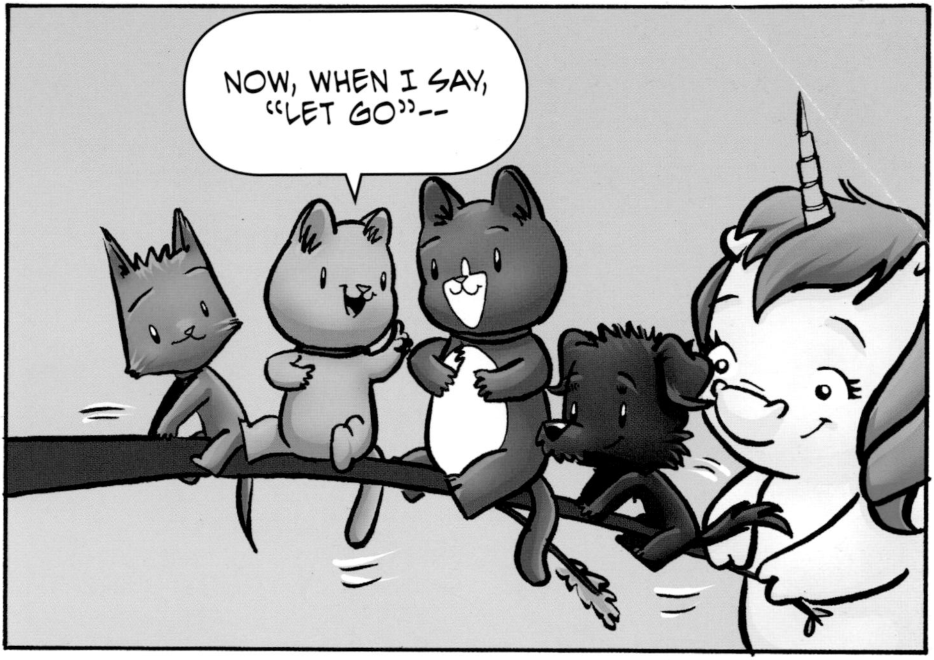
NOW, WHEN I SAY, "LET GO"--

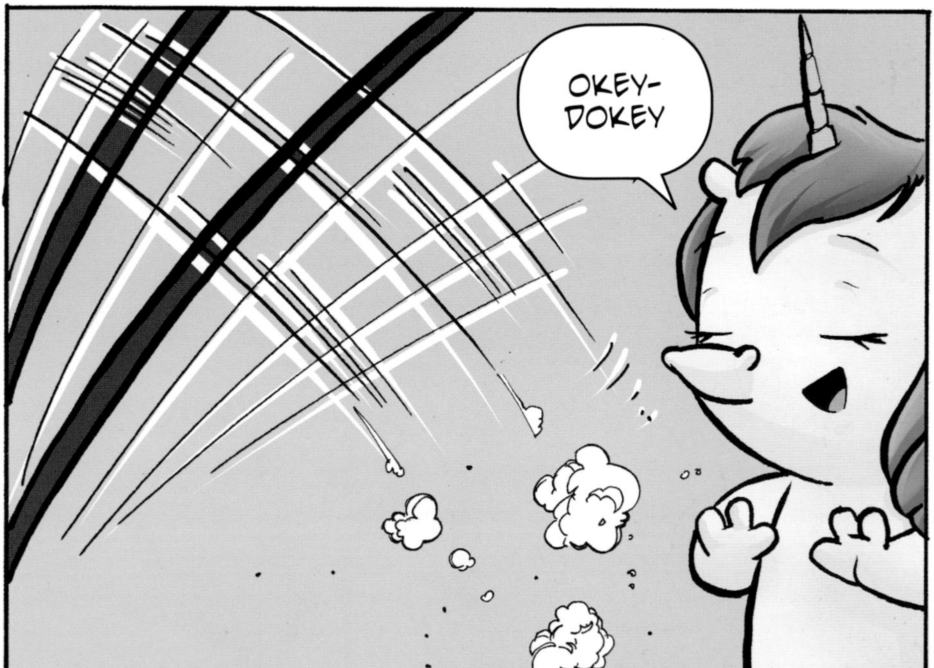
OKEY-DOKEY

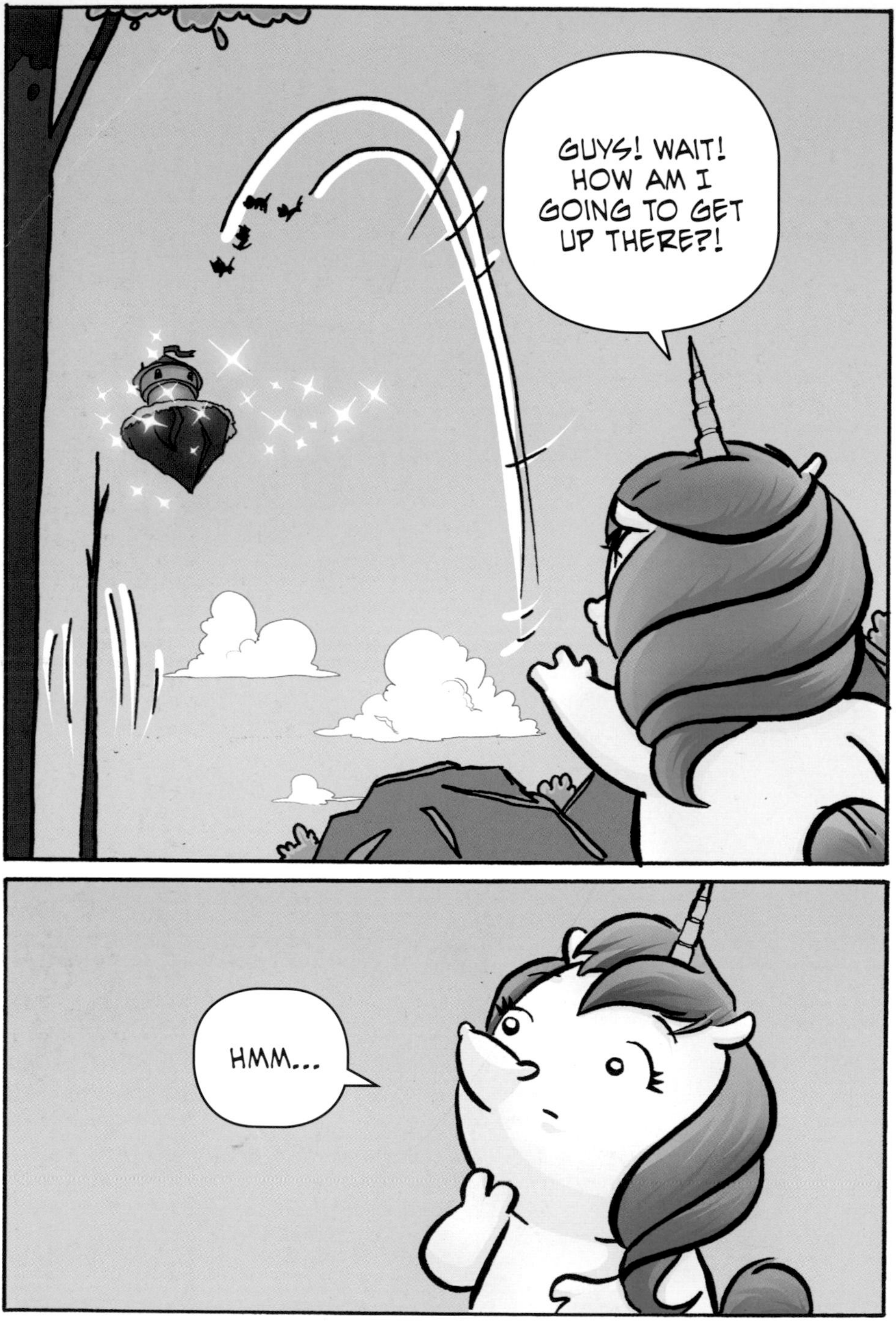
GUYS! WAIT! HOW AM I GOING TO GET UP THERE?!
HMM...

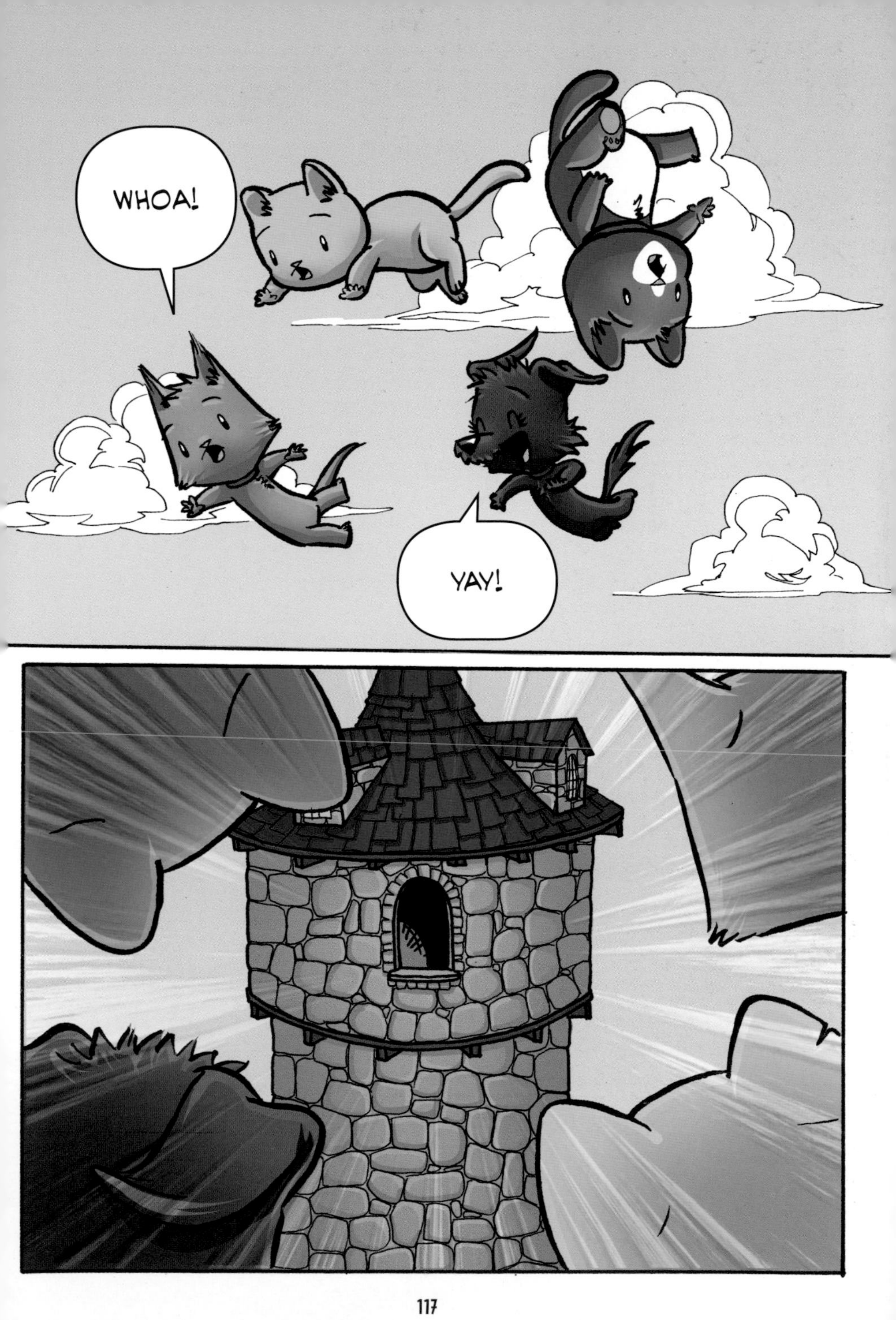
WHOA!
YAY!

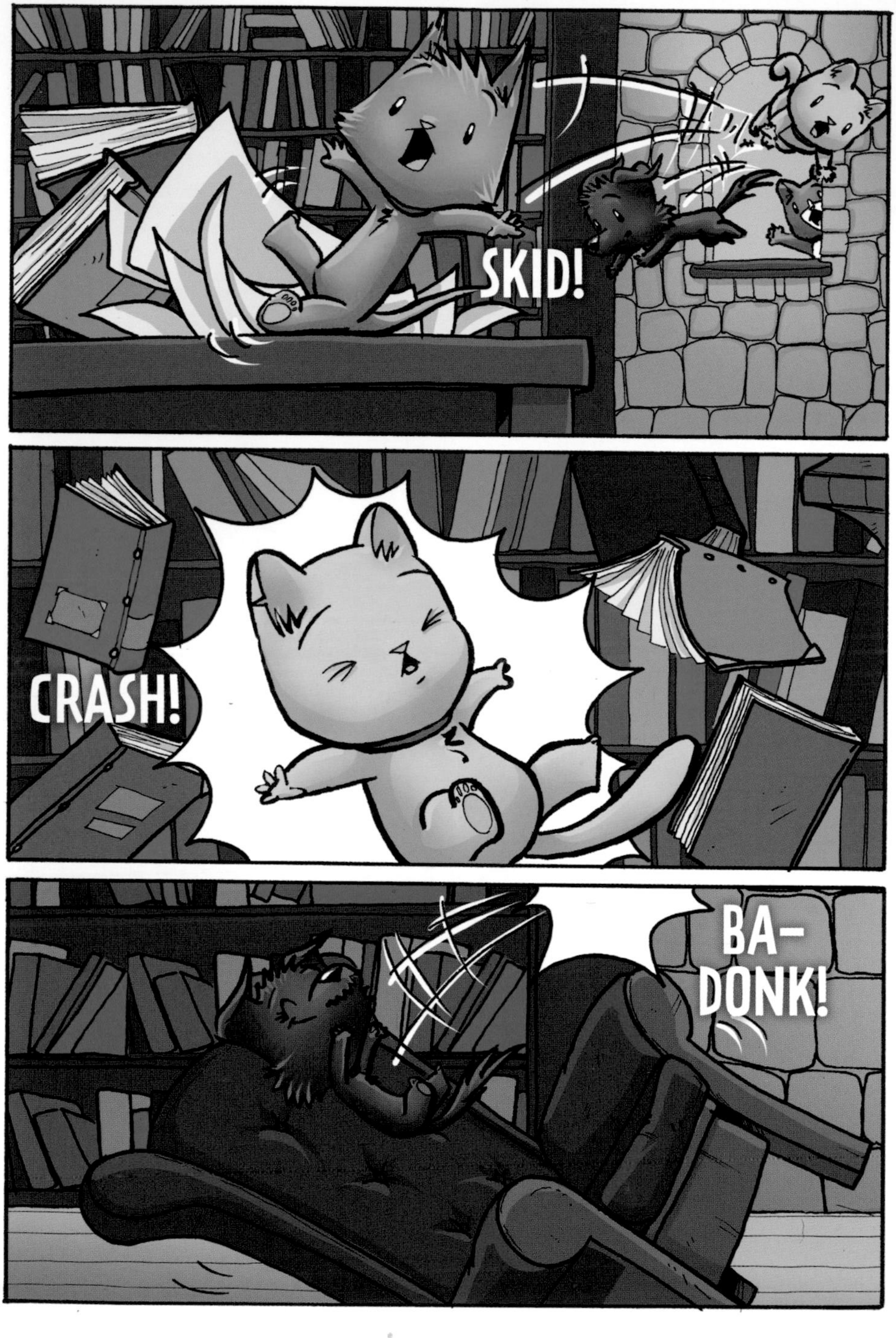
SKID!
CRASH!
BA-
DONK!

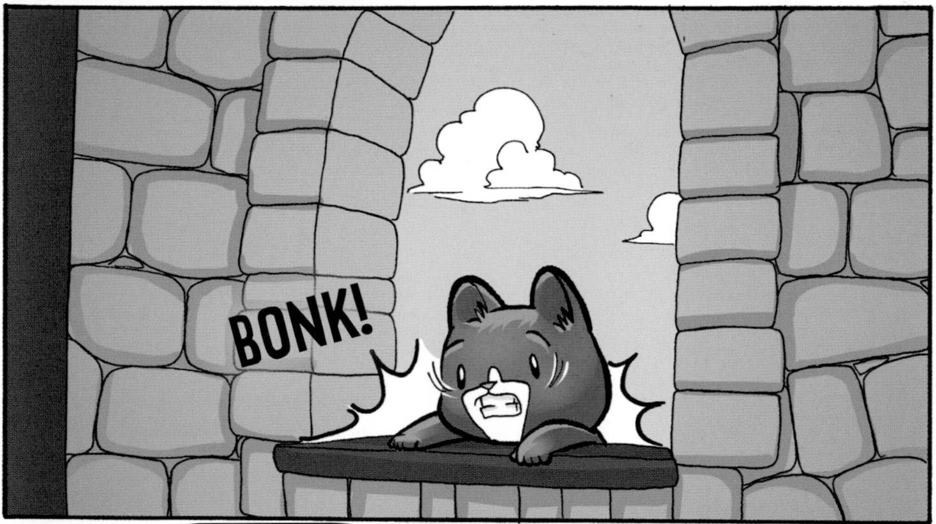
BONK!

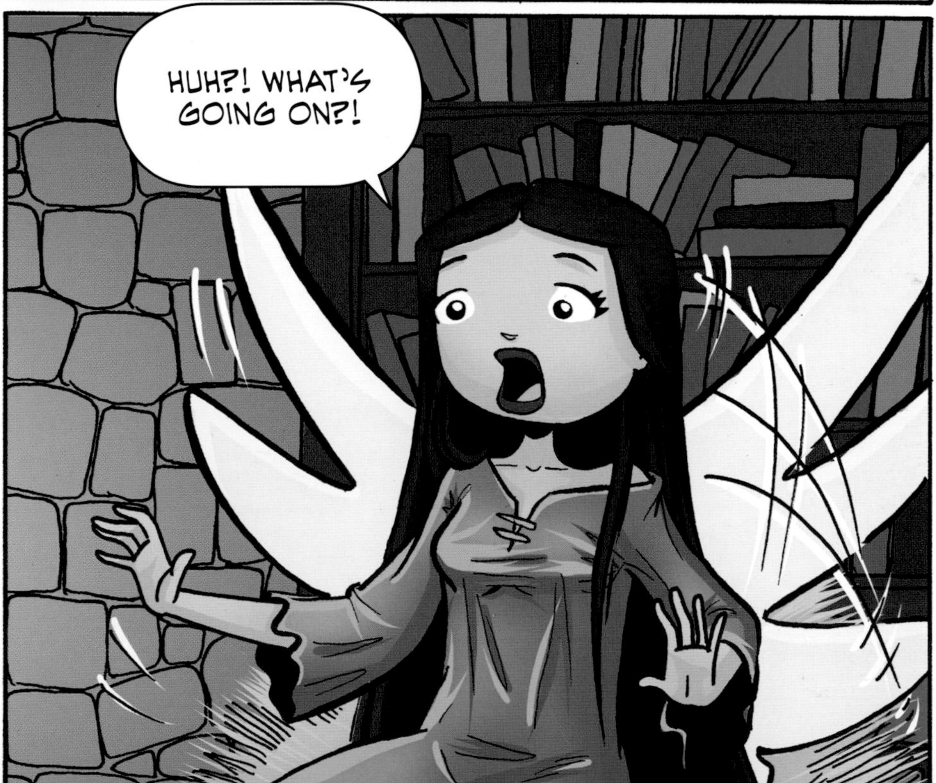
HUH?! WHAT'S GOING ON?!

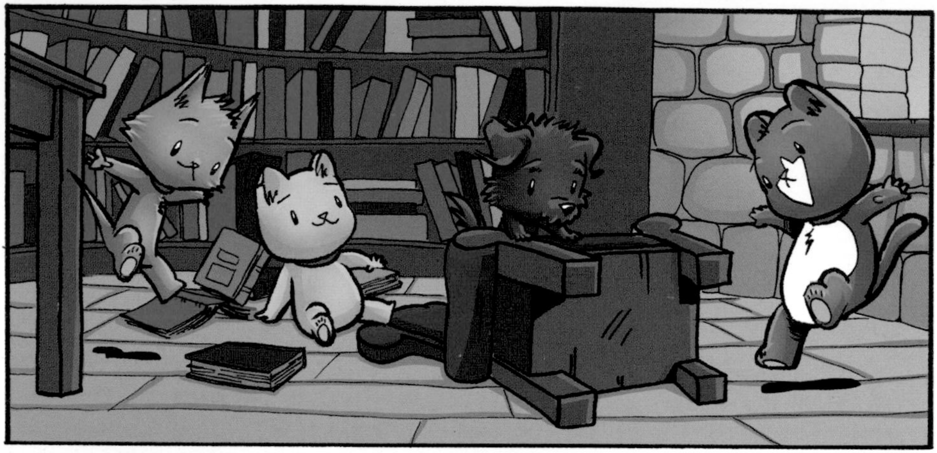

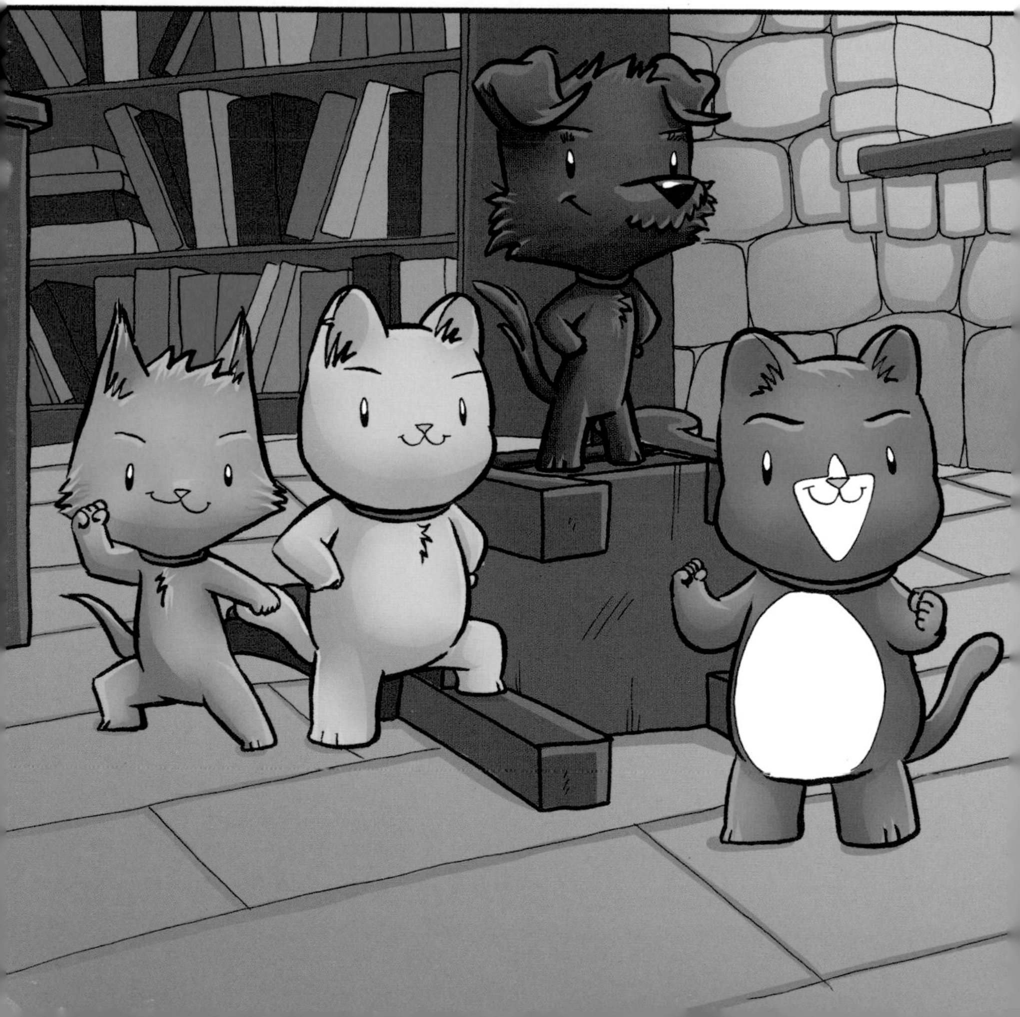

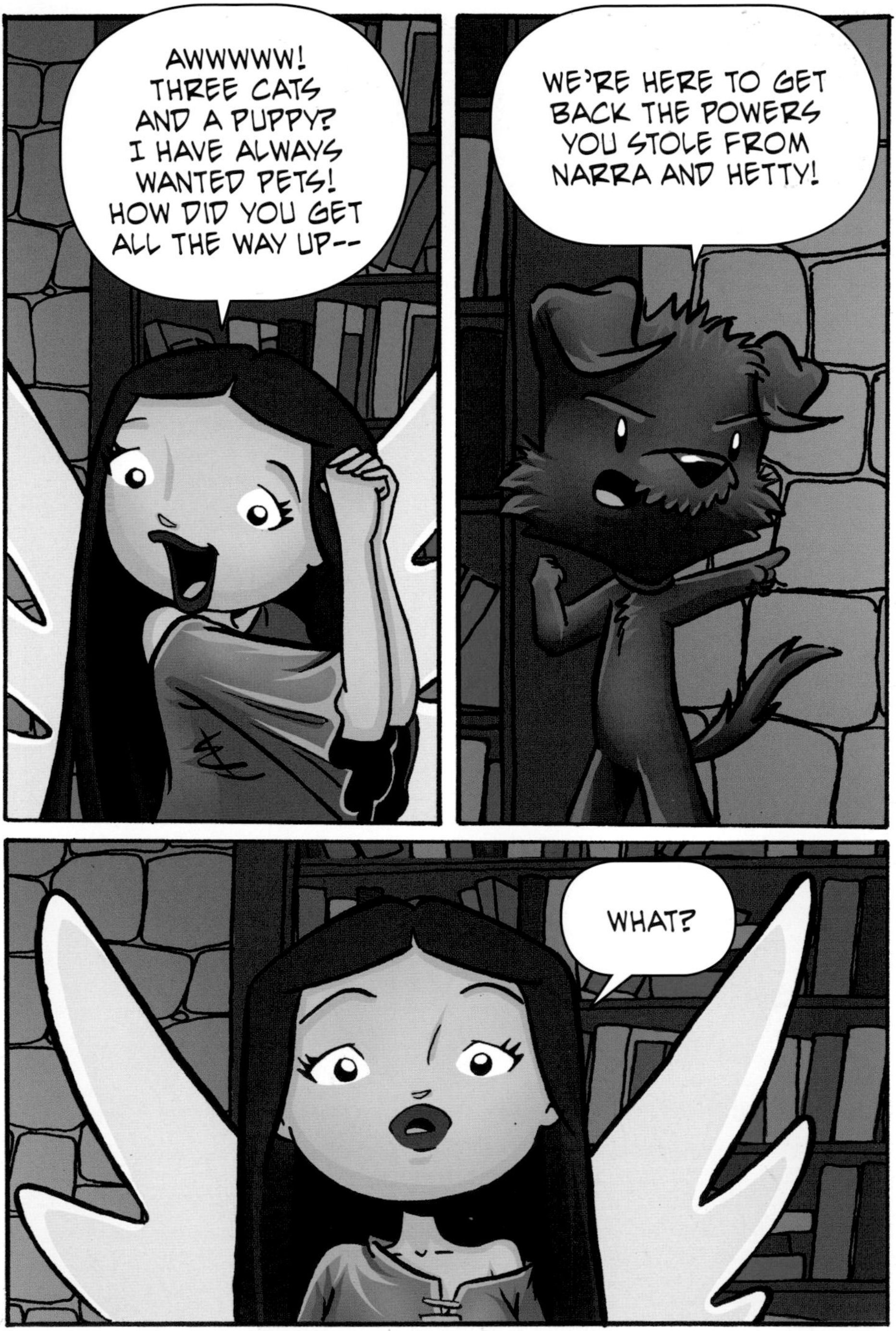
AWWWWW! THREE CATS AND A PUPPY? I HAVE ALWAYS WANTED PETS! HOW DID YOU GET ALL THE WAY UP--
WE'RE HERE TO GET BACK THE POWERS YOU STOLE FROM NARRA AND HETTY!
WHAT?

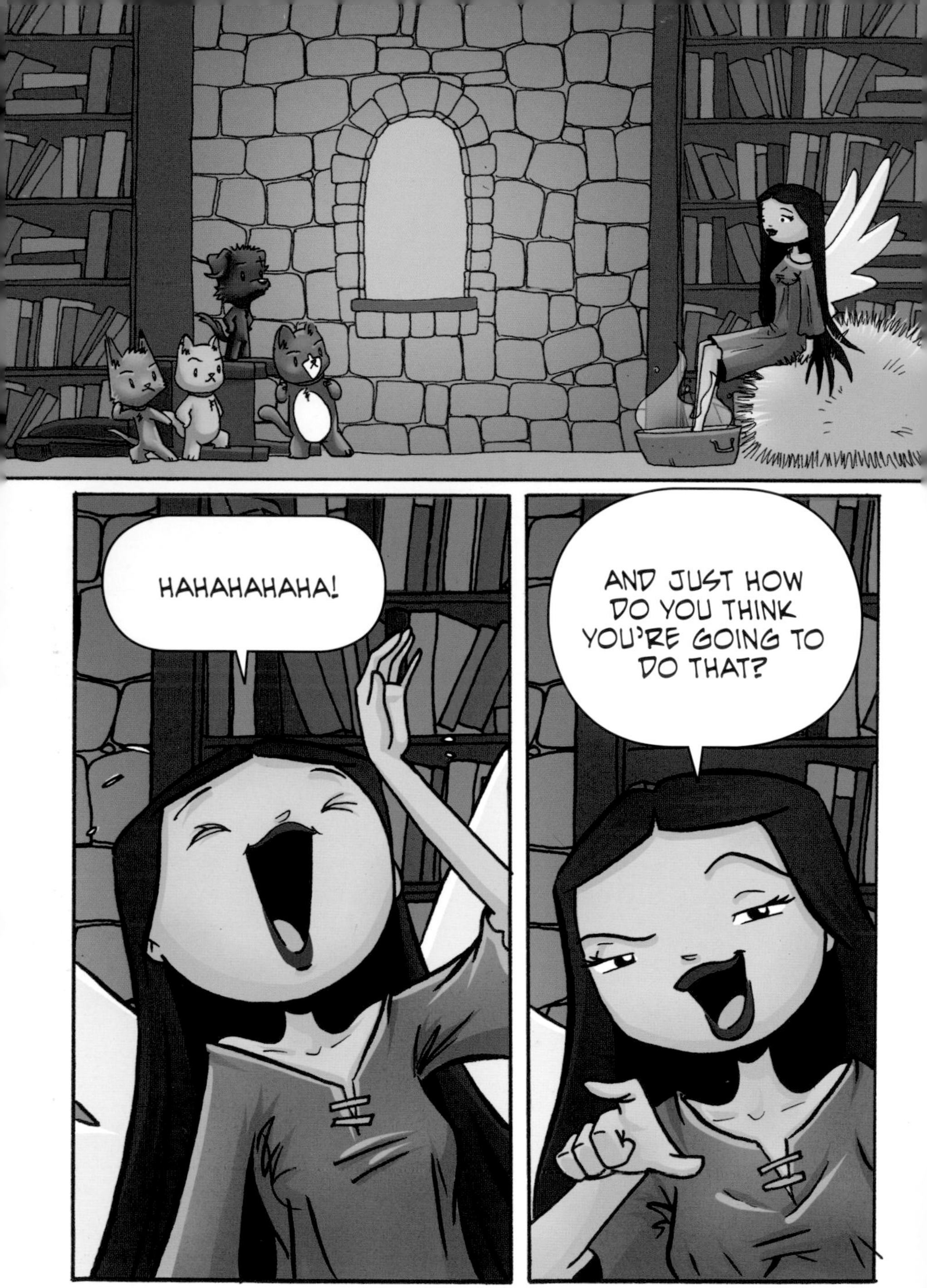
HAHAHAHAHA!
AND JUST HOW DO YOU THINK YOU'RE GOING TO DO THAT?

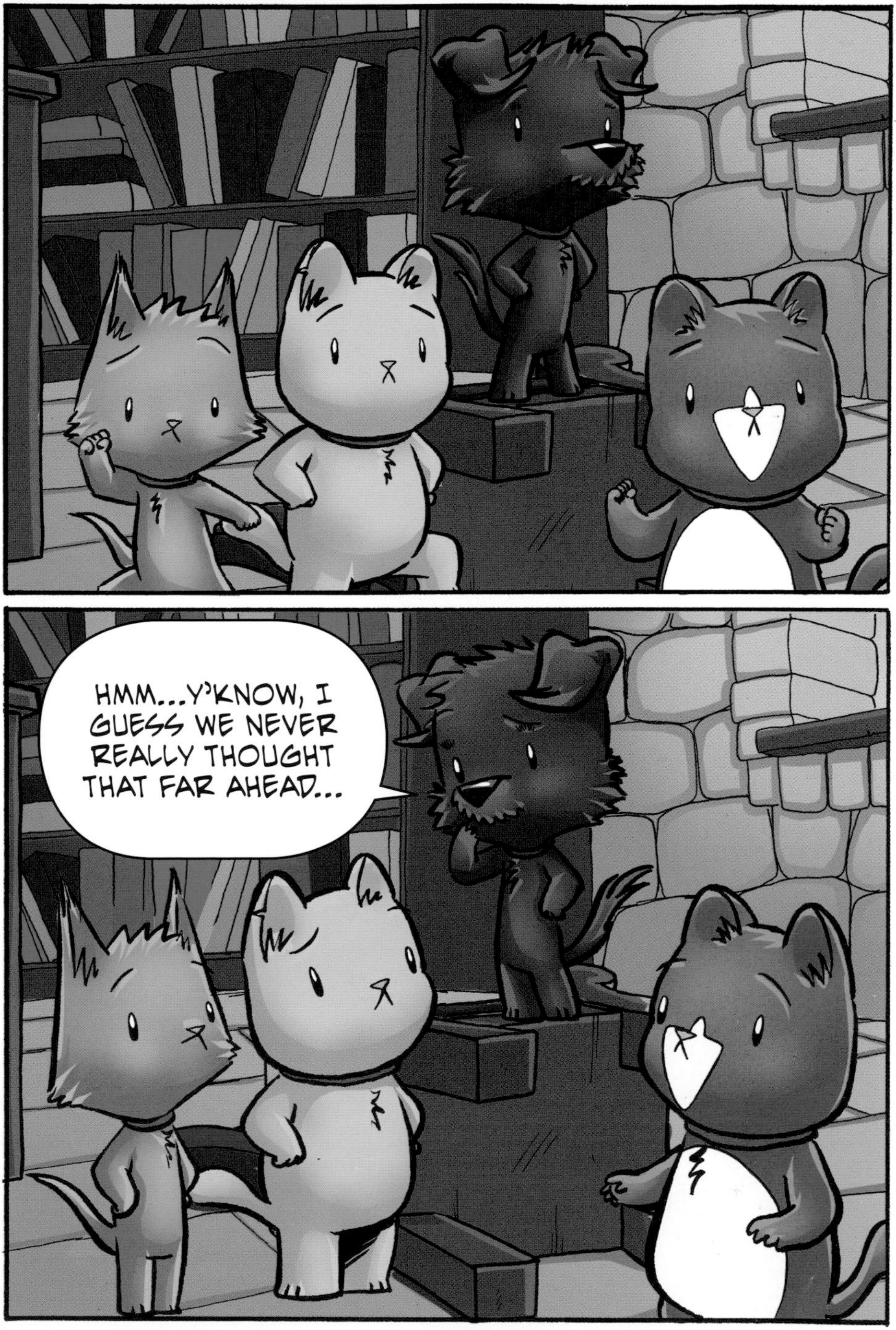
HMM...Y'KNOW, I GUESS WE NEVER REALLY THOUGHT THAT FAR AHEAD...

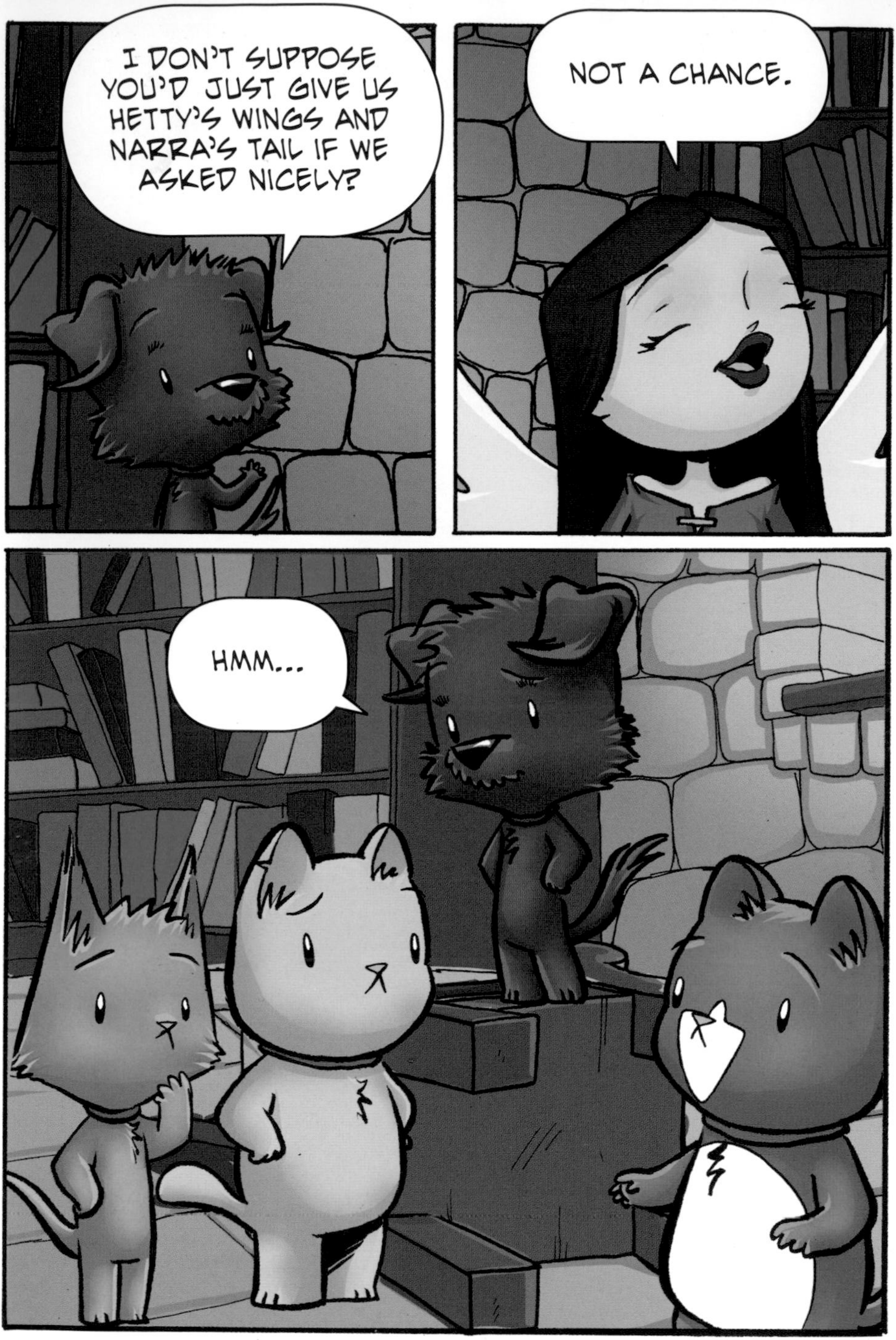
I DON'T SUPPOSE YOU'D JUST GIVE US HETTY'S WINGS AND NARRA'S TAIL IF WE ASKED NICELY?
NOT A CHANCE.
HMM...

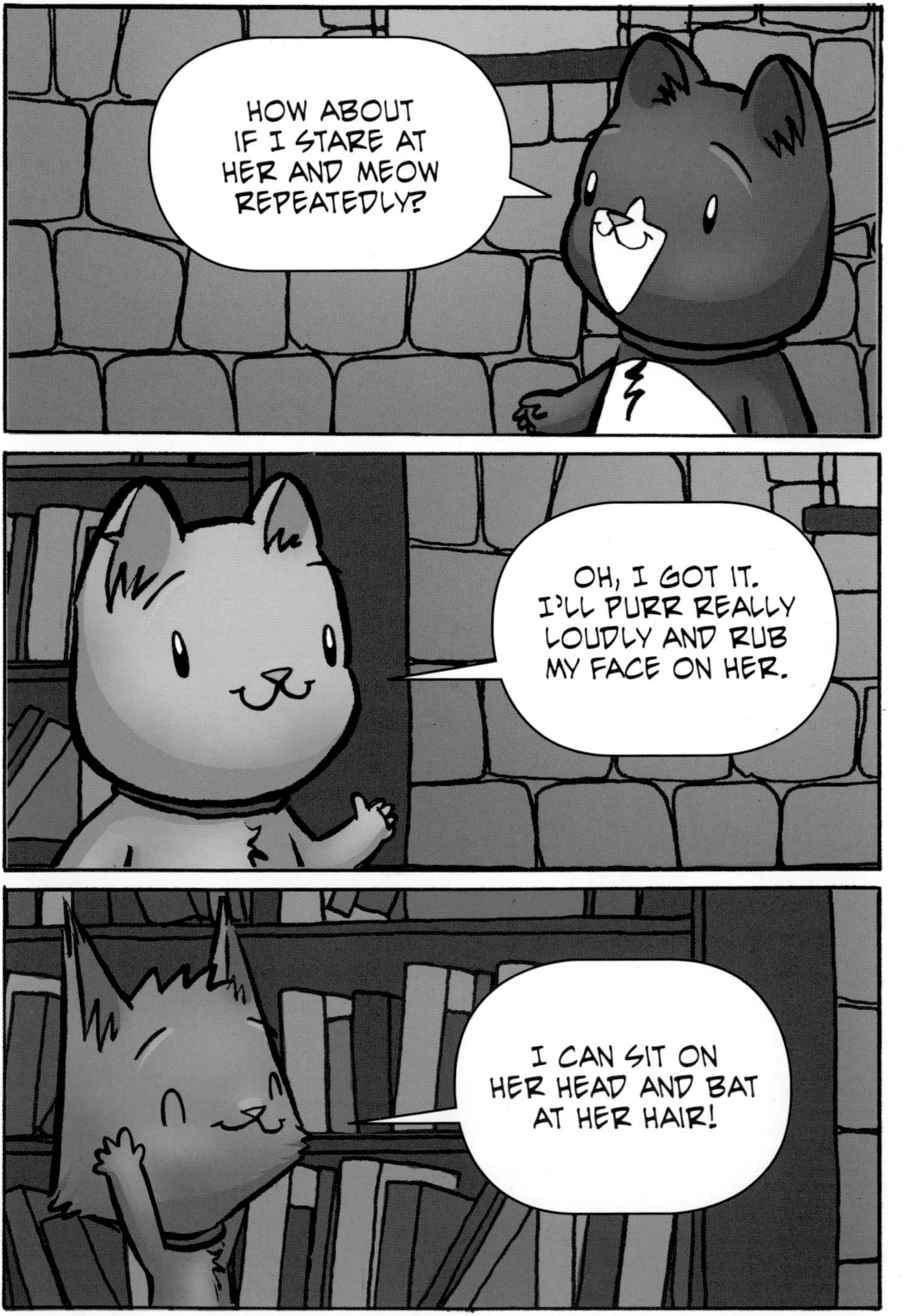
HOW ABOUT IF I STARE AT HER AND MEOW REPEATEDLY?
OH, I GOT IT. I'LL PURR REALLY LOUDLY AND RUB MY FACE ON HER.
I CAN SIT ON HER HEAD AND BAT AT HER HAIR!

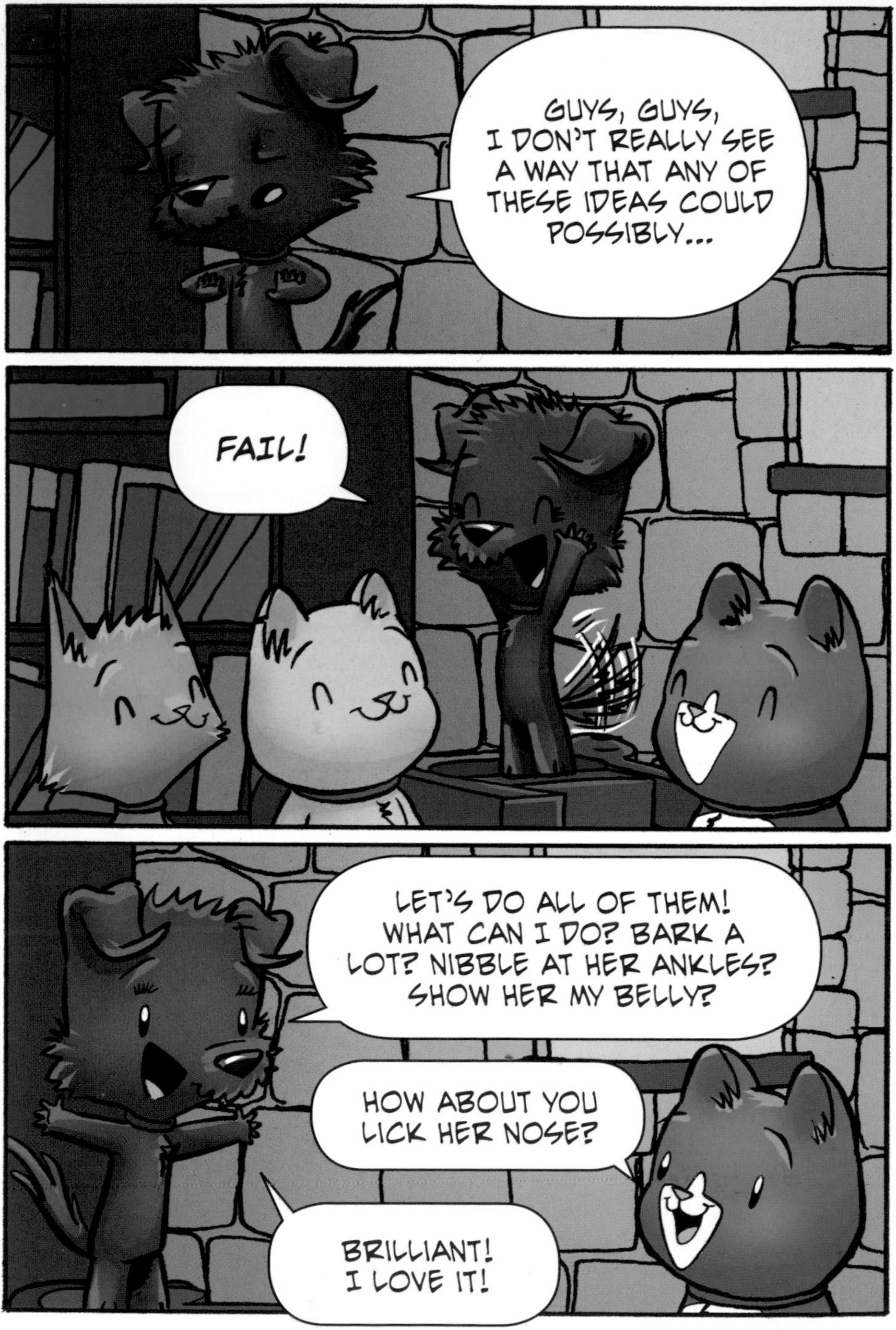
GUYS, GUYS,
I DON'T REALLY SEE A WAY THAT ANY OF THESE IDEAS COULD POSSIBLY...
FAIL!
LET'S DO ALL OF THEM! WHAT CAN I DO? BARK A LOT? NIBBLE AT HER ANKLES? SHOW HER MY BELLY?
HOW ABOUT YOU LICK HER NOSE?
BRILLIANT! I LOVE IT!

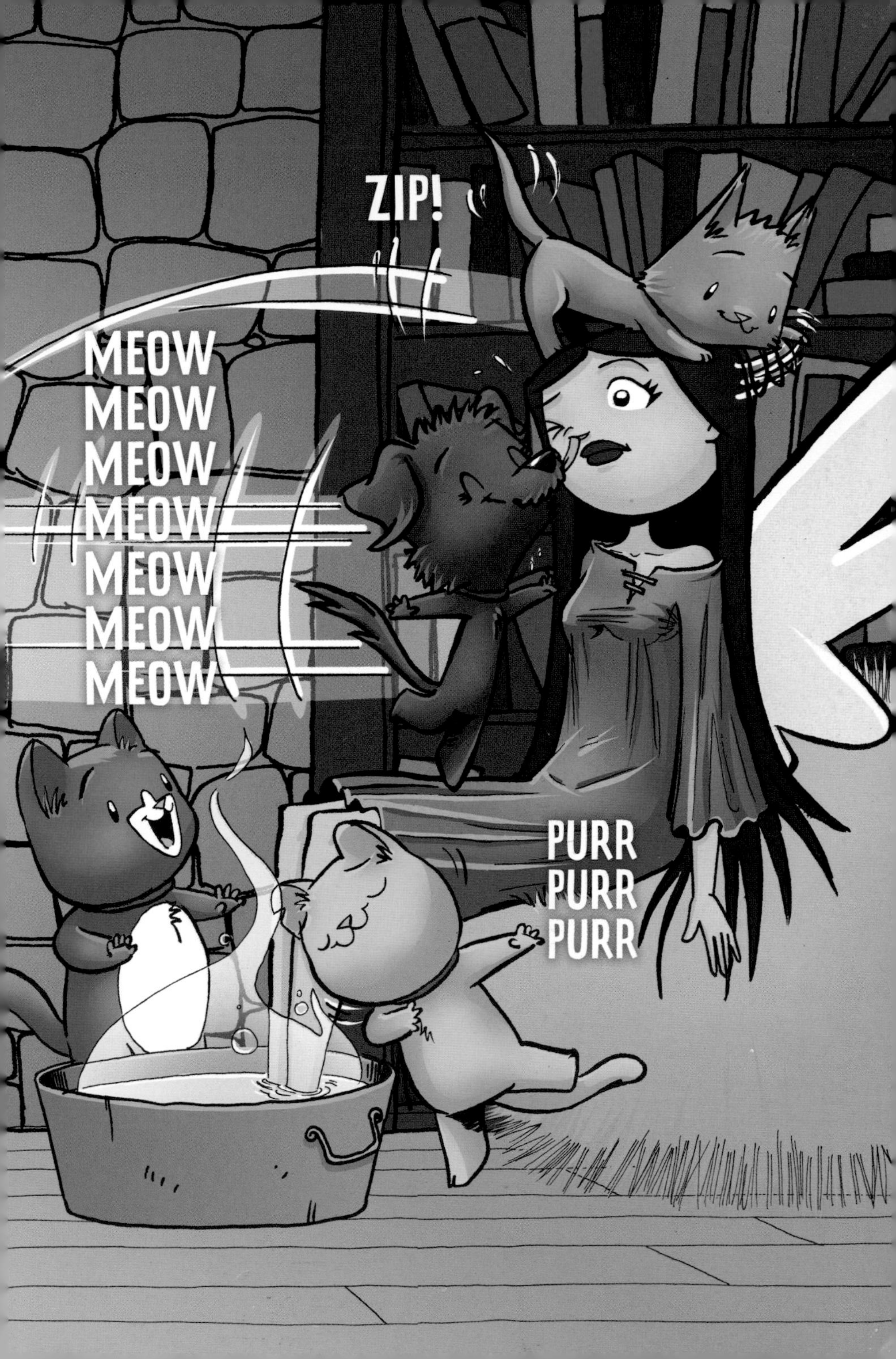
ZIP!
MEOW
MEOW
MEOW
MEOW
MEOW
MEOW
MEOW
PURR
PURR
PURR

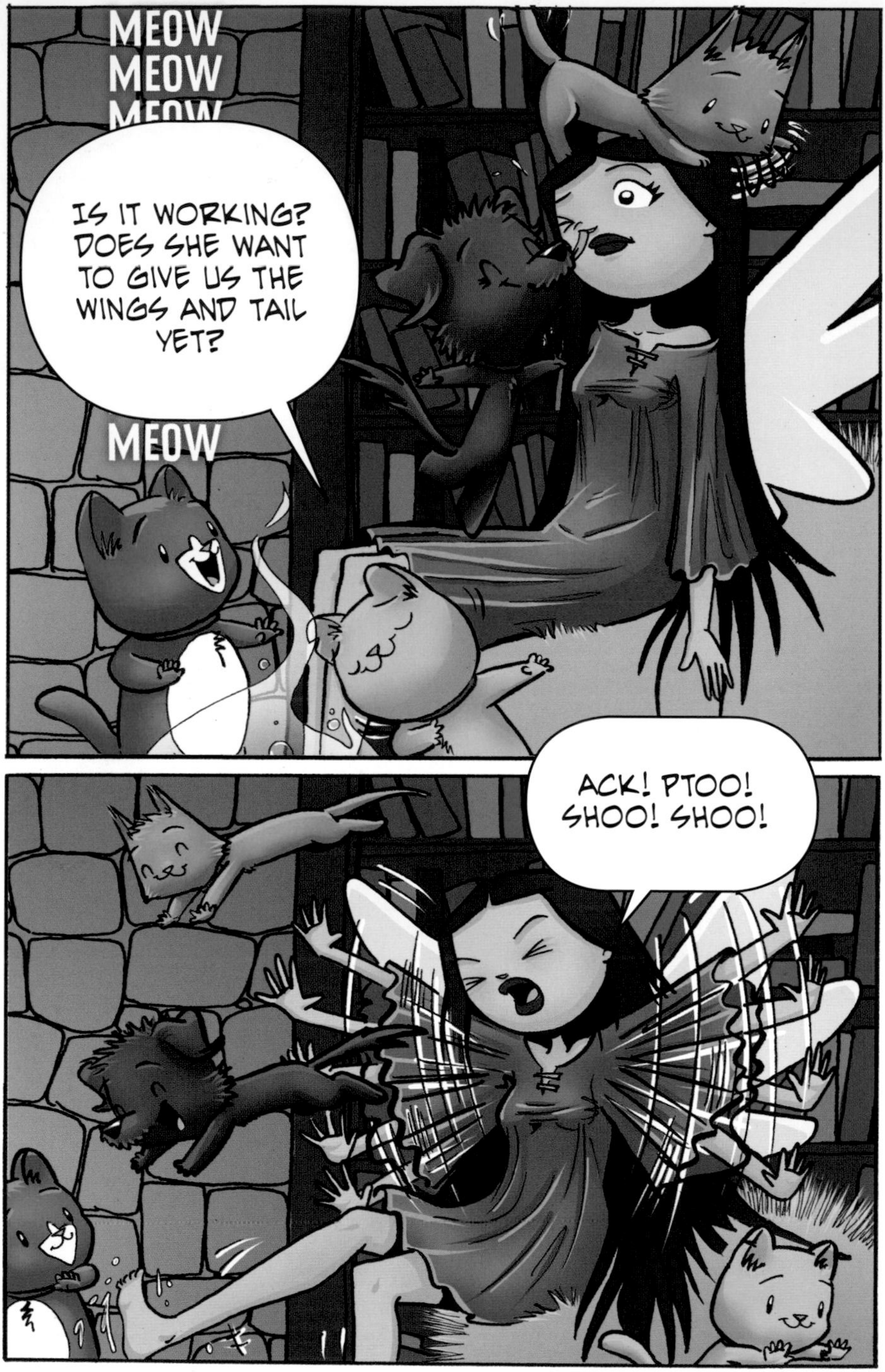
MEOW
MEOW
MEOW
IS IT WORKING? DOES SHE WANT TO GIVE US THE WINGS AND TAIL YET?
MEOW
ACK! PTOO! SHOO! SHOO!

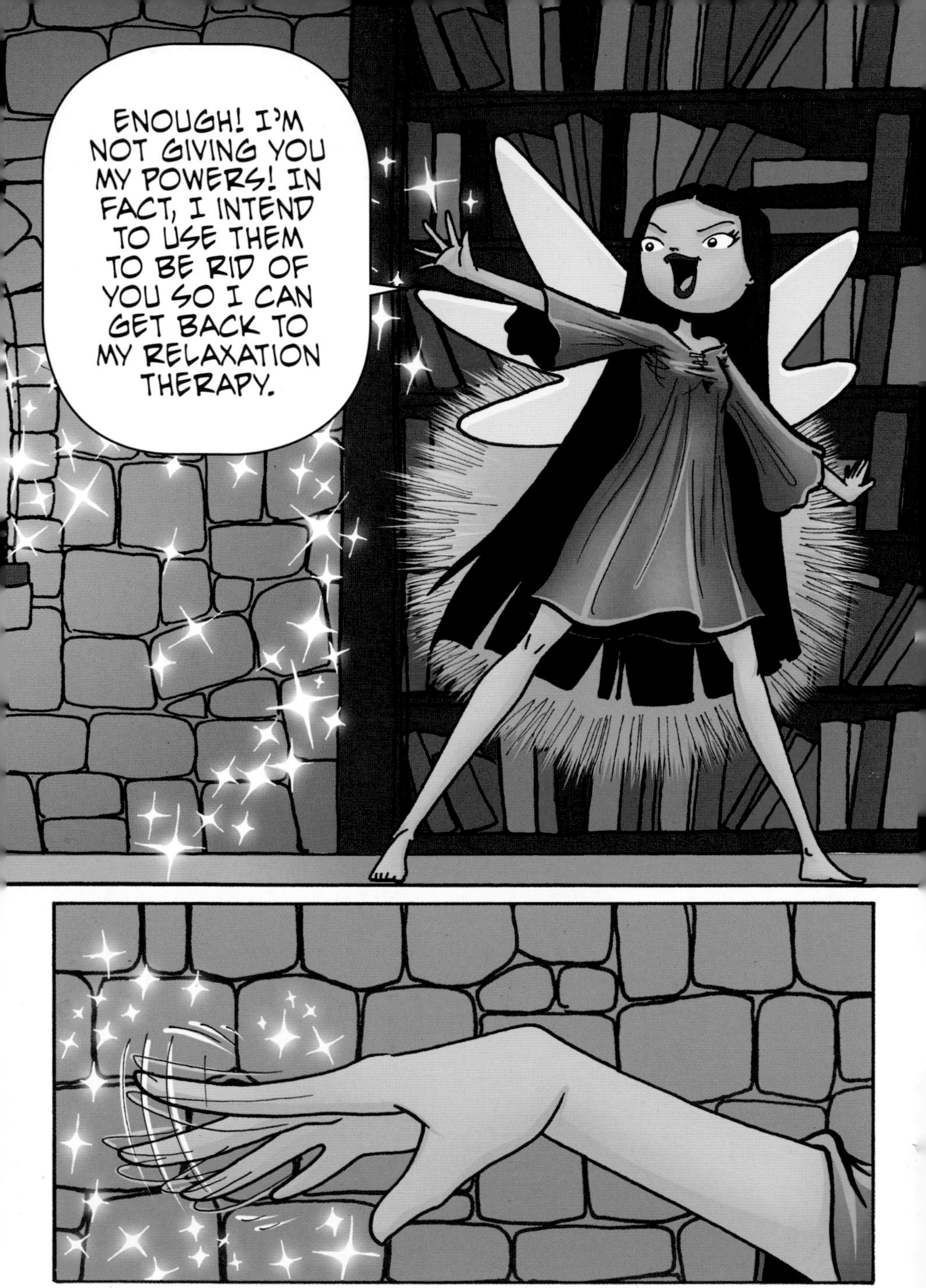
ENOUGH! I'M NOT GIVING YOU MY POWERS! IN FACT, I INTEND TO USE THEM TO BE RID OF YOU SO I CAN GET BACK TO MY RELAXATION THERAPY.

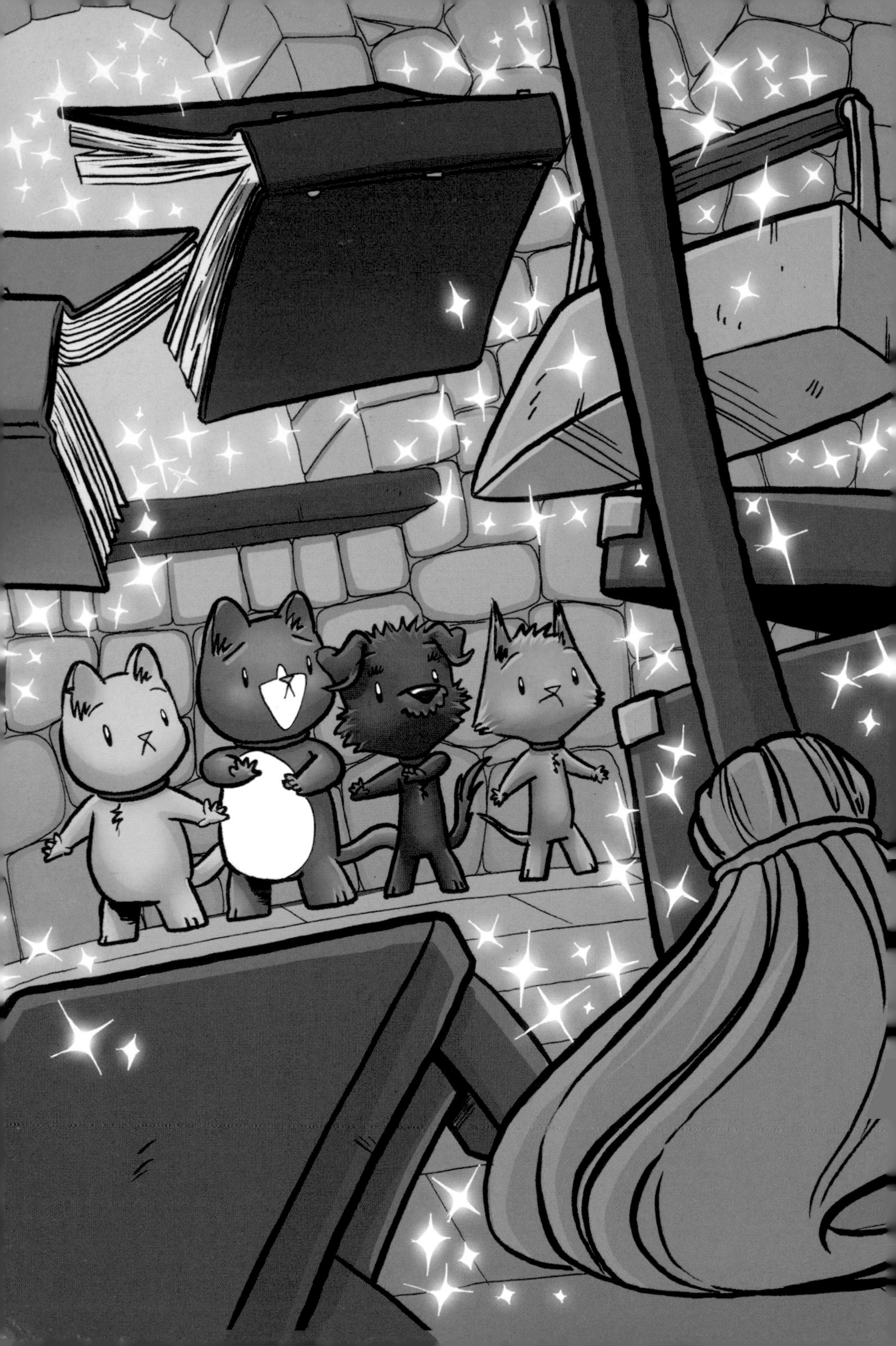

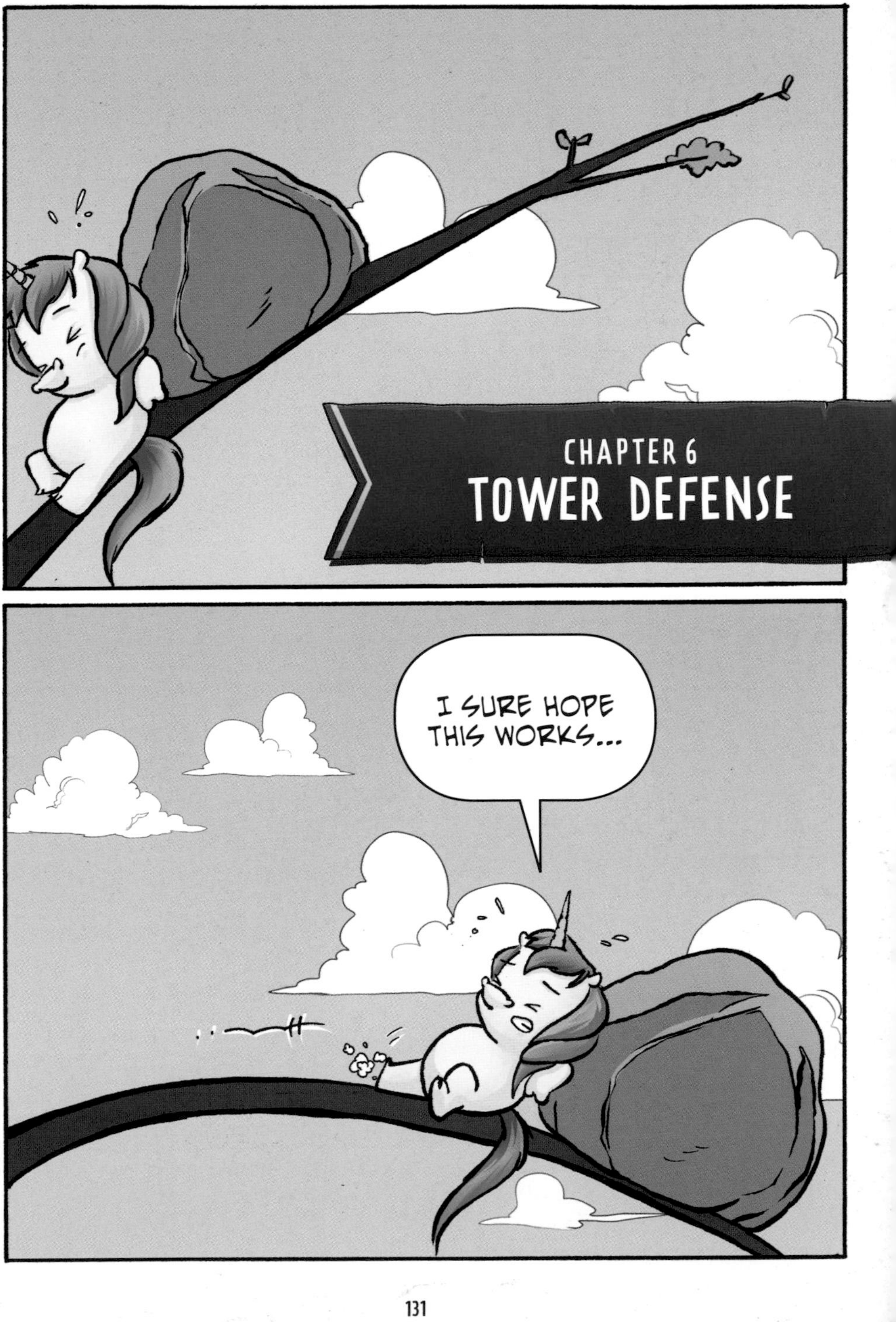
CHAPTER 6
TOWER DEFENSE
I SURE HOPE THIS WORKS...

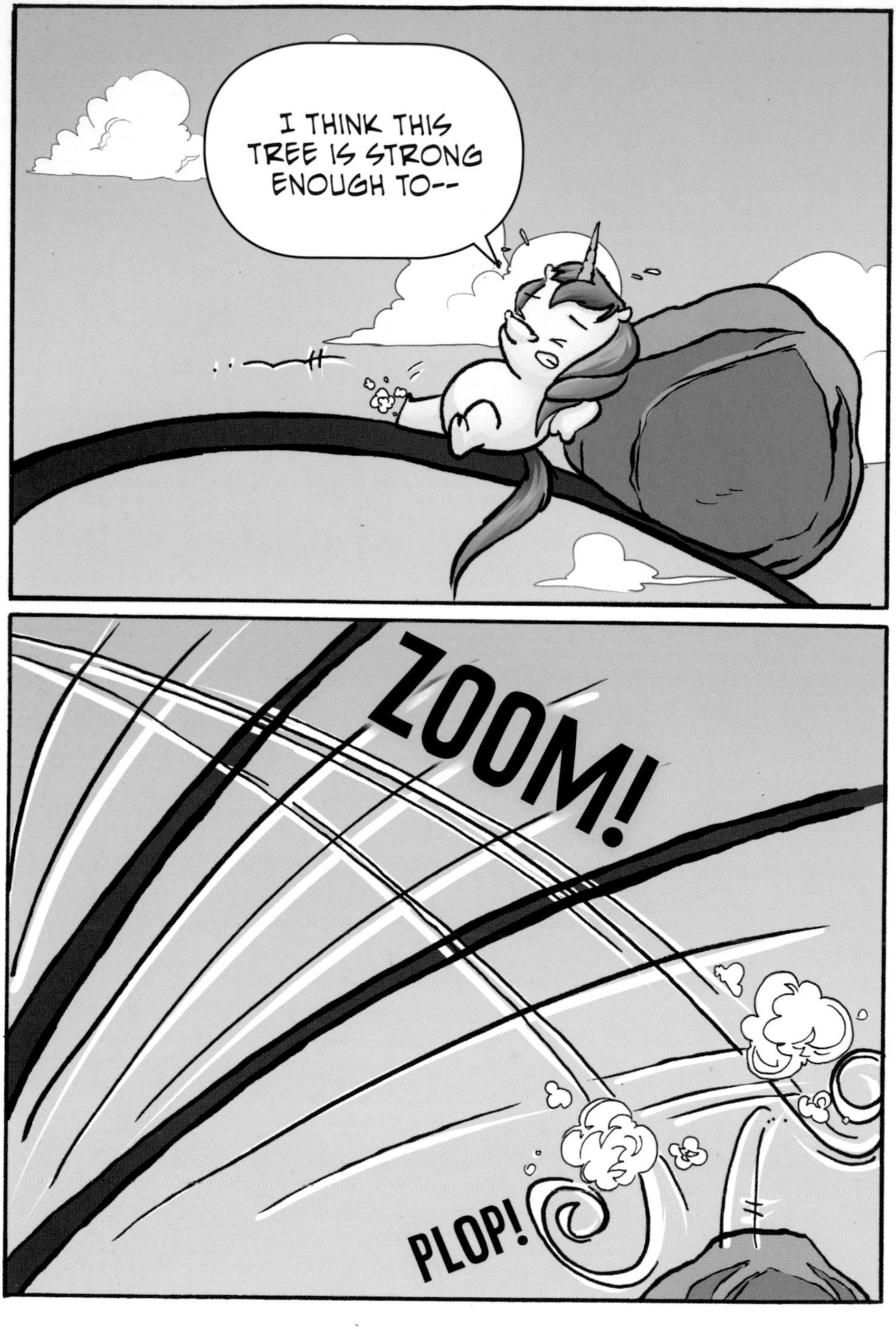
I THINK THIS TREE IS STRONG ENOUGH TO--
ZOOM!
PLOP!

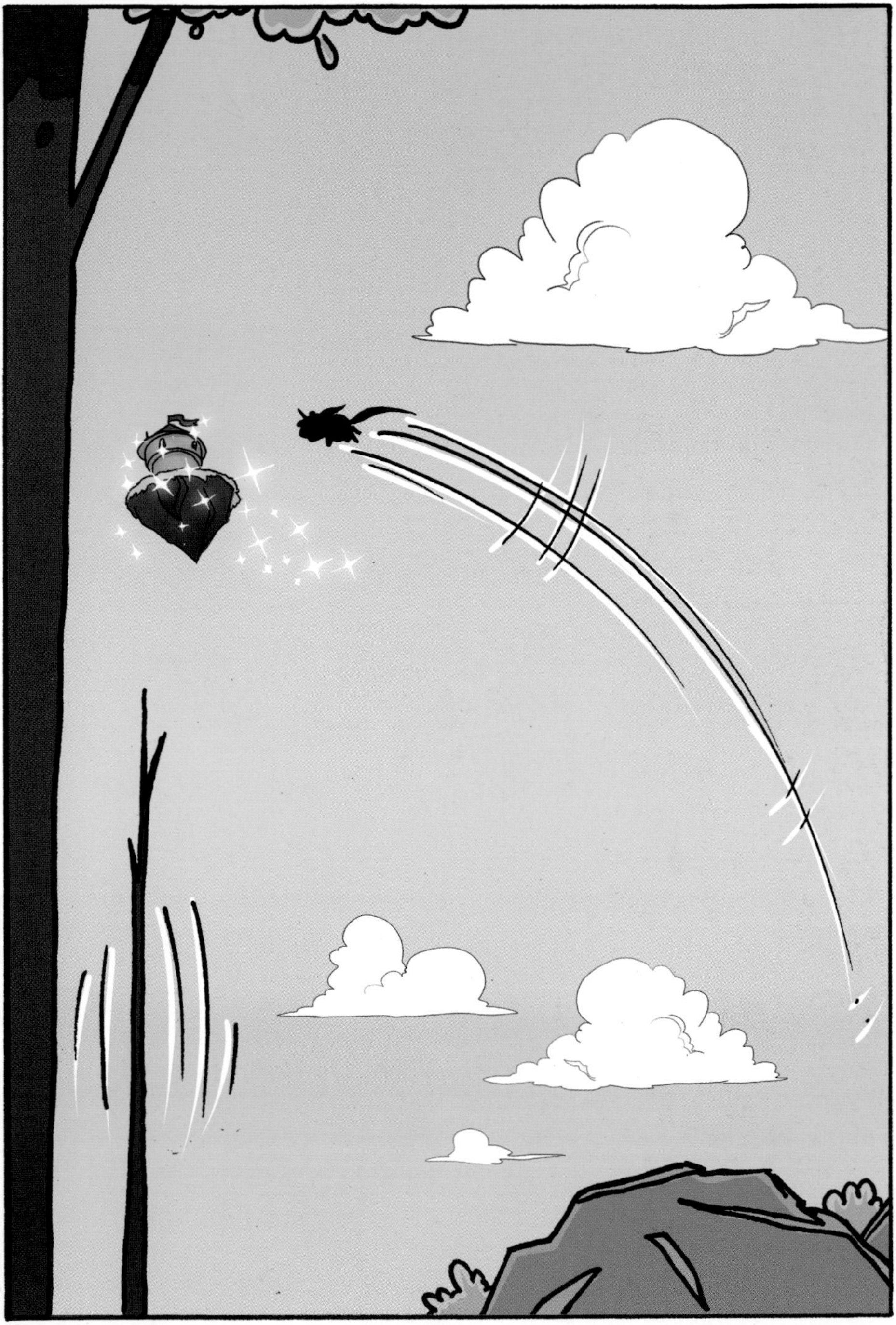

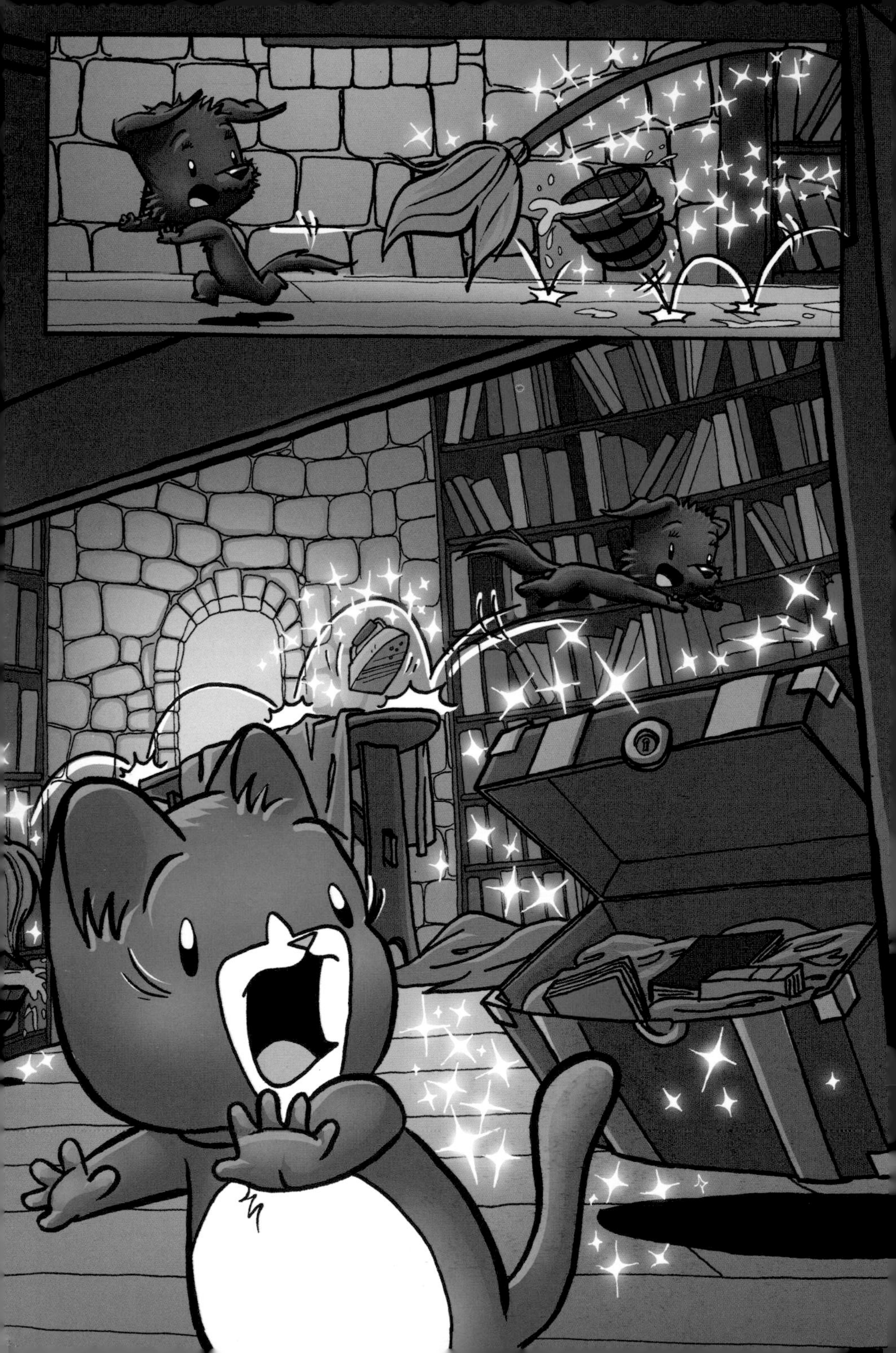

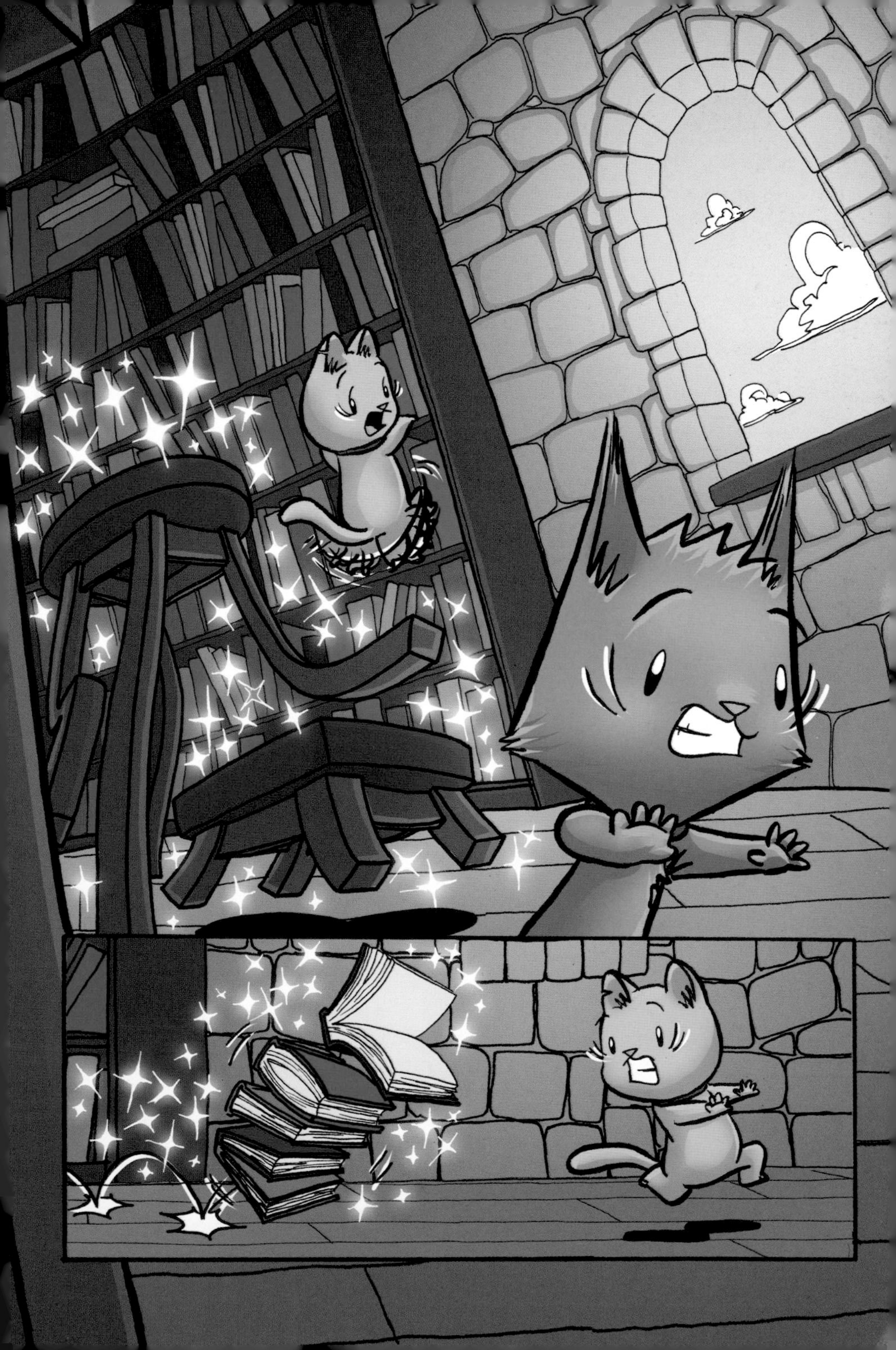

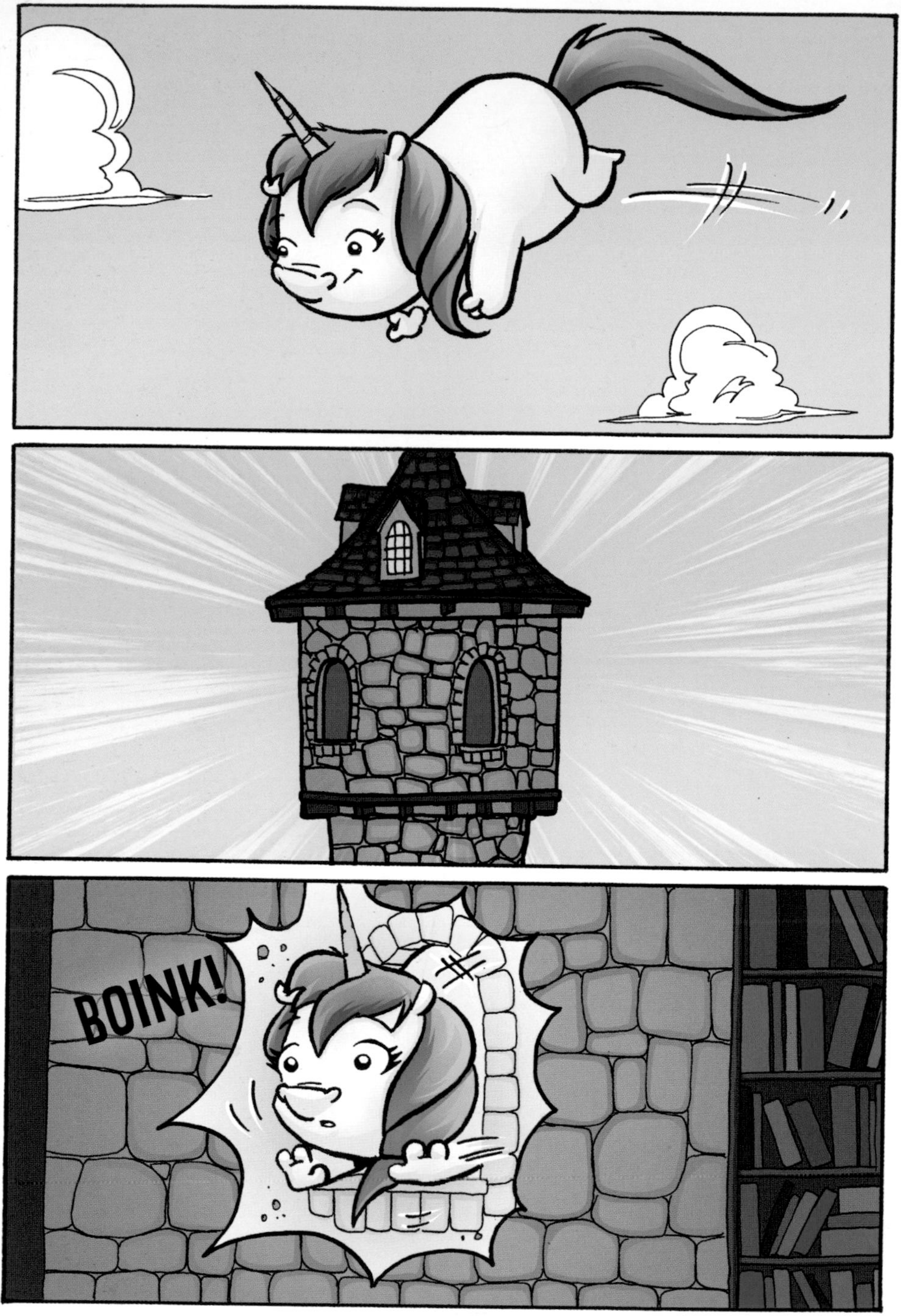
BOINK!

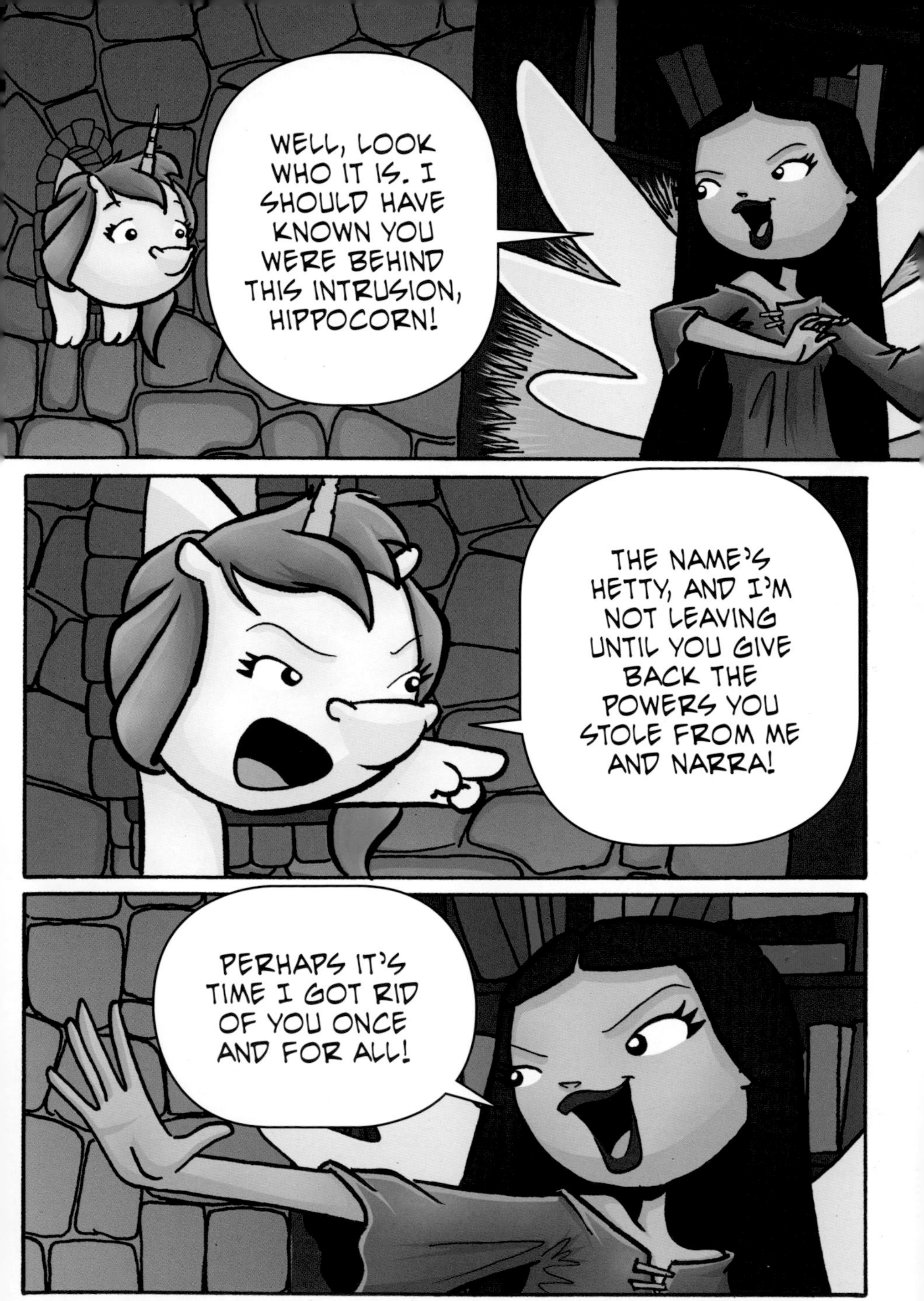
WELL, LOOK WHO IT IS. I SHOULD HAVE KNOWN YOU WERE BEHIND THIS INTRUSION, HIPPOCORN!
THE NAME'S HETTY, AND I'M NOT LEAVING UNTIL YOU GIVE BACK THE POWERS YOU STOLE FROM ME AND NARRA!
PERHAPS IT'S TIME I GOT RID OF YOU ONCE AND FOR ALL!

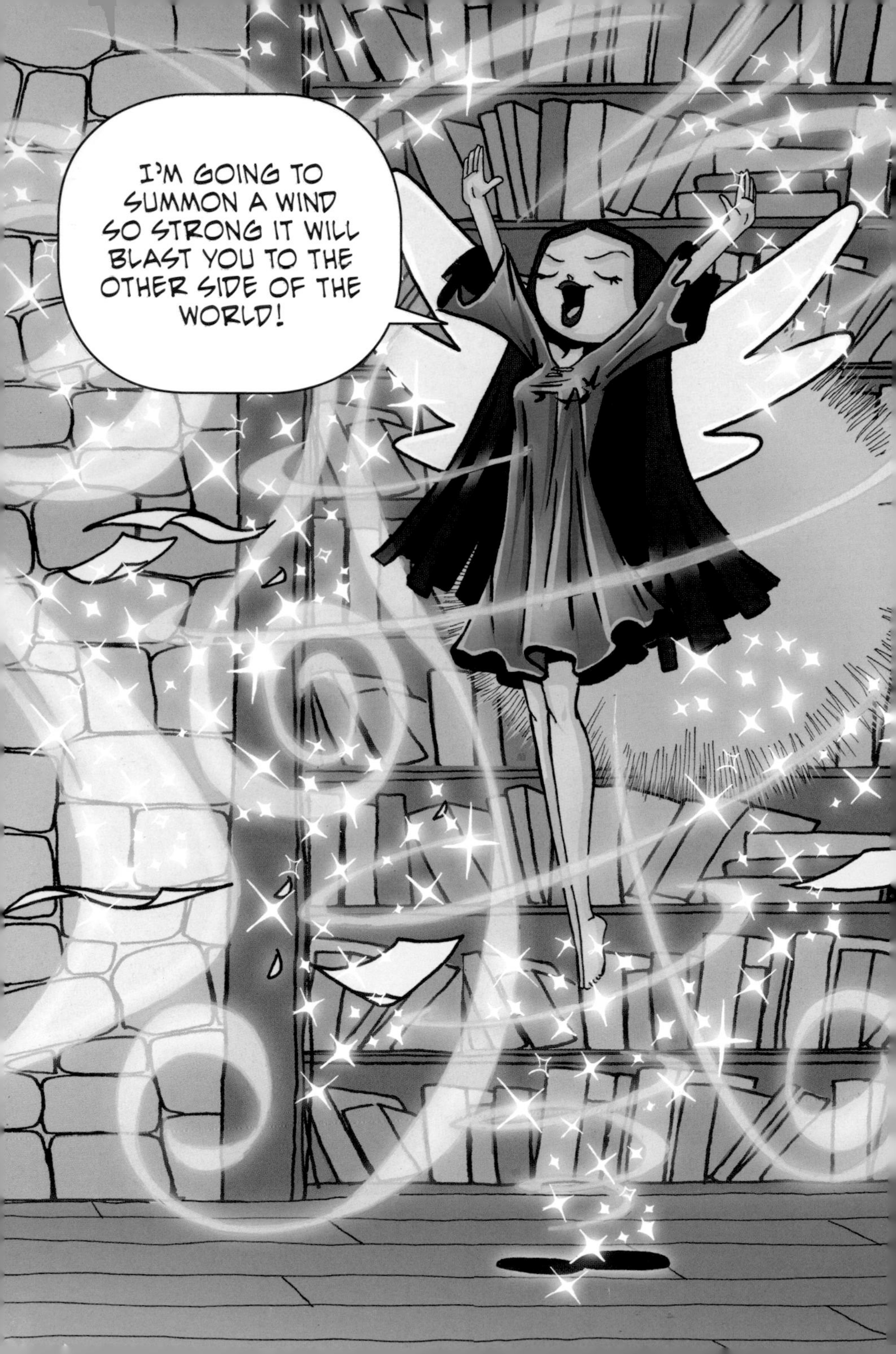
I'M GOING TO SUMMON A WIND SO STRONG IT WILL BLAST YOU TO THE OTHER SIDE OF THE WORLD!

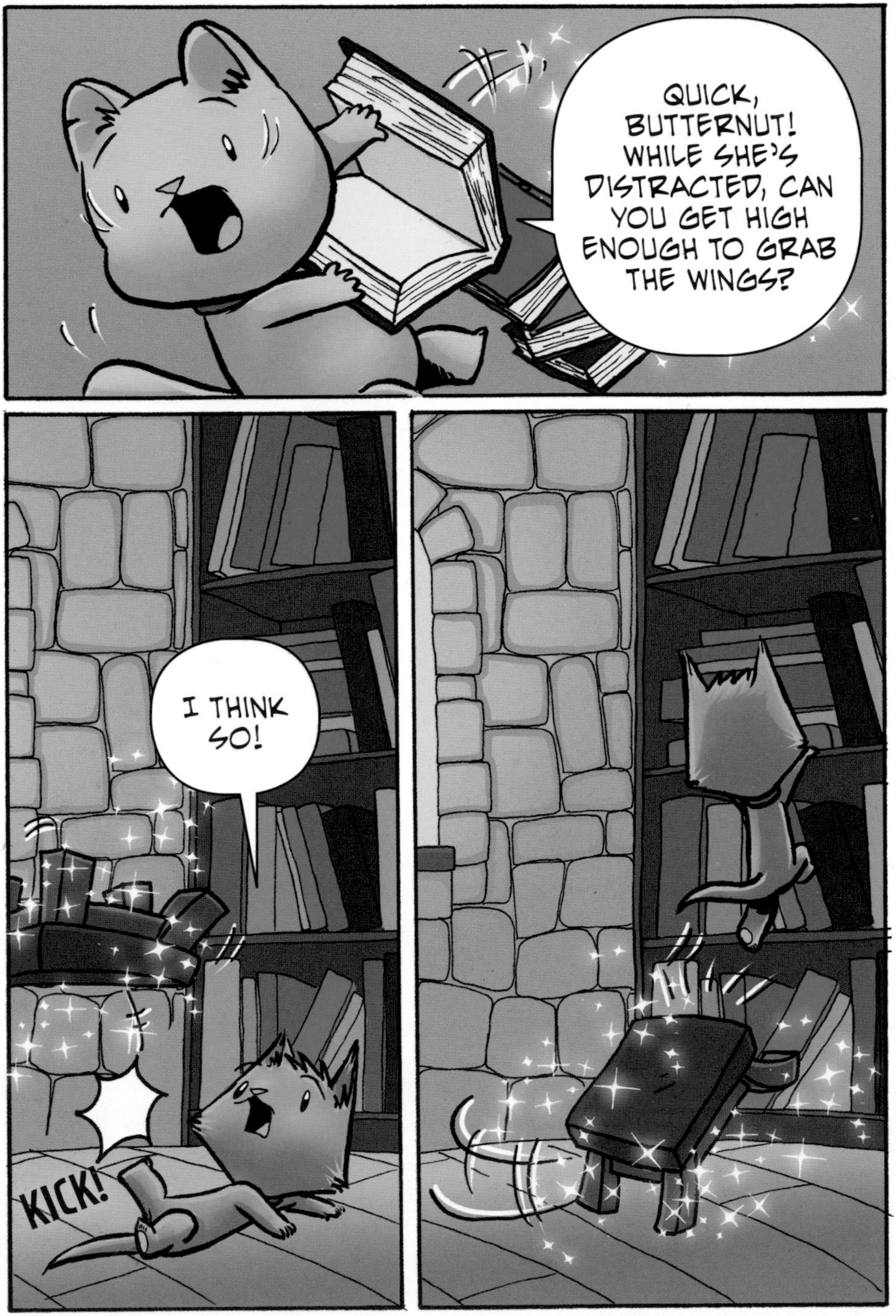
QUICK, BUTTERNUT! WHILE SHE'S DISTRACTED, CAN YOU GET HIGH ENOUGH TO GRAB THE WINGS?
I THINK SO!
KICK!

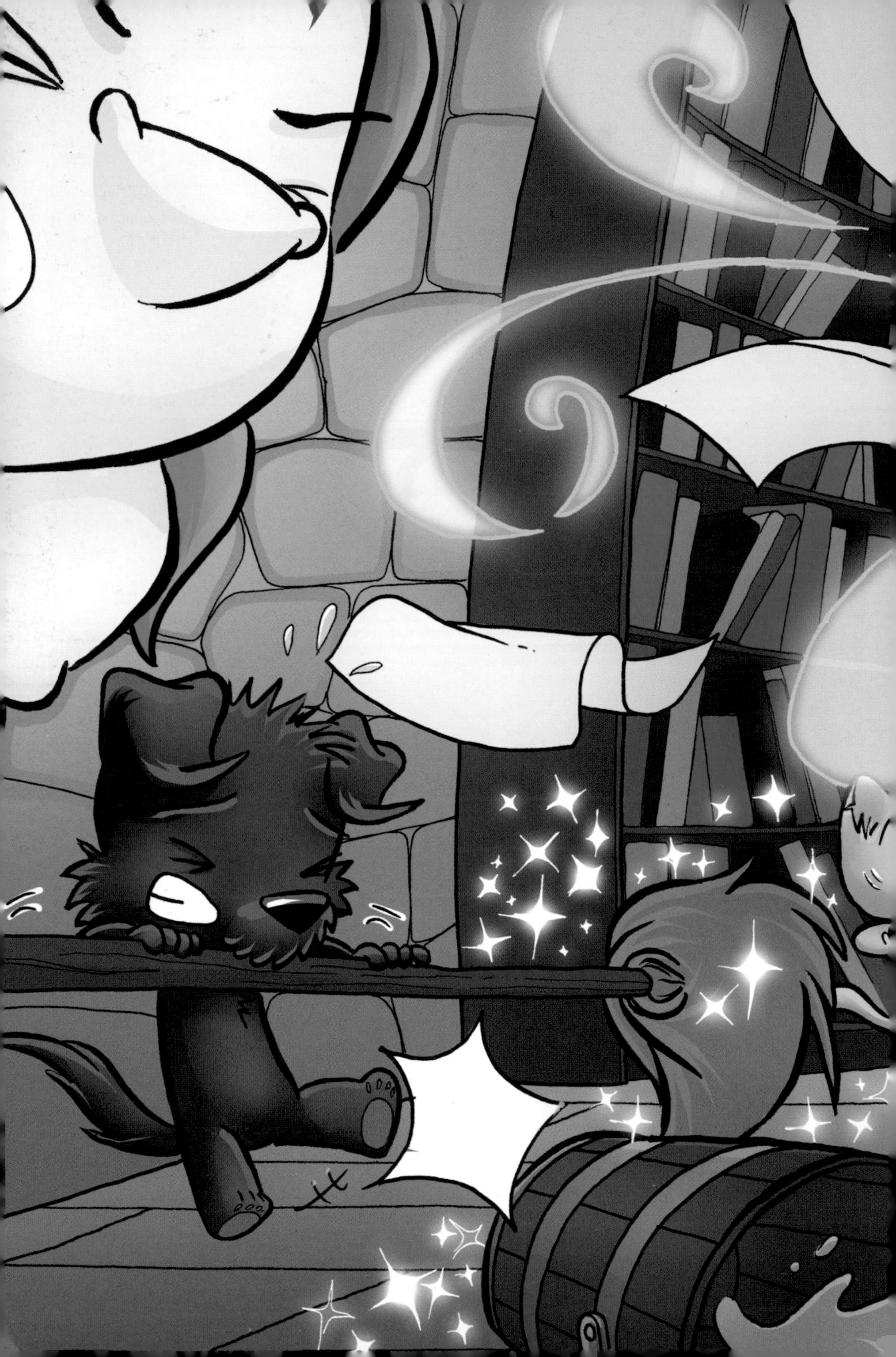

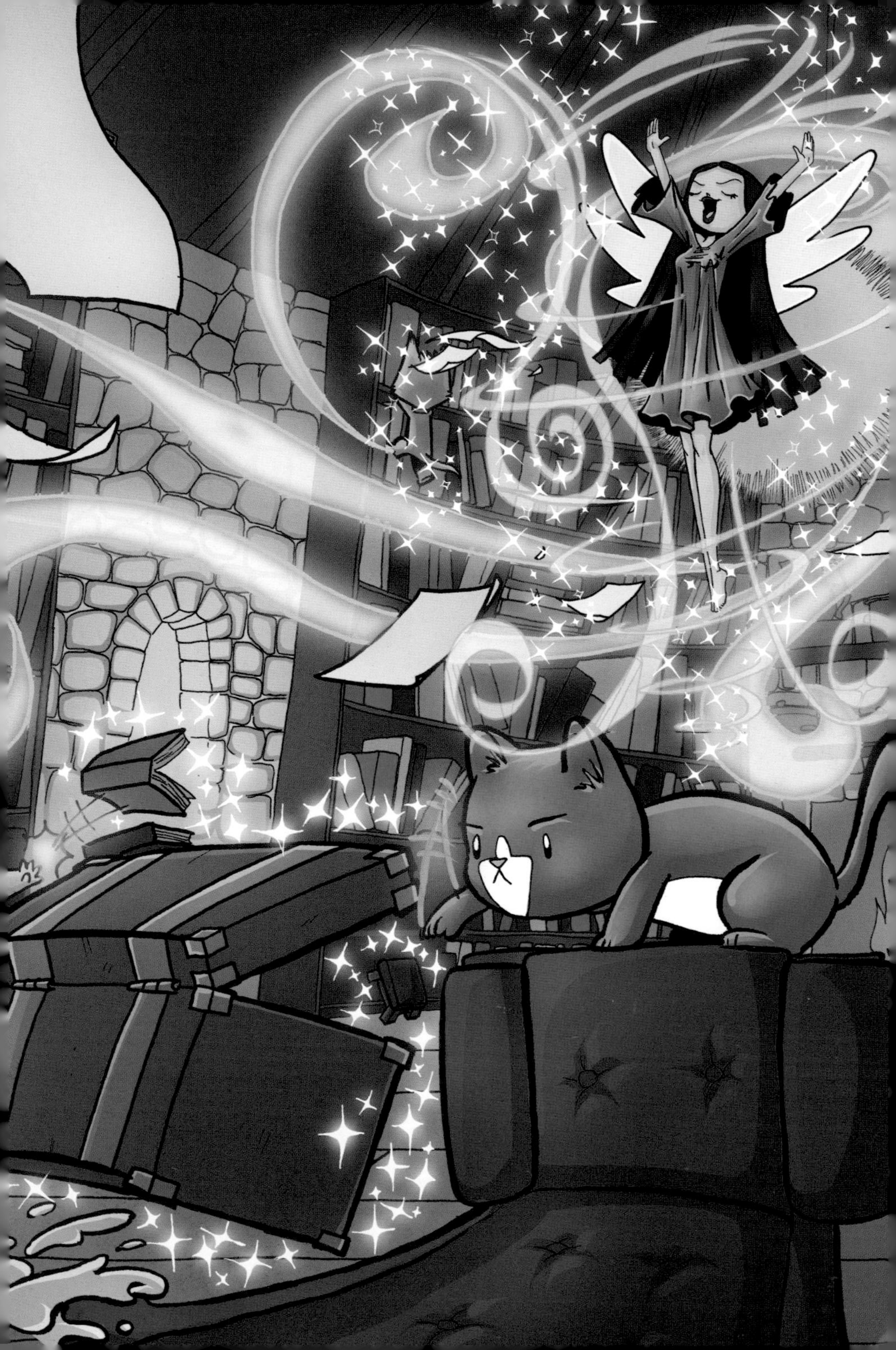

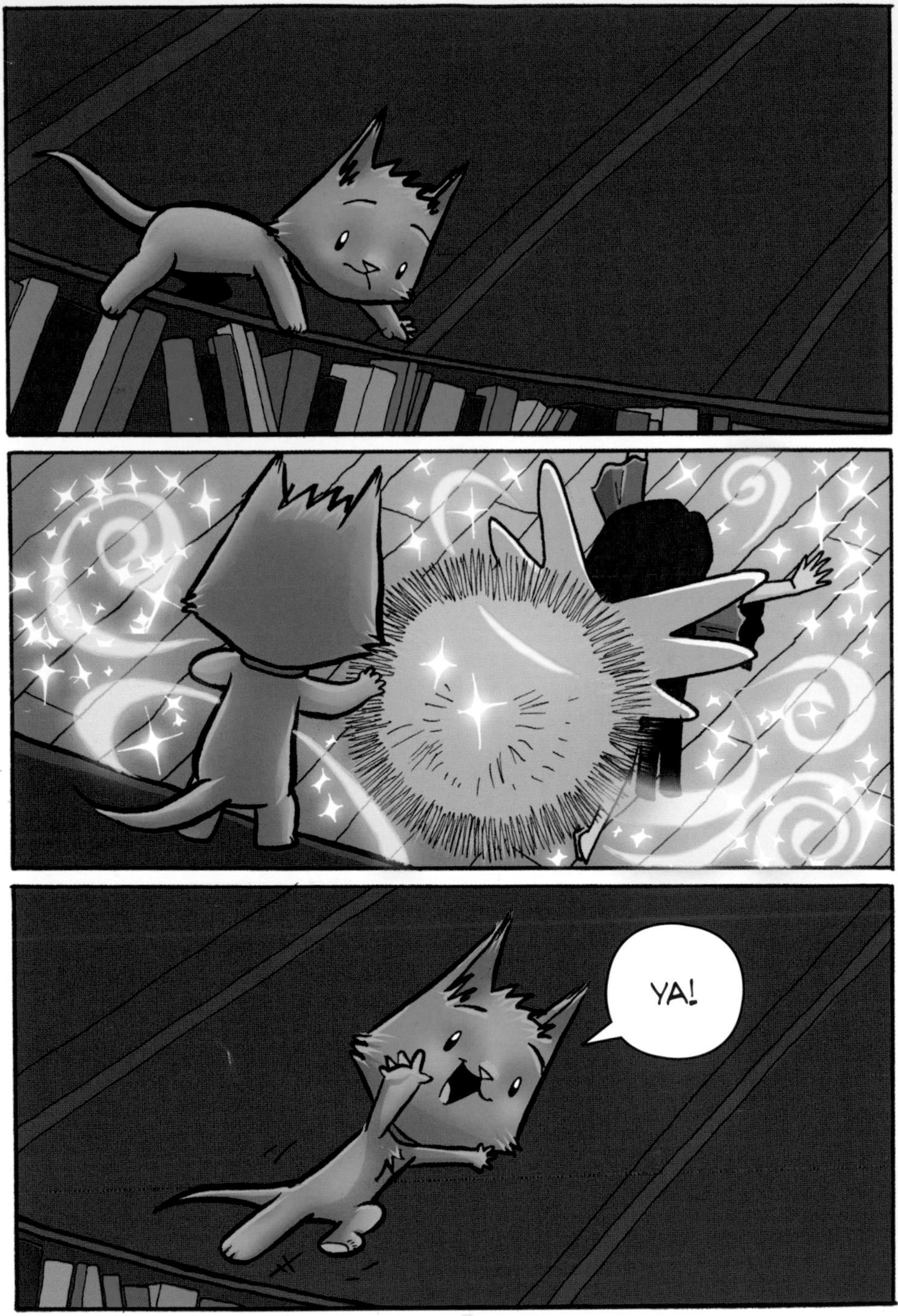
YA!

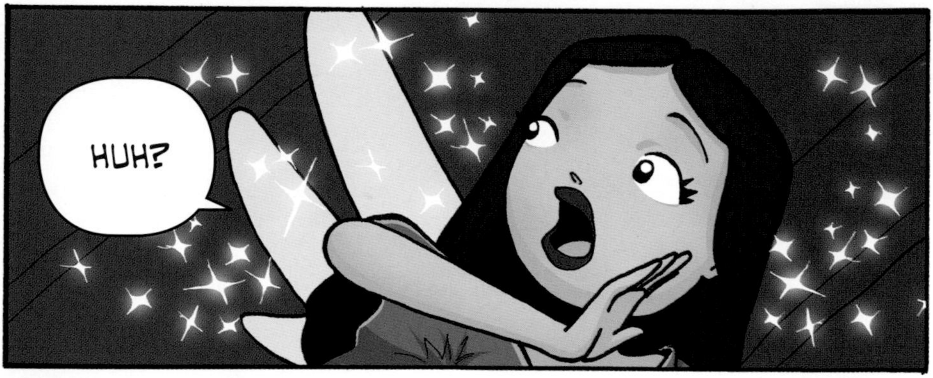
HUH?

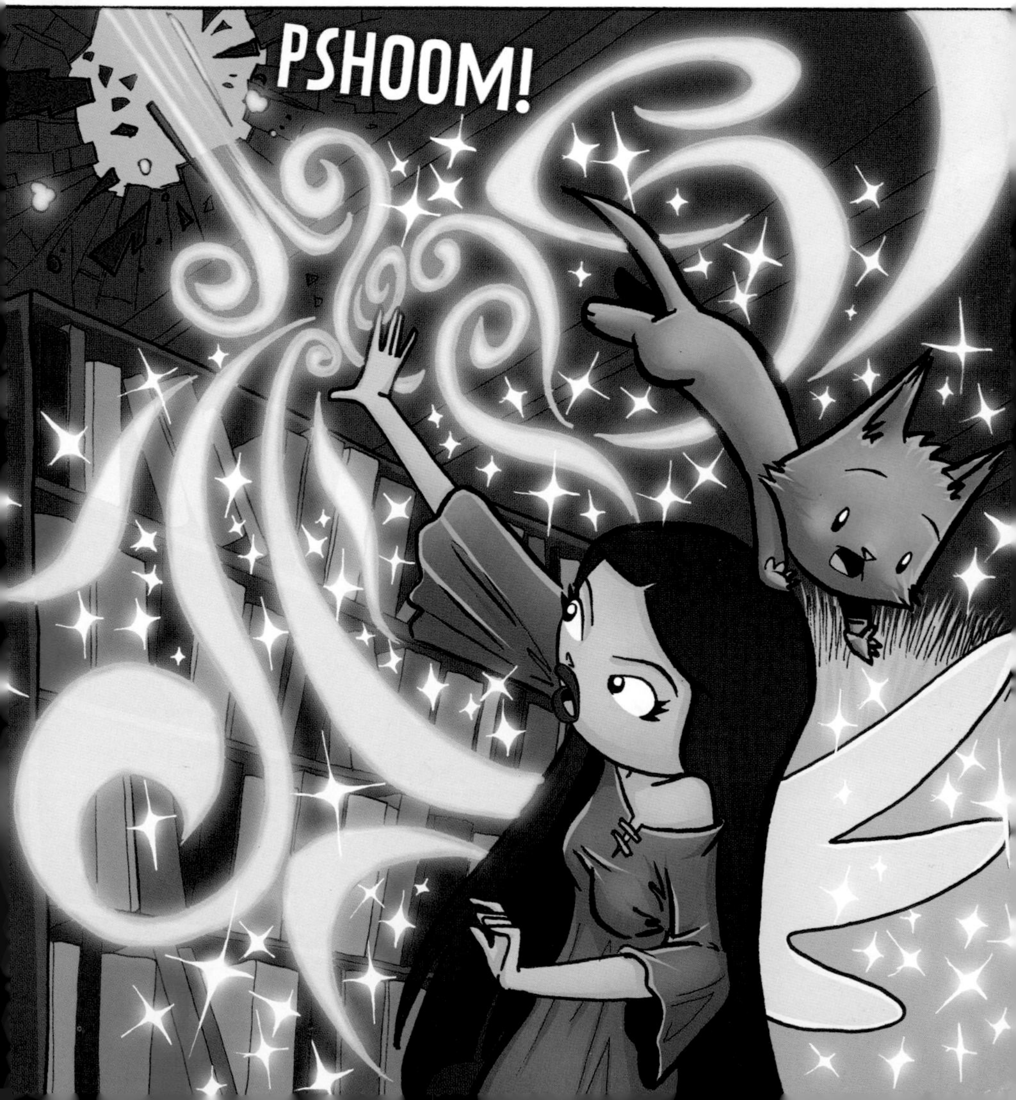
PSHOOM!

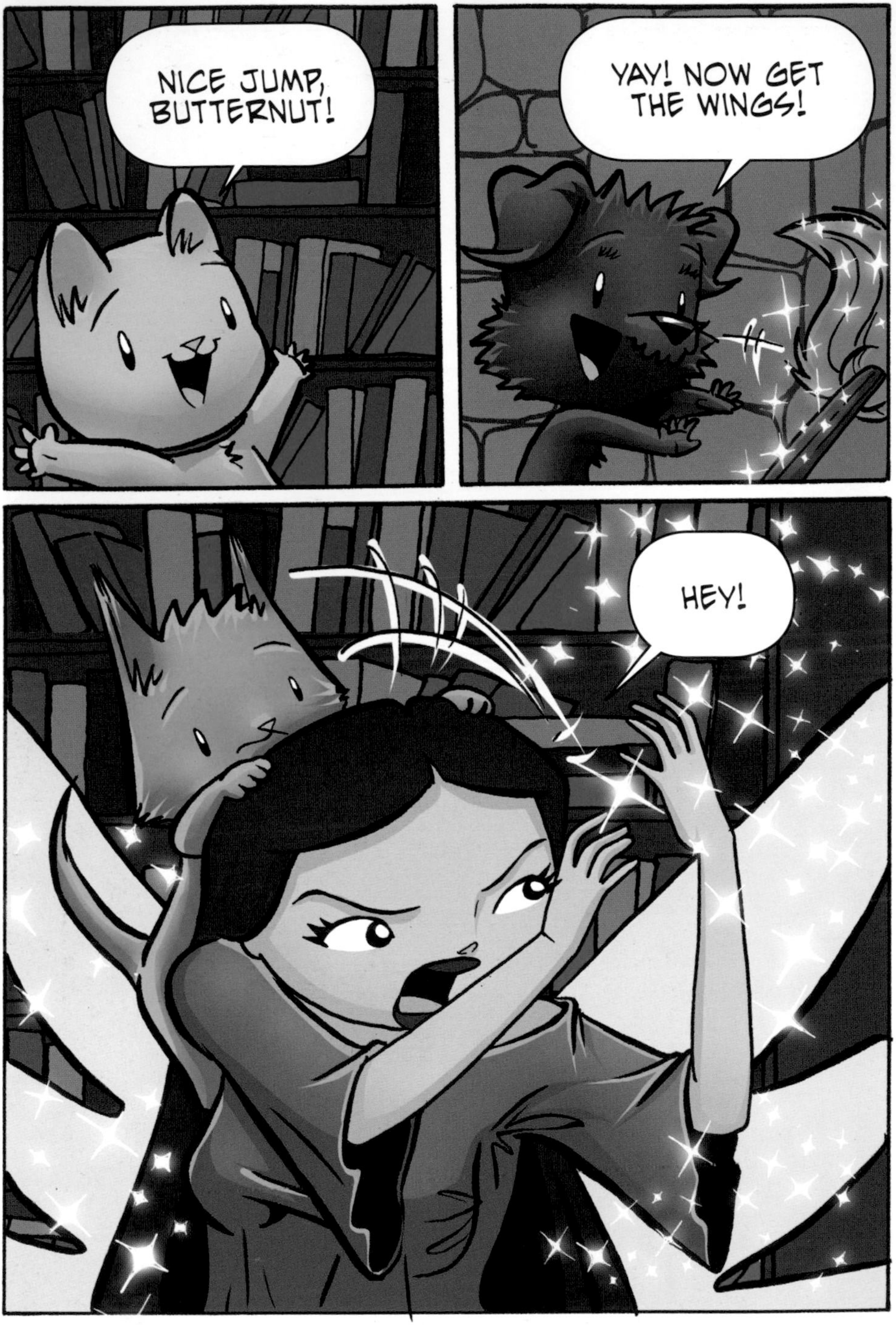
NICE JUMP, BUTTERNUT!
YAY! NOW GET THE WINGS!
HEY!

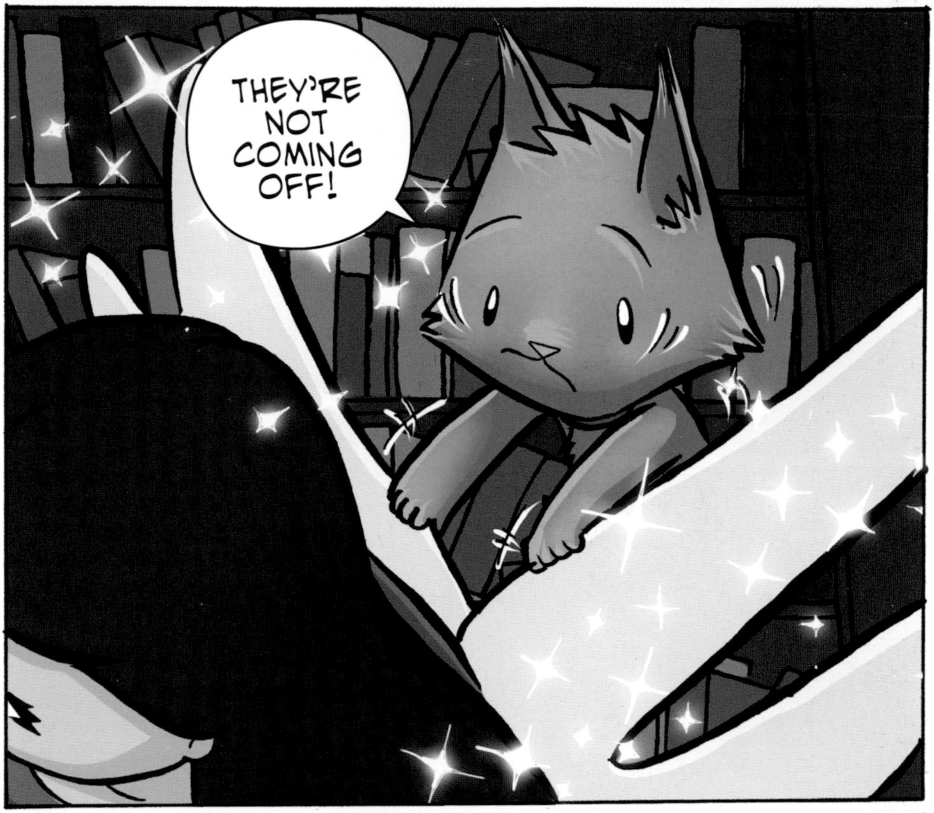
THEY'RE NOT COMING OFF!

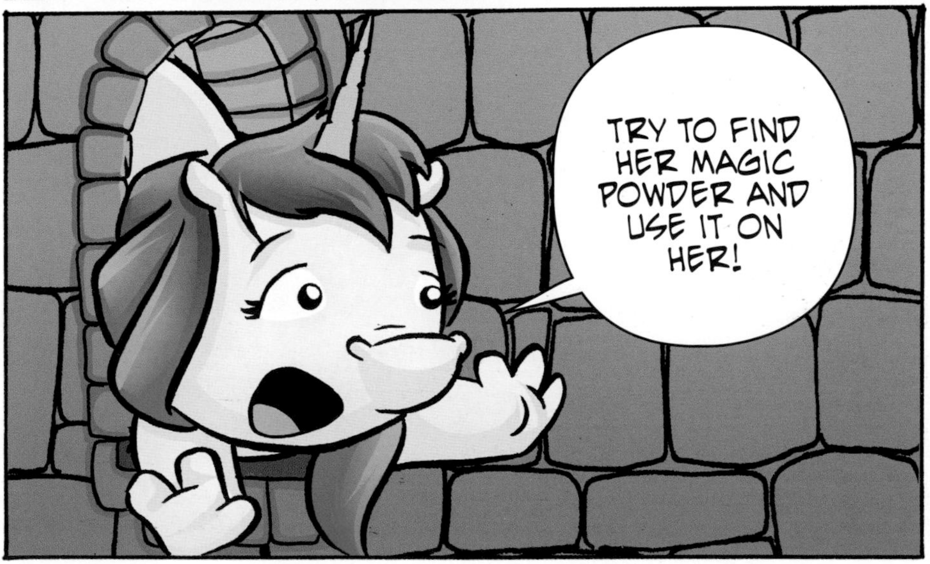
TRY TO FIND HER MAGIC POWDER AND USE IT ON HER!

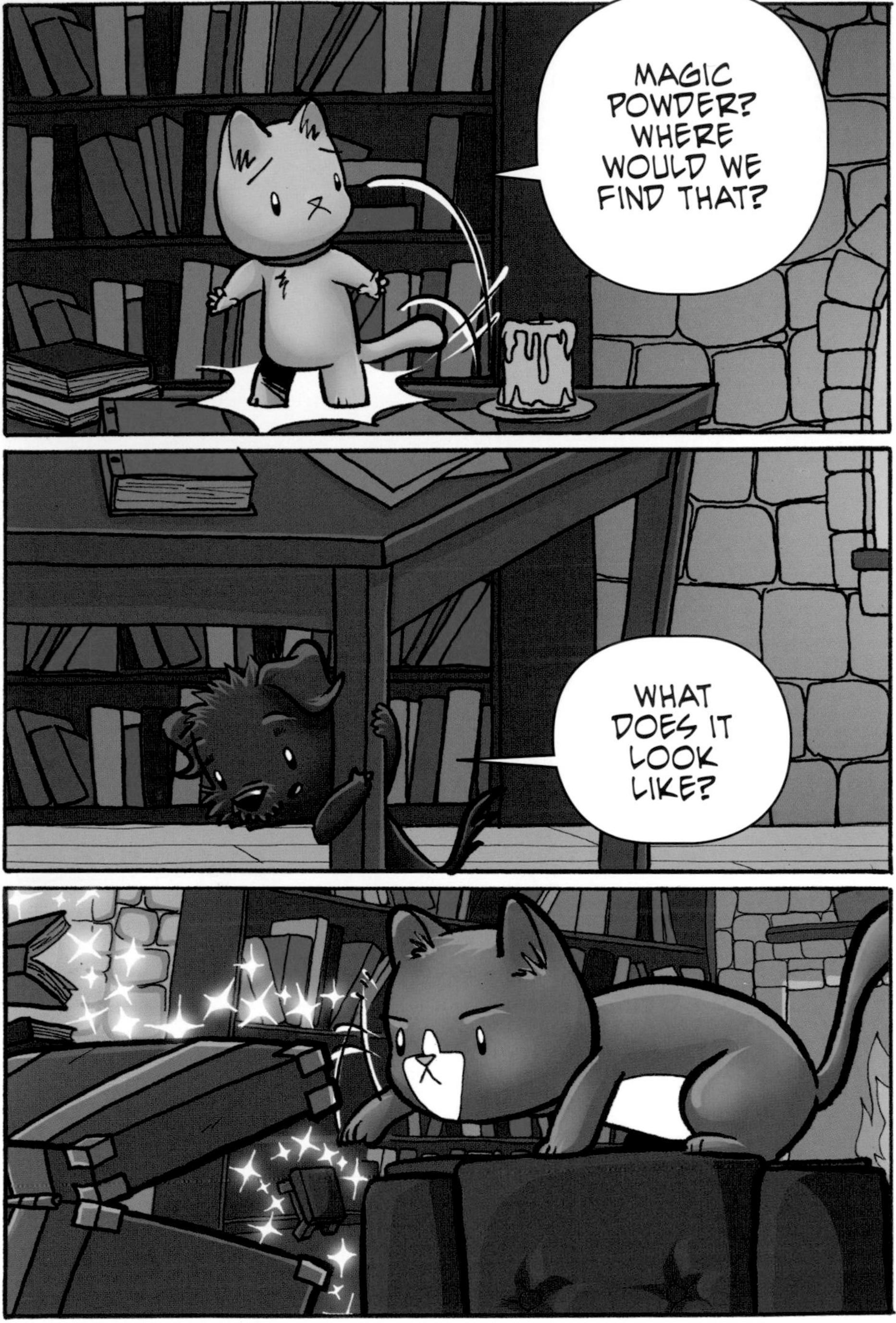
MAGIC POWDER? WHERE WOULD WE FIND THAT?
WHAT DOES IT LOOK LIKE?

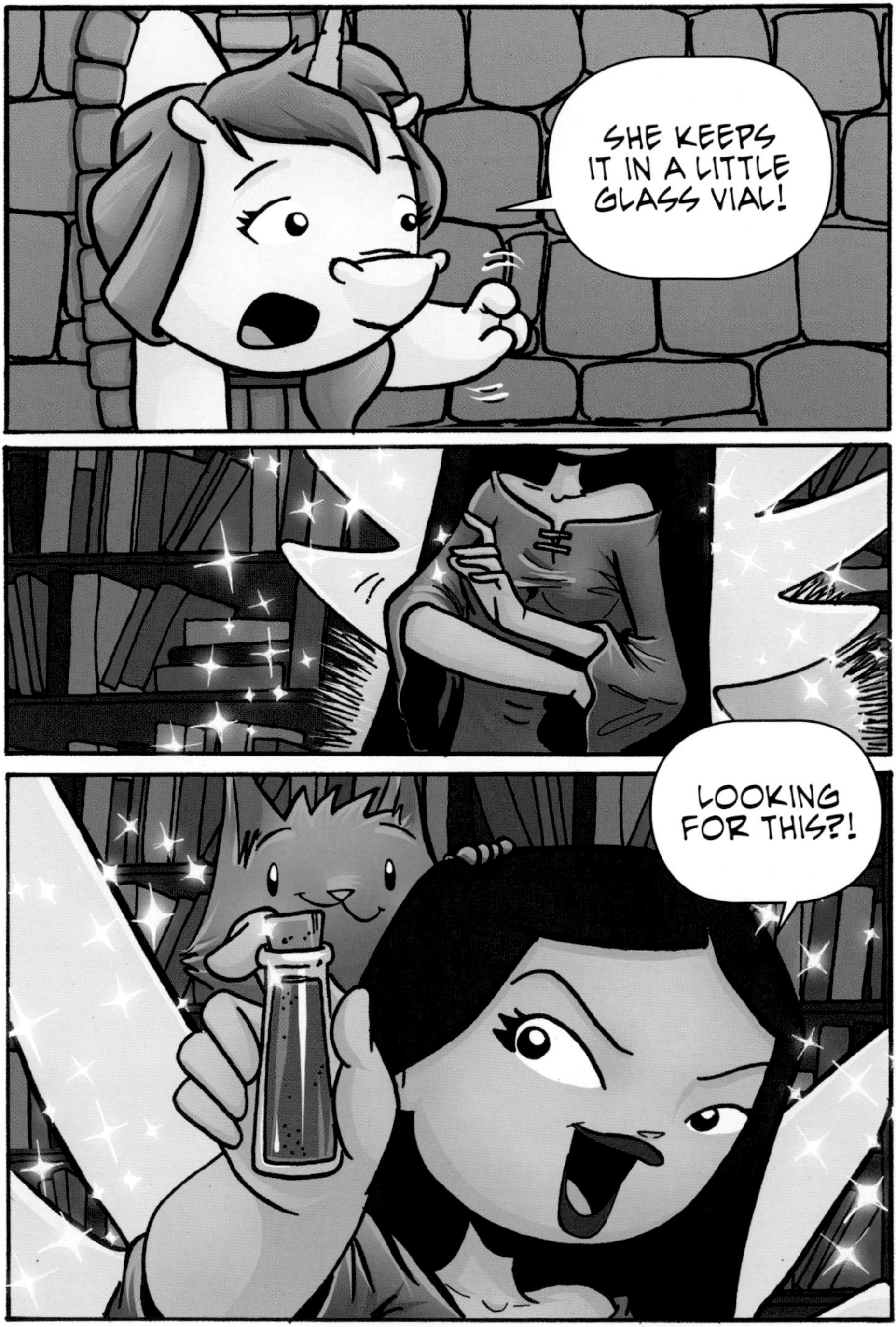
SHE KEEPS IT IN A LITTLE GLASS VIAL!
LOOKING FOR THIS?!

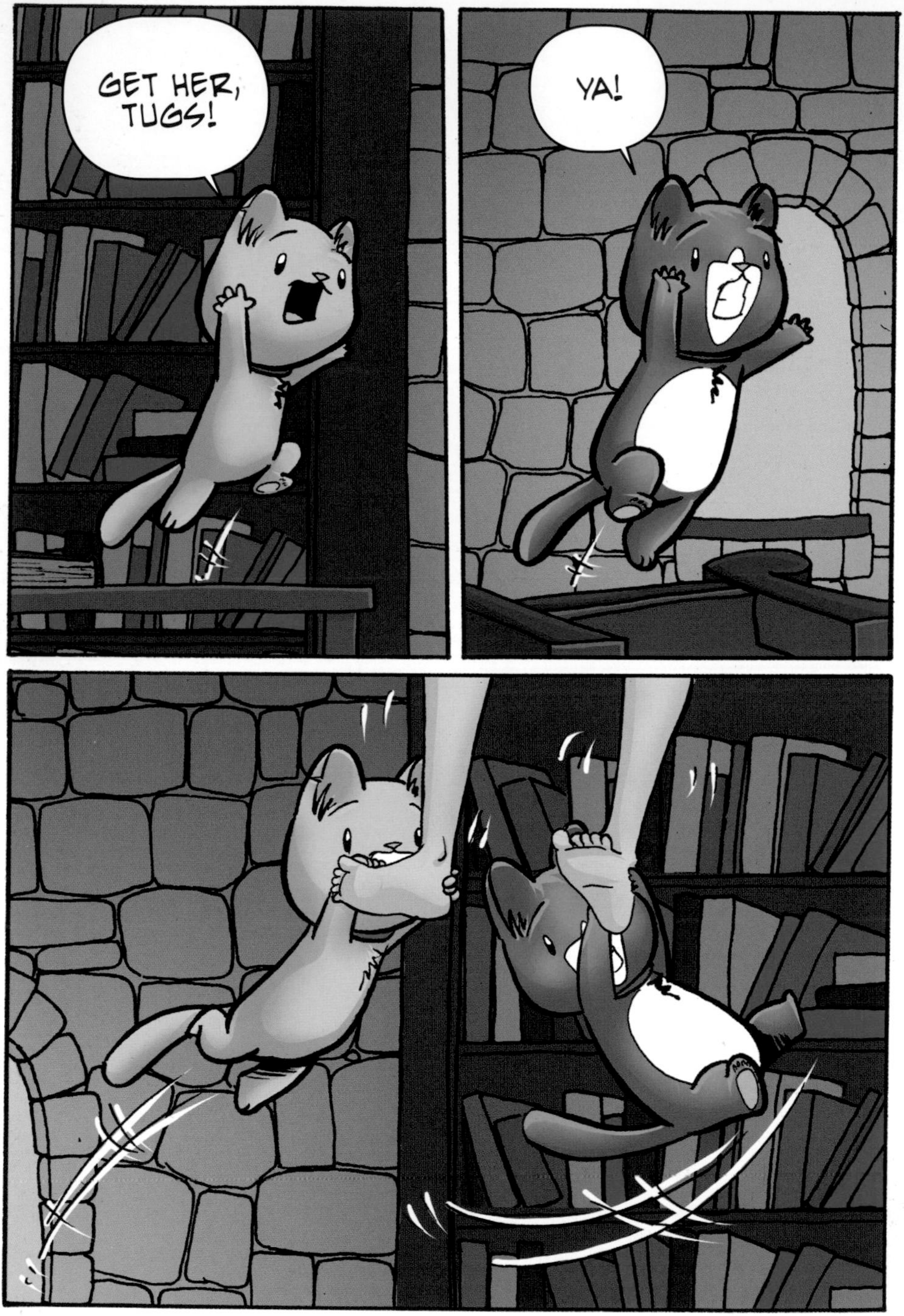
GET HER, TUGS!
YA!

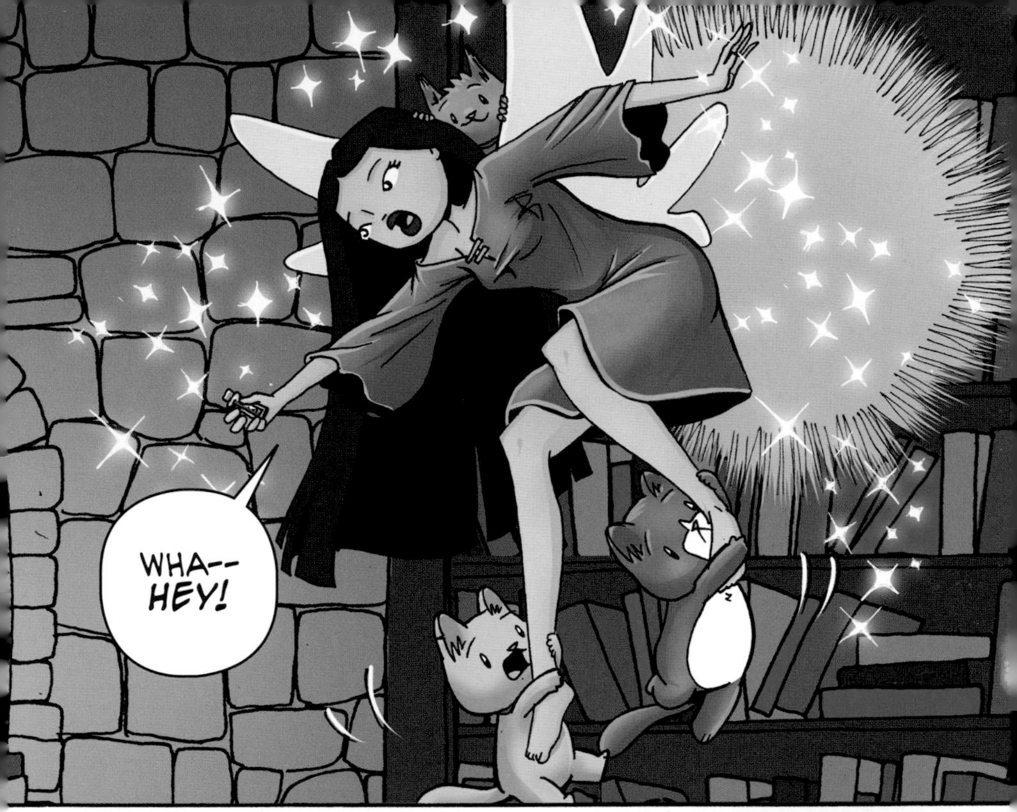
WHA--
HEY!

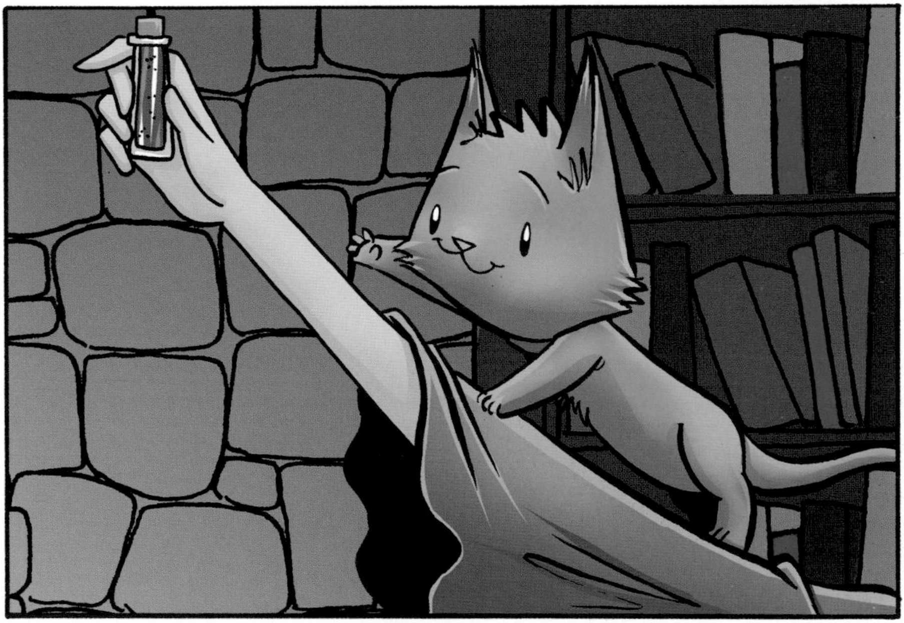

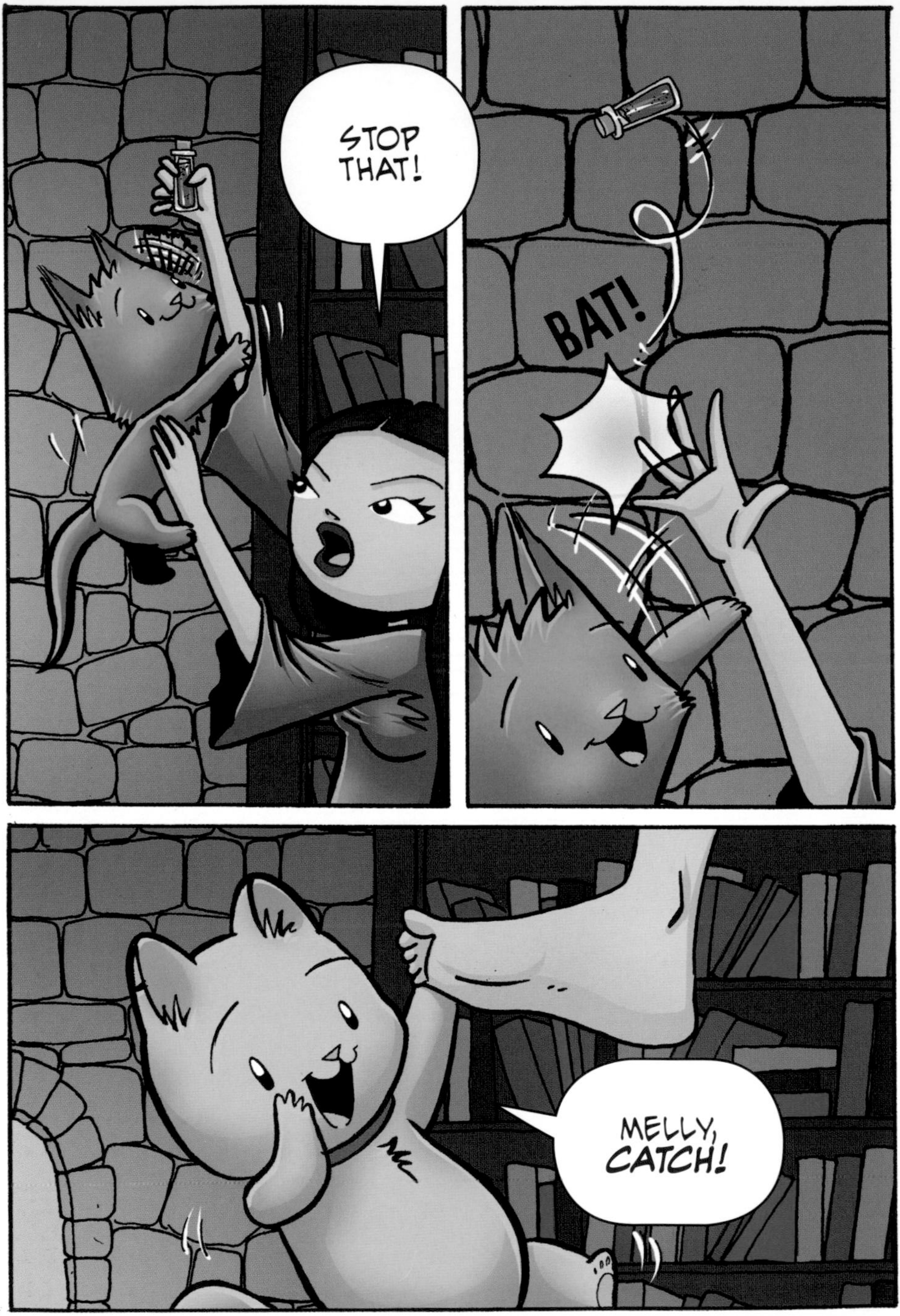
STOP THAT!
BAT!
MELLY, CATCH!

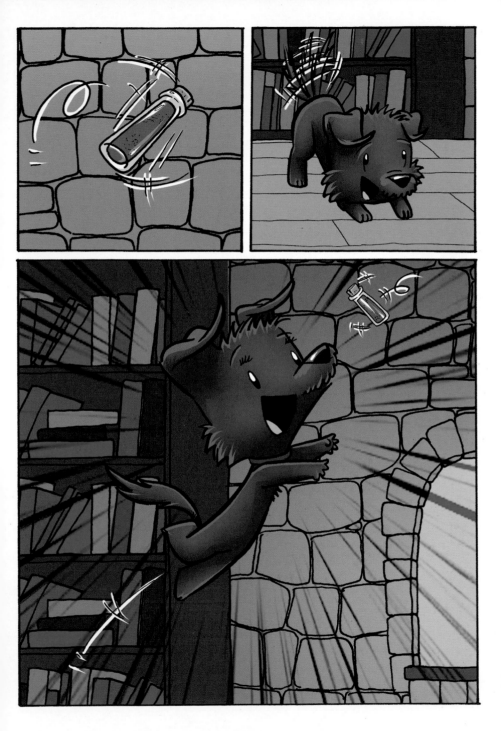

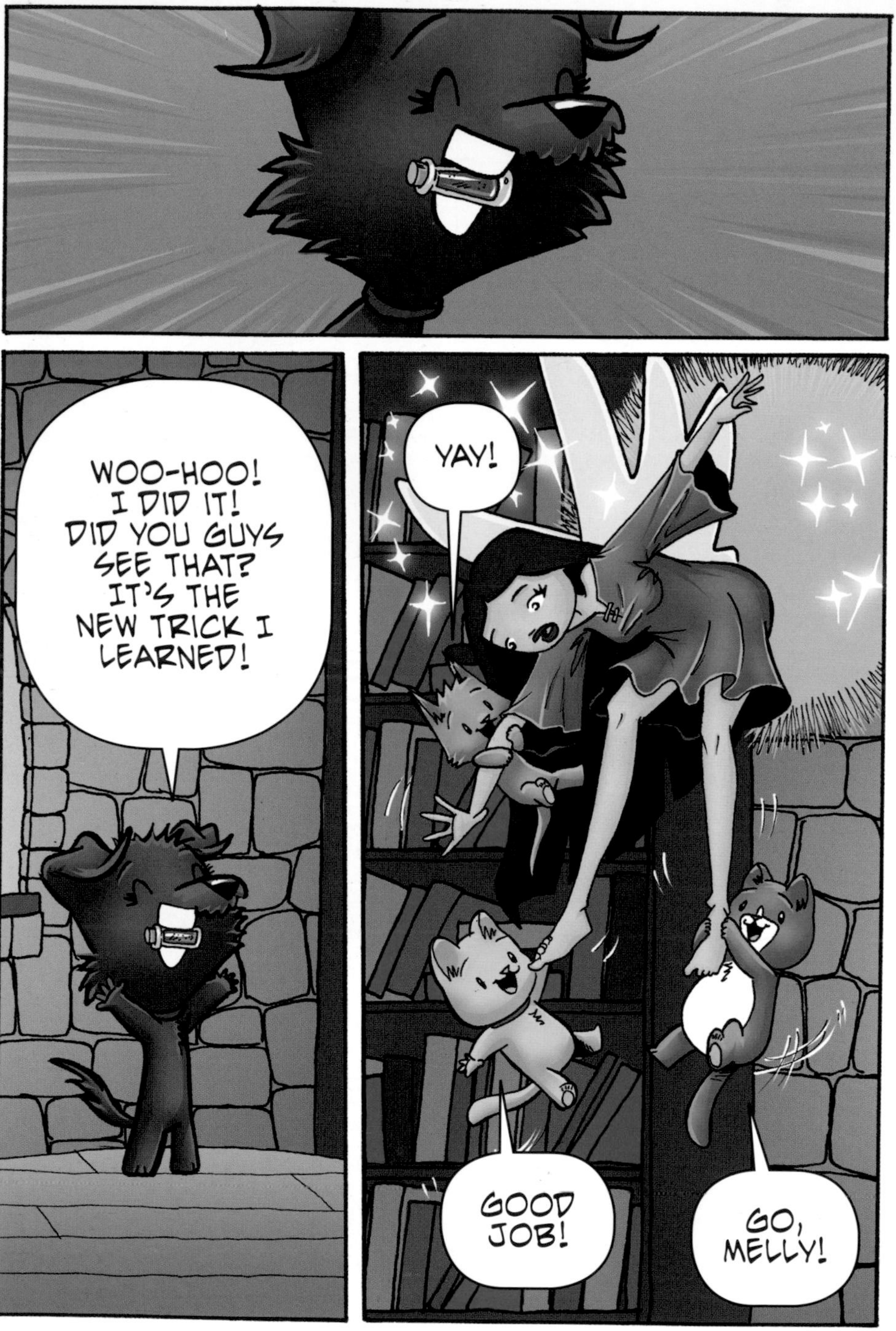
WOO-HOO! I DID IT! DID YOU GUYS SEE THAT? IT'S THE NEW TRICK I LEARNED!
YAY!
GOOD JOB!
GO, MELLY!

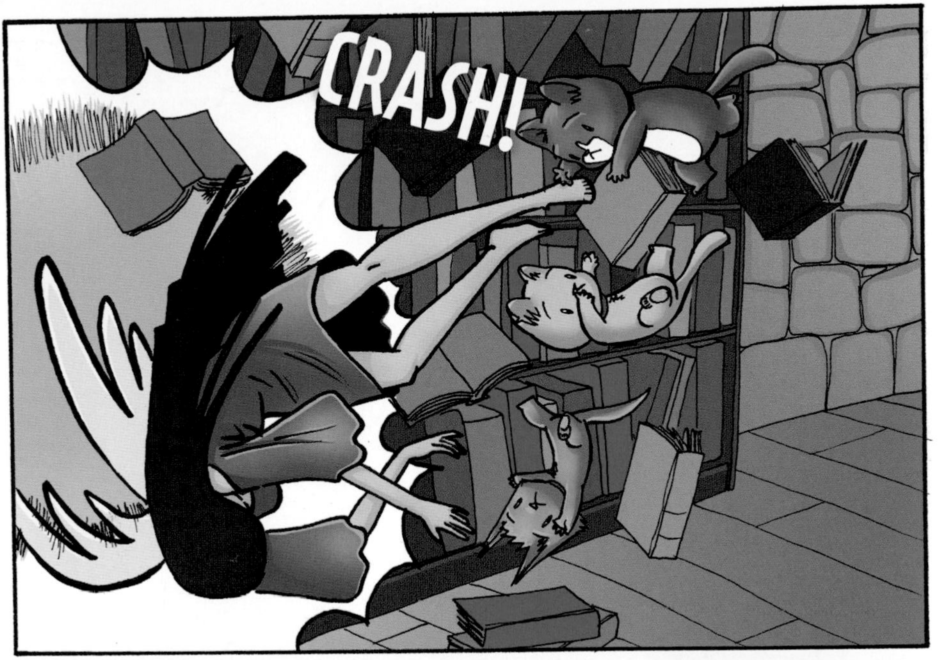
CRASH!

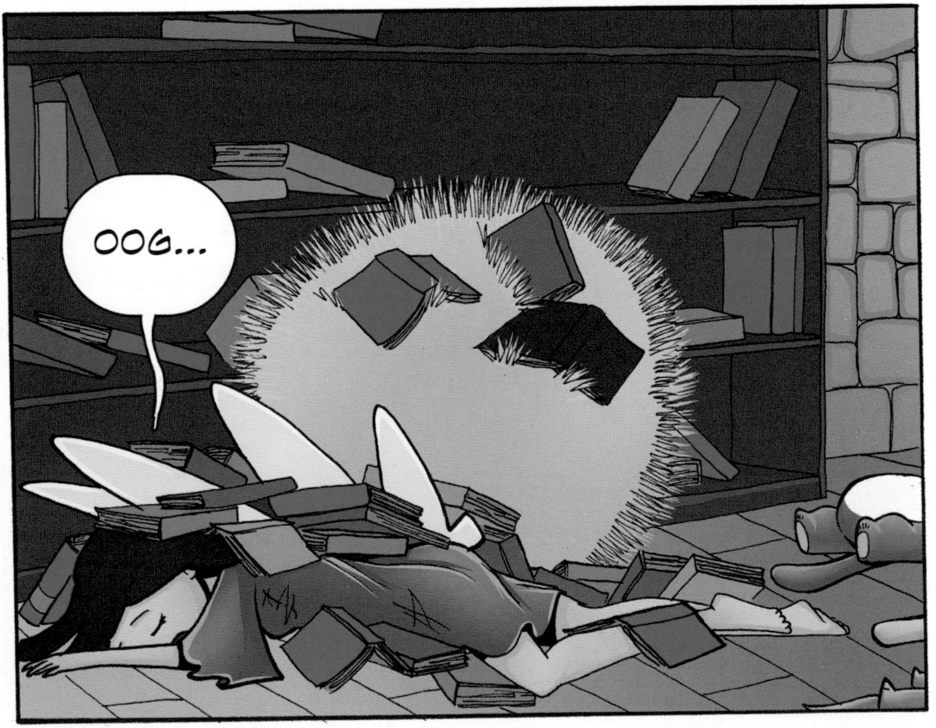
OOG...

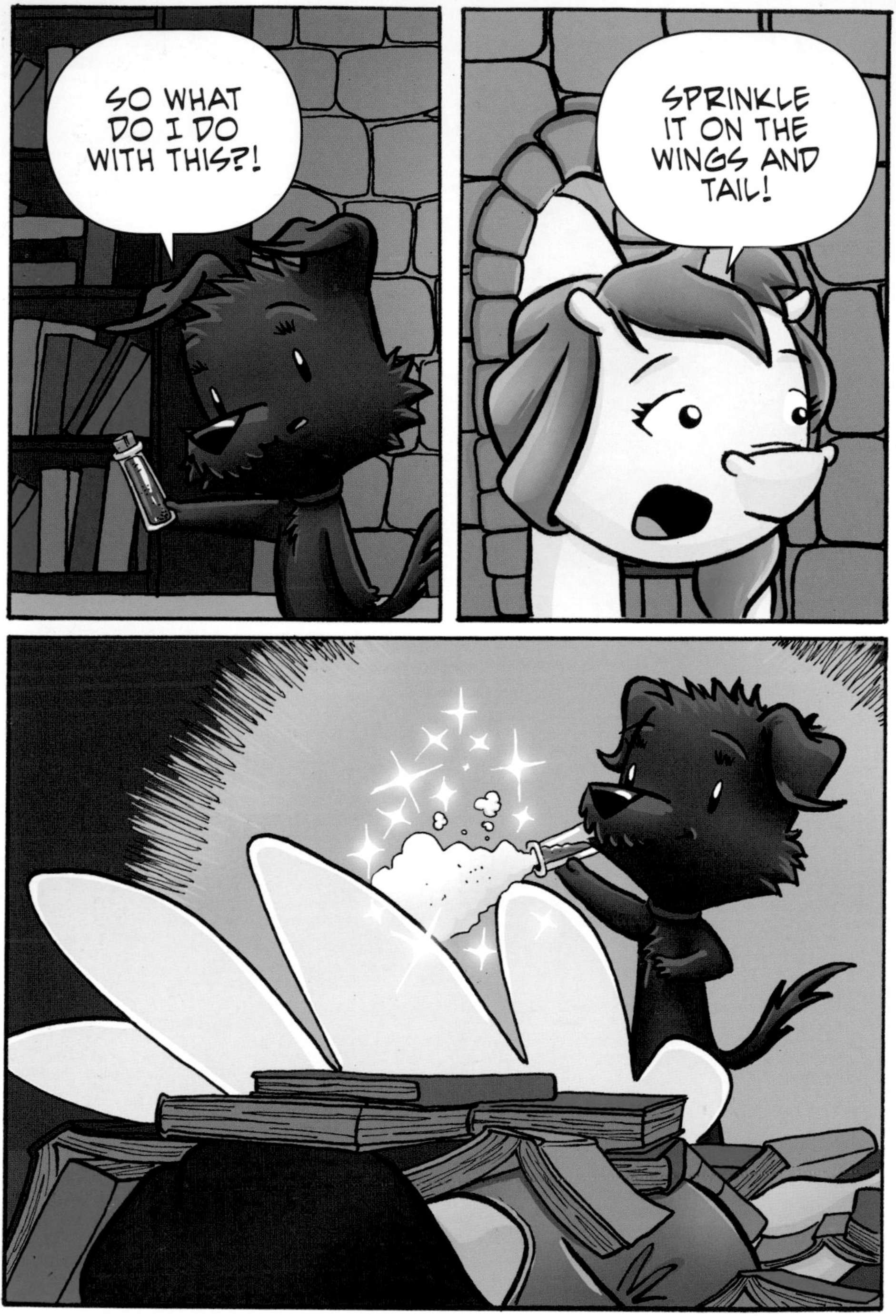
SO WHAT DO I DO WITH THIS?!
SPRINKLE IT ON THE WINGS AND TAIL!

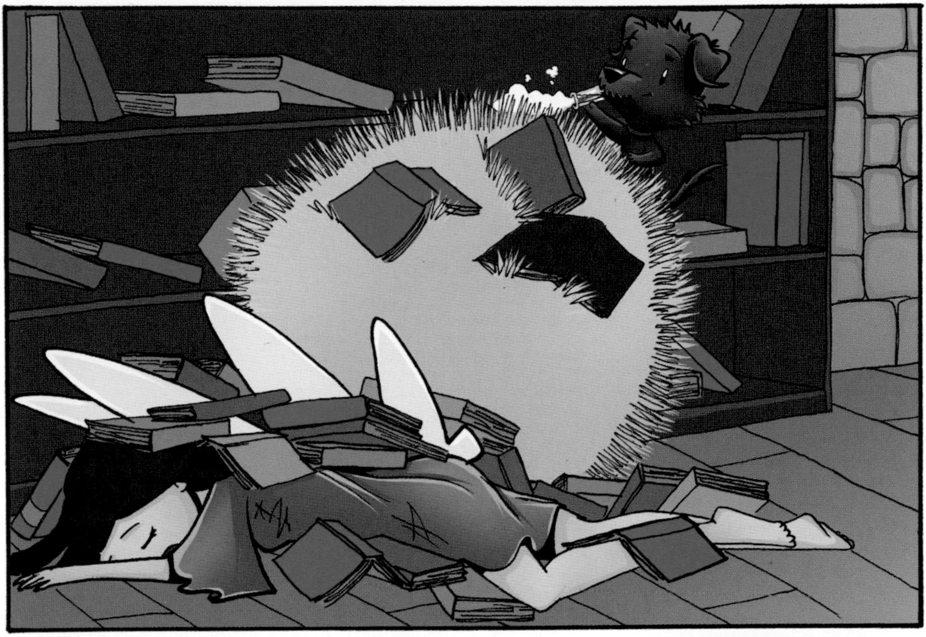

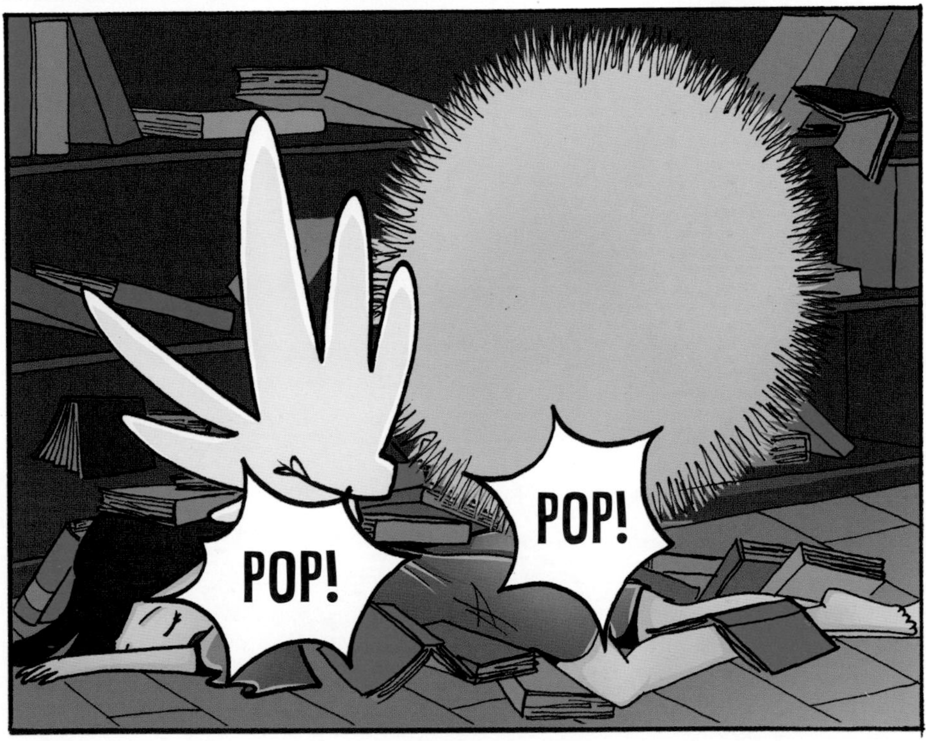
POP!
POP!

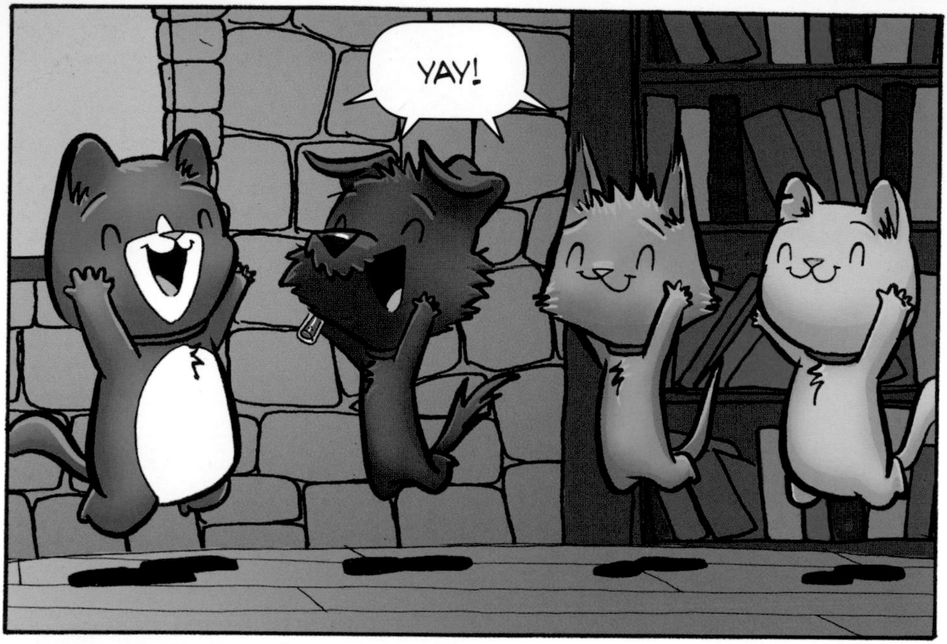
YAY!

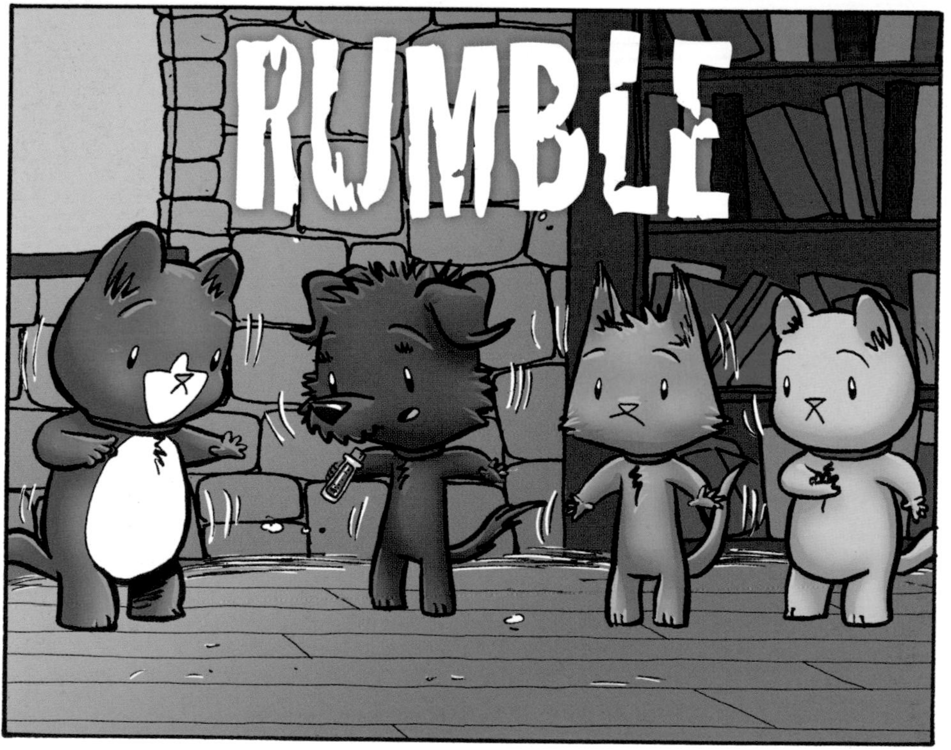
RUMBLE

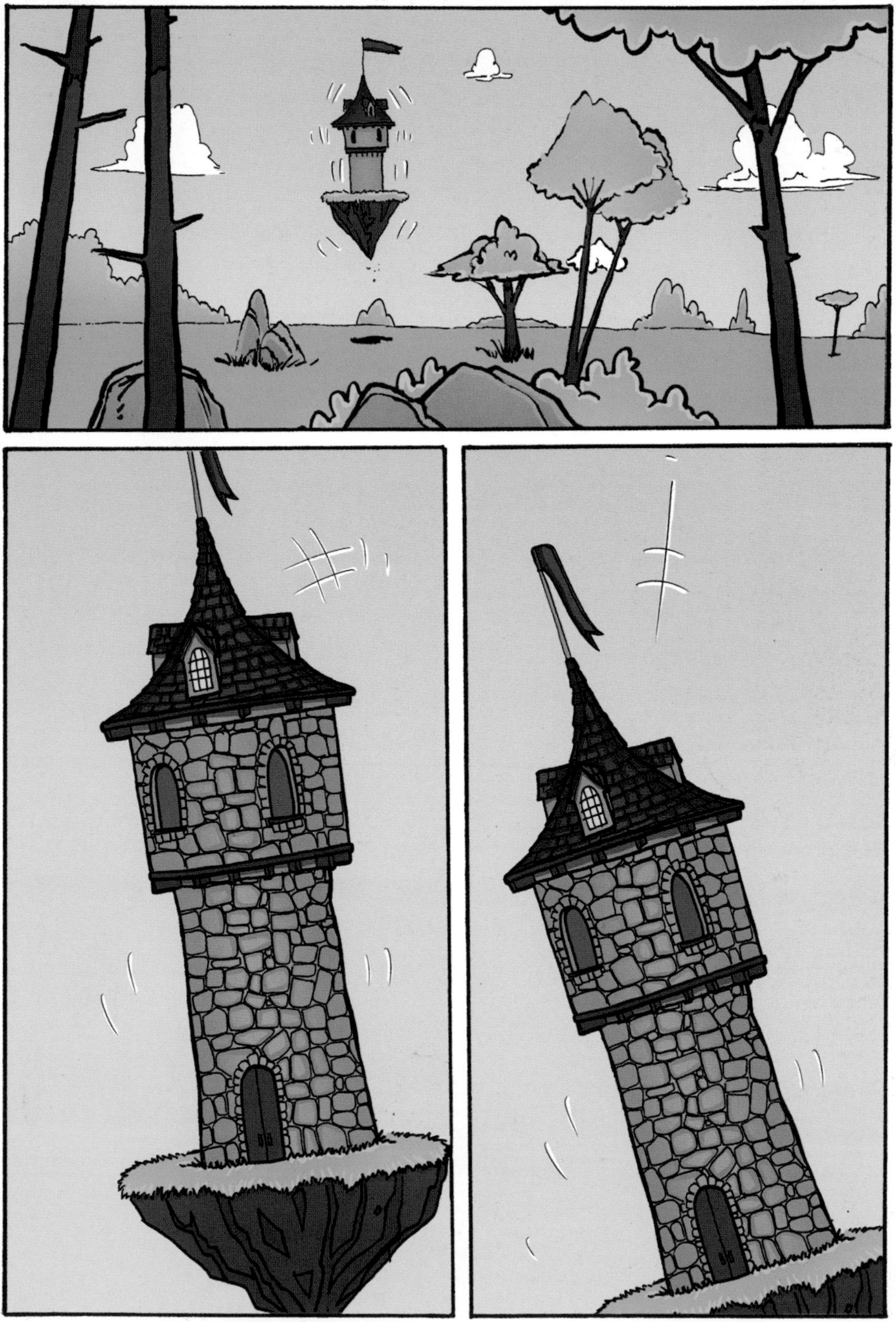

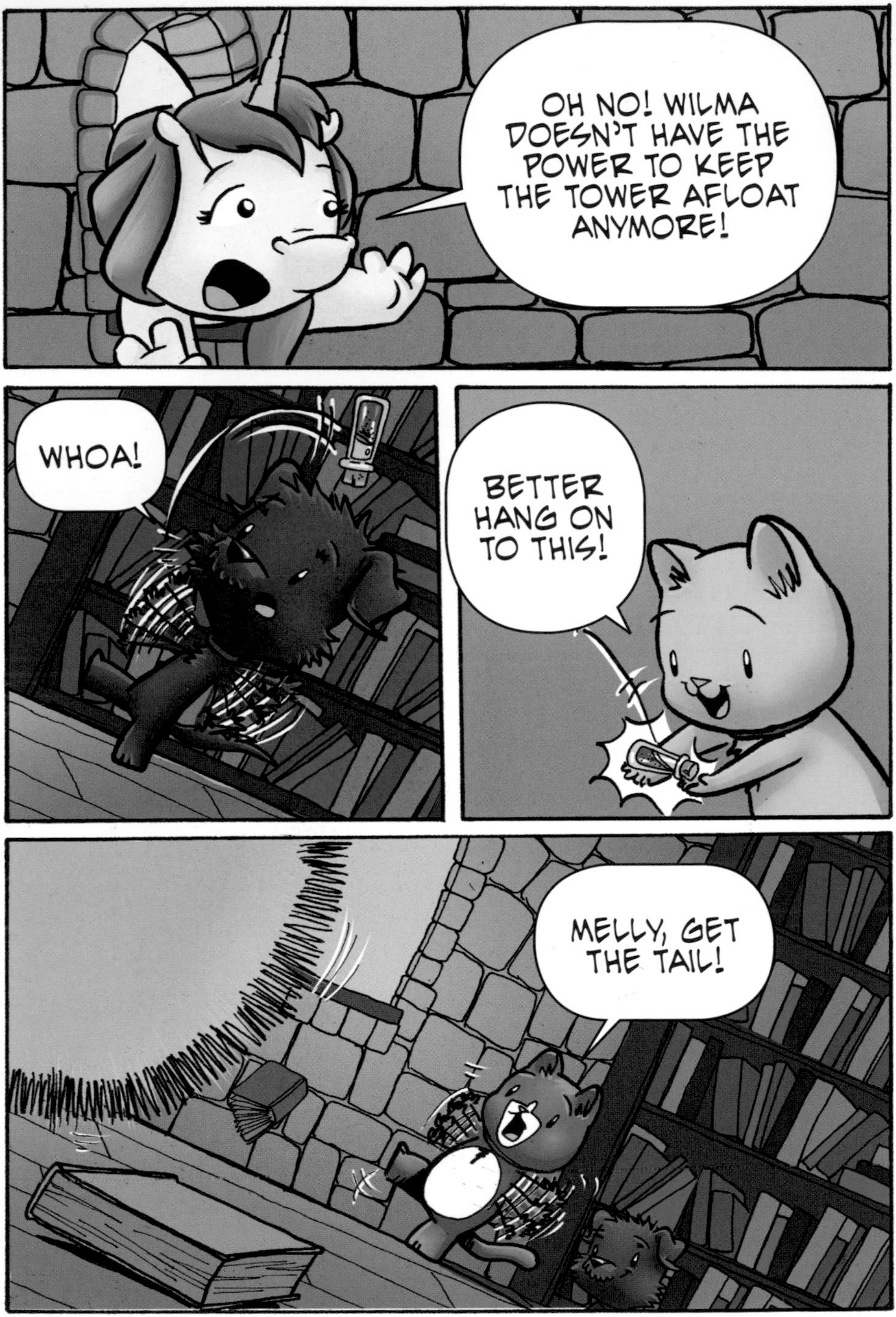
OH NO! WILMA DOESN'T HAVE THE POWER TO KEEP THE TOWER AFLOAT ANYMORE!
WHOA!
BETTER HANG ON TO THIS!
MELLY, GET THE TAIL!

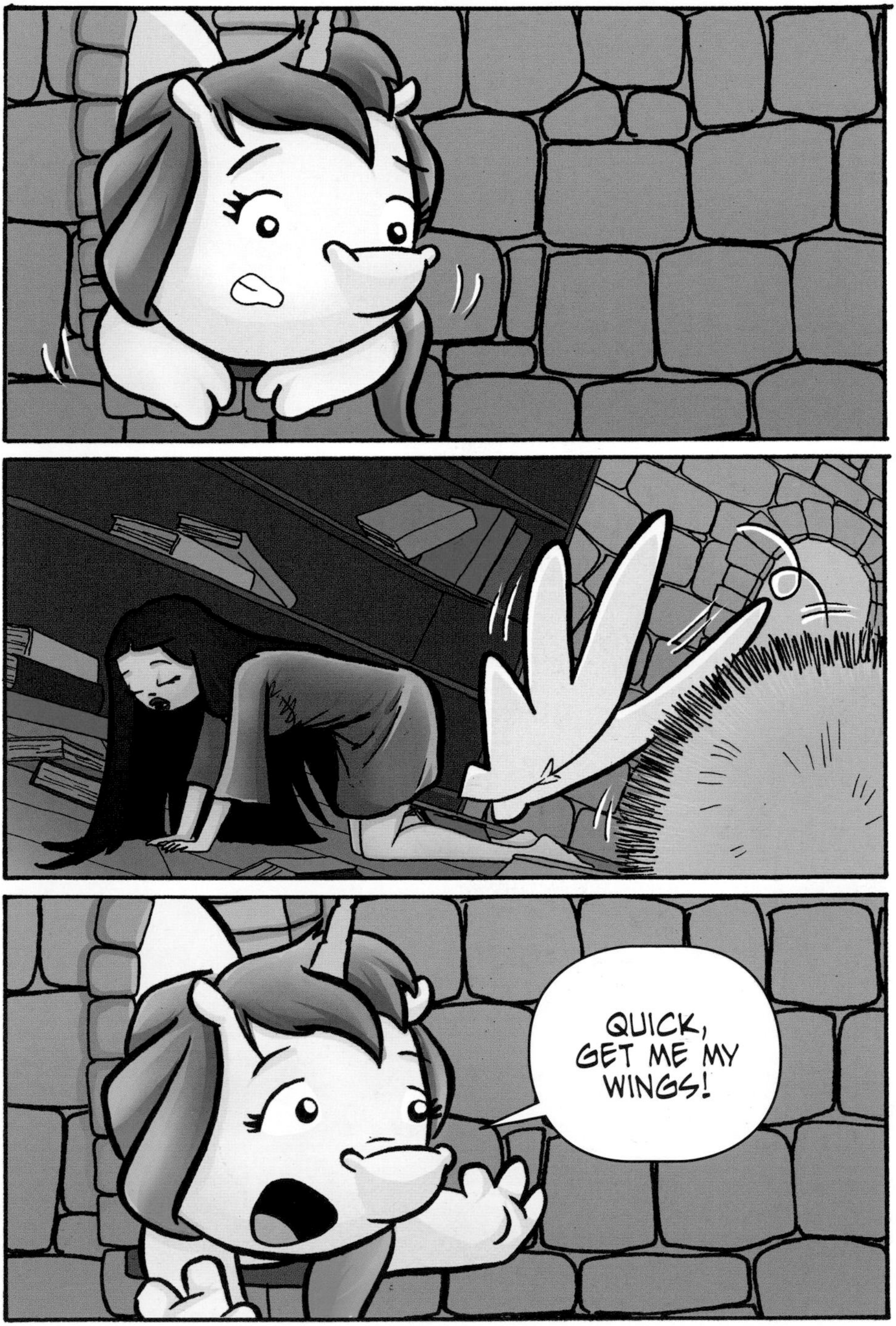
QUICK, GET ME MY WINGS!

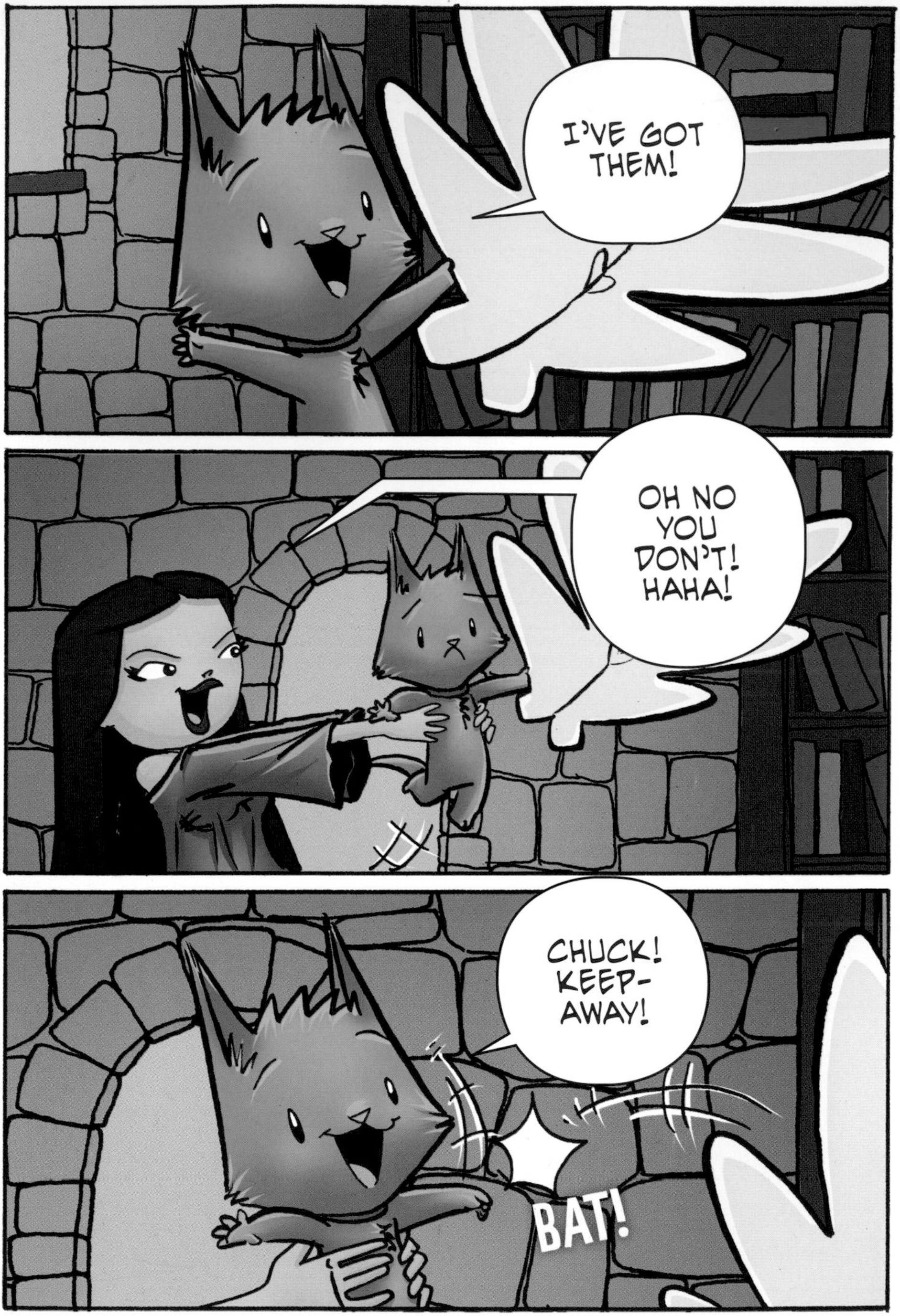
I'VE GOT THEM!
OH NO YOU DON'T! HAHA!
CHUCK! KEEP-AWAY!
BAT!

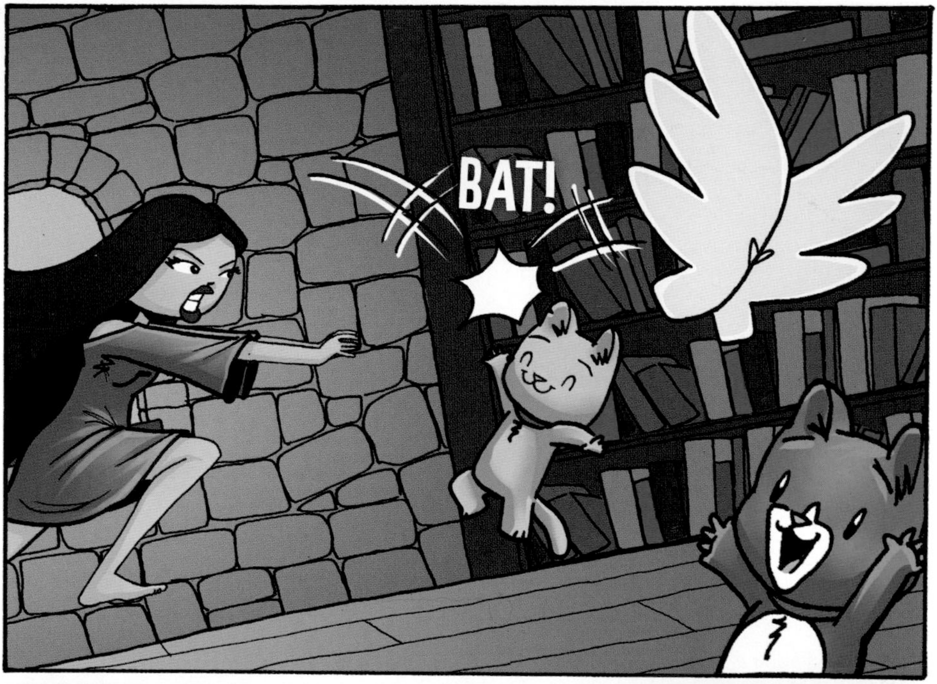
BAT!

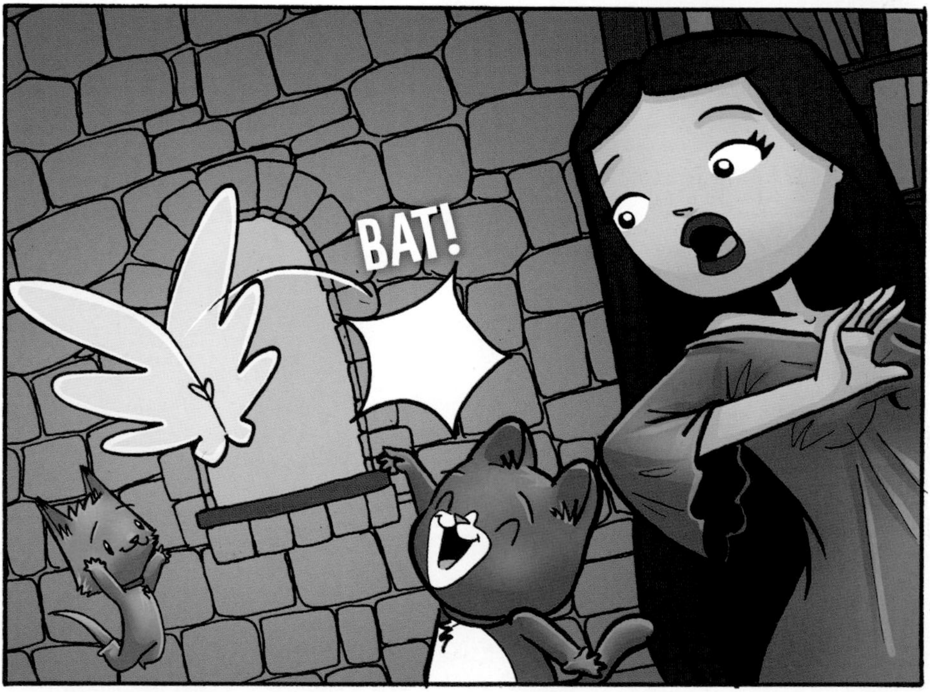
BAT!

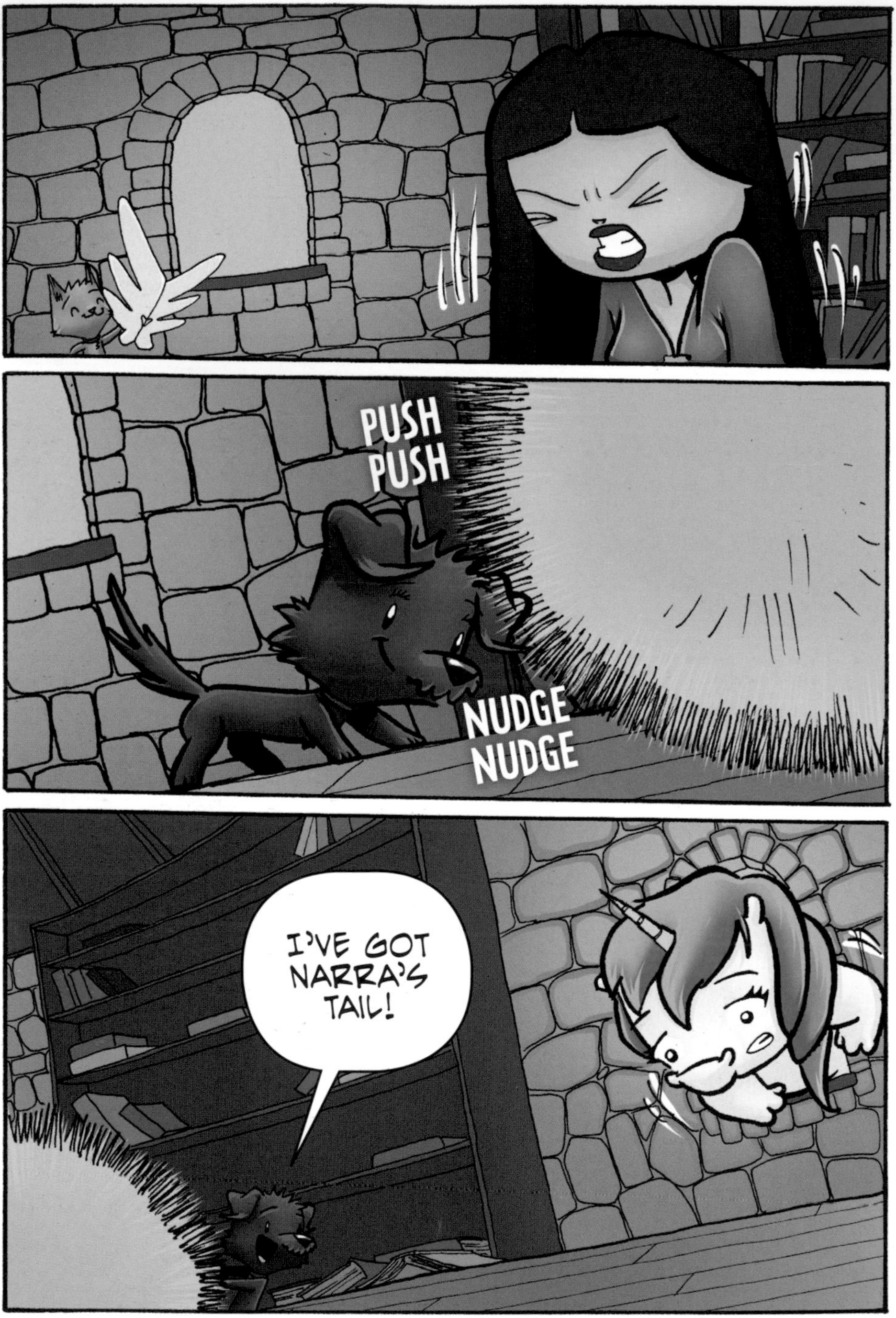
PUSH
PUSH
NUDGE
NUDGE
I'VE GOT NARRA'S TAIL!

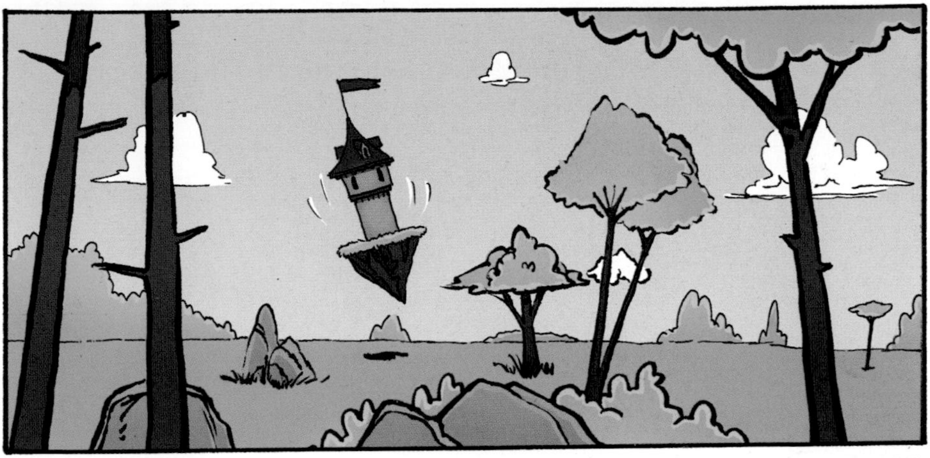

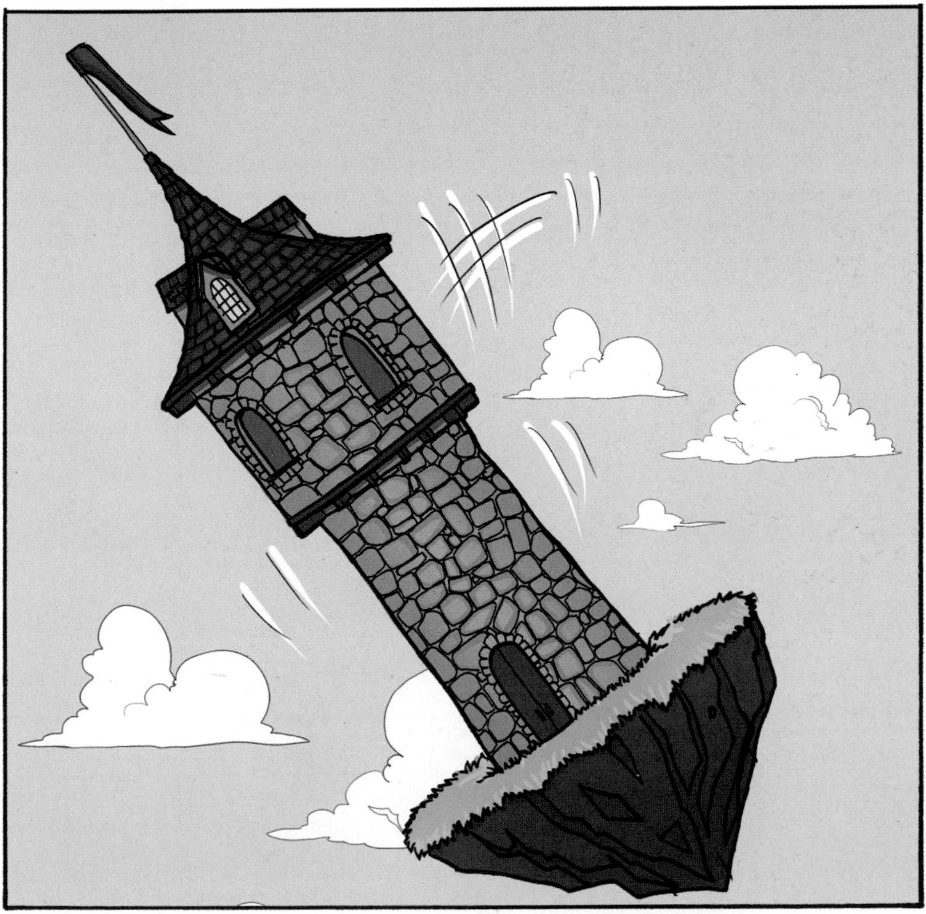

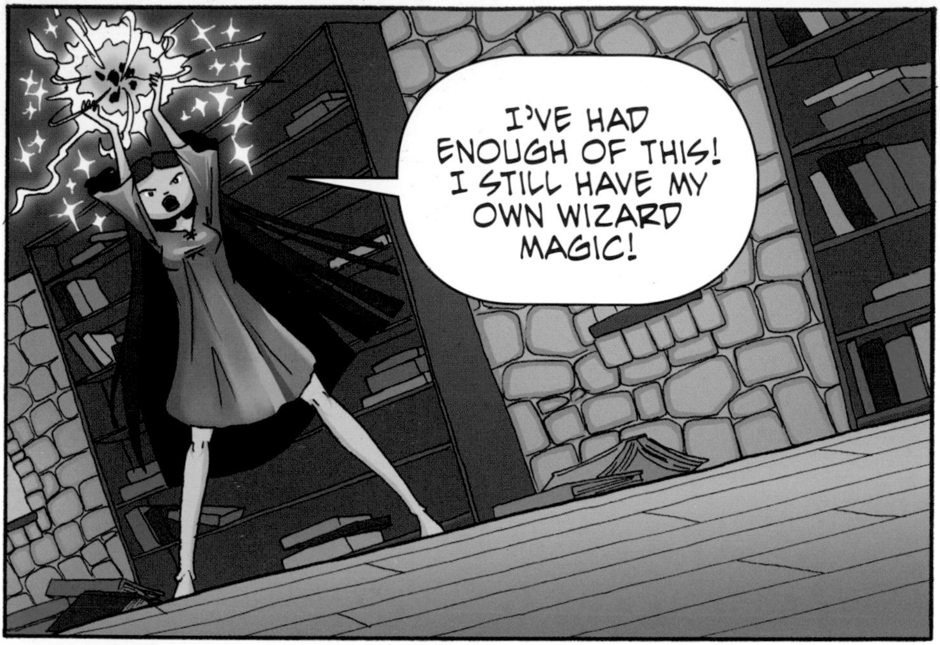
I'VE HAD ENOUGH OF THIS! I STILL HAVE MY OWN WIZARD MAGIC!

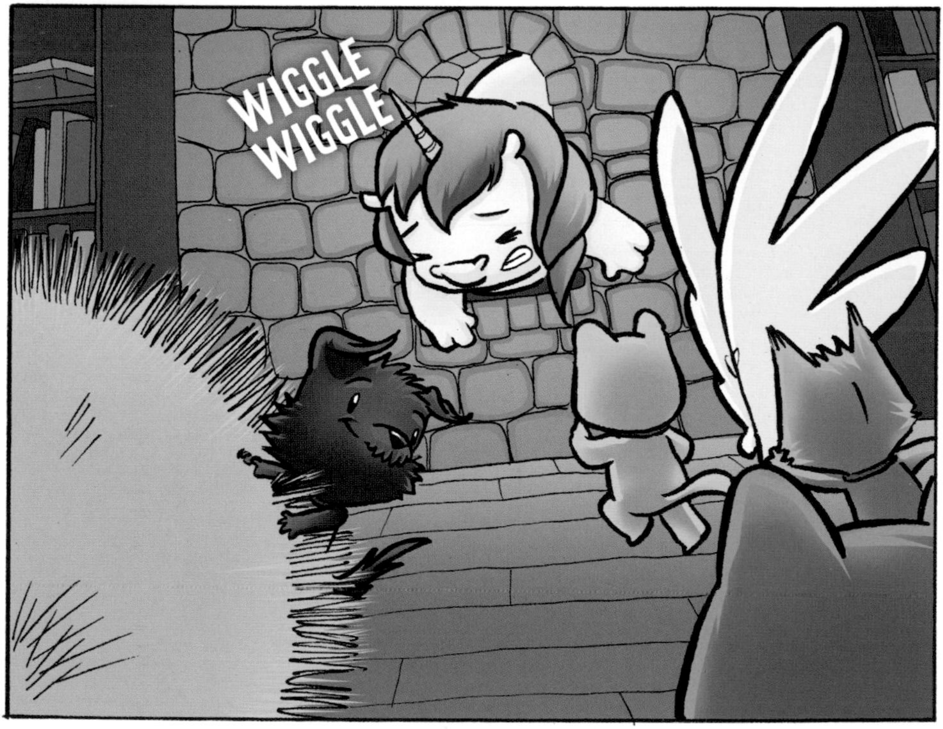
WIGGLE WIGGLE

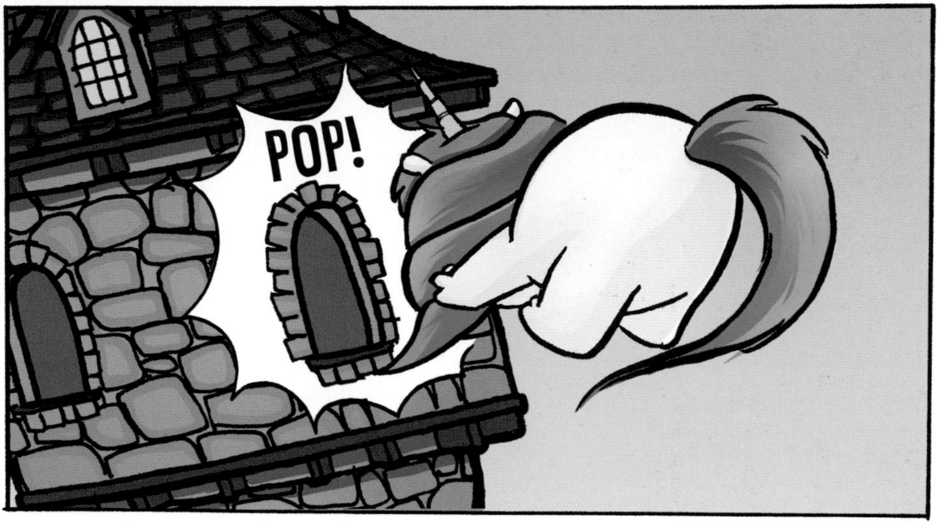
POP!

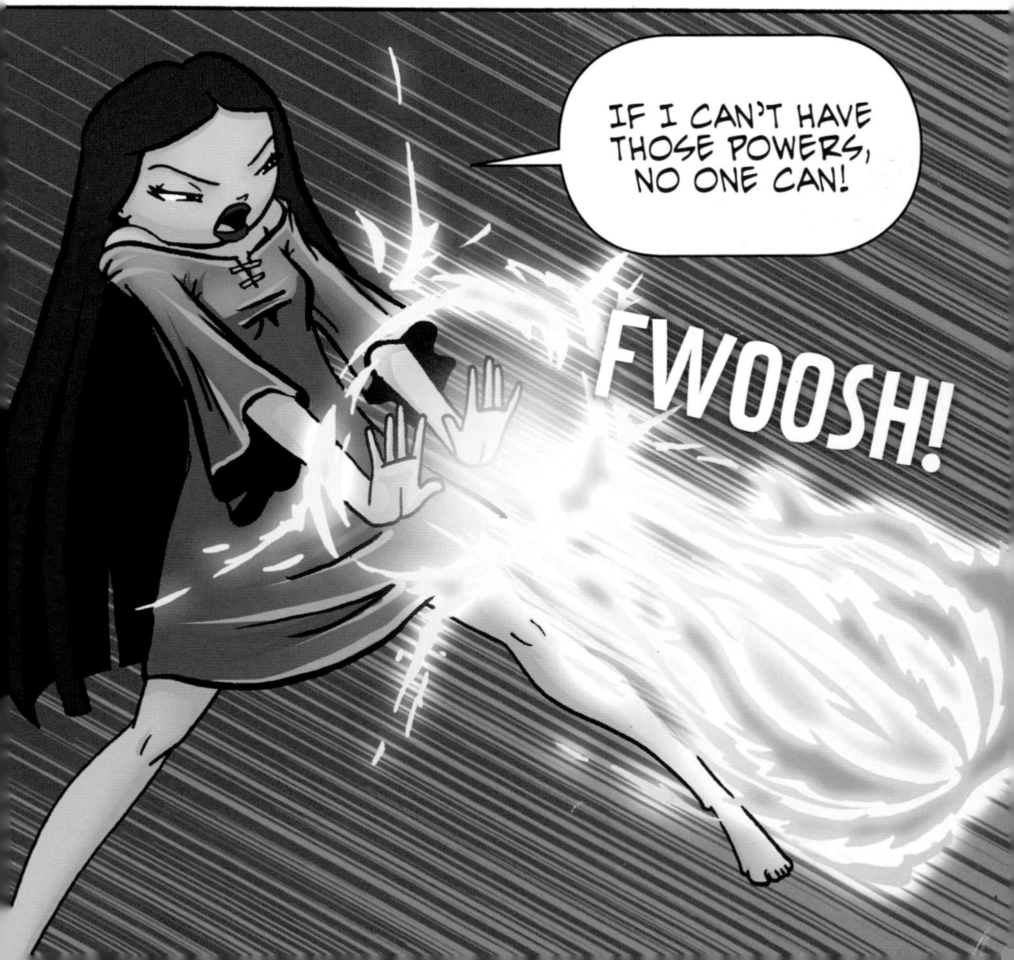
IF I CAN'T HAVE THOSE POWERS, NO ONE CAN!
FWOOSH!

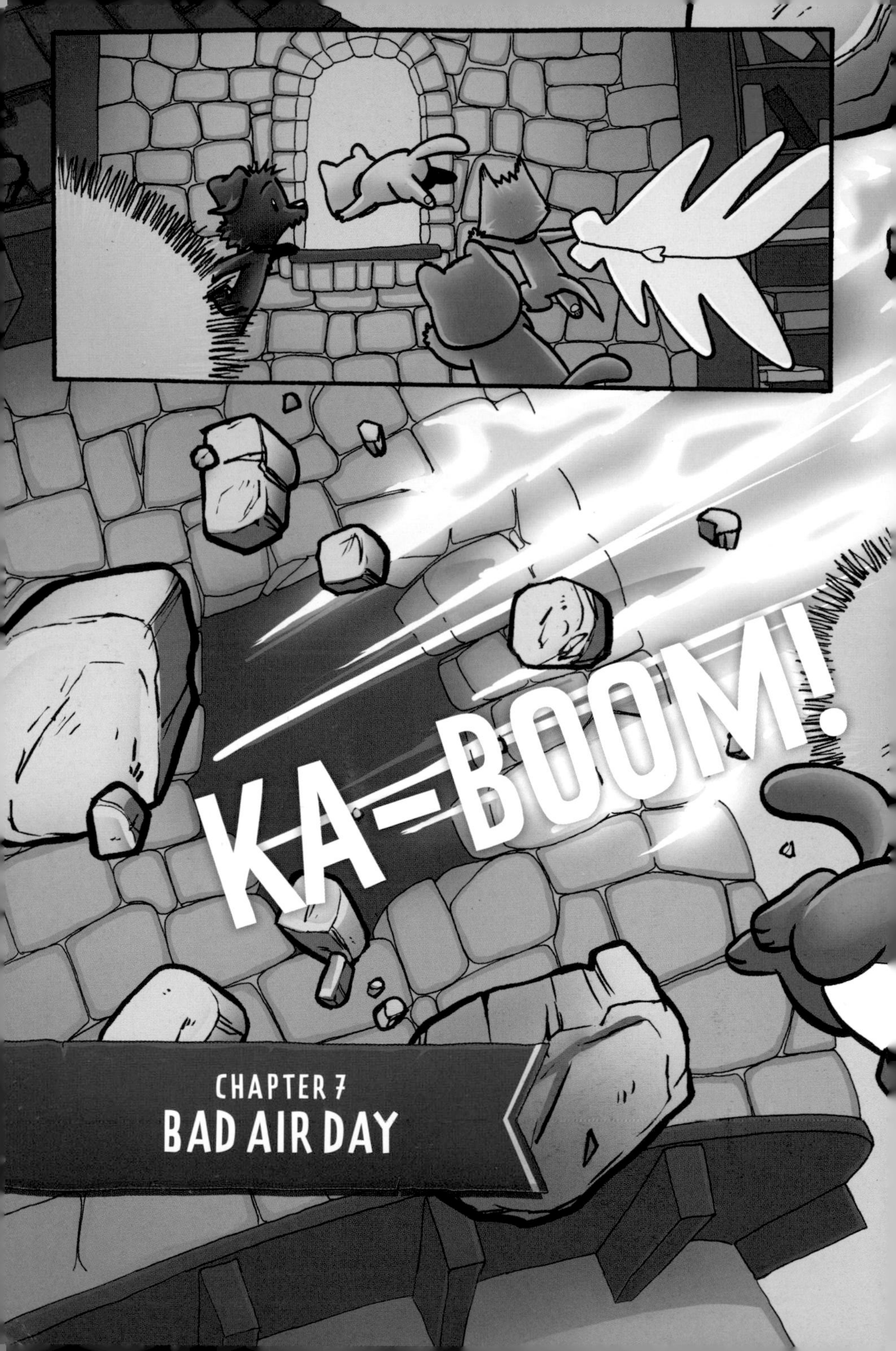
KA-BOOM!

CHAPTER 7
BAD AIR DAY

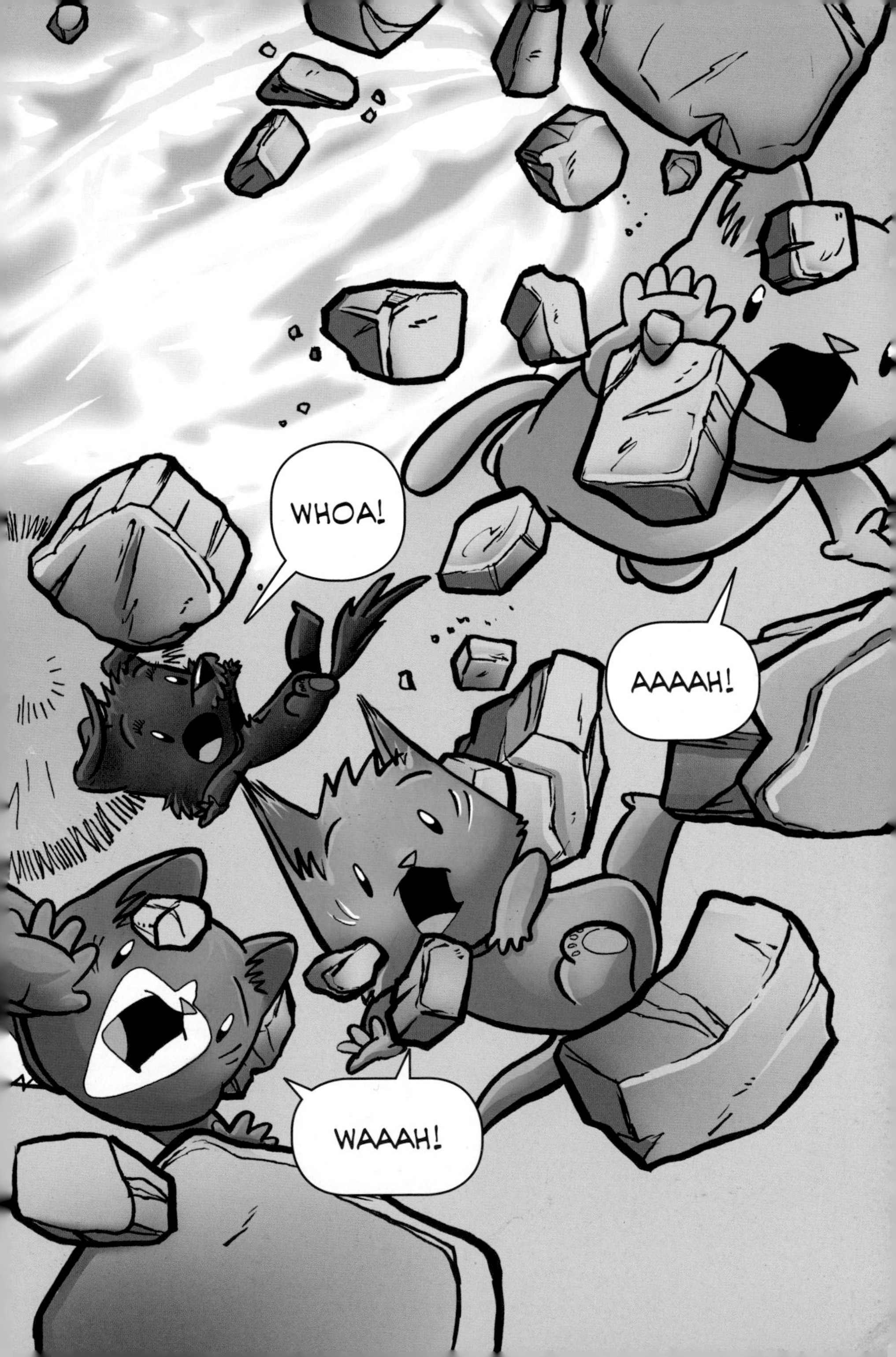
WHOA!
AAAAH!
WAAAH!

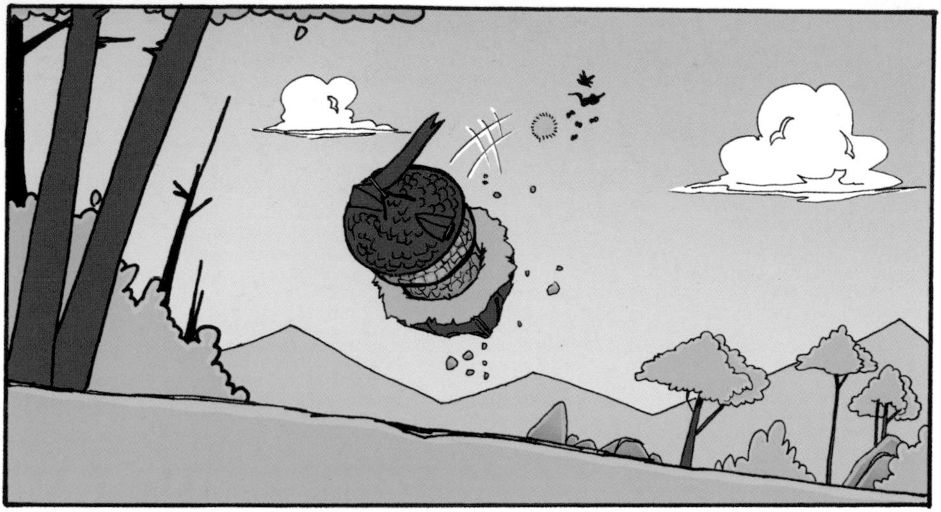

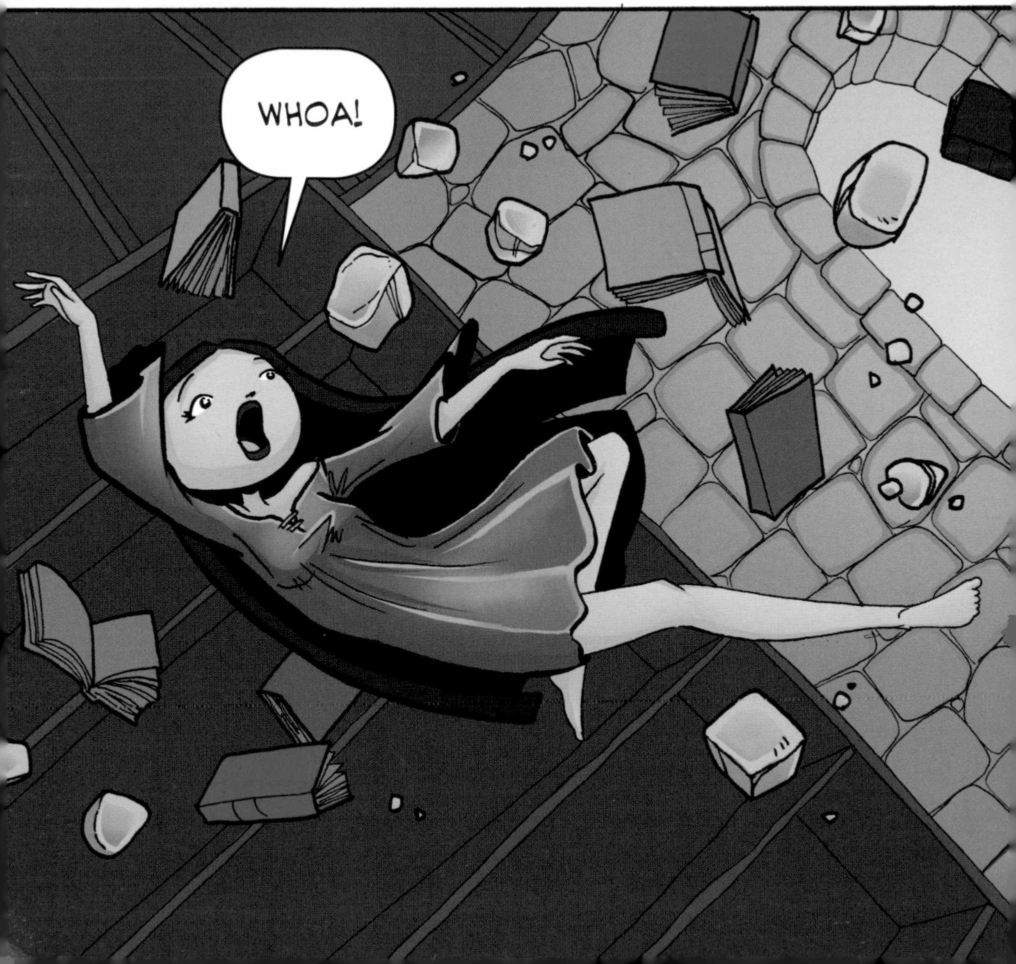
WHOA!

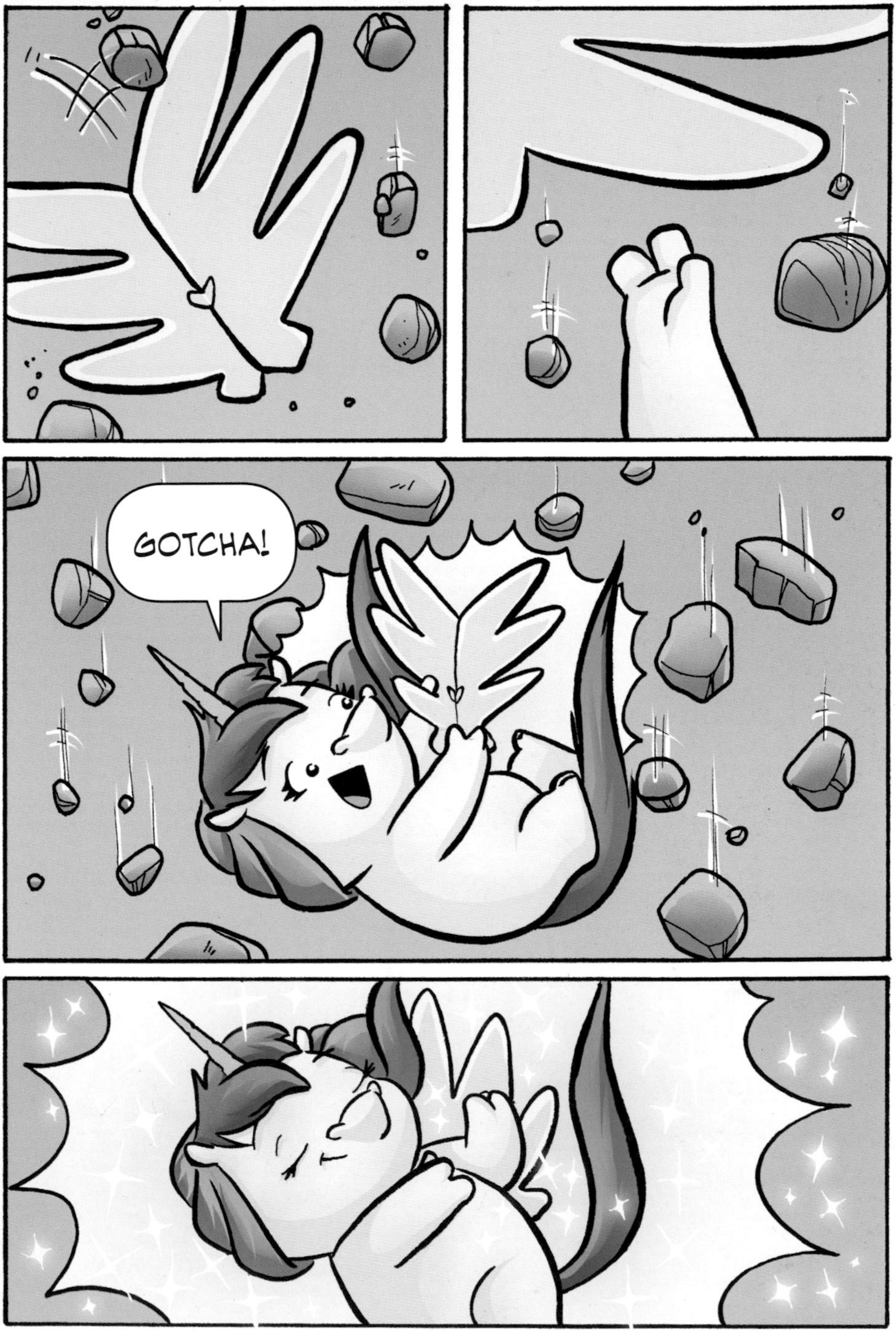
GOTCHA!

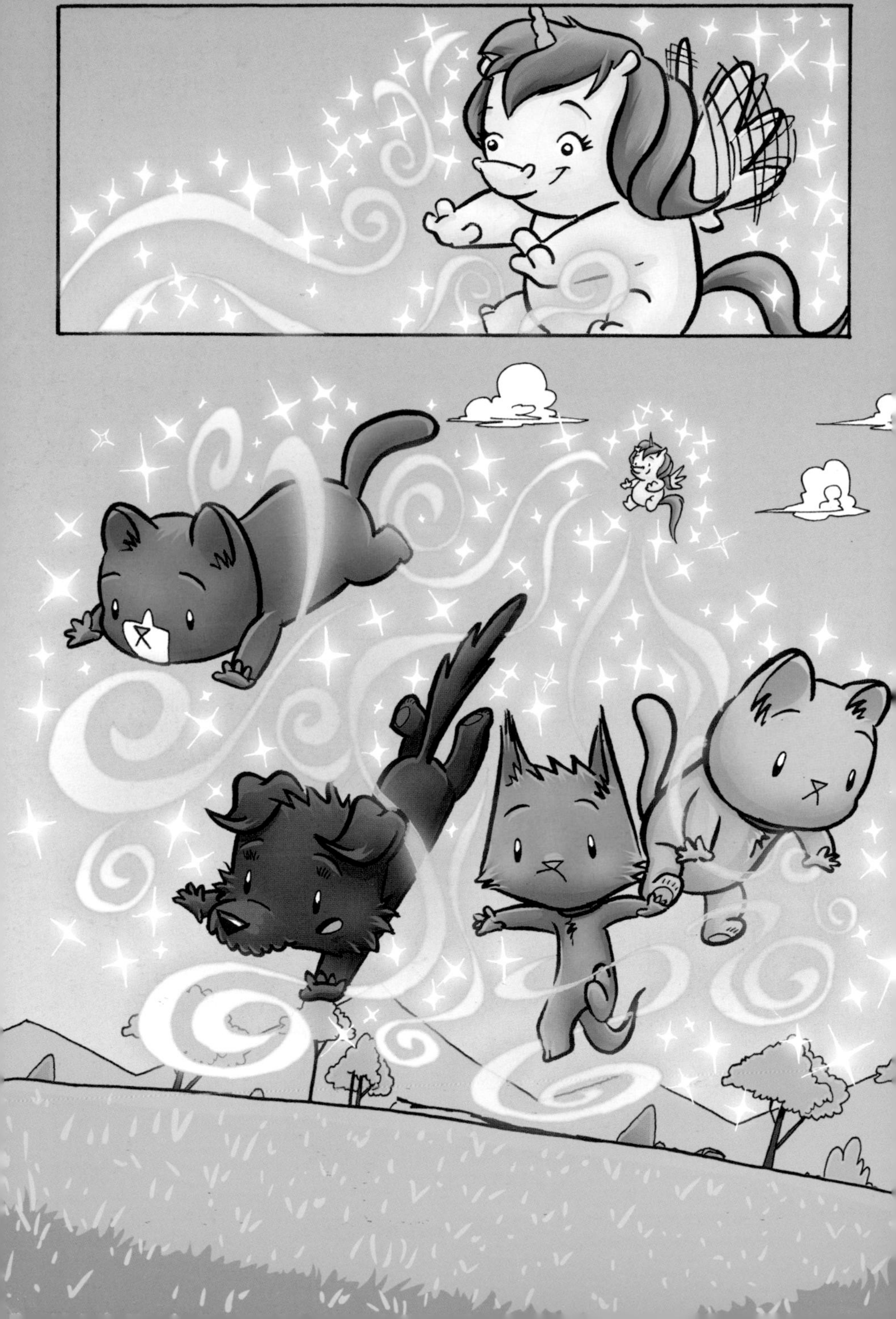

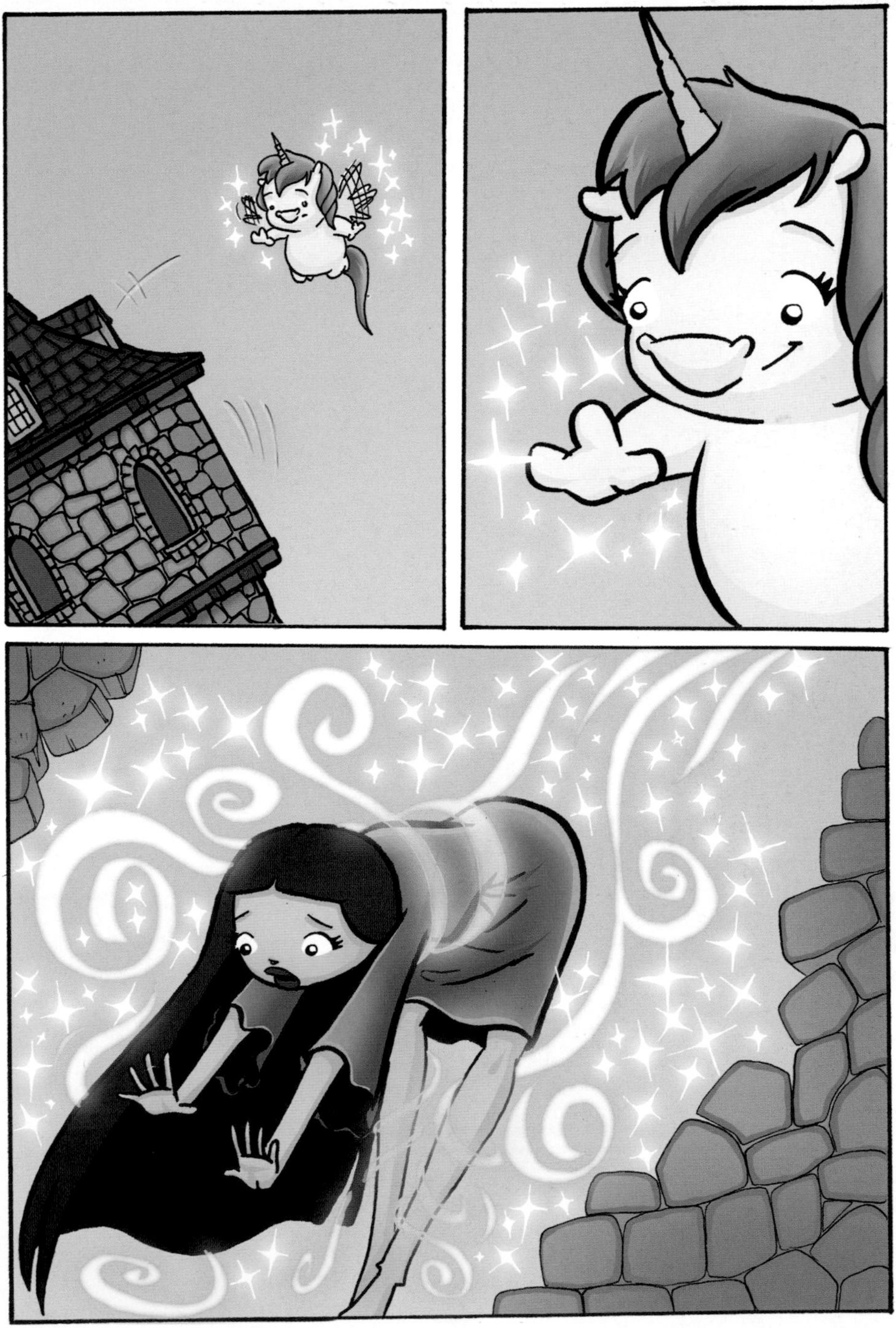

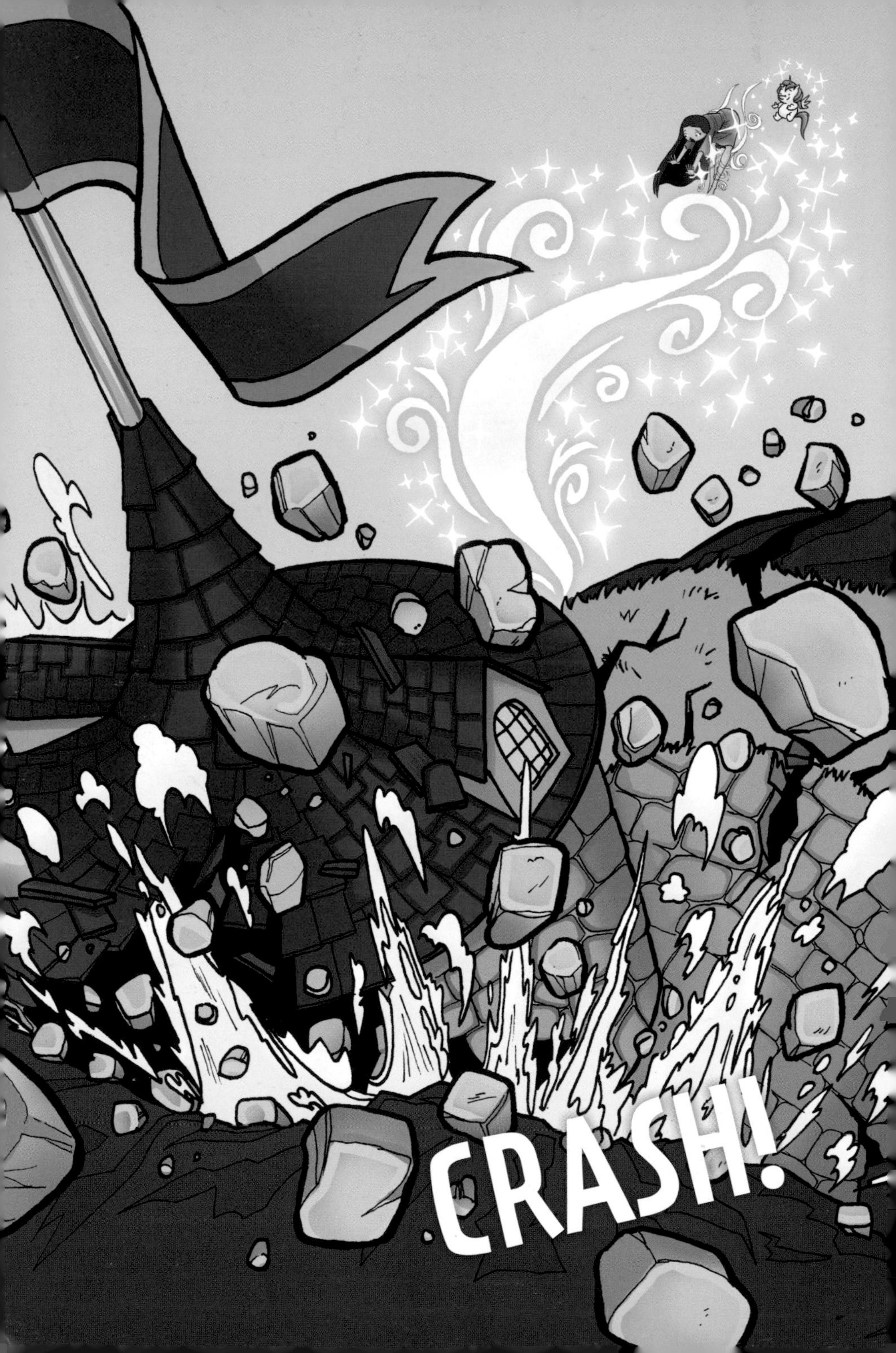
CRASH!

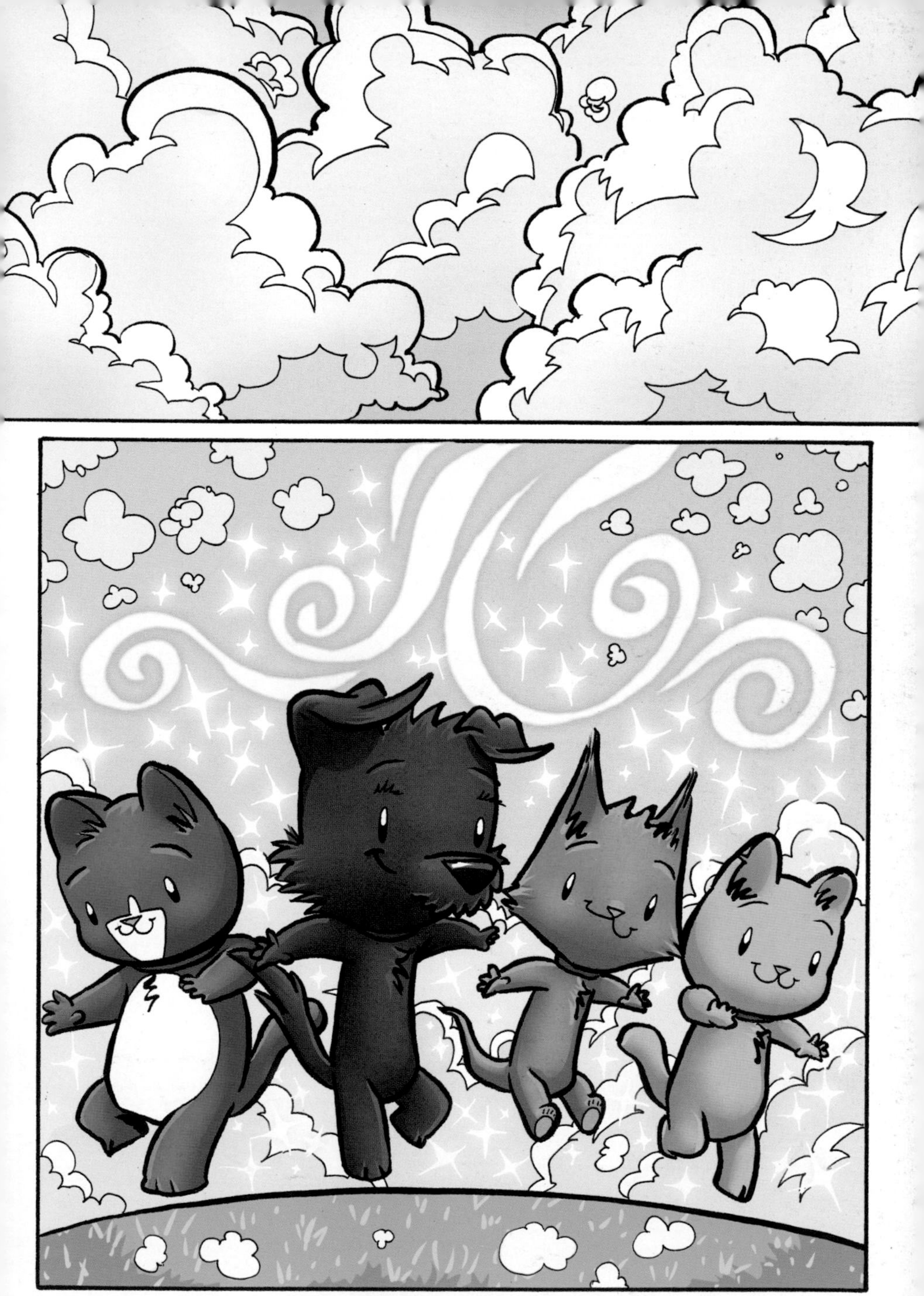

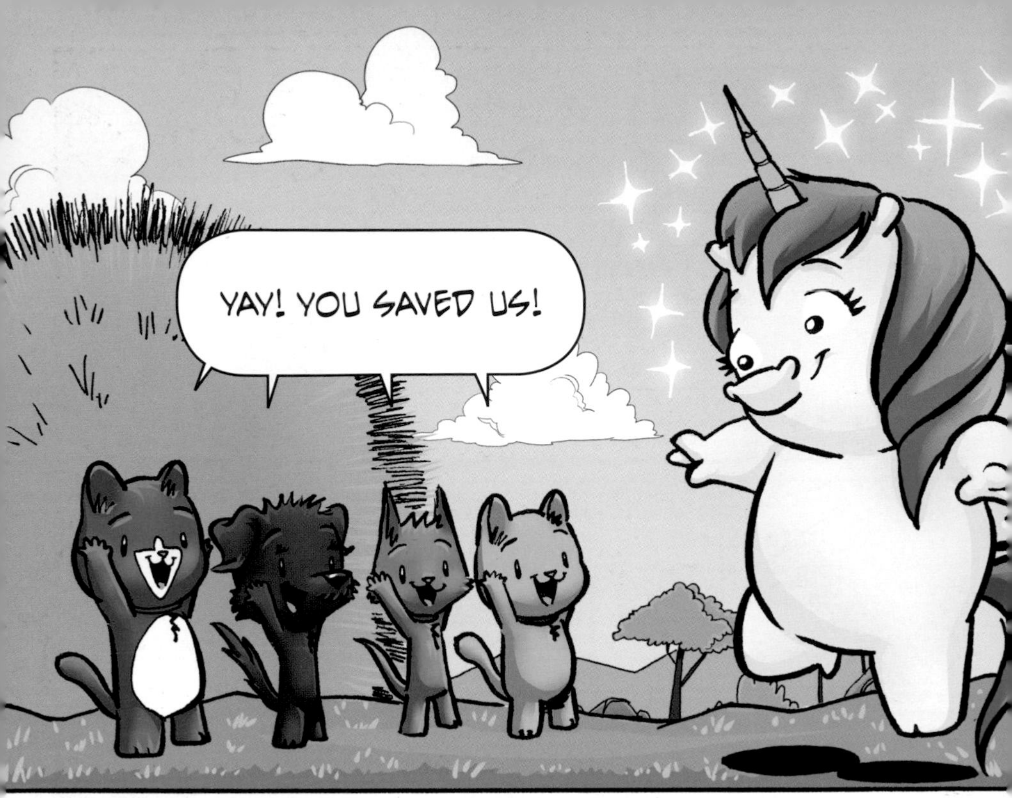
YAY! YOU SAVED US!

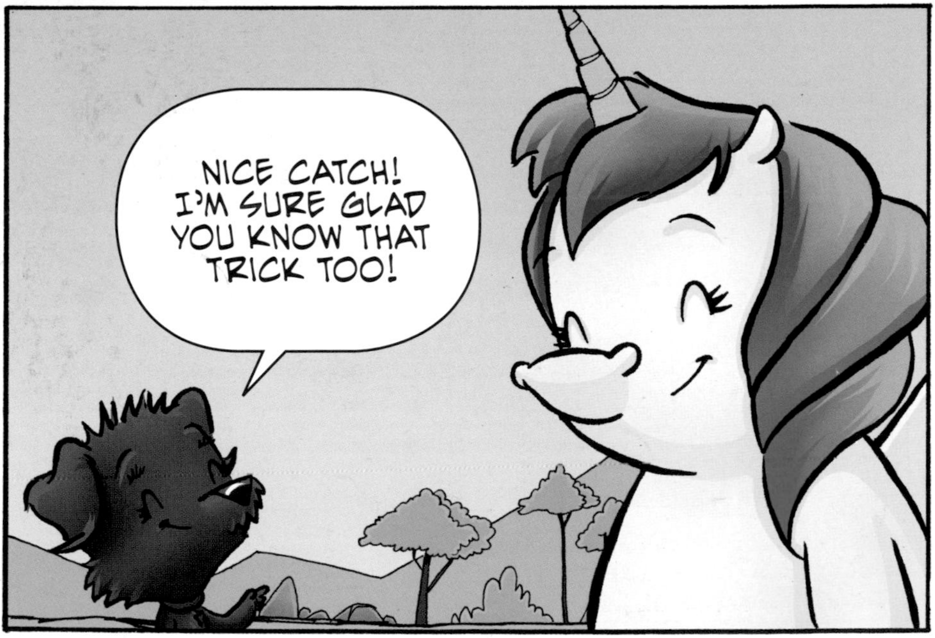
NICE CATCH! I'M SURE GLAD YOU KNOW THAT TRICK TOO!

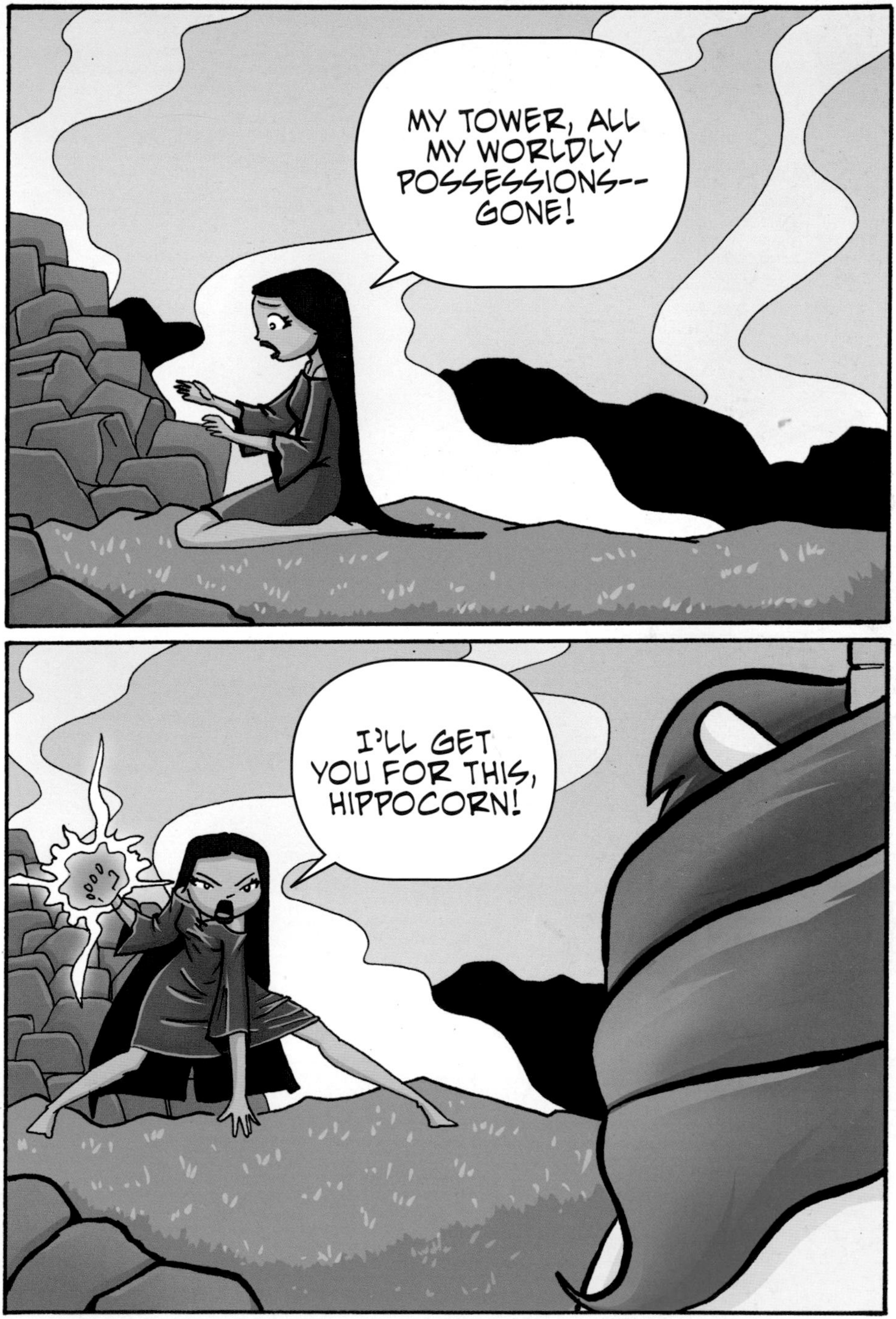
MY TOWER, ALL MY WORLDLY POSSESSIONS-- GONE!
I'LL GET YOU FOR THIS, HIPPOCORN!

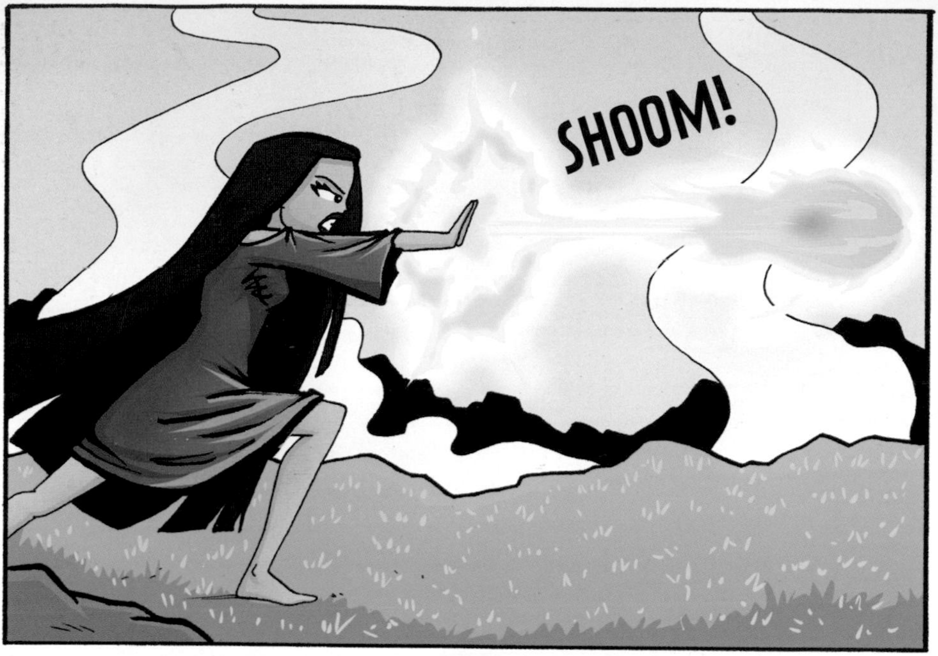
SHOOM!

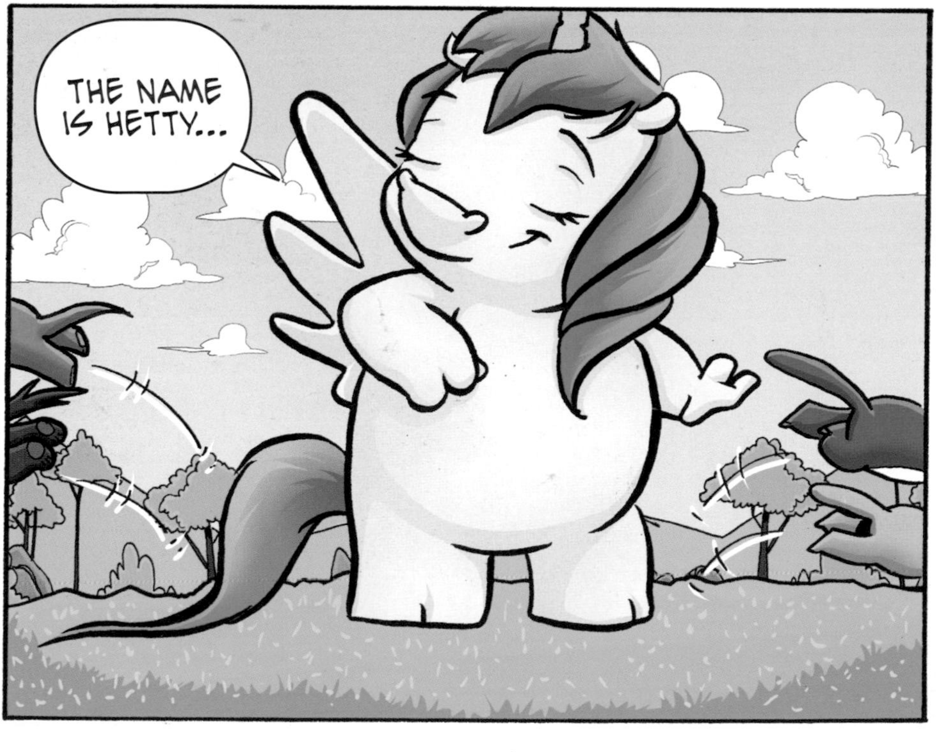
THE NAME IS HETTY...

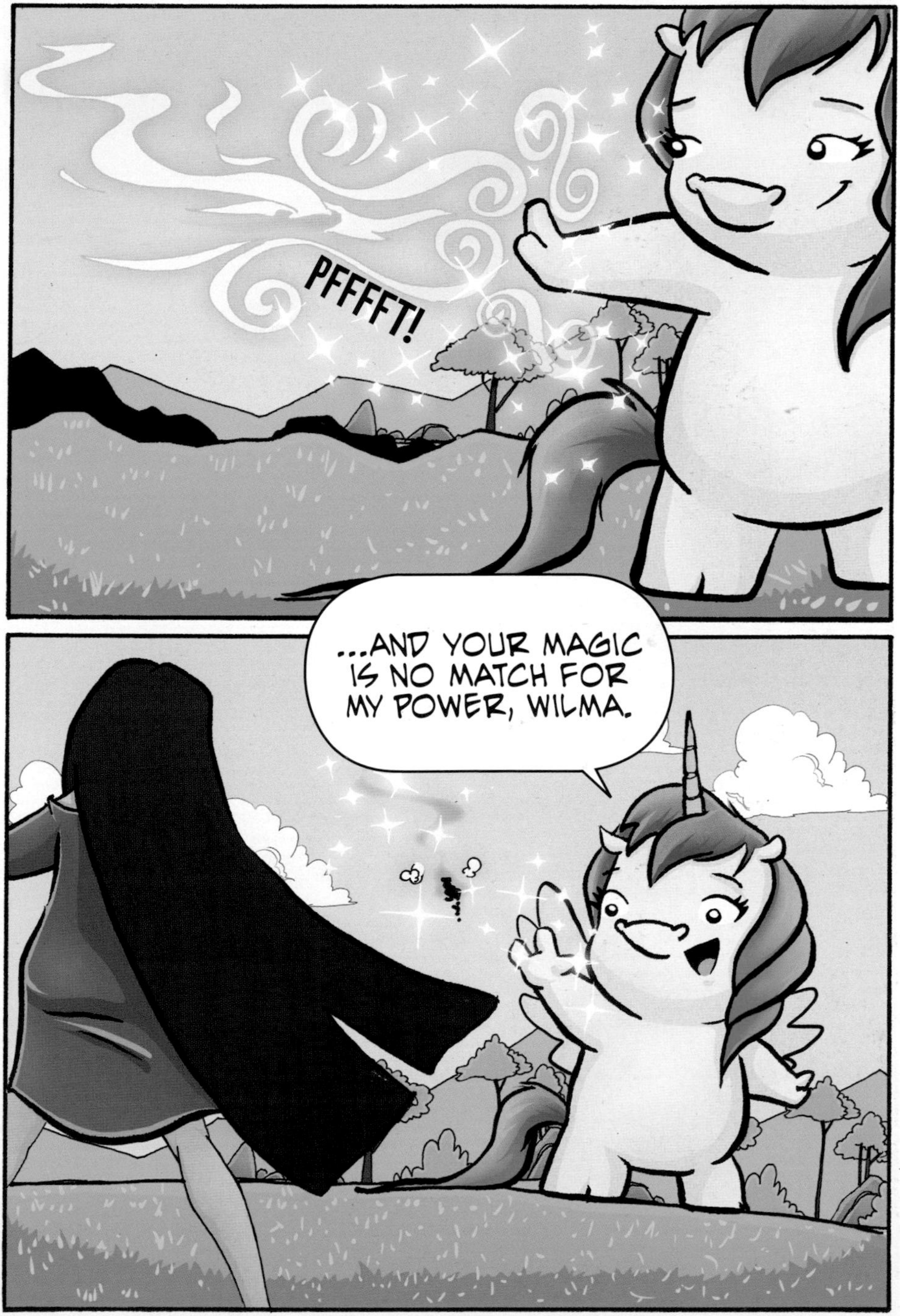
PFFFFT!
...AND YOUR MAGIC IS NO MATCH FOR MY POWER, WILMA.

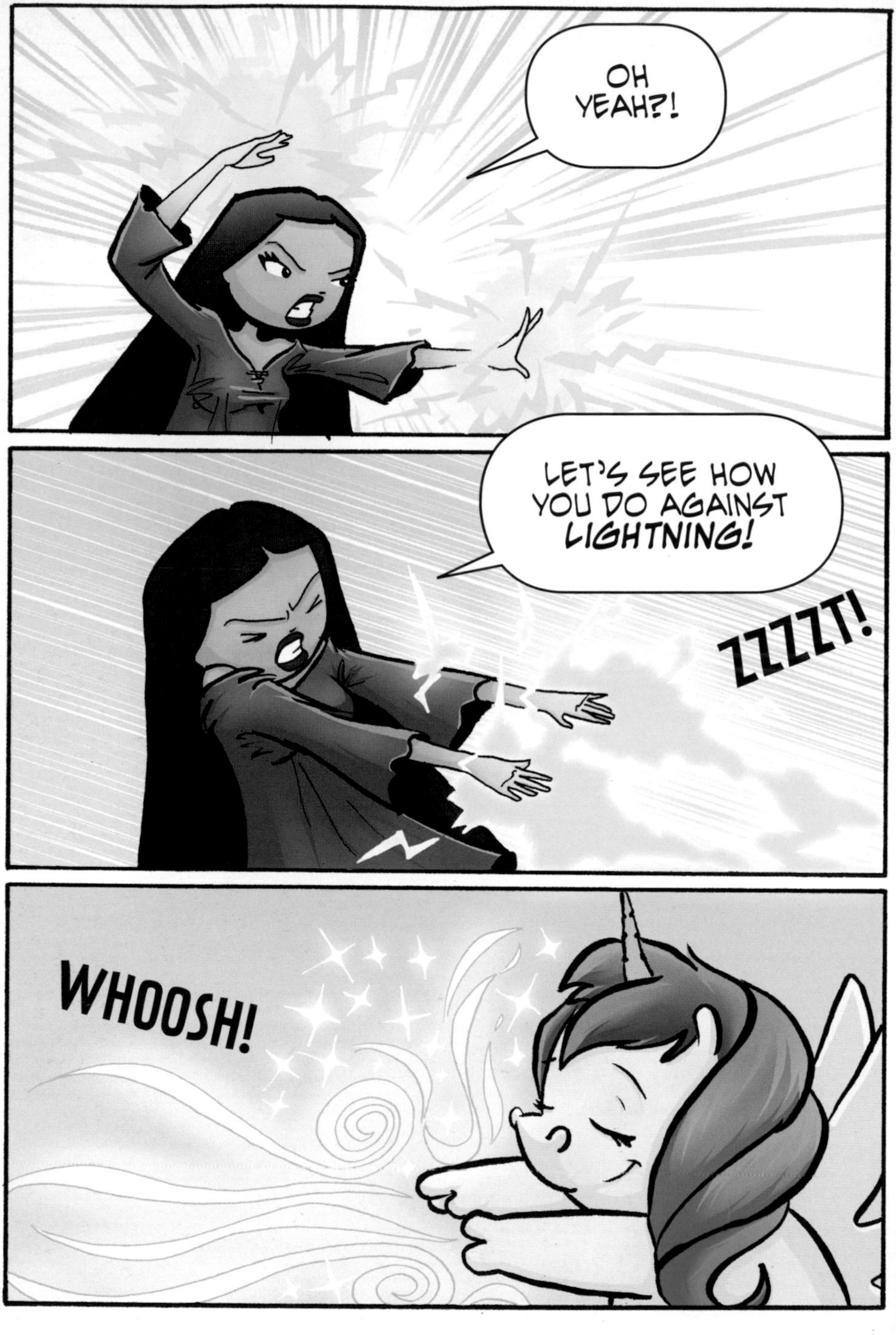
OH YEAH?!
LET'S SEE HOW YOU DO AGAINST LIGHTNING!
ZZZZZT!
WHOOSH!

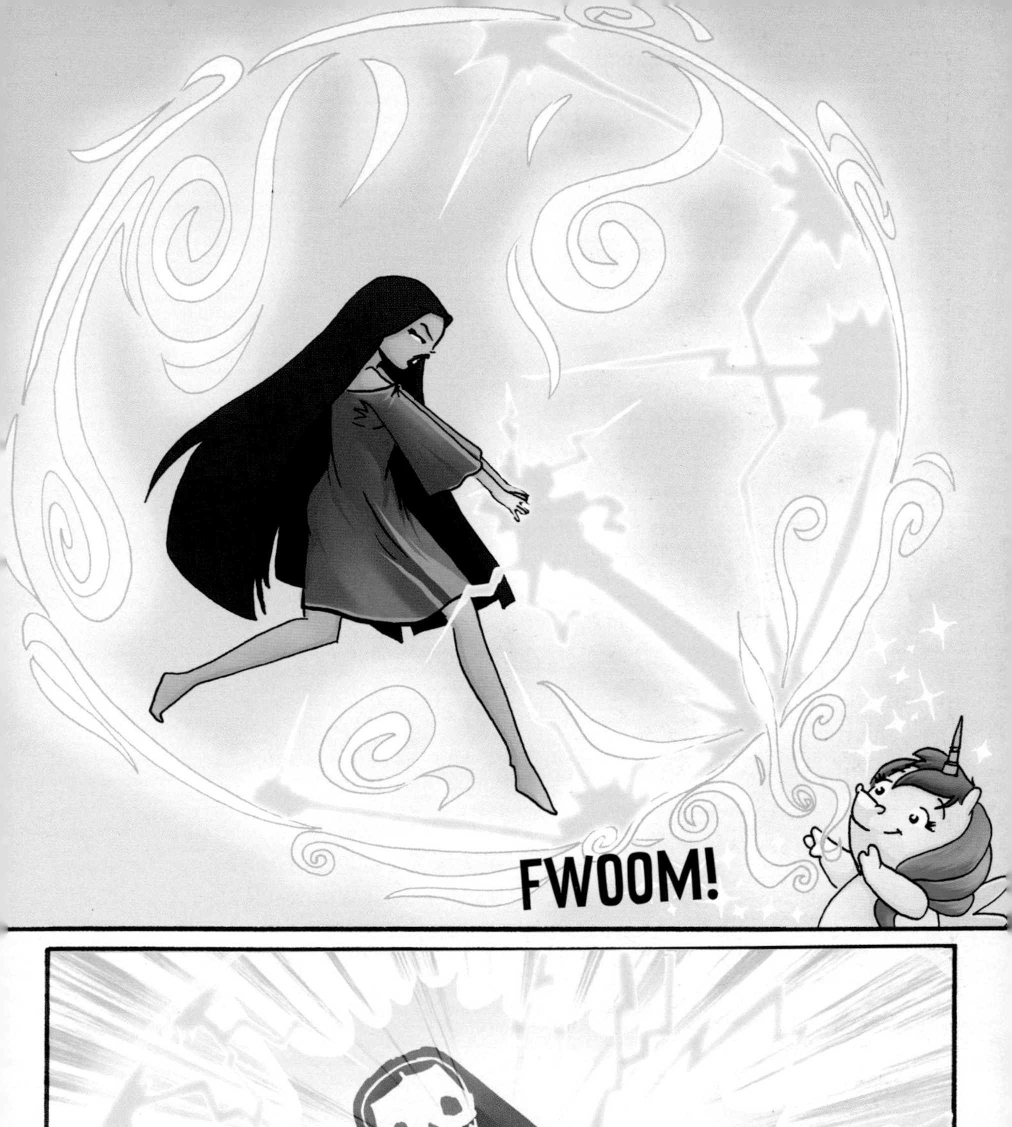
FWOOM!

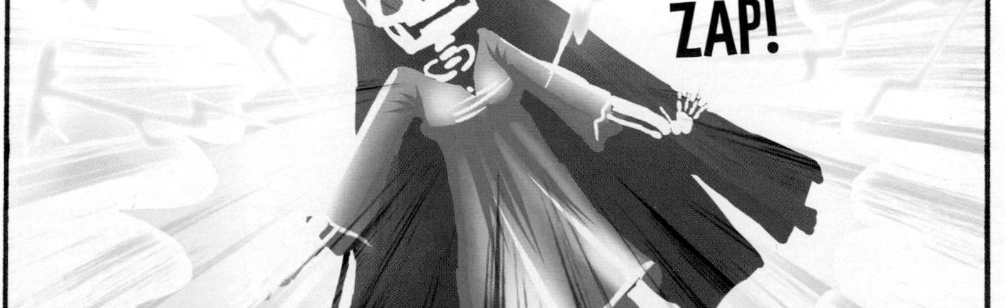
ZAP!

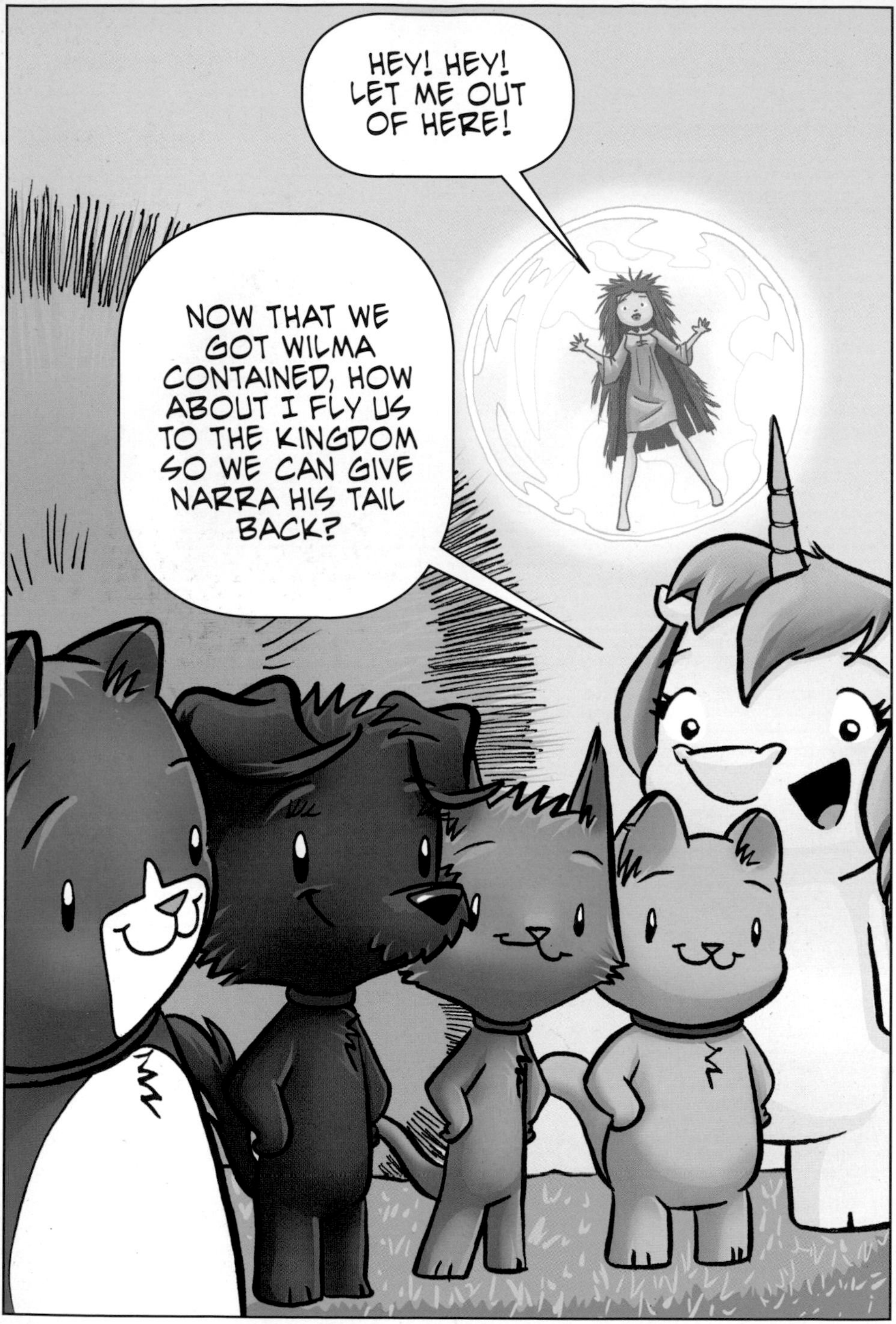
HEY! HEY! LET ME OUT OF HERE!
NOW THAT WE GOT WILMA CONTAINED, HOW ABOUT I FLY US TO THE KINGDOM SO WE CAN GIVE NARRA HIS TAIL BACK?

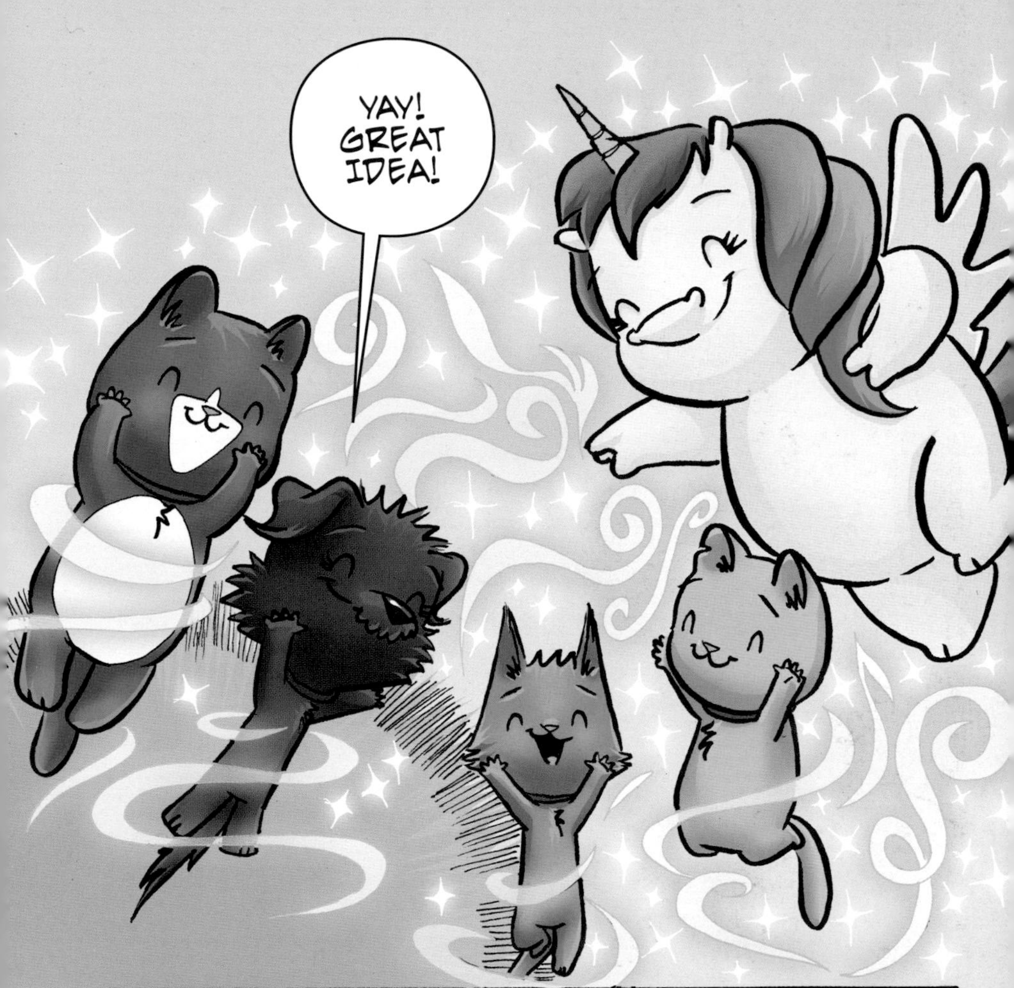
YAY! GREAT IDEA!
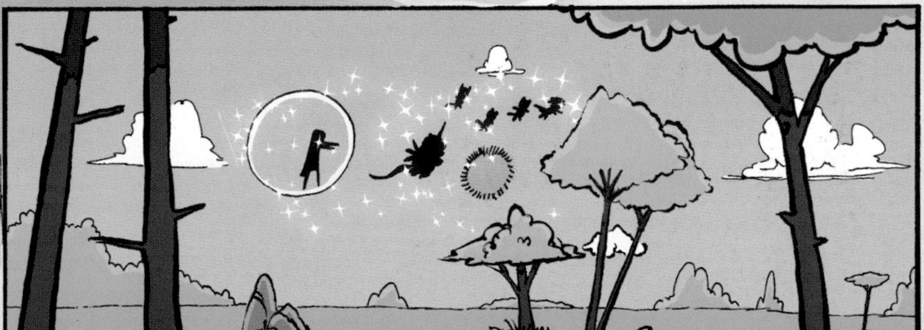

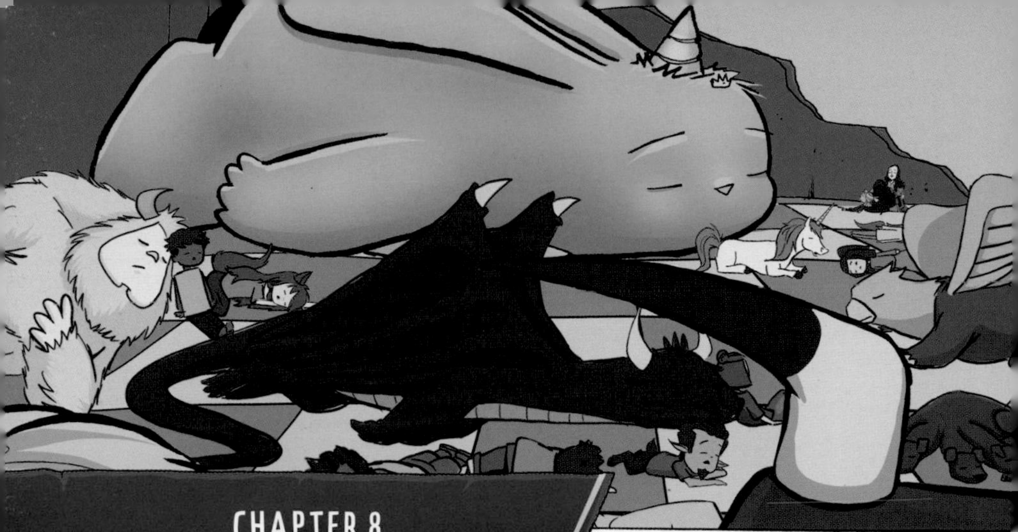

CHAPTER 8

WHOLE AGAIN

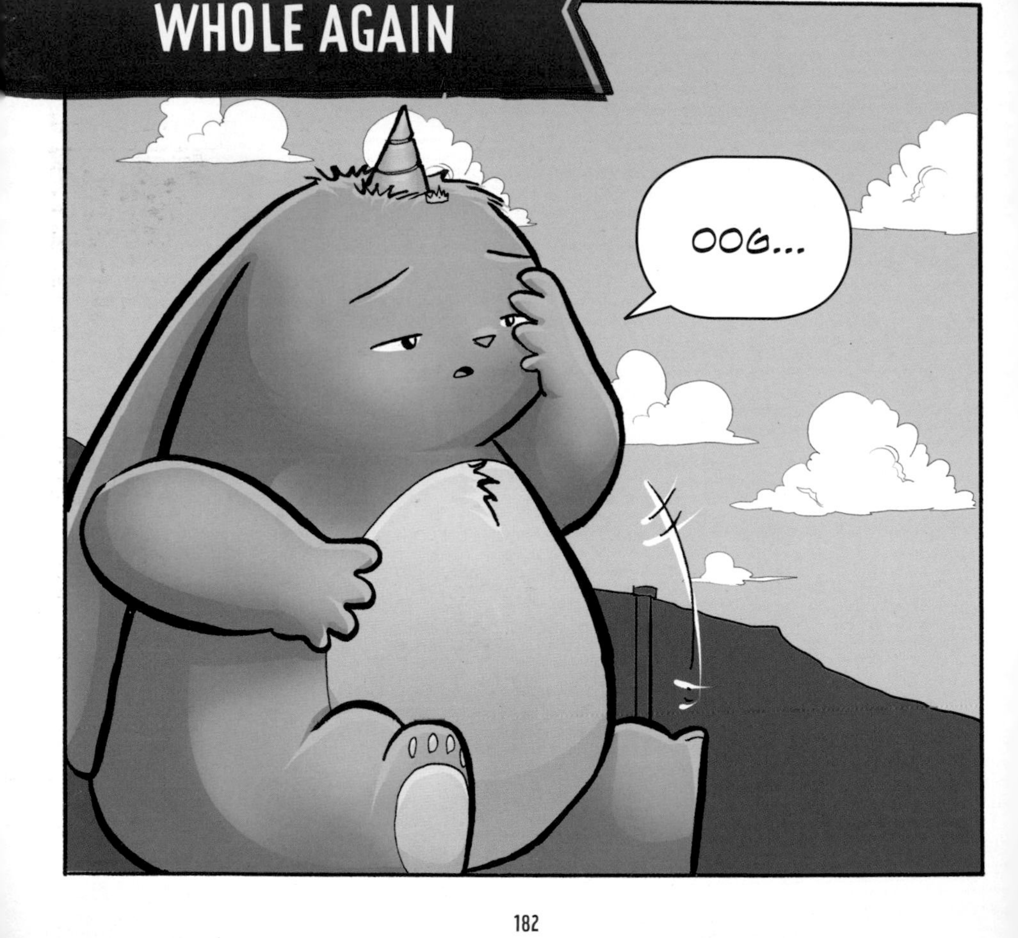
OOG...

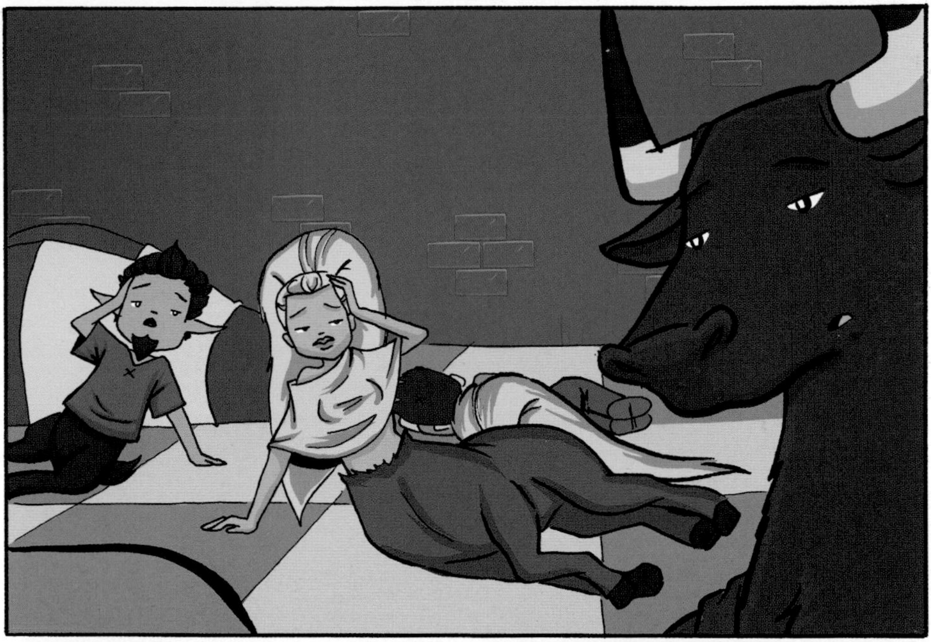

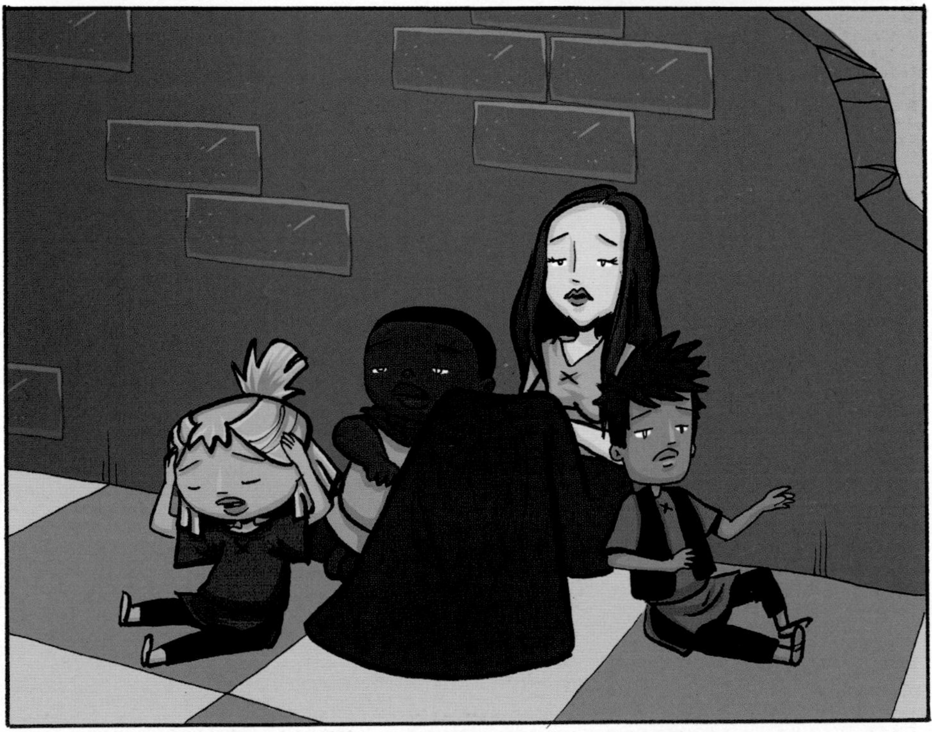

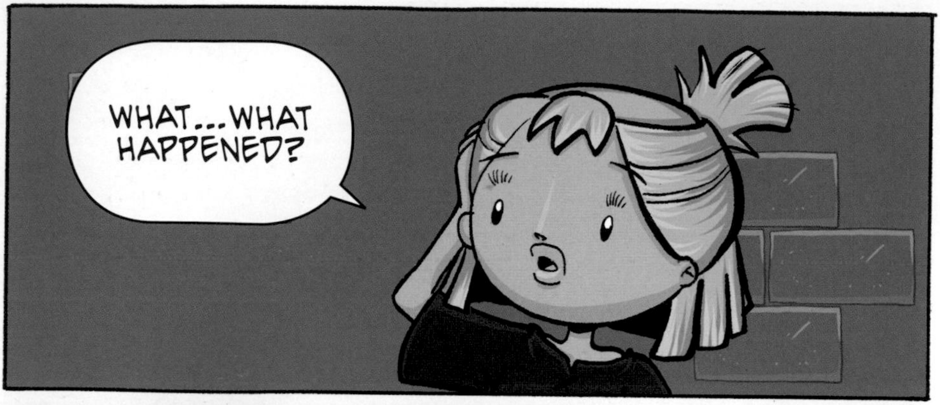
WHAT...WHAT HAPPENED?

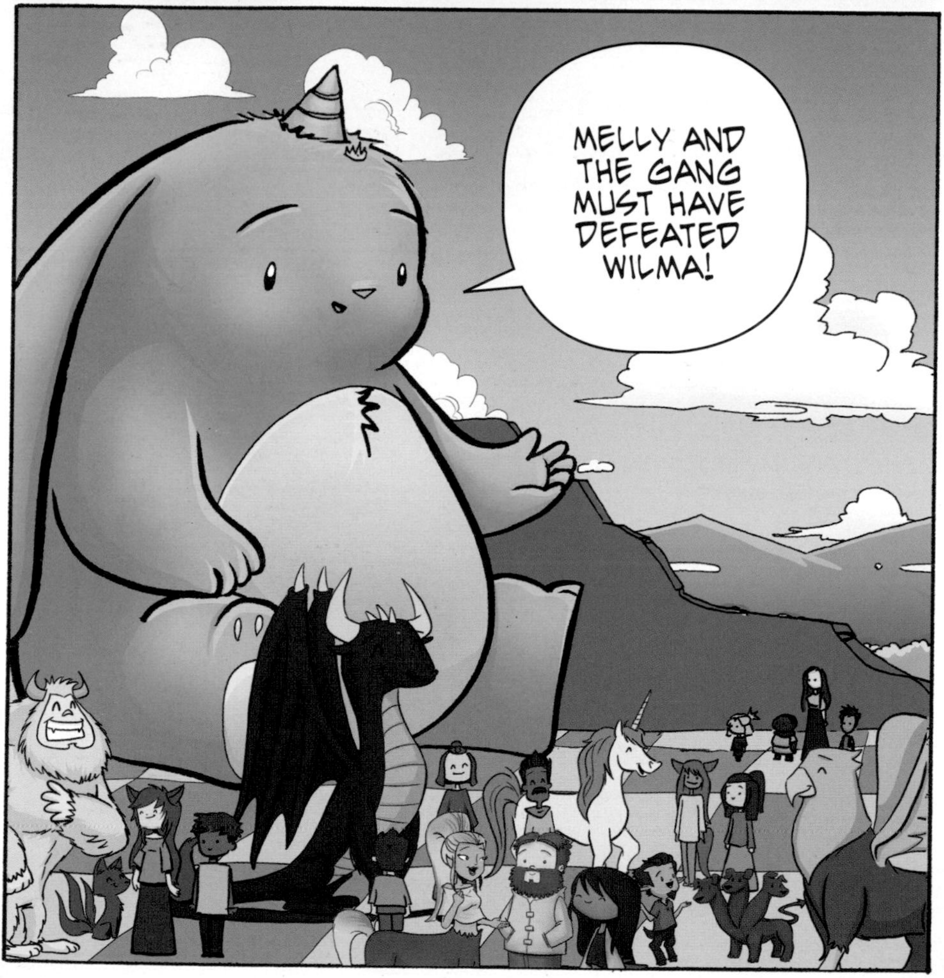
MELLY AND THE GANG MUST HAVE DEFEATED WILMA!

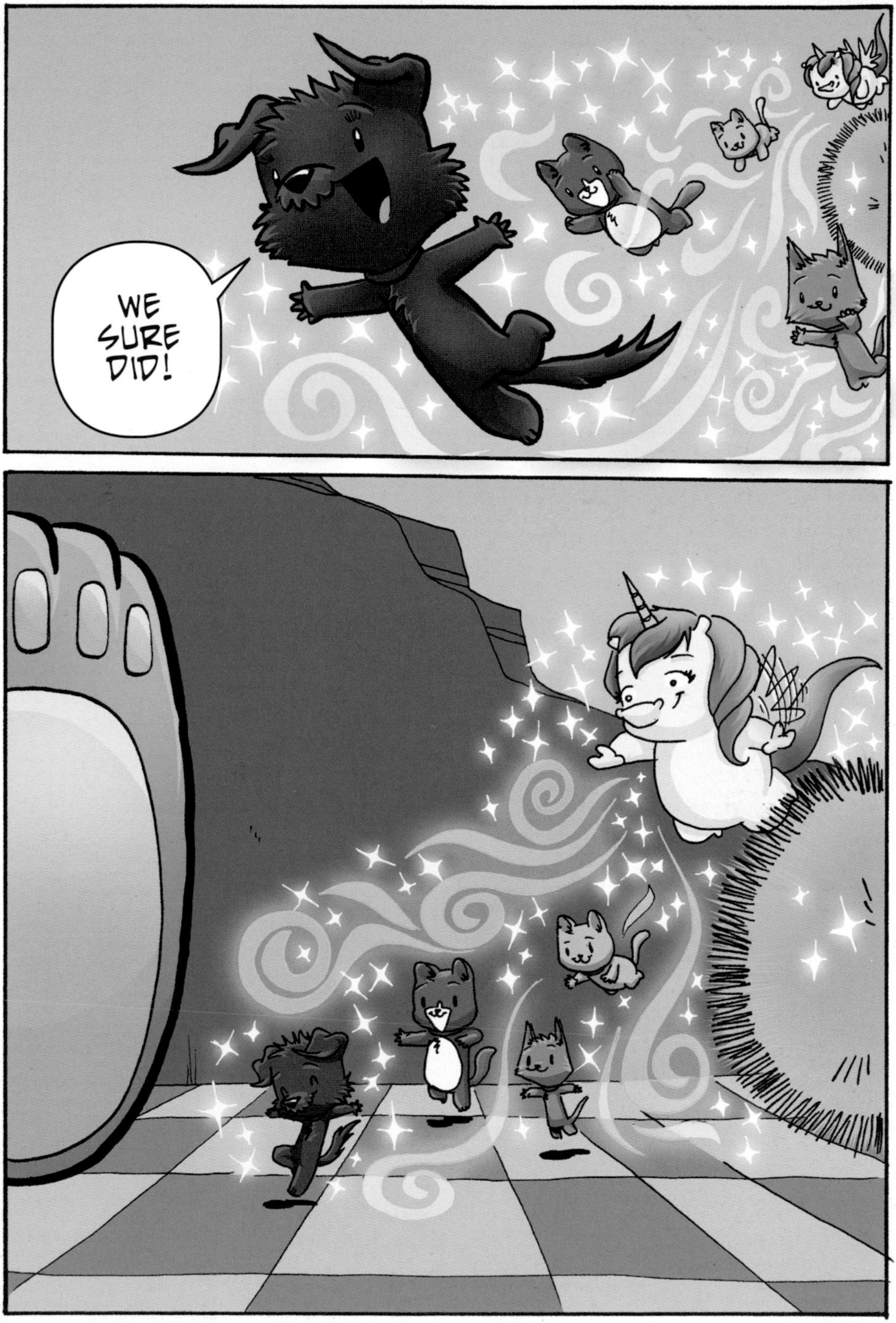
WE SURE DID!

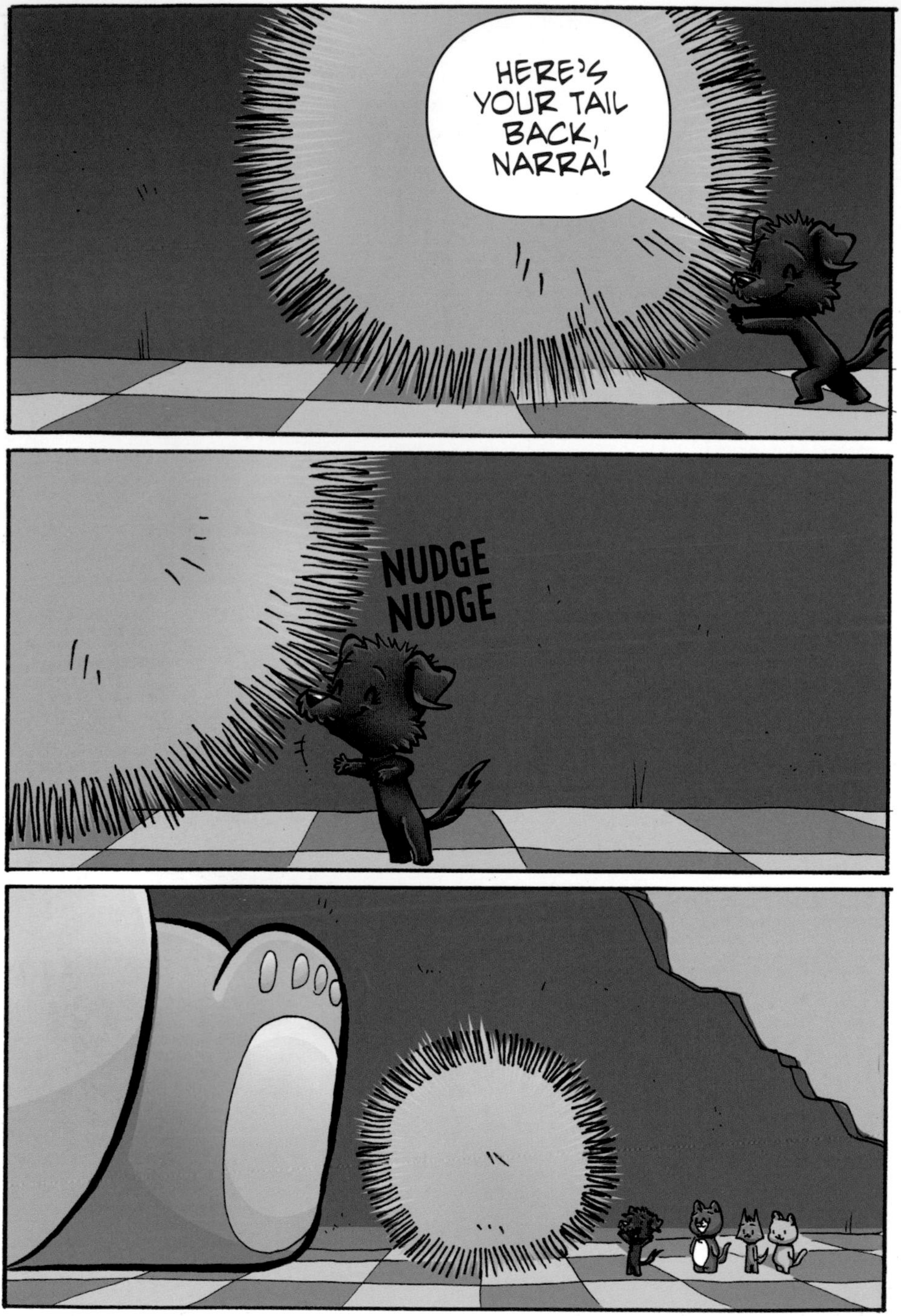
HERE'S YOUR TAIL BACK, NARRA!
NUDGE NUDGE

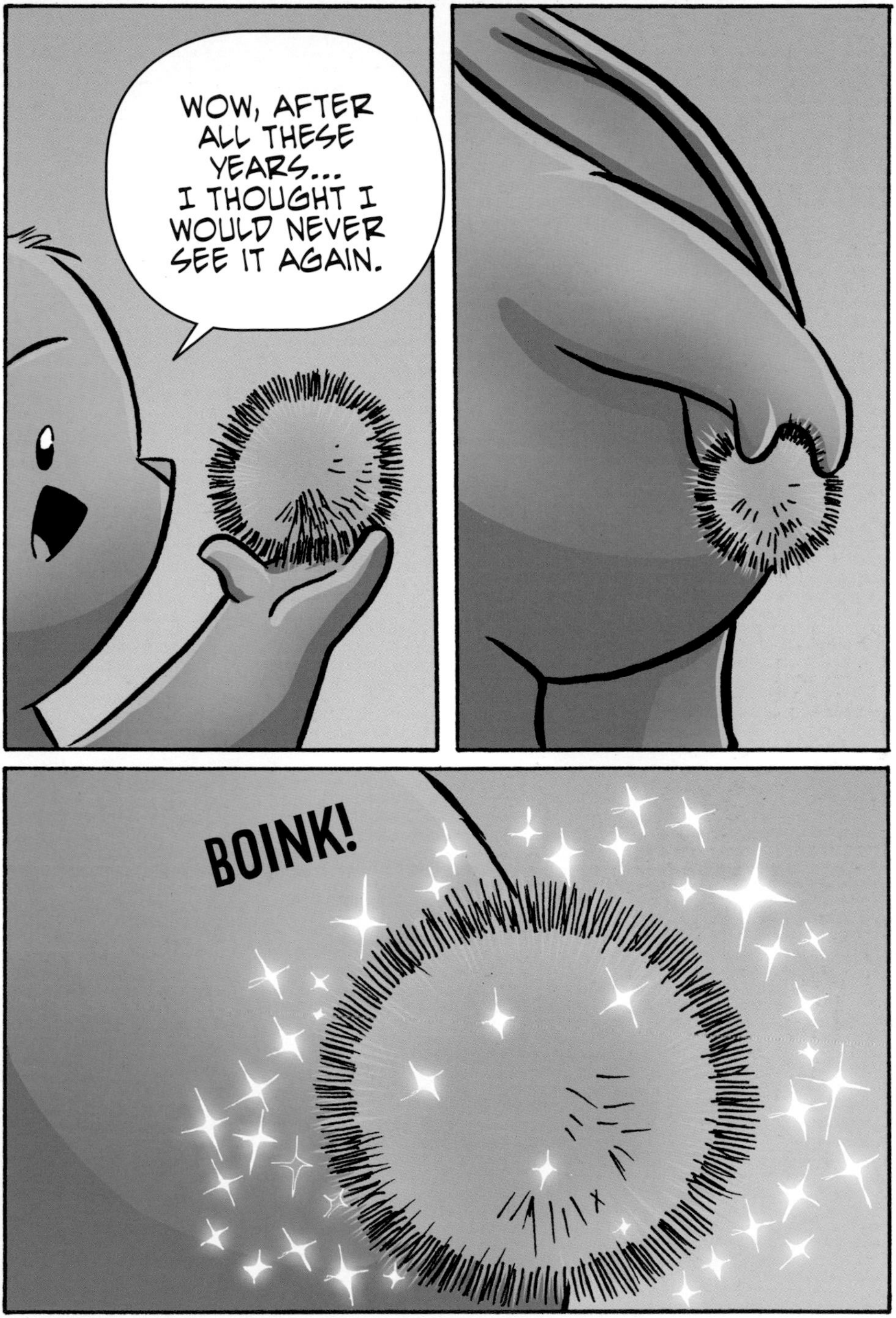
WOW, AFTER ALL THESE YEARS... I THOUGHT I WOULD NEVER SEE IT AGAIN.
BOINK!

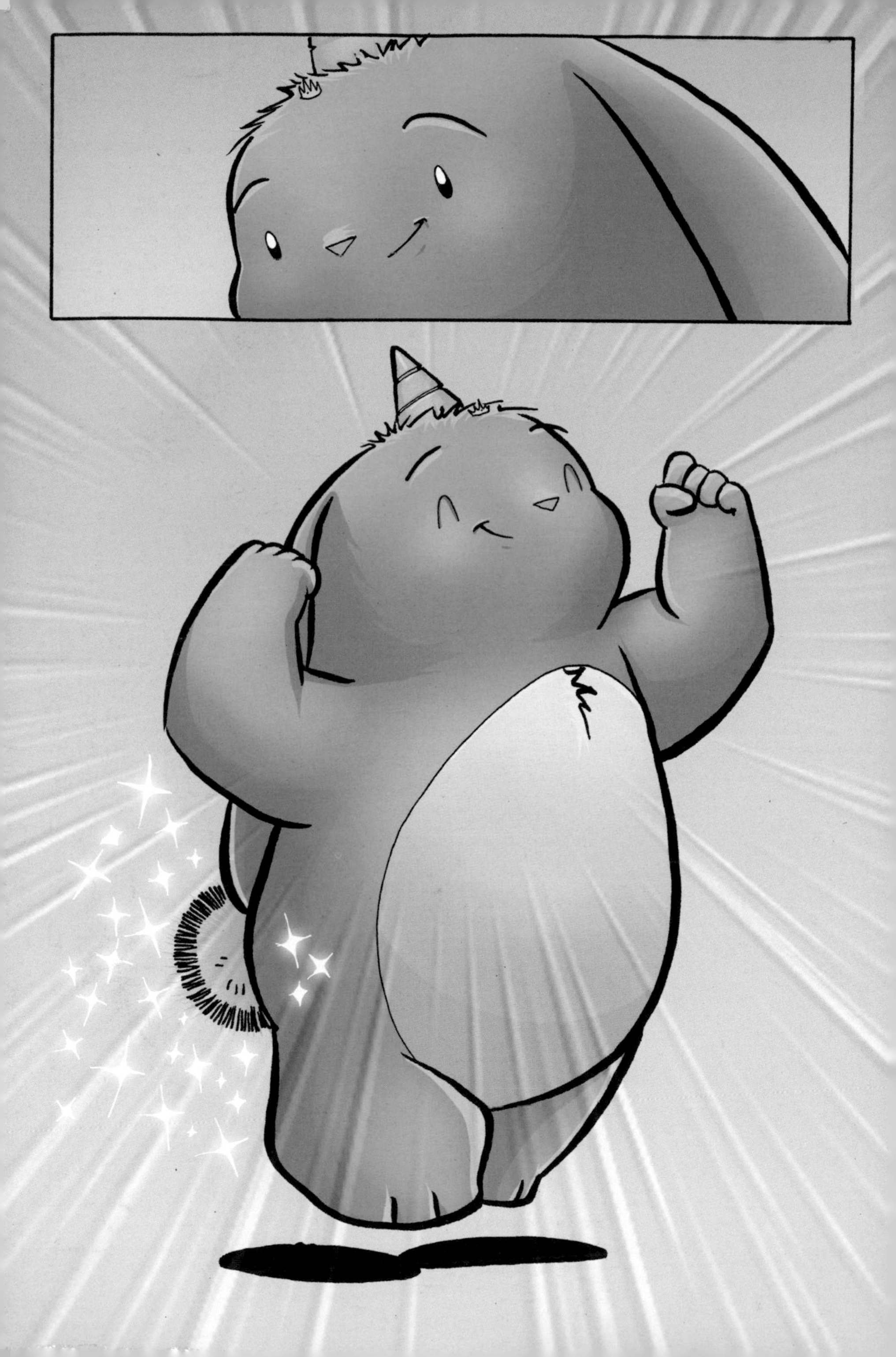

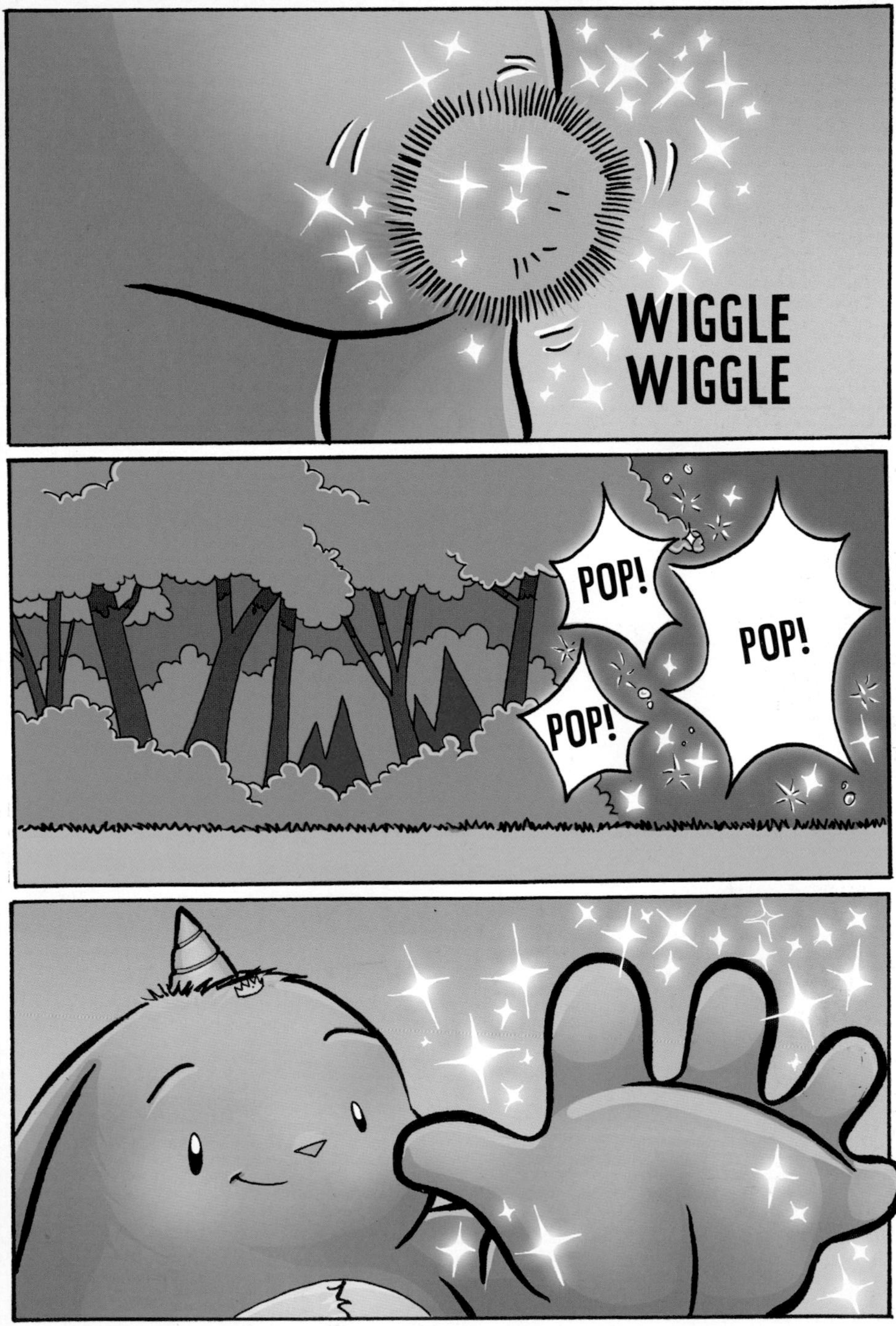
WIGGLE
WIGGLE
POP!
POP!
POP!

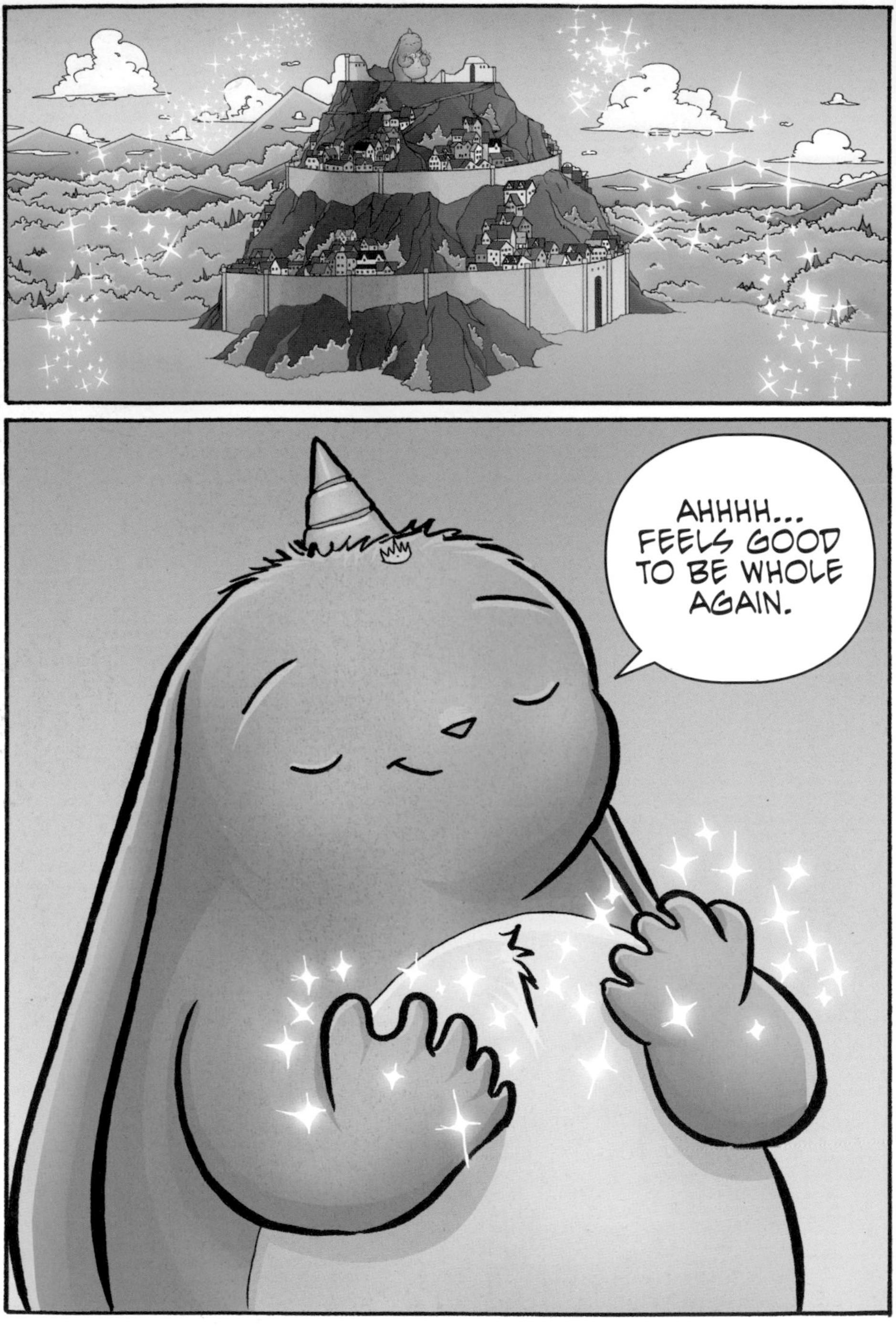
AHHHH... FEELS GOOD TO BE WHOLE AGAIN.

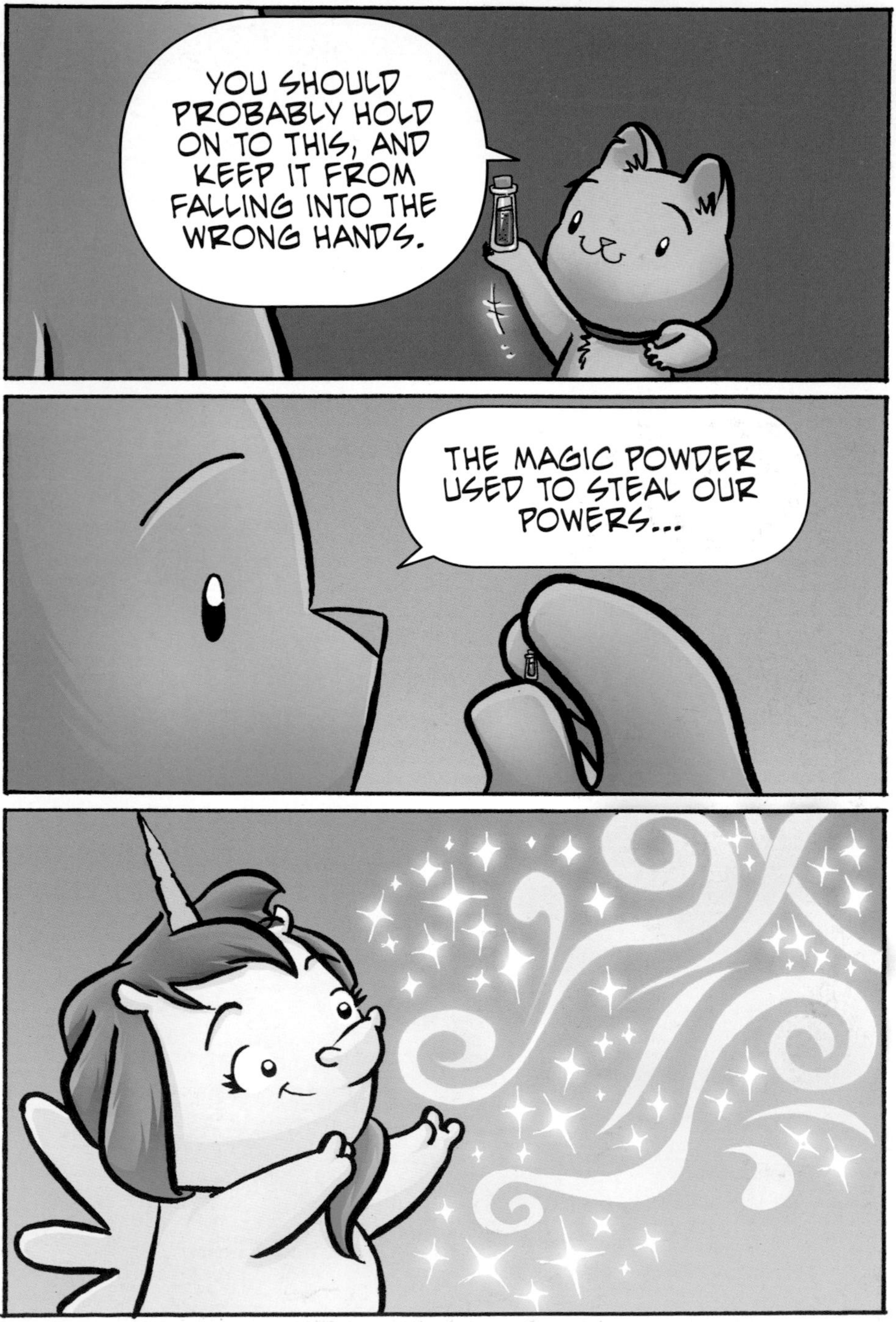
YOU SHOULD PROBABLY HOLD ON TO THIS, AND KEEP IT FROM FALLING INTO THE WRONG HANDS.
THE MAGIC POWDER USED TO STEAL OUR POWERS...

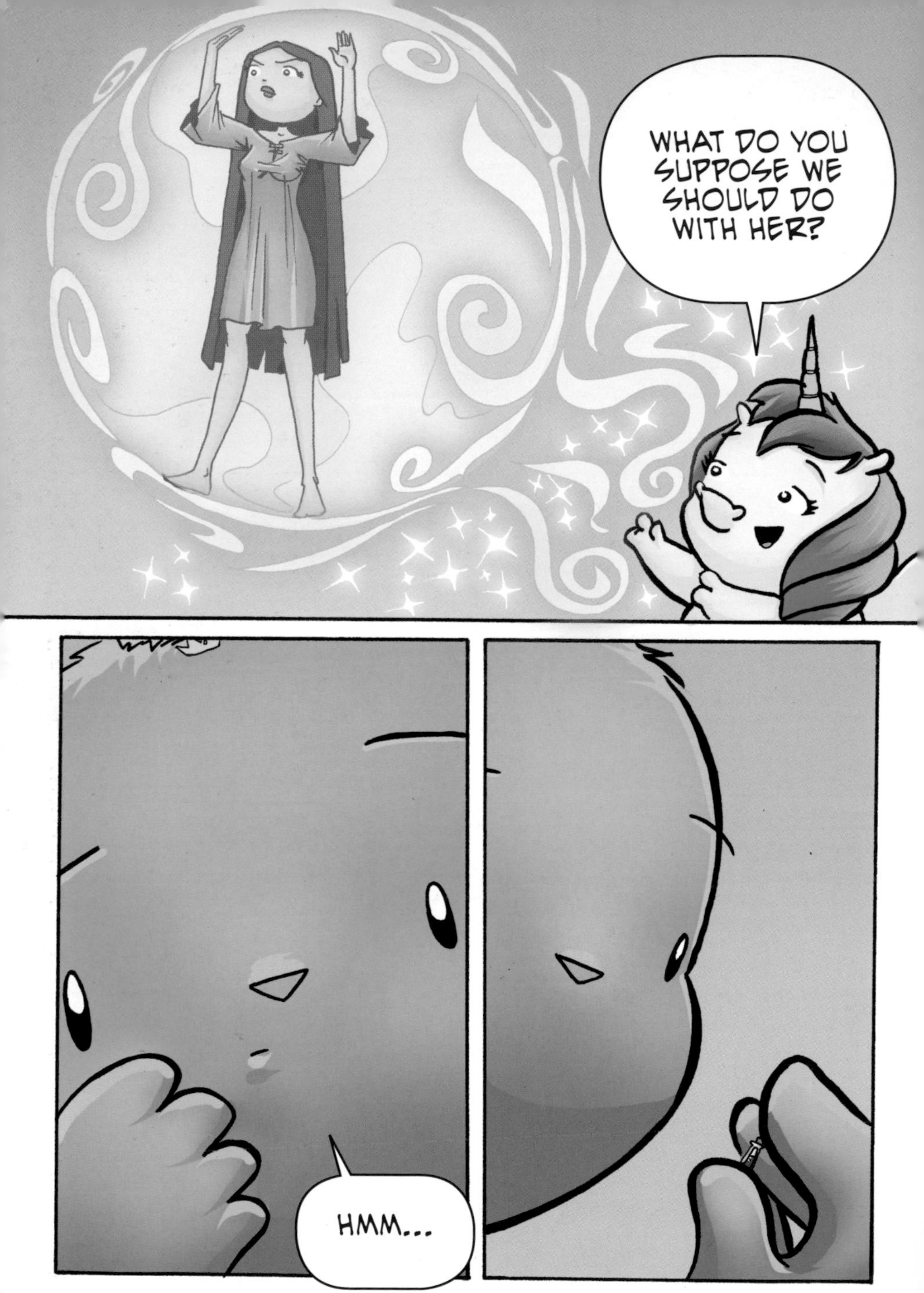
WHAT DO YOU SUPPOSE WE SHOULD DO WITH HER?
HMM...

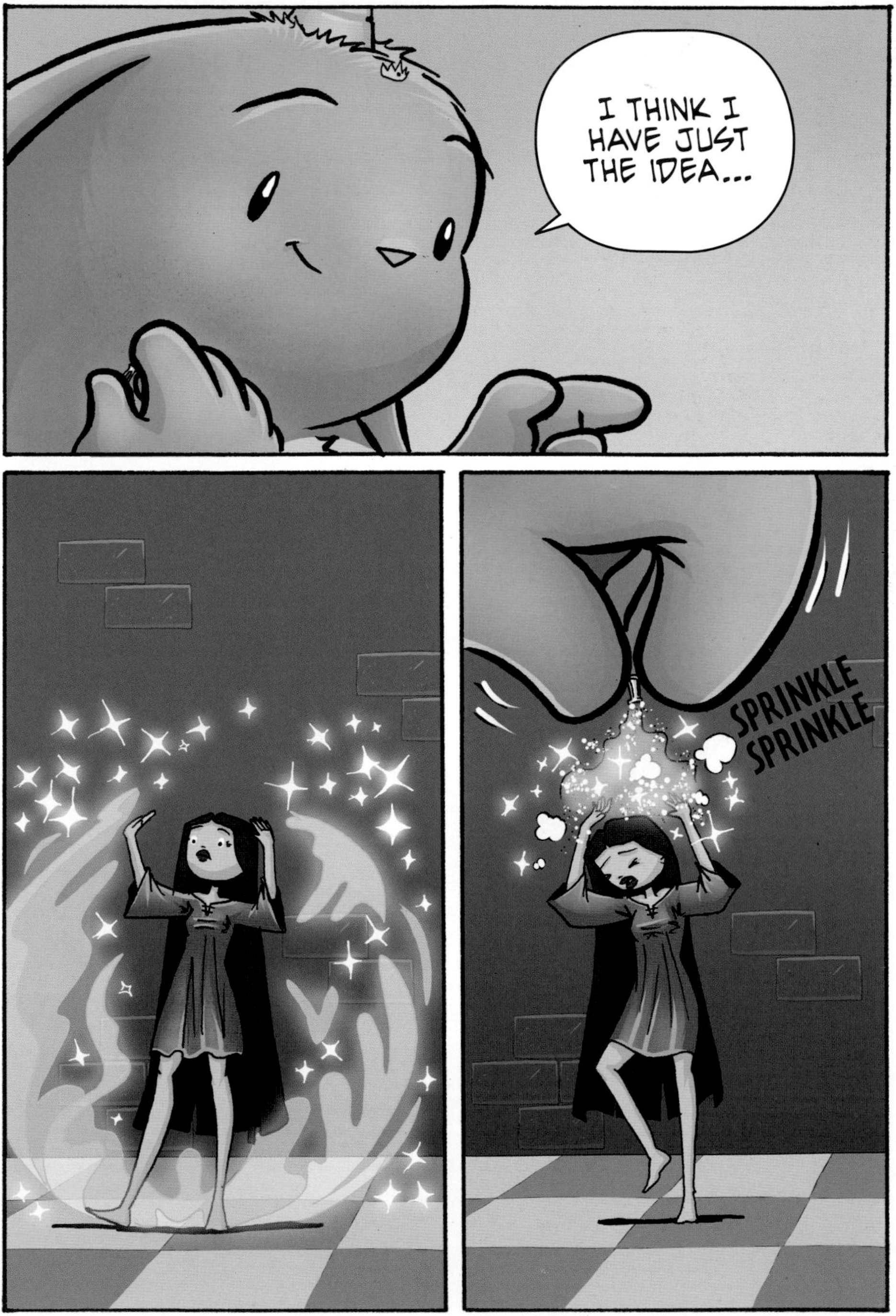
I THINK I HAVE JUST THE IDEA...
SPRINKLE SPRINKLE

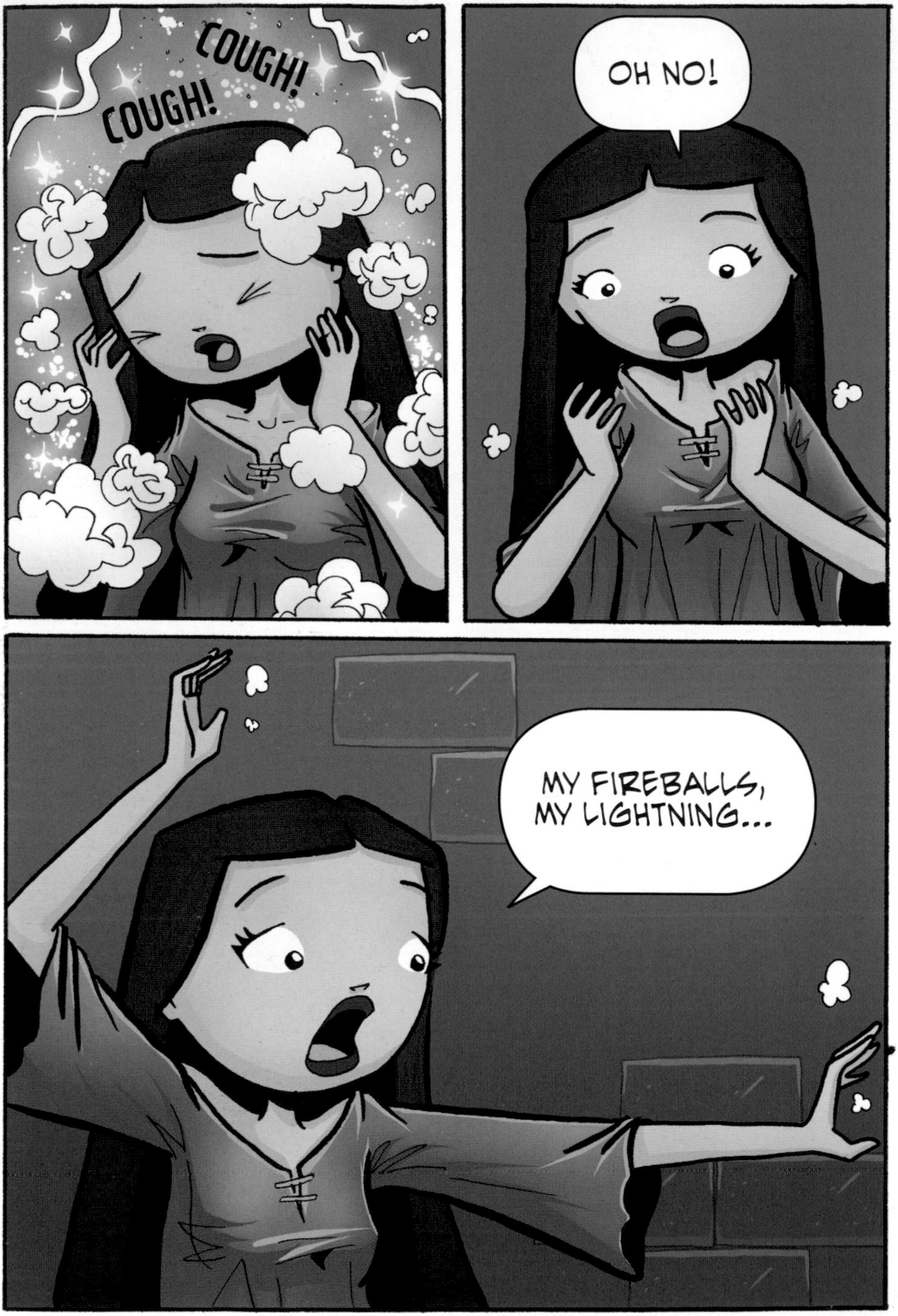
COUGH!
COUGH!
OH NO!
MY FIREBALLS,
MY LIGHTNING...

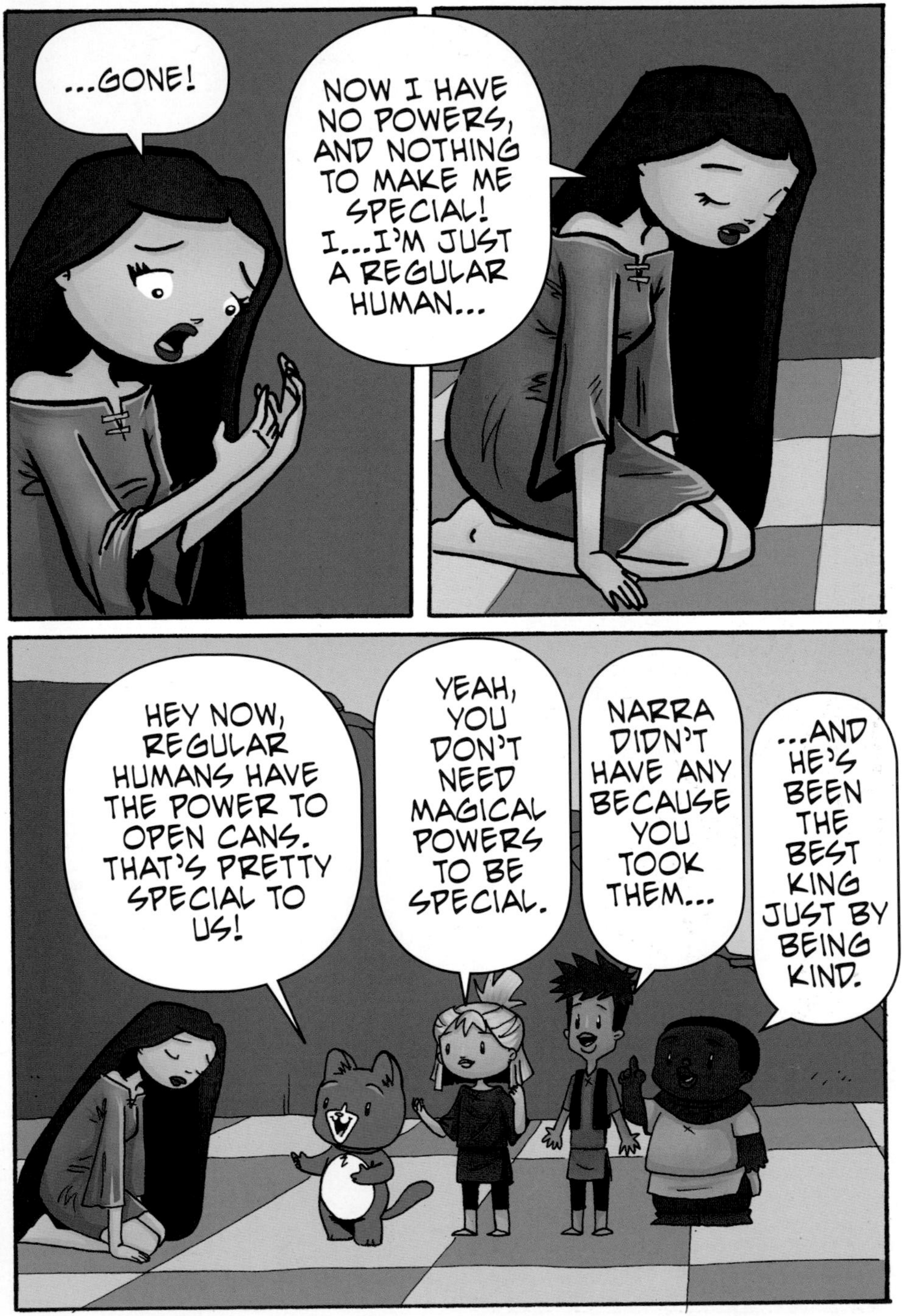
...GONE!
NOW I HAVE NO POWERS, AND NOTHING TO MAKE ME SPECIAL! I...I'M JUST A REGULAR HUMAN...
HEY NOW, REGULAR HUMANS HAVE THE POWER TO OPEN CANS. THAT'S PRETTY SPECIAL TO US!
YEAH, YOU DON'T NEED MAGICAL POWERS TO BE SPECIAL.
NARRA DIDN'T HAVE ANY BECAUSE YOU TOOK THEM...
...AND HE'S BEEN THE BEST KING JUST BY BEING KIND.

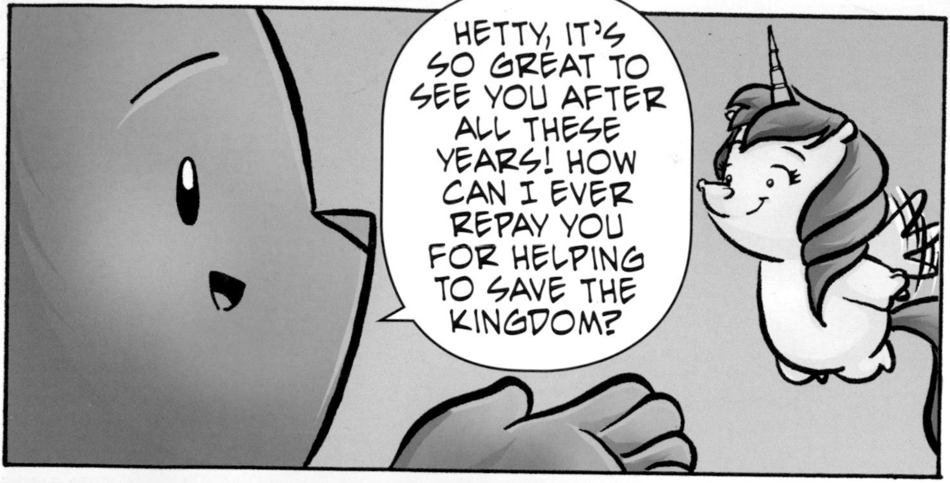
HETTY, IT'S SO GREAT TO SEE YOU AFTER ALL THESE YEARS! HOW CAN I EVER REPAY YOU FOR HELPING TO SAVE THE KINGDOM?

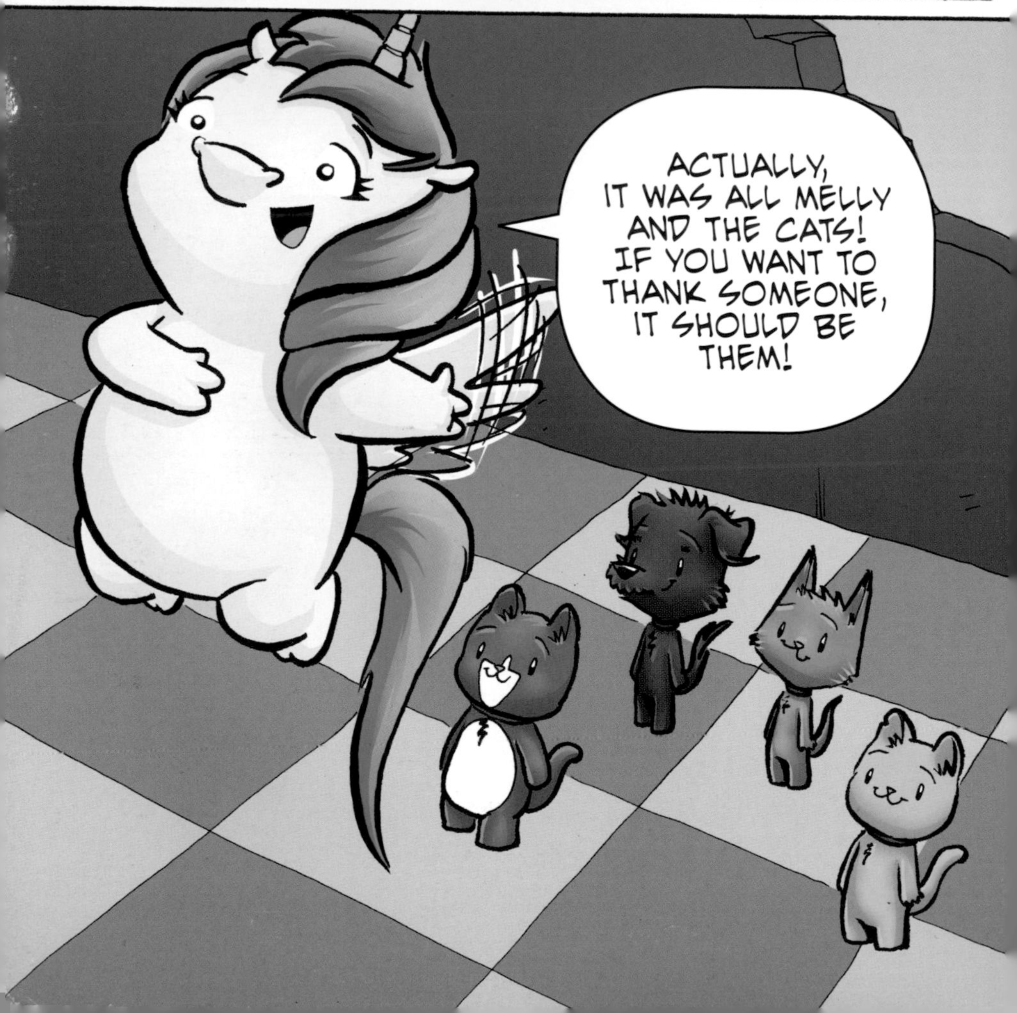
ACTUALLY, IT WAS ALL MELLY AND THE CATS! IF YOU WANT TO THANK SOMEONE, IT SHOULD BE THEM!

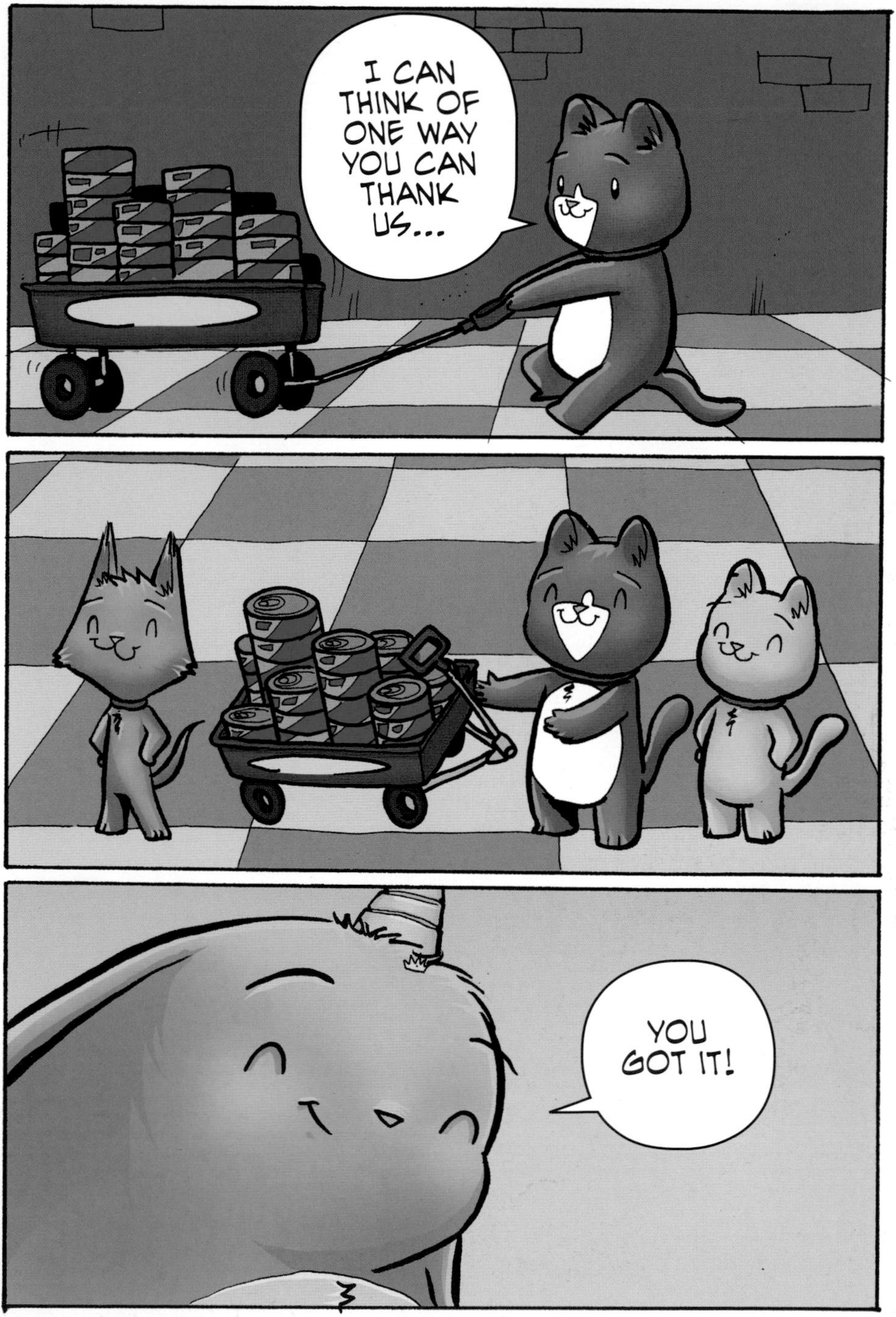
I CAN THINK OF ONE WAY YOU CAN THANK US...
YOU GOT IT!

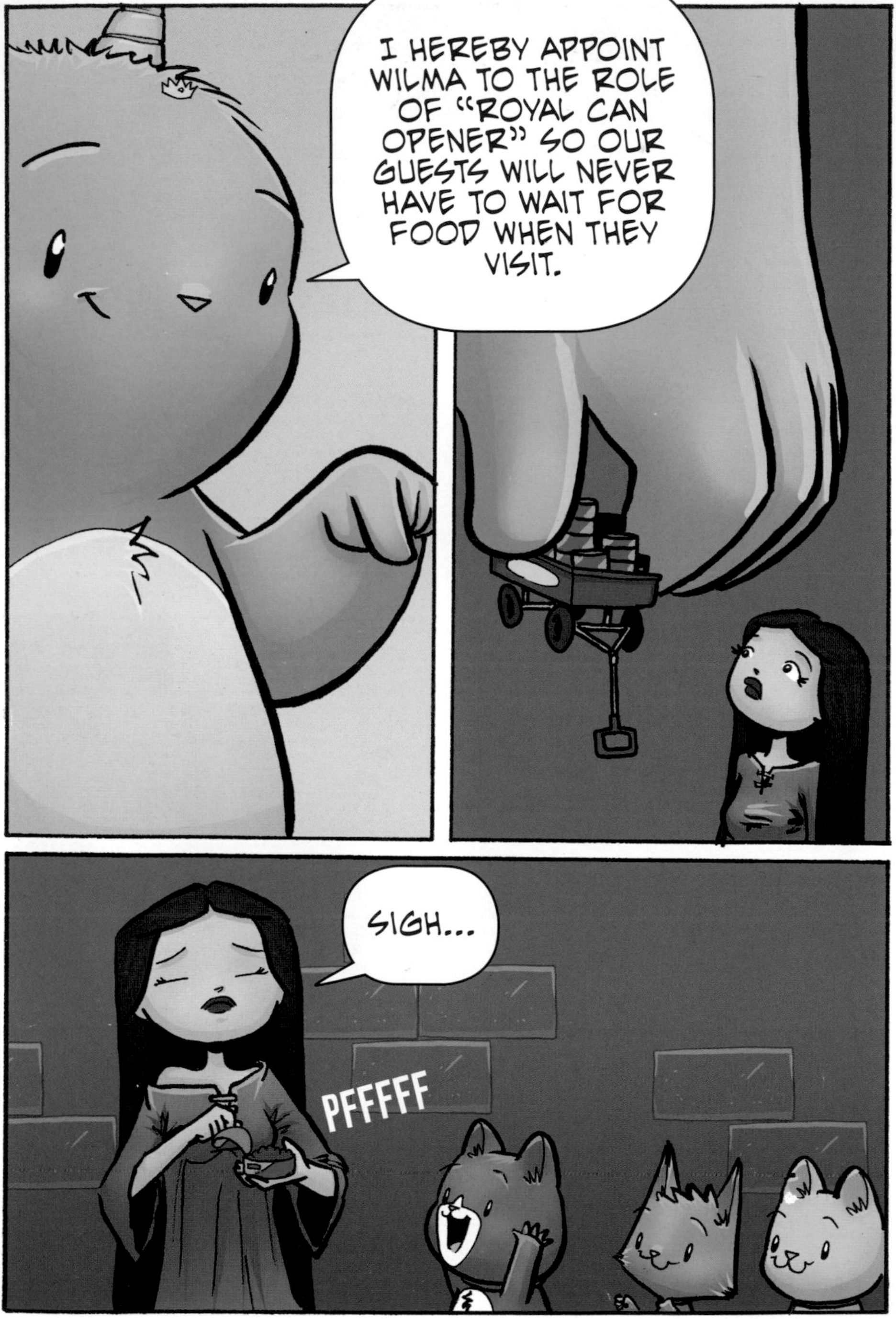
I HEREBY APPOINT WILMA TO THE ROLE OF "ROYAL CAN OPENER" SO OUR GUESTS WILL NEVER HAVE TO WAIT FOR FOOD WHEN THEY VISIT.
SIGH...
PFFFFF

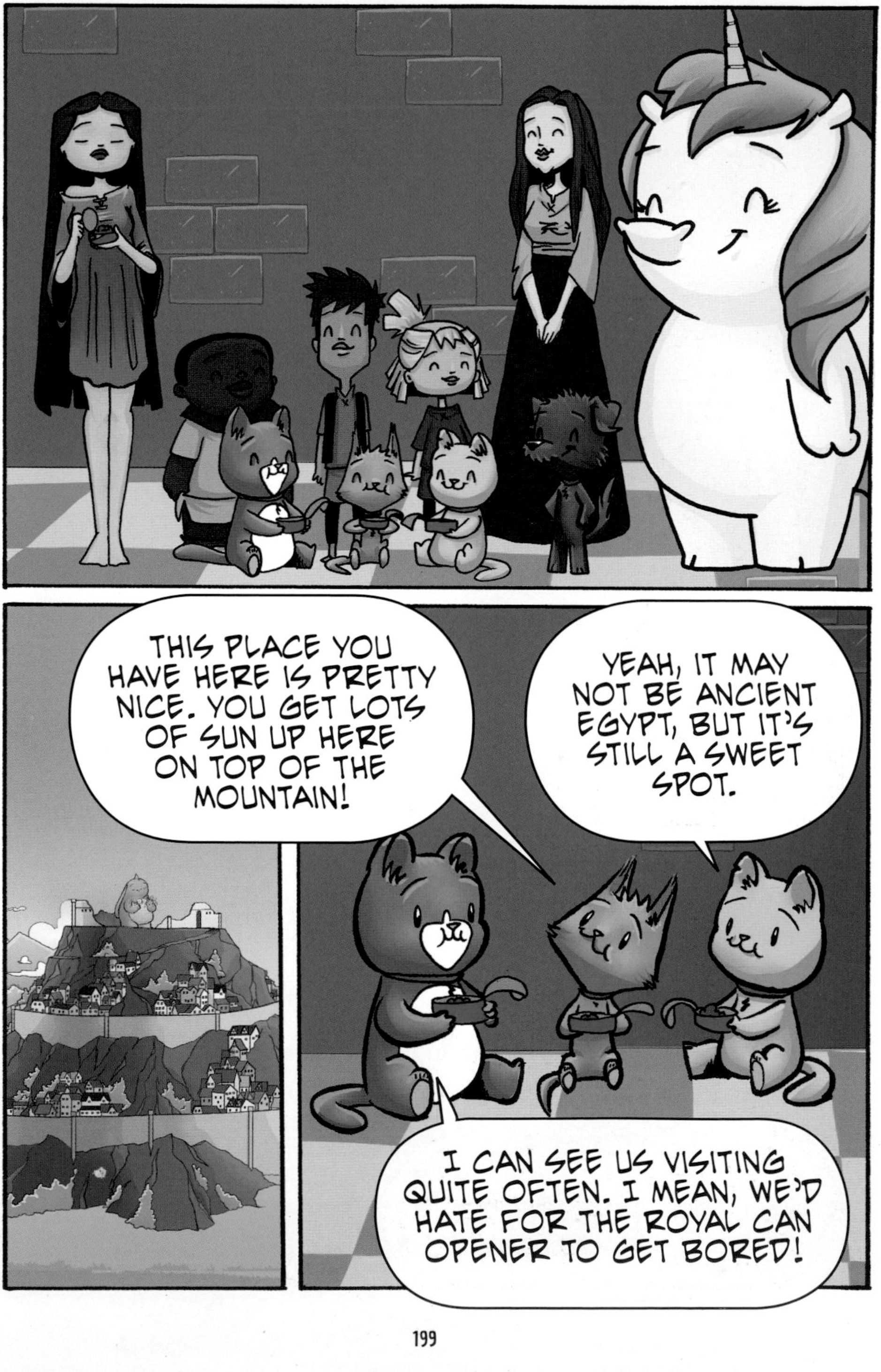

THIS PLACE YOU HAVE HERE IS PRETTY NICE. YOU GET LOTS OF SUN UP HERE ON TOP OF THE MOUNTAIN!
YEAH, IT MAY NOT BE ANCIENT EGYPT, BUT IT'S STILL A SWEET SPOT.
I CAN SEE US VISITING QUITE OFTEN. I MEAN, WE'D HATE FOR THE ROYAL CAN OPENER TO GET BORED!

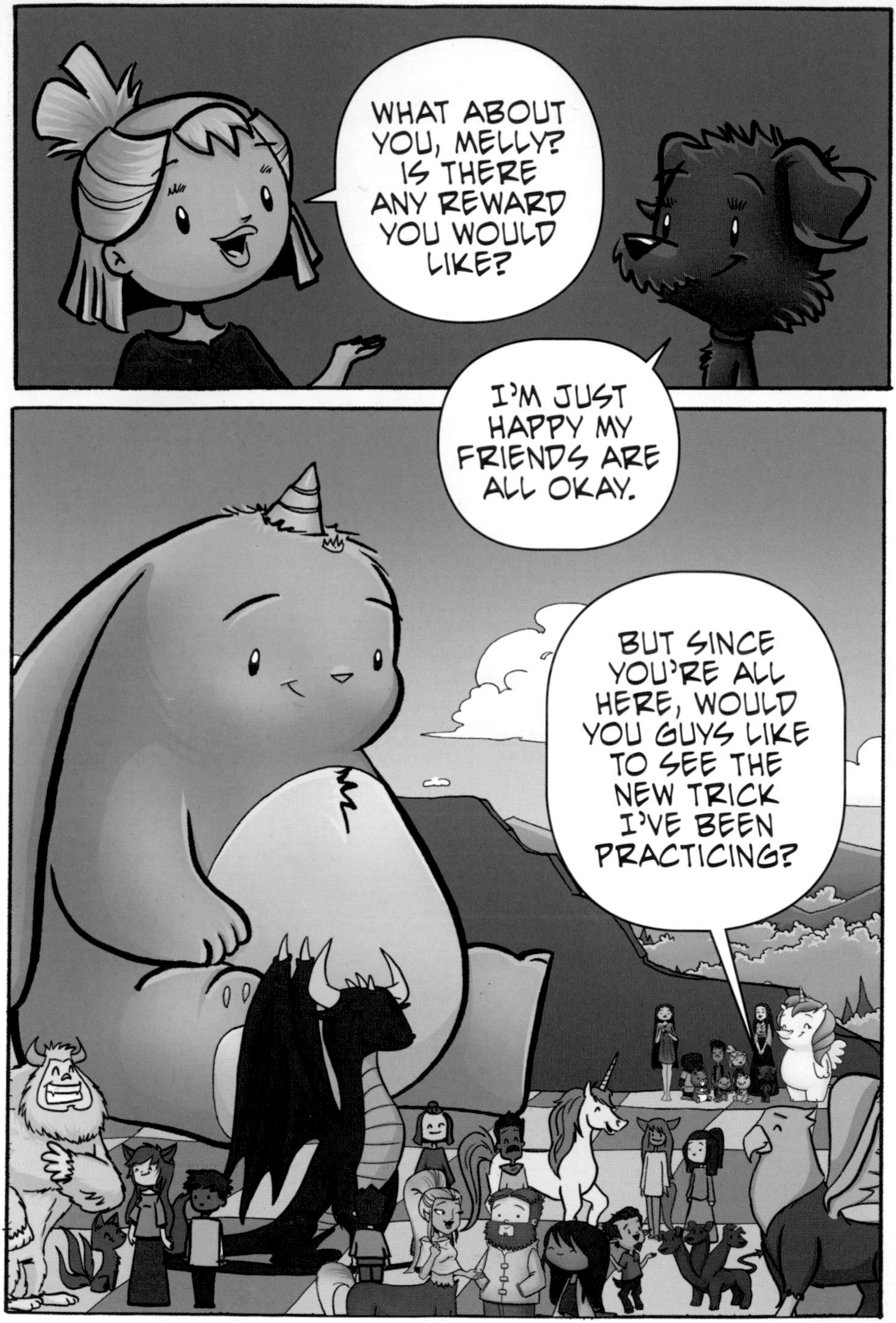
WHAT ABOUT YOU, MELLY? IS THERE ANY REWARD YOU WOULD LIKE?
I'M JUST HAPPY MY FRIENDS ARE ALL OKAY.
BUT SINCE YOU'RE ALL HERE, WOULD YOU GUYS LIKE TO SEE THE NEW TRICK I'VE BEEN PRACTICING?

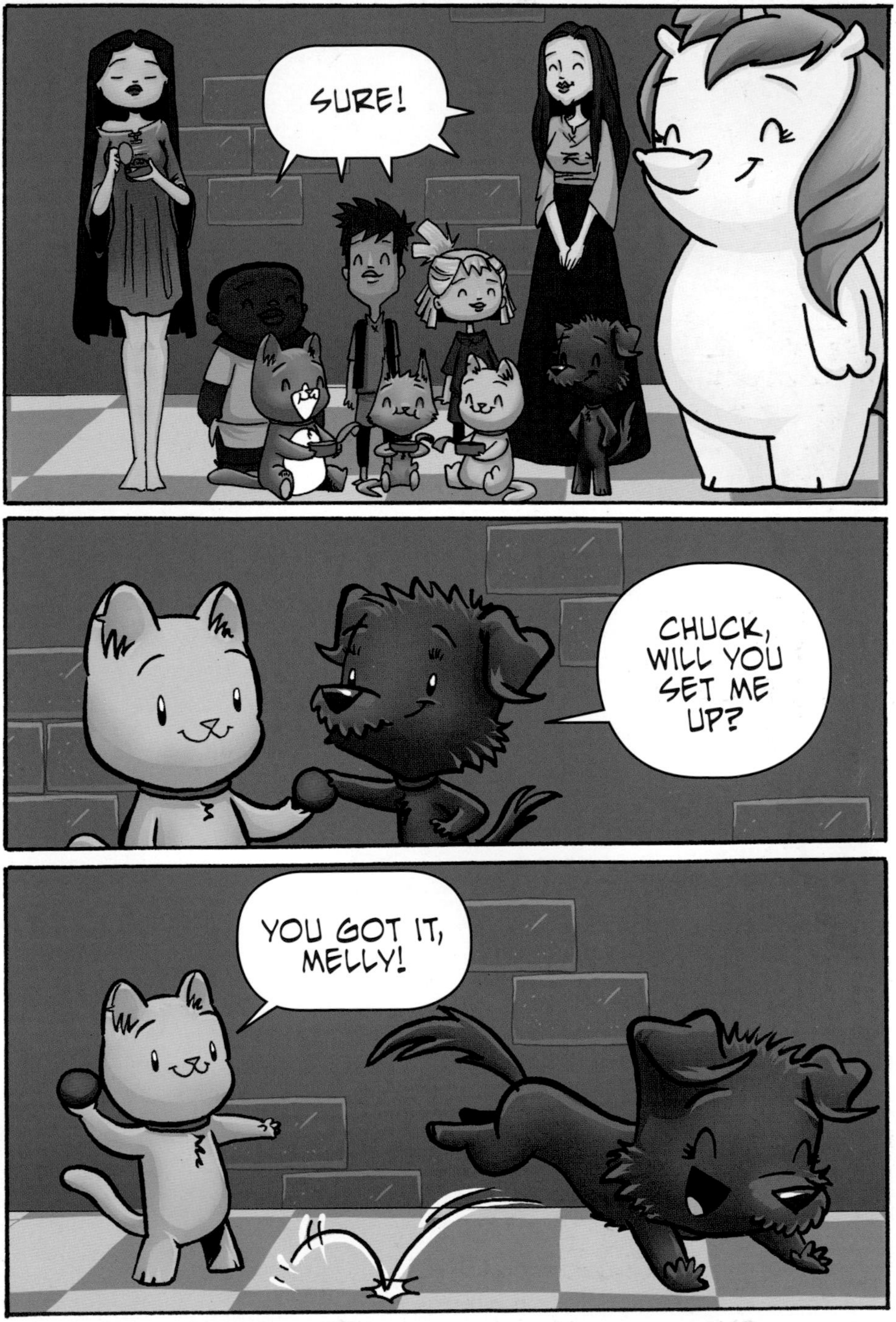
SURE!
CHUCK, WILL YOU SET ME UP?
YOU GOT IT, MELLY!

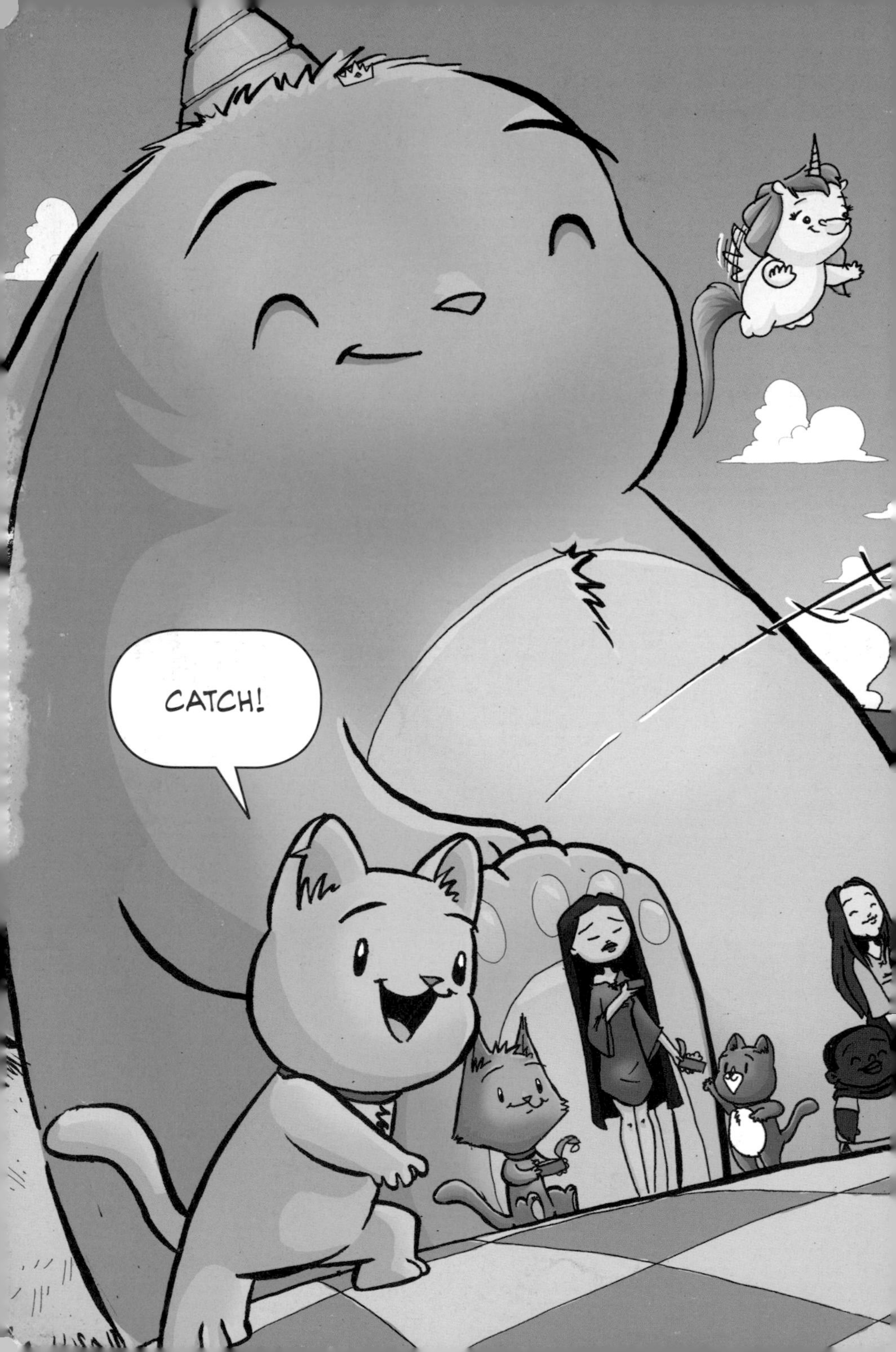
CATCH!

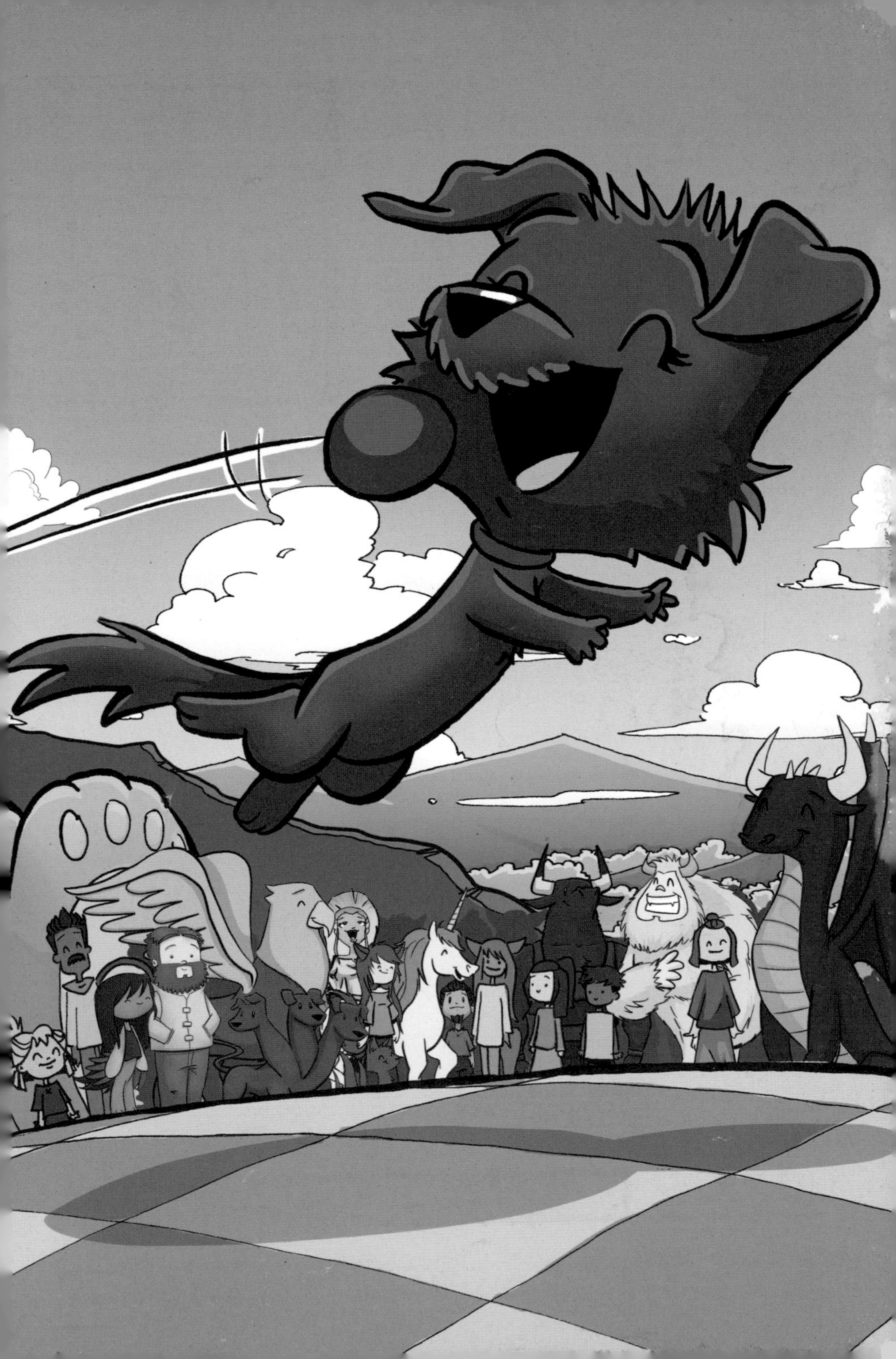

AUTHOR'S NOTE

Hello again! Thank you so much for joining me on this second adventure with Mellybean and her friends! It continues to be a dream come true to make these books, and I'm so happy you've read them.

This time around, it was so much fun to have the cats join Melly on her trip to the magical kingdom and to have them save the day together as a team. As you might already know, Melly and the cats are based on my own pets. Butternut and Tugs came with me when I moved from Canada to San Francisco, and that's where we met Charlie (aka Chuck), who belonged to my now fiancée. A few years later, we adopted Melly and became one big kooky family.

When writing these books, I try to capture each of their real-life, individual personalities. For instance, ever since Butternut was a kitten, he liked to climb. Trees, cat towers, shelves, ladders—even on top of my shoulders while I cooked. Tugs, on the other hand, would prefer being on the ground, where he could supervise the food bowl. He'd meow nonstop whenever it was empty until we filled it. Not out of hunger—he just wanted to make sure food was available. And Chuck is the most logical of the group. He'll often sit right on top of you, no matter what you are doing, so he can be the center of attention.

The cats helped save the day in this book by bringing all those skills to the table. And just as important, they completed their mission of finding a royal can opener! (Which is a key detail, because my real cats—and even Melly—have always shared a loved of canned cat food.)

One of the things I love most about this series is looking at the world through the eyes of my pets and sharing that with you. I hope you had fun reading, because that's what this is all about. I can't wait for you to share in the many adventures to come!

PHOTOS COURTESY OF THE AUTHOR.

3 1901 06210 4445